Mariana Zapata is a *New York Times*, *USA Today*, and a multiple No. 1 Amazon bestselling author. She is a five-time Goodreads Choice Awards nominee in the Romance category. Her novels have been published in thirteen languages.

Mariana lives in a small town in Colorado with her husband and beloved Great Dane, Kaiser. She loves reading, anime, and dogs. When she isn't writing, you can usually find her picking on her loved ones.

Website: **www.marianazapata.com**
Facebook: **/marianazapatawrites**
Instagram: **@marianazapata**
Twitter: **@marianazapata_**
TikTok: **@marianazapataauthor**

By Mariana Zapata

Under Locke
Kulti
Lingus
Rhythm, Chord & Malykhin
The Wall of Winnipeg and Me
Wait for It
Dear Aaron
From Lukov with Love
Luna and the Lie
The Best Thing
Hands Down
All Rhodes Lead Here
When Gracie Met The Grump

MARIANA ZAPATA

HEADLINE
ETERNAL

First published in 2022 by Mariana Zapata

First published in Great Britain in this paperback edition in 2022
by HEADLINE ETERNAL
An imprint of HEADLINE PUBLISHING GROUP

1

Cataloguing in Publication Data is available from the British Library

ISBN: 978 1 0354 0492 6

Book Cover Design by RBA Designs

Illustration on page 611 by nextgirl91

Editing by Hot Tree Editing and My Brother's Editor

Typeset in 10.75/13.75pt Minion Pro by Jouve (UK), Milton Keynes

Printed and bound in Great Britain by Clays Ltd, Elcograf S.p.A.

HEADLINE PUBLISHING GROUP
An Hachette UK Company
Carmelite House
50 Victoria Embankment
London EC4Y 0DZ

www.headlineeternal.com
www.headline.co.uk
www.hachette.co.uk

I love you, Ernie

Chapter One

Oh boy, my stomach hurt.

Grimacing, I pressed my hand against my abdomen as I tried to stop panting . . . but fuck, that didn't feel right. It wasn't a cramp. It was a twisty kind of pain that made me push my hand harder against my abdomen like that would make it better. All day my stomach had been feeling funky, but the minute I'd walked outside, it had gone straight into kind of painful.

Running already wasn't my favorite thing to do in the world. I wouldn't say it was in the top ten. Really, it wasn't even in the top twenty. If I had to rank it, I'd put it after scrubbing my bathtub. Maybe even after cleaning the baseboards, and nobody liked doing that. But I could probably count on two hands the number of times I'd taken the day off from squeezing a run in over the last fifteen years.

Just thinking I had been doing it for so long in the first place made my stomach hurt even more.

But that was beside the point.

Unfortunately, running was one of those things anybody could do anywhere, so it was hard to come up with a legitimate excuse to skip going for one that didn't leave me feeling guilty afterward. It was too easy to picture my grandma tilting her head to the side and piercing me with one of her signature glares as she silently reminded me why I had to suck it up and go.

If I ever had to run, I was going to have to *run*. Not jog. Not sprint. Run like my life depended on it, because it would.

So, slacking off wasn't really an option, even though I wished it could be. It was bullshit, but it was what it was—reality.

I winced as I tried taking a deep breath, pressing my hand tighter against the middle of my stomach. *Yeah, that definitely isn't a cramp.* And that couldn't mean anything good either. The last time it had hurt like this . . .

Stopping right where I was, in the middle of my long drive-way, I did a slow circle, looking around. I listened, but there was nothing other than some crickets somewhere in the distance. The usual.

I'd had a grilled cheese with bacon sandwich for lunch. Maybe it was gas? The cheese had only been expired about a day, but . . .

I listened again.

Slowly, I turned in another full circle, taking in the trailer sitting in the middle of the five acres that made up the property I'd been renting for the last three years. Next, I stared at the greenhouse building, then focused on the small shed set off to the side. There were bushes scattered around, but most of them were right along the fence line, giving the mobile home some privacy from the road.

Then I listened some more.

There wasn't anything out here.

Which was exactly how it should have been. I'd been careful. I was always fucking careful. Cautious might as well have been my middle name. I was just being paranoid.

Taking another deep breath in through my nose, I let go of my stomach and palmed the pepper spray I'd stuffed into my pocket after I'd turned into the driveway at the end of my run. *I should probably stop doing that.* I should keep it in my hand the whole time, at least until I got inside and locked the door. I didn't love running at night, but I hated waking up early, and I sure as hell hated running in the heat. Temperatures in New Mexico were no joke.

Keeping my ears peeled, I finished catching my breath the rest of the way down the driveway, but there really wasn't anything or anyone out there other than the crickets. Even the clouds were hiding the stars, and if there was a member of the Trinity up in the sky creeping on me, I couldn't see them. The thought almost made me snicker as my stomach suddenly hurt a little more sharply.

It's the cheese. It has to be the fucking cheese, I thought as I unlocked the door and went inside, engaging the dead bolt and the flimsy bottom lock that was mostly for decoration. There was a gallon of rocky road ice cream in the freezer that I'd been dreaming about tearing up all day, so my stomach needed to quit its bullshit.

After toeing off my sneakers and setting my keys and pepper spray on the nightstand, I picked up the towel I'd left there and wiped myself down before slipping my hoodie from earlier back on so I wouldn't sweat up the couch. Only then did I take a nice, deep, even breath, and almost immediately stopped in the middle of it as I eyed the coffee table. Specifically, the map I'd left on top of it before I'd gone outside, telling myself I needed to get my run over with. I wanted to watch some TV while I cooled down. Then I'd have dinner, shower, squeeze in my last lesson, maybe finish reading my book while I ate that rocky road, and finally go to bed.

Just like every day.

And if that made my chest get a little tight, then it made my chest get a little tight.

C'est la fucking vie, right? But even knowing that, I couldn't help peeking at the atlas, which was almost as old as I was, as I circled around the couch and plopped down in the middle. Right in front of it.

It was already open, just waiting for me.

I can do this.

All I had to do was choose somewhere. Fucking anywhere, or just about anywhere, as long as it was within the continental U.S.

Eyeing the stained pages, I tried to decide if I should close my eyes and randomly point at a place or eeny-meeny-miny-moe like I'd used to when I'd been a kid and my grandparents had let me pick where we'd head to next. They'd tried to make moving around as much of a game as they could, at least at the beginning. To be fair, I hadn't really seen it as too much of a chore until about middle school. Bouncing from town to town had been fun for a really long time.

Then, in high school, it had become a necessity.

Now, it made my eye twitch.

And made me want that ice cream even more.

But I *knew* I needed to move, and I really was planning on it. It was just easier said than done. Six months ago, I'd told myself I couldn't leave because I wanted to harvest my garden first. I'd put so much work into it; I couldn't let it go to waste. Then, I had convinced myself that I should wait until after the holidays. Moving during winter would suck. What if it suddenly snowed? My car wasn't all-wheel drive, so I needed to take that into consideration too.

Then there was the biggest factor: I hadn't been able to pick a place yet.

It might have not helped that every time I'd sat down to make a decision, I'd done the same thing I had tonight—I spent all of two minutes total looking at the map before I'd come up with something else that needed to be done that was just as important. Like running. Or folding the mound of clean laundry that always seemed to pile up even though I was the only person in the house and I usually wore my pajamas all day unless I had video lessons with my students. Then I got real fancy and put on a nice shirt while I sat in front of my computer in sweatpants or shorts.

It wasn't like it mattered where I went. It was time to bounce.

It was one of the rules I'd been raised with after all: *Don't stay in one place for too long.*

Lifting the back of my palm to my face, I dragged it across my forehead before dropping it onto my lap as I blew a raspberry with my mouth.

My stomach clenched again.

It doesn't mean anything. It was a coincidence; my body was being annoying and had nothing to do with me moving. There was no reason for me to believe I needed to panic, get in my car, and peel out of here. It had been a long time since my stomach had done this funny shit. *It doesn't mean anything.* It was the cheddar. Or *maybe* it was a sign that, yes, I needed to get out of here at some point in the very near future.

That made sense.

Maybeee . . . I could spice it up and move east. As long as it wasn't anywhere warmer than here, I might even be able to run during the day instead of risking my life every night. I had never been farther east than Texas.

I needed to think about it a little longer to be on the safe side.

But *just* a little longer. A day or two max. No more than three. It was a good plan, I thought, as I picked up the glass of water I'd left on the edge of the table and took a big gulp. In the middle of taking another drink, I grabbed the remote from beside the map and turned on the TV.

"*. . . I'm tellin' you it was got-damn ANGELS! The po-lice tried to say it had to be some weather phenomenon. Call it whatever the h-e-double-l you wanna call it, but that weren't no storm out there. It were angels!*"

The reporter on the screen blinked, and at the same time, the corners of his mouth twitched almost unnoticeably, but I caught it. "*Sir, why would you think it was angels and not a member of the Trinity you saw through your window?*"

The elderly man lifted his arms and let them drop at his sides. Behind him was an arid landscape with some blurry horses in a corral. "*Come on, boy, use some common sense. Ain't no lightnin' blottin' out the got-damn sky the way this'un did. D-uh. Tried to tell me too it was one of dem cape-wearers. What them 'heroes' gonna be doin' around here? Nothin'! That's what! Lived here my whole [beep] life and never have I seen one of dem comin' 'round these parts. We ain't got no crime worth dealin' with. Puh-lease. This here was HUGE! You couldn't see nothin' but this light in the sky. No reason it woulda been one of 'em Trinity. They can't do that kinda thing. Folks been watchin' too many movies.*"

That was . . . interesting. I remembered one of them had been spotted in Albuquerque helping with a fire, but that was nearly three hours away and about a year ago. There was crime here, in the town I lived, like everywhere else, but nothing that kept me up at night.

It was one of the benefits of living in Chama, New Mexico, population about 1,000.

Which was exactly why I lived here.

On the screen, the older man's hands moved animatedly as he went on to say that his neighbors had claimed to have seen *something* out of their windows, but by the time they had gotten up to look, there hadn't been anything out there. It was only because he'd been washing dishes and had a window above the sink that he'd seen the "*big ol' glow move across the sky.*"

I'd always wondered if angels were real. Some people said they existed—and I mean, if you really thought about it, there were superhumans or whatever the Trinity were, why wouldn't there be angels? When I was little, we lived in a house that my grandma swore was haunted. But angels?

I changed the channel, trying to decide if I was in the mood to watch a movie or not, but I paused on the footage that seemed to have been recorded on a cell phone.

"The Primordial made a rare appearance today at a hospital in Chicago. Workers said the hero spent several hours at the facility, distributing gifts to children."

Taking another sip, I eyed the woman standing beside a hospital bed, smiling at a little girl tucked into it.

Rumor had it she was six foot two or three, but it wasn't like anyone had ever held a tape measure against her. She had broad shoulders rounded with muscle, and beneath the dark green, skintight suit that covered everything from her throat to the tips of her fingers and toes, the most well-known member of the Trinity was r-i-p-p-e-d. Everyone had, at some point, watched the footage of her holding up the Golden Gate Bridge when an earthquake had done the unthinkable and nearly caused it to collapse ten years ago.

I wanted to be her when I grew up.

If I magically became superhuman. And grew over a foot and gained forty or fifty pounds of muscle. And had magnificent bone structure and flawless skin.

Miracles could happen.

The incredible woman had hair so brown it couldn't be mistaken for any other color and a skin color so golden, if she had any human in her, which was widely debatable, I was pretty sure a DNA test would have come up with a mix of ethnicities to pinpoint how it came to be. The face of the strongest woman in the world could only be described as striking.

She was a beacon of strength, femininity, and just plain being amazing, for not just little kids but for people of all ages. They all were, if you wanted to get technical. Most of humanity thought the three superbeings, called the Trinity for that reason, were incredible.

Not plain, normal people with a million lies on which they'd built their lives.

I was going to play myself a sad little violin.

"... among outcry from the families of those who were injured during the fire that left dozens hospitalized. Newly recovered security footage shows The Defender arriving ten minutes after ..."

And here I'd literally just been thinking about that fire. I couldn't believe they were still going on about it. It was a miracle he had even been able to help in the first place. He'd saved so many people. I rolled my eyes and switched the channel one more time before freezing.

There was a man with rich, brown skin surrounded by at least four heavily armored police officers moving toward one of those vehicles that SWAT teams used. "The trial for Camilo Beltran began today. Otherwise known as El Cerebro, the former drug lord and leader of the Arenas gang is finally being brought to justice on charges of drug trafficking, money laundering, and bribery ..."

Swallowing back the anger and the little bit of fear that suddenly built up in my throat, I pressed the button on the remote again and decided I might as well eat now and watch a movie. That would be good. I had some time to kill before my lesson with my newest student, a twenty-three-year-old named Jo Ji-Wook who was moving to Toronto in a few months. His English was improving every week, and I was really proud of how far he'd come. What I *should* do was fold laundry while I sat there, but suddenly I felt extra tired and bummed out.

I'd spent half the day trying to replace the garbage disposal that had stopped working. The online manual I found claimed it would only take thirty minutes, but that hadn't been the case. One of the screws had arrived stripped, and it had gone to shit from there.

Which was basically the story of my life. *When You Think Things Can't Go Any More Wrong, Hold Your Horses: The Gracie Castro Story.* Coming to theaters never. Shinto Studios would shoot the screenplay down before they even finished reading the title. *Gracie Castro: The Sorceress of Secrets* might work, I thought glumly. Except I didn't have any powers, if you didn't count my rare but epic stomachaches.

Like the one I had right then, that I hoped was actually gas or just uneasiness about moving.

I cast a long look around the living room of the mostly bare single-wide trailer that had been home for years. Then I probably sighed for the tenth time in the last ten minutes and settled deeper into the couch for comfort. It was the closest thing to a hug I was going to get anytime soon, after all.

I missed hugs. I missed them a lot. Hugging yourself didn't release any oxytocin in your body, so it didn't have the same effect as getting one from another person.

I knew that from experience.

Squeezing the remote, I eyed the atlas on the coffee table one more time and sighed *again*. If I followed the instructions my grandma had left me, I should have relocated a year ago. For a while there, during high school, we had bounced around every semester. After I'd graduated, we had milked our stays for a year. Then we'd upped it a little more after that. *Two years maximum, mi corazón. As long as you keep your head down and tell no one, you should be okay.*

That was another rule: *keep your head down.*

I had. It was a lot of work to keep it that way, but I was alive, and that was the point. That had been the point of all this shit.

But this place was the closest thing to home I'd known in forever. I'd settled in. I had found peace and, honestly, part of myself too while being on my own. It wasn't exactly at the top of the list of places I would want to live, but I still didn't want to leave. I was comfortable. I didn't want to start over for the twentieth time. But . . .

There was always the chance one day I wouldn't have to. That's what I kept hoping for. It was just another miracle I could dream of.

And maybe, eventually, someday, things might change. Maybe I would be able to get a passport and travel and meet someone awesome who didn't ask too many questions. Find a companion . . . a friend. More than a friend would be great.

If I had to pick, that would be at the top of the list of things I'd want—someone.

He'd have to be okay with me being . . . me. Just shy of thirty. Mostly nice. I had a mostly steady job, even if I was never going to be rich. I could have done worse in the face department, I thought. I could have done a lot better, but I could have been unluckier. There was plenty of other stuff I could complain about, so facial features and the size of my waist weren't worth worrying about.

And that was part of my problem. The source of all my problems actually. There wasn't a plastic surgeon in the world who could fix my problems with a surgical knife.

I needed a whole new life, new DNA, for that shit.

I was in the middle of thinking that depressing shit when I saw it out of the corner of my eye.

A flash of pure purple light through the blinds that had me flinching it was so damn bright.

And it was a split second after that, that I felt it—the rumble. The frame of the single-wide shook. My cup rattled. The walls trembled.

What in the hell *was that?*

WHAT THE HELL WAS HAPPENING?

The interview on the TV suddenly popped up in my head.

Was it . . . an angel?

No, *no*. It wasn't.

Was there a meteor shower tonight? Was a plane falling apart? Oh shit. *Oh shit, shit, shit.*

Did that explain the blinding light? No. I was pretty sure nothing other than a spotlight could glow that brightly, but what the hell did I know? Did it explain the mini earthquake that had just rattled the trailer? Maybe . . . ? But there *was* something, and whatever it was, it had to be big to make the ground shake. I couldn't think of anything off the top of my head that *could* be that big, other than Godzilla, but kaijus weren't real, so . . .

There was nothing to be scared of unless it really was chunks of an airplane falling out of the sky, on the verge of crushing me.

Forcing myself to get up, I headed around the couch and went straight for the front door. I grabbed my flashlight, unlocked the door, and peeked before going out there.

But in the same way I should have expected, in the only way that seemed to work in my life, what I expected wasn't what I actually got.

Down the steps of my tiny deck, I looked around the yard and didn't see a thing. I hadn't imagined the light or the shaking. Had I? I'd always wondered if I'd end up going nuts since I spent so much time by myself, but *no*, I was too young. And there weren't active tectonic plates around here; I was pretty sure. I went around the side of the trailer and stopped. Midstep and everything because . . .

Oh *shit*.

Oh shit, oh shit, *oh shit*.

Tiny purple fires were scattered across my yard.

Hand already shaking, I lifted my flashlight and aimed it at the center of them.

I gulped.

I turned it off, then turned it back on, thinking I'd imagined it.

I hadn't.

I fucking hadn't.

There was a body there. On the ground. In the dirt.

A human body.

A big one.

My hand shook like crazy as the beam of light settled on

what looked like a piece of cloth spread out under what I was fairly certain was a male frame from the muscle proportions I could see.

A piece of cloth that looked an awful lot like . . . like . . . a *cape*.

A cape.

Oh *shit*.

A fucking cape that was torn and tattered, but it was either a tablecloth or that.

And it was attached to a half-bared chest by a wish and a prayer.

My hand shook even more as I took in the color of it.

Oh boy.

Oh no.

It had been years since the last time I'd done the sign of the cross, but I did it right then.

I recognized the color of the suit that was more than half ripped off the body there.

Charcoal.

I knew exactly what shade of blue the cape was too.

The whole world did.

Cobalt fucking blue.

There was only one person who wore a cape and a suit with those colors, and it wasn't a character from a Shinto Studios movie or comic book.

It was . . .

It was . . .

One of the members of the Trinity.

It was . . .

The Defender.

It was The fucking Defender.

Chapter Two

Fuck.

Shit.

Oh shit, shit, shitttt.

I opened my mouth to either squeal or scream—later on, I would probably be proud of myself for not straight-up fainting in the first place—when the body lying there started to writhe, then cough.

He coughed?

The figure, who I was 99.99999 percent sure was the being known to the world as The Defender—holy fucking shit—made another hoarse sound that sounded like clear and total pain. His hand extended out to the side, his fingers sifting through the dirt beneath and around him. He moaned. A deep cough rattled through his body, followed by a brutally pained sound.

What in the hell was going on? How the hell had he made it here? Where the hell had he come from?

I tipped my head to the sky again to make sure there was nothing up there, nothing coming after him. Only the clouds were there, at least as far as I could see.

How had this happened? I'd watched The Centurion survive a skyscraper falling on him. It had been all over the news for weeks. The world had witnessed The Primordial walk out of a building that had exploded without a single hair out of place.

I was going to cry.

Maybe throw up.

Maybe both.

The Defender had to have the same kind of invincibility too, shouldn't he?

All three members of the Trinity were icons of seemingly limitless strength, speed, and a variety of other incredible powers, who remained a mystery even after so many years. That was part of the reason why so many people were obsessed with them. Why any footage of them instantly went viral.

The Primordial had been the first to make her existence known. The film of her carrying a "misfired" nuclear bomb into space was considered the most life-changing moment in history. This incredible, seemingly human woman in a forest green suit had shot through the sky out of nowhere as millions panicked from the ground, wrapped her arms around the weapon, and carried it through the atmosphere and so far out it couldn't harm anyone or anything. Out of the view of thousands of cameras that had been aimed toward the sky, trying to follow her. There hadn't even been a pinprick of an explosion visible. All anyone knew was that there hadn't been mass casualties, as had been expected.

For months, it was all anyone had been able to talk about— the flying woman who had saved the world and disappeared afterward. Had she lived? Had she died? No one knew. But she had flown! She had saved thousands, if not millions.

It was almost a year before she made another appearance, setting off another round of complete disbelief that someone, or something, like her could exist. That she hadn't been destroyed. My grandpa had told me all about how people had been equally in awe and terrified of her at the time; I'd been too young to really understand how complicated her appearance in the world had been.

Then, over the next few years, two more beings, seemingly just like her, had appeared during other extreme times of need, performing incredible acts of heroism that stunned the rest of us normal people. I could remember the exact moments I'd seen videos of them for the first time. I was pretty sure everyone could.

They were superheroes brought to life.

Electro-Man and every other character ever created only paled in comparison to what these very real beings could do.

A whole decade went by without any of them ever communicating with anyone; they simply showed up, did what they had to do, and then disappeared. Sometimes it would be months before they were seen again. Then, about ten years ago, things changed, and they actually started talking to people a little bit, but the three of them remained the greatest mystery of all time.

The public had come up with their "titles." She had never called herself The Primordial or called the other two by any official name. Someone had come up with The Primordial, The Centurion, and The Defender, and the names had stuck. Then, some television anchor had been the first to call them the Trinity, and shortly after that, someone somewhere drew up a symbol for them—three black, equilateral triangles in a horizontal row.

So really, who wouldn't be obsessed? I used to have a bobblehead of The Primordial on my shelf. I'd seen a guy at the grocery store with a tattoo of The Defender's silhouette on his neck a week ago. The last town I'd lived in had a mural painted of The Centurion on the bank's wall.

On the other hand, some people thought they were a danger to mankind. My own grandma had done the sign of the cross any time they were mentioned. There were weekly protests with people claiming they needed to be destroyed, but those people probably wiped from back to front. Not my grandma obviously; she had just been really religious. Before my grandpa's dementia had progressed, he had thought they were amazing.

But of the three of them, The Defender was the one people

knew the least about. He'd been the last of the Trinity to appear. He never did appearances. Never, ever, spoke to the media. He just . . . did what he did and disappeared afterward. Drones had tried following him countless times, but every single one abruptly stopped working almost immediately. Footage of him was rare. A good view of his face was an anomaly that I wasn't sure even existed; the best shot I'd ever seen had been a distant picture of a dark-haired man with a clean, sharp jaw. For whatever reason, every photo and video of him came out distorted. He was the only one of the Trinity that came out like that. Some people speculated they were all capable of it, but he was the only one who did it.

But even without a good view of his face, the rest of him was unmistakable. The man in the shredded suit wasn't just long and muscular, he was built like a classical statue. What remained of the material was a charcoal gray color, and the cape and boots were dirt-smudged but blue. My flashlight landed on that incredible, unforgettable shade again. Not regular blue, a deep, bright blue.

Oh boyyyy.

This couldn't be happening.

It couldn't.

The man in my yard, surrounded by embers of *bright purple fucking fires* that were shrinking by the second, groaned again. His fingers stretched and curled, and he arched his neck back, a long, low moan escaping his body in a way that felt so, so wrong.

It was him.

Normal people didn't wear capes and boots around.

Their bodies didn't fall from the fucking *sky*.

It was him.

He grunted so quietly that I barely heard him.

But I *did* hear him, and it didn't make any sense. I was one of the last people in the world who needed one of the Trinity in their backyard, but the little, tiny bit of compassion in my heart wouldn't let me head back inside and pretend like this wasn't happening. Which was exactly what my grandma would have told me to do. Run the other way and pretend like I didn't know anything, pretend I hadn't seen anything. She would have told me to pack a bag and leave his ass there.

Survive had been the last thing my grandma had asked of me. *Do whatever you have to do* was the unspoken addition that had lingered between us. It was how she'd raised me.

On the ground, The Defender's fingers raked through the dirt as he gasped again.

Shit, shit, *shit*.

Before the reasonable part of my brain reminded me of why this was an awful idea, of what I had fucking promised, I ran over, skidding to a stop, just barely managing not to step on the figure there.

I stopped beside his thigh and dropped to my knees. Just as I was about to reach out and touch him, I slapped my palm down on my own leg and leaned over the man trying to breathe.

He was struggling.

"Oh, fuck me," I muttered to myself before setting my hand gently on top of his. "Hey." His skin was so hot it was almost uncomfortable, but I really didn't like the look on his scrunched face. Much less the state of the rest of him. "Are you okay?"

Broad fingers flexed in mine, almost more convulsively than on purpose, and The Defender tried to take another breath that sounded like a wheeze.

I wasn't even sure he knew I was there.

"Do you want me to call 9-1-1? Or . . . or is there a hotline to call the other members of the Trinity?" I was trying my damn best not to panic. Normal people could go to a hospital, but this man wasn't normal. What was a hospital going to do for him? He was missile-proof, for fuck's sake. It wasn't like a tiny little needle or even a big-ass needle was going to pierce his skin.

What do I do?

His face scrunched up, and his eyes squeezed closed. "No . . . hospital," The Defender grumbled in a voice that was barely audible. "No . . . one . . ."

Oh God, he was talking to me. He was actually talking to me. And I didn't like what he was saying.

"You don't want me to call anyone?" I tried my best not to shriek.

His fingers jerked in mine, and I barely heard him, but I managed to catch just enough to hear him whisper, "No." His throat bobbed. He gasped, then groaned. "In-inside . . ."

Inside? *My house?*

This was the last thing I needed. The absolute last thing. There was *the* last thing, and this would have come after that.

The Defender let out another rattling breath; it was the most pained sound I'd ever heard.

Focus, Gracie. Focus.

I could go back in and let him deal with his situation on his own. Technically, this wasn't my responsibility . . . but that wasn't the kind of person I wanted to be. It was the opposite of the kind of person I wanted to be. Okay, *okay. Don't panic.*

He didn't want me to call 911, and he wanted to go inside. I could do that much.

I had to.

Lifting my hand off his and sounding almost calm, even though part of me wanted to cry, I said, "Okay, okay. There's no way I can carry you. I think I have a wheelchair, but I need to get it. I'll be right back, okay?" I couldn't believe this shit was happening.

What might be the strongest person in the world—it was widely debatable among the Trinity—groaned again, and I took that as an okay. It wasn't like we had another choice. There was no way I could carry him, and I wasn't positive what he could manage. Not much from the look or sound of it.

He also didn't want to be out here for a reason, and I had to fight the urge to look toward the sky again. If there was something up there . . . Fuck, I didn't want to know.

Fuck, fuck, *fuckkkk*.

Okay, *calm down*, we'd figure it out. *I* would figure it out.

I jumped up, and even though my legs were worn out, I ran as fast as I could toward the outbuilding where the owner had left some things stored. I pushed in the code to the keypad and waited for the lock to turn. It was easy to find the wheelchair in the corner; I hadn't put anything new in the shed. Covered in dust and spiderwebs, I pulled it out anyway, figuring a little spider bite wouldn't do shit to a man who was immune to radiation. I was going to have to gamble it, but that was the least of my worries. It might be a blessing to get bit by a brown recluse right now. It'd be an excuse to get the hell out of here without feeling like a total piece of shit. I hated how much of a coward that made me, but it was the truth.

Picking it up and out the door, I set it down outside. Spreading it, I tipped it backward and pushed it all the way back around the house. I was panting by the time I made it to those damn dwindling purple fires. Then I stopped.

Because The Defender wasn't where I'd left him.

He was on his hands and knees. The man who was so much more than a man, who could break my neck just as easily as a twig, was *crawling*. Even in the dark and at a short distance, I could tell his entire half-naked body was shaking.

The sight of it stunned me.

I had never seen any of the Trinity even stumble before. Never, ever, ever. Hadn't I seen him carrying a fully loaded tanker?

Yet here he was, letting out these bone-rattling breaths as he struggled to move one knee, then the other, one hand, then the next, in front of him. Over and over like it was the single most difficult thing he'd ever done. Alarm pierced through my chest and skull and even my freaking soul as I watched him struggle before I snapped out of it and pushed the wheelchair the rest of the way to him.

The Defender dropped his head, panting shallowly, his fingers digging into the dirt.

"How can I . . . ?" *Get it together. Get it together.* "Tell me what I can do to help you," I told him breathlessly in the weirdest voice of my life.

I was panicking, okay. I was panicking.

One of the greatest powers on the planet, and more than likely in the universe, couldn't walk, and he'd fallen from the fucking sky like an asteroid in *Armageddon*, and there were a handful of small, purple fires smoldering around us.

And this shit was taking place in my *yard*.

How the hell were these fires purple?

This wasn't supposed to be happening.

He didn't answer, but he did manage to put another hand in front of the other until he slapped one onto a footrest, groaning so deep in his throat I was surprised the ground didn't shake.

Knowing this wasn't the time to hesitate and figuring the worst that would happen would be that I'd fall face-first on the ground or just, you know, break my back, I ducked under the arm that was on the footrest. "Let's get you up," I told him.

I could do this. I'd helped my grandparents countless times. In and out of bed, in and out of the shower, the car, the couch.

He was just . . .

A flying, invincible, super-fast, super-strong being that was breathing like he'd had half the bones in his body broken.

Was that possible? No. No way.

The Defender said nothing, and I took it as acceptance.

Please, Jesus, don't let me snap my spine in half.

"Ready? On three. One, two, three!"

He hissed long and low, so painfully that part of me expected him to faint, and I think I might have peed myself a little bit as his weight settled. I tried to stand, but the being leaned into me, and I damn near collapsed.

I huffed and I puffed, and if my house had been made of sticks, it would've gotten blown down from the strain he put on me, because *oh shitttttt.*

What the hell were his bones made of? Concrete? I groaned, my knees shaking, and chances were, I was going to end up with a bulging disc in my spine, but too bad.

I swore he leaned into me even more as his loose hand slapped the armrest wildly, giving me most of his five-hundred-pound weight—at least that's what it felt like. I strained. I huffed and puffed some more. My knees shook and sweat popped up on my back and under my arms instantly, but the tall man who I was confident now couldn't stand, moved his feet just enough to tell me he was trying to turn. He was trying to get into the wheelchair.

And that's when I recognized that my knees weren't the only things wobbling. His whole body was. His lungs rattled, and I wanted to peek at his face to make sure it wasn't turning blue, but even that was too much trouble.

We moved together, turning in place little by little. Just as we were barely shifting away from the chair, one of his knees buckled completely, and I knew. I knew he was going down, so I did the only thing I could think of.

I pushed his ass. Or the side of it.

It felt like all muscle too, but that was beside the point.

I shoved him toward the wheelchair just as he started to fall, and it was honestly a miracle that he moved that big frame enough to land butt first onto it. I dropped to my knees at the same time I heard him grunt.

"Oh fuck me," I panted, tucking my chin down to catch my breath. I was never going to be able to move again. Seriously, how much did he *weigh*?

He moaned at the same time the wheelchair groaned. He had boulders in his pockets. He had to. Lifting my head, I watched him tilt his head back, his arms going wide over the sides of the chair like he was absolutely exhausted. That terrible wheezing sound was back in his chest.

Waddling over on my knees, I stopped at his feet as I struggled to catch my breath.

I risked a glance up at the sky again and squinted. Then I squinted some more. Had I seen something? A glimmer of . . . something?

Oh hell no.

We needed to get inside. Now. A strong wind could probably lift the trailer, but it felt safer than staying out here in the fucking open.

I'd just been joking earlier when I thought *Things Going Wrong* was the story of my life.

I was never going to joke about that shit again.

Struggling back up to standing, I stumbled around the side to grip the handles just as The Defender dropped his head forward to hang loosely. As fast as I could, I turned and pushed the wheelchair forward. I was pretty much bent at the waist, pushing with every single ounce of my strength, heading for the ramp that was fortunately right there. When I was close enough, I started running toward it to build up momentum.

It only barely worked, and my hamstrings were on fire as we did the turns and made it to the door. It only took a second to punch in the code. Then I huffed even more to push him through the doorway and into the kitchen, grateful I hadn't set the dead bolt there. I'd beat myself up later for forgetting, for being lazy. Setting the wheelchair against the wall right beside the door, I kicked it closed harder than I needed to. I flipped the lock, even though I realized that wouldn't do shit against someone like him.

. I wasn't going to worry about that. Not yet. I was pretty sure I hadn't seen anything. Definitely not a pale purple twinkle that had to be a star.

Running into the living room, I grabbed a throw pillow and then went back into the kitchen, tucking it in behind his head to support it a little.

Finally, I dropped back to my knees, back to struggling to catch my breath. I'd thought I was in better shape than this. *Then again, when the hell had I ever trained to push someone this heavy around?*

Never, that's when.

I was going to need to go to a chiropractor. Maybe get an X-ray.

After a moment, when my chest was still rising and falling like crazy but I could actually breathe through my nose almost steadily, I lifted my head and planted my palms against my thighs. Then I shuffled around.

In front of him.

The Defender's head was drooped, but his frame wasn't shaking as badly as it had been.

Maybe that wasn't a good thing though.

Setting my hand over his wrist, I snuck it under and pressed my fingertips to where his pulse would be and waited.

A thump.

One second, two seconds, three . . . one too many before another.

One, two, three, four, more and more, and then another *thump.*

"Are you kidding me right now?" I choked. I hoped that was normal. I mean, he wasn't human-human, so his heart shouldn't beat the same way, right? Easing my fingertips away, I sat back on my heels and finally got a good look at him.

The familiar suit was mostly torn away from his body. A lot of tan chest was exposed; his bottoms clung to his legs for dear life. The entire right side of his cape was gone, like someone had ripped it right down the middle out of anger.

That wasn't terrifying.

Okay. No reason to worry about that. Lifting my gaze—

Oh.

It suddenly made a lot of sense why his face was so blurry in pictures and videos. It almost didn't seem possible to me either to be seeing what I was seeing, and I was looking at him, face-to-face. I had to blink twice for my eyes to absorb him. Maybe camera lenses couldn't handle what they focused on. What he really looked like.

It shouldn't have been a surprise. The Primordial was beautiful, and The Centurion looked like he could have been some kind of sun god to an ancient civilization. He was unbelievably handsome.

But The Defender . . .

He was the most beautiful person I'd ever seen.

Gorgeous wasn't the right word to describe the smudged, dirty face. Thick, dark eyebrows highlighted a smooth forehead and sharp, lean cheekbones. His hair was so dark I wasn't sure whether it was brown, black, or a shade in between. His perfect nose, rectangular jaw, and the fullness of his mouth tied all the pieces of him together into a package that was almost too fucking much. He was rugged and elegant at the same time.

He was big. Not hulking. Not bodybuilder sized, just . . . muscular but proportionate. Like a light heavyweight boxer that wasn't actually light weight.

The most surprising part about him though was his bright red, almost sunburnt cheeks.

His eyes opened, and I stopped breathing.

The Defender's irises glowed purple like stained glass held up against the sun.

Not blue, not gray, purple-purple. Violet maybe. Intense and bright, and 100 percent not human.

I felt like a deer in the headlights as that intense focus settled on me.

"Are you okay?" I asked like an idiot once I'd snapped out of it, like I hadn't just seen him struggle to simply move. "Should I call an ambulance? I don't know if I can get you into my car, but I could probably drive you to the hospital, even though I'm sure the military or someone would come pick you up in a helicopter. Or . . . or The Primordial would come get you. Or The Centurion."

I was rambling. I was fucking rambling, but I couldn't stop. It was a curse; it always had been. There was a reason I didn't initiate talking to strangers. I had no self-control.

I had a big mouth.

Once you got me going, it was almost impossible to stop me. Everything just started coming out. What I'd watched on TV, what I liked eating for dinner, how bad the flies were. And then under pressure? I was scared and fascinated, and my body didn't know how to handle either. It wasn't just my brain in shock; it was every part of me.

The Defender—*The* fucking *Defender*—stared at me with glowing purple eyes, and I was pretty sure they were watering from pain. His chest rose and fell in small gasps that were terrifying. Those eyes moved to a spot just behind my head, locked there for a moment, before they fluttered closed. His mouth moved, but nothing came out.

Was he *dying*?

I choked. "Please tell me what to do," I begged, desperate.

"No hospitals," the being gritted out. Bright white teeth flashed in a bared expression that wasn't a smile, making me gulp. "My . . . back . . ." he confirmed in a hiss I barely heard, the muscles at his cheeks flexing on and off as he let out a rattling, weak exhale. "Weak . . ." His throat bobbed roughly.

I stopped breathing.

Pale lavender lids framed with pure black eyelashes fluttered over those unreal eyes as another savage groan ripped its way up his throat.

"You need help. The hospital, something, someone," I whispered, scared. He couldn't be dying. He couldn't. He was invincible, wasn't he? What in the hell could hurt him this badly?

His head barely moved, but I took it to be him shaking it, telling me no. Then he confirmed it. "No. Tell . . . no one."

He wanted to stay *here*? In . . . in secret?

I already knew this was a shitty idea, and part of me knew damn well I was going to regret it, but . . .

So much of my life had been determined by the choices of others. Literally, almost every aspect of it had. All I had to do was look around to see the signs of it.

But I had made my own decision a long time ago. It was a small one, but it was mine. It lived in the back of my head every day with every beat of my heart and most of the thoughts in my brain. I knew exactly who I wanted to be. Who I *should* be, even if it battled against every paranoid, protective instinct that had been built up in my body over the years.

This man wasn't just a man. He had helped millions. He was an icon. A hero. What kind of person would I be if I didn't help him?

I knew that kind of person, and I fucking refused to be it.

The Defender didn't want help, didn't want a hospital, didn't want . . . anything, it seemed, other than secrecy. I didn't know why. I didn't know how this had happened or what danger we might possibly be in.

It couldn't matter. I'd worry about it later.

If there was a later.

Because I couldn't tell him no. I couldn't have left him out there. Not even for my grandma.

Even though he couldn't see me, I nodded at the man who had been made into little action figures that graced countless little people's bedrooms. The man who had inspired characters in television shows and movie after movie. A champion of the earth, he'd been called.

There was a giant statue of him in São Paulo in gratitude for his help after a massive earthquake.

And the same son of a bitch was in a wheelchair in my kitchen, injured and asking *me* for help.

"I'll help you," I promised him. Promised myself. "Tell me what to do. What do you need?"

A shake rattled through his body, his fingers twitched, and he whispered, "Time . . . food . . ."

"That's it?" No unicorn tears or some healing herb that could only be found on a remote island in the Pacific?

He grunted, and I wanted to cry. I had to strain to hear him grit out, "Don't . . . betray me."

Like I hadn't just dislocated my arms and given myself a bulging disc pushing him into my house while trying to help him.

This weird, weird feeling suddenly filled my stomach, but it was totally different from the one earlier. It wasn't dread . . .

But it made me really, really wary. "I won't. I promise."

The Defender slightly opened those glowing eyes and stared at me through the crack of them for a moment, and I was pretty sure I felt hot all of a sudden. The Centurion could shoot lasers from his eyes, but I'd never heard of The Defender being able to. Could he?

But before I could wonder over it any longer, his lids lowered again and he was out.

His head dropped back against the pillow as another shake rattled through that athletic frame.

I reached forward and found his slow, pumping pulse.

"What the hell did you get yourself into?" I wondered out

loud before leaning back onto my heels, worry, dread, and confusion battling it out in my chest.

Slowly lowering his hand back to his thigh, I took in the width of his wrist. The bones there were big but not abnormally huge. His skin had a deep golden tan to it that was lighter than mine. And as I looked at his fingers and then visually swept up his arm, I noticed his bones were the same all the way up. Sturdy. His shoulders were broad, just like they seemed on television. With most of his chest exposed thanks to the torn suit, I could tell the bones at his sternum were thick and his chest was padded with muscle.

He was unreal. A wet dream in the flesh. Perfection.

A very fit, athletic-looking man. He didn't have diamond skin or a third eye. Maybe he had a third nipple, but I wasn't going to look for it.

Part of me had expected him to look . . . different—inhuman, maybe, whatever that meant. But he didn't.

He was normal.

But what the hell had happened to him?

Where had he *been*?

Should I have put him in bed or the couch instead?

Could I move him?

I was in over my head. Taking care of my elderly grandparents was one thing. Taking care of all . . . this . . . was something totally different.

But he was already here, and I didn't believe in fate, but *he was here.* Of all the millions of fucking places he could have landed in, it was with me. And out of all the things he could have asked for, it had been time and food he'd brought up.

How could I let him down?

My stomach twisted, and the hairs on the back of my neck rose.

Was this what the hell my stomachache had been about?

It didn't matter.

First things first. He'd said he needed food, and even though I had groceries, it wasn't enough for both of us, but I'd worry about that tomorrow.

Did he want to be fed now? Or had he just meant in general?

Struggling to my feet, I hobbled toward the fridge in the corner of my little kitchen. I pulled out the soup I'd eaten with my sandwich and tried to think while I warmed up a bowl in the microwave. He'd asked for food and hadn't said it in a passive way like *let's wait until I'm awake*. Hadn't he?

I poured the soup into the blender and waited until the potatoes were pureed and figured it couldn't be so bad. Baby food it was going to be, because I wasn't willing to risk him choking on chunks if he didn't wake up to chew. Because that would be my luck, finding one of the most well-known people in the world and then having him die in my house immediately afterward. I'd bury the body and a cop would come by, find his bones, and then I'd go to jail for murder.

Or The Primordial and The Centurion would search to the ends of the world for me, rip me apart limb by limb, and toss me into the ocean as a shark buffet.

I knocked on the cutting board I'd left on the counter.

It took me a minute to set up a workstation. I dragged the coffee table from the living room and set the cup on it. I'd never fed a baby before; I'd never even been around a baby in more than passing, but I'd fed my grandparents. I could feed him.

If I had good luck, he'd wake up and muster up enough energy to chew and help me out, but I didn't. So I opened his mouth a little by pressing on the hinge of his jaw—a dull buzz ignited over my fingers, but I was also going to think about that later—and reached over to spoon a bit of soup between his lips. They were a pretty dark pink color. His mouth was perfect.

And I had no business helping him.

I pushed that thought aside and focused on what I was doing. Fortunately, he didn't wake up, but his throat bobbed, so maybe I wasn't totally shit out of luck. Slowly and surely, I spooned more and more soup into his mouth while soaking up the angles and bones that made up his face.

The urge to poke at his cheek and feel its texture was right there, but I held back. Better not. My thumb felt a little weird where I was touching him already.

I stopped after about ten spoonfuls, not wanting to overdo it until I knew he could keep it down. I'd give him a little more later.

With a towel under his chin, I poured a little bit of water into his mouth, and he didn't let me down then either; he swallowed that too. Convenient. And weird, but I wasn't going to over-think it.

I had to help him. Whatever I had to do, I would. If anyone deserved it, he did.

It was the least I could do. The least anyone could do.

And, hopefully, this superbeing wouldn't shit himself, even if that was at the bottom of the list of things for me to worry about—at least until I knew how he'd ended up like this. How he'd ended up here.

I rubbed my face and turned to eye the atlas still sitting there on the table. *Sorry, Grandma*, I thought. *I'll get out of here as soon as I can.*

Chapter Three

He didn't wake up. Not that day or the next or the one after that.

But it wasn't the sleeping part that scared me; it was the fact he didn't pee or poo. For *three* days. I would've been headed to a hospital. I wasn't exactly crazy over the way I had to go about checking him either, but I wasn't about to go prying at the remains of his suit, trying to look at more than what was already exposed. I'd spent enough time staring at him, but I figured it wasn't every day that a being some people referred to as a god sat in an old wheelchair in my house, injured and in what seemed like pretty close to a coma with a Hello Kitty blanket draped over his chest.

I fucking hoped it wasn't a coma. I was trying to be positive and call it a nap. A nice, long, regenerative nap.

What I had done was poke at his calf. The material there was thick and almost felt like really flexible crocodile skin. It was textured and cool to the touch. The Defender didn't smell, and there was no wet spot anywhere on the material beneath his butt, and that was my scientific proof that he hadn't pooped or peed. He *ate*, so he had to digest his food somehow. Did beings like him even go? Did they have . . . buttholes?

I had so many questions.

Questions I had no business having in the first place, but curiosity was my second greatest flaw, after running my mouth.

The fact was, the less I knew about him and he knew about me, the better. And saying nothing was easier than lying. It was how I'd gotten through life without giving away the things that needed to stay a secret.

He was still eating and drinking water, and even though he felt warmish, it didn't feel high enough to be a fever. He'd been pretty hot the first day he'd arrived, but I figured that had something to do with those purple fires that hadn't left a trace. I hadn't taken his temperature because there was no way that would be accurate anyway considering his heartbeat. While he hadn't gotten any better, he hadn't gotten worse. *I thought*. So there was that.

I would only do what he asked for, and I had to hope it was enough. Part of me had been worried leaving the house the day after he showed up to go buy groceries, but nothing had happened. The Centurion and The Primordial hadn't dropped a submarine on me.

I did skip my runs to be on the safe side, even though it felt wrong.

I fed him slowly, every three hours, five times a day. Soup—always soup—that resembled baby food. I slept on the couch to be close in case he needed anything. It was where I'd slept every night since. I'd made a deal, and I wouldn't back out on it.

And if this went against everything my grandparents had instilled in me, it was for a good cause, and I could only hope I wouldn't live to regret it.

The important part was, I wasn't about to let him die on me. He'd probably haunt me for the rest of my life if that happened, and that would be awkward. There were things I did in my bedroom that I didn't want anyone else to witness. With my luck, he would end up being some kind of poltergeist superghost or something.

Wiping off his mouth with a warm, damp towel after feeding

him liquefied chicken, ten-vegetable, and rice soup, I sat back on my heels and took in the features of the sleeping being in my house. I figured I now knew how people had to have felt when they'd first discovered fire. It was hard not to stare.

His cheeks still had a hint of a sunburnt color to them, and he hadn't stirred at all since that first day. His fingers had twitched once or twice. His toes did the same a couple times too, but that had been the extent of his movements.

It didn't make sense. None of this did. I couldn't move past it.

I sighed and took in all the bones that built up his face for about the fifteenth time since he'd shown up. He looked like he might be somewhere in his thirties, but I wasn't really that good with ages, so I might be totally off. It was hard to tell since his skin was red but had no signs of deep wrinkles.

He was stupid handsome.

And a fucking mystery.

I'd always been a sucker for a good mystery.

"How much longer until you wake up?" I asked him. "Aren't you supposed to have some kind of regeneration power, or does that just happen in comics?"

He didn't answer, of course, so I leaned back and soaked up his stunning face a little longer.

I hadn't been this close to anyone since my grandma had passed away. The only conversations I'd had in the last few years were with my students and the occasional extra-friendly person at a store. And here I had him. The Defender of all people.

It really was one of the last things I needed.

I wasn't one to pray, but I closed my eyes for his sake—and a little bit for my own—and wished he woke up soon.

"Have a good day," I told my student, Ha-ri, as I leaned back in my chair.

The sixteen-year-old dipped her head forward. "Have a good night," she replied, sounding out the syllables as best as she could.

She had come such a long way over the last year we had been working together, and I was really proud of her. In three months, she was going to be traveling to England to study abroad, and her family wanted her to be as prepared as possible for the trip. I had worked with her sister a few years ago, and that's why they had reached out to me for her.

I gave her a quick wave back and ended the chat session. She was my last student of the day. Luckily, the other night, I'd been able to reschedule my lesson with Jo Ji-Wook, and I'd squeezed him in at two in the morning. I was trying to be as quiet as possible not to bother the man in my kitchen, but I had to work, and unfortunately for him, almost all my lessons were in the evening, night, or basically the middle of the night for me.

Pushing away from the desk, I flipped my head forward and gingerly took my wig off and set it on the mannequin head on the corner of my desk. Just as carefully, I tugged off the nylon hose that kept my hair plastered to my head and set that beside the wig before raking a hand through the strands. I could never get used to wearing a wig, even after so long. It was one of those things that was probably totally unnecessary, but I wore it anyway.

With a yawn, I got up and picked up my computer, knowing exactly what the hell I was going to do for a little while. The same thing I'd been doing before my back-to-back students. I'd even left my bag of Cheetos on the couch so it would be ready for my next round of investigating.

It only took a second to creep down the hall and into the kitchen, eyeing The Defender still motionless in the chair, his chest rising and falling so slowly. Quietly, I opened the fridge and grabbed a can of soda before tiptoeing back out into the living room. I cracked open my Dr Pepper, unrolled my Cheetos, and opened my laptop.

I'd already spent an hour looking up more information on them—the Trinity. I'd thought about looking up just The Defender, but that was too risky, and I was too paranoid even using the browser page that didn't save your history. You never knew who could hack into your shit. I logged out of all my accounts after every time I used them and deleted my cookies and browser history. I didn't even have an app on my phone for my email or bank account.

I wasn't going to be the one to give him away if someone was looking for him.

And selfishly, I wasn't going to put myself into a shittier situation either. This was already thin-ice territory. Like the thinnest of thin ice.

That's why I was doing research, to hopefully learn something that might help me help him.

But the thing about the internet was that, while there was a lot of information about the Trinity on it, a ton of it made no sense. Some of it seemed like it could be legitimate, or at least that it *could* be possible. But other theories?

People had some active imaginations.

That or they were really, really bored.

Some of it had merit though. There were two fields of thought about their background. Some people believed they were from another planet. Others thought they were a lab experiment.

Some believed they had been born to human mothers and then genetically modified. Others thought they had been "made" by someone, like the military or a pharmaceutical company. I could see, in a way, how that could make sense. But the conspiracy theorist in me thought if that had been the case, there would be a hell of a lot more of them by now than just the three. Unlike in movies, no other beings with powers that rivaled theirs, much less came close to them, had ever come forth. There weren't battles or evil villains. For all anyone knew, they were the only ones who could do what they did.

I hummed and clicked back on my browser window. There was just so much information—rumors and theories, pictures and videos—to wade through. Fascinated, I kept getting sucked into the wild tales about them.

Someone claimed to have grown up on a ranch beside a family with triplets that she swore looked like younger versions of them. Someone else claimed that forty years ago, they'd seen a UFO crash nearby, and when they got to the site, there had been little kids climbing out of it. Stories like that were endless. People claimed to have seen something suspicious in a cornfield, out of their window while going through Death Valley, and while flying in an airplane.

Scrubbing my cheek, I picked up my can of Dr Pepper and took a sip before focusing on the search results on my screen. I'd left off on page four of . . . I didn't even know how many.

The sound of creaking in the kitchen had me leaning over to the side to take a look.

Someone was awake.

The Defender was sitting there, hand in the air, head still propped against the pillow stuffed behind him. He spread his fingers wide before forming a fist. He was blinking slowly, the white-and-pink blanket that had been on him before pooled at his waist.

There's no reason to be nervous. There's no reason to be nervous.

But I was still fucking nervous.

I shut my computer and got up. "Are you okay?" I called out.

The superbeing didn't look away. His attention was fixed on his fingers, turning them one way and then the other before sliding his gaze toward me, his expression groggy. And . . . grumpy?

I almost tripped.

Because I hadn't imagined it the other night. His eyes weren't just kind of purple; they were a pure, royal purple. Indigo maybe. In that moment, they weren't violet like I'd thought. There was a dot of black for a pupil, but that was it. They weren't glowing, but they were still incredible.

And the man with the most beautiful eyes I'd ever seen, settled into the most handsome face I had also ever laid eyes on, looked in my direction, blearily.

Was he out of it? Stopping right in front of the chair, I picked up the glass of water I'd refilled for him earlier and crouched.

"Are you okay?" I asked again. "You good? You . . . got here a few days ago," I reminded him, watching his face carefully, trying to see his eyes. Maybe he had a concussion?

Was that possible? He couldn't have brain damage, could he? I'd been too worried about his back to think about his head.

I didn't think I imagined the fact that, at the sound of my voice, he blinked once and something in those crazy-colored eyes seemed to focus, to snap into place, and suddenly, I knew he was finally seeing *me*.

And just as quickly as I processed that, the most ferocious fucking scowl formed over that gorgeous face while I crouched there. I almost wanted to look over my shoulder to make sure there wasn't some kind of demon behind me, but there wasn't.

What the hell was with that expression?

There wasn't anything on my face; I'd just seen it during my video call. Did he really not remember what happened? Had he been in so much pain?

"You asked to stay here. You said not to call anyone." My voice came out high and shaky because I was fucking nervous.

His eyelids dropped to a sliver, and the scowl on his mouth got even deeper. His nostrils flared. My skin . . . why was my skin buzzing? Why did he look about ready to fucking kill someone? Was he breathing harder too?

"I didn't kidnap you or anything, swear." I was starting to ramble. His lip curled back just enough for me to see his canine exposed. *I'm Gracie*, formed on the tip of my tongue, but I changed my mind and swallowed it down. *The less information, the better.* Right. That was another rule I'd followed my whole life.

He growled.

I suddenly wished I had a knife on me. Not that that would stop him, or much less slow him down, but it wouldn't make me feel so helpless when he was sitting there staring at me like I'd smashed his headlights. I swallowed hard as that pink mouth went flat and my skin tingled even more.

He was definitely breathing harder.

And he was mad at whatever he had to be mad at. It couldn't be me. I hadn't done shit.

The Defender's nostrils flared again, and that gaze flicked back to a spot behind my head before he closed his eyes, so, so tight that lines formed at the corners of them. He swallowed hard. That broad chest rose and fell once, and the muscles at his cheeks flexed like he was gritting his teeth.

"You good?" I asked slowly, concerned.

He couldn't really think I'd kidnapped him, could he? I wasn't that dumb. I didn't think anybody would be dumb enough to try and kidnap someone who could bat a 50 caliber round away like it was a gnat.

On the other hand, people ate laundry detergent, so . . .

Another shaky breath later, he spread his fingers wide again just as he opened his eyes too, that pissed-off expression still on his features.

The Defender stared at me. Hard.

I started to open my mouth again to ask if he was okay, but I shut it right back.

Those dark purple eyes moved over my face as his mouth went flat, and after a long, long glare that made my heart start beating fast, he finally flicked one of his fingers toward the glass of water I was holding.

Okay . . .

My hand shook as I held it out toward him.

He didn't take it, but those eyes settled back on me heavily with what seemed an awful lot like contempt for some reason. Or maybe he was just mad at the situation and I was the lucky motherfucker to have to be around him while he calmed down? I'd never pictured myself meeting a member of the Trinity, and I sure as hell hadn't imagined getting glared at by one of them.

It made me gulp.

Cupping my hand under his chin, I raised it and brought the glass to those pink lips. But this time, instead of the small trickle I poured so he wouldn't choke, his throat bobbed, ready, and he drank greedily. The whole glass was gone in two big chugs.

"Want more?"

The Defender grunted, his gaze lingering on me in a way that made me even more nervous.

Could he read my mind?

I went and refilled the glass, thought about it, and grabbed the fruit salad I'd cut up that morning, keeping my mind blank the whole time. Back at his side, I held the cup as he chugged down that one too. Then I offered up the bowl.

He was still glaring.

All righty then. I speared a piece of reddish fruit with a fork and held it up to his mouth, my hand still trembling. Bright white teeth bit into the watermelon. The Defender chewed slowly, almost thoughtfully, his gaze staying where it was the entire time before briefly flicking back to the bowl. Out of the corner of my eye, I saw his fingers flex then straighten, over and over again.

I speared another piece and held it out. He took it and chewed that slowly too, eventually eating another five before whispering out an "Enough" that sounded absolutely grouchy and rough, like I was inconveniencing him or something.

I set the bowl aside and tried to be reasonable, like he was a normal stranger who needed my help and not one of the most well-known people on the planet who could also smash me like a bug when he was at his best.

Fuck me.

"So . . . do you . . . need to pee? Go number two? Want to eat something that's not fruit or soup?" I offered, wanting to ask him if he pooped or not but figuring with that glare, this wasn't the right moment.

Chances were, there was no perfect moment to ask him about his poo.

The man I'd watched stop a moving train made a sniffing sound and literally said one word. "Chicken."

If he wasn't going to worry about not using the bathroom regularly, I guess I didn't need to either. "There's chicken in the soup, but that's all the chicken I have right now," I told him, watching his features closely.

The Defender stared at me as he whispered, "Steak," the one word sounding brittle.

Was that his version of compromising?

"It's frozen. I left the first day after you got here, but I haven't gone shopping again since then because I didn't want to leave you alone. How about slices of turkey breast?"

How he managed to tell me to fuck off with my turkey breast without actually moving his lips, almost impressed me.

If it wasn't so startling, it might have been irritating too, honestly. Beggars can't be choosers, and there had to be millions of people who would kill for this experience. To nurse a member of the Trinity back to health. To be so up close and personal with one. It was like coming across a unicorn. The thing was . . .

I just wasn't one of those people. Maybe at a different time. In a different life.

"That's all I've got, I'm sorry," I explained as mildly as I could, even though he was kind of being difficult. Wasn't he? I hadn't been over to that many people's houses in my life, but I'd always eaten whatever it was they gave me to be polite.

What I got in response was a pissy expression on the most perfect face on the planet.

But no matter how symmetrical his features were or how nice his skin was or who the hell he was and what he was capable of, I pressed my lips together to keep from making a face back at him.

Good thing I was used to keeping control of my expressions when my grandma would ask me to do something I didn't want to or say something I didn't want to hear.

He's in pain. He's probably used to people bending over backward to do his bidding. I couldn't handle a migraine without getting grouchy, and I didn't even have people around to deal with my bullshit.

I'd thought about it, and short of pawning him off on someone despite his request, it wasn't like I could call emergency services to come pick him up. That would raise too many red flags and bring way too much attention on me. Mostly though, he had asked. Even if he didn't remember, I did.

I had to suck this shit up and do it. It was the least I could do after everything he'd done. And if he wanted chicken, I'd get him chicken. He wanted steak? I'd give him steak. Just not this instant. I wasn't his maid. "I can see about picking some up tomorrow," I tried to compromise too.

From his expression, that wasn't soon enough, but the nearest store still open was an hour and a half away.

He might be The Defender, and he might deserve the world for the things he'd done, but *driving* that far at *night*?

No.

"The store is closed already."

I'd always thought my grandma's glares could say a million words, but from the look of it, she wasn't the only one with that power.

Unfortunately for him, I thought he was amazing but not amazing enough to drive in the darkness to go buy groceries.

"Unless your body is totally different than mine, which I don't think it is since you didn't throw up when I fed you blended-up vegetables with airplane noises"—Oh boy, I hadn't meant to tell him that—"I have soup, or I can make you a sandwich with the sliced turkey. I can put some avocado in it too," I offered carefully, calmly. "That's all I have. I was scared to leave you alone for too long. So . . ." I'd closed and locked the gate to stop people from crossing the property just to be safe—at least from other humans.

His eyes glowed for about a second before going back to normal. To plain beautiful, not unreal. I gulped.

Was that a yes then?

I'd take it. While he was responsive, though I knew I shouldn't ask him anything, I couldn't help myself. This was important. "Do you remember? What happened?"

His incredible glare gave me nothing at all.

Moving on then. Okay. There were a couple other things I could ask that weren't too personal, one of them being the thing that had been sitting on my chest from the moment he'd first passed out. "Is there anything I can do right now? To help?" *Please tell me to call someone. Please tell me to drive you somewhere so that somebody else can help you.*

My prayers went unanswered when he gruffly said, "For now . . . nothing."

For now. I didn't miss that part. I tried my best to keep my face blank so he wouldn't see how badly I didn't want him here. "Are you sure there's no one you want me to call?" I tried again.

His gaze flicked to the wall behind me again as he said in a crab-ass voice that sounded oddly resigned, "No."

All righty then. I could do this. It wouldn't be the first time I'd taken care of someone.

It wouldn't exactly be hard to look at his face a while longer. I'd probably never get to see bone structure so perfect again in my life. Might as well appreciate it now.

His gaze moved around the kitchen and beyond. I knew what he was looking at. The worn table to his left was covered by an embroidered tablecloth that my grandma had made before I'd been born. It hid the dings and marks on it that had already been there when I'd moved in with just my suitcases and a few boxes. There was an old cat clock with a swishing tail on the wall behind me that I was pretty positive was what he kept focusing on.

The kitchen was small with Formica counters and cabinets that were a shade of tan that had been popular in the eighties. I'd never bothered replacing the checkered valance curtains above the one small window in the kitchen or the ones above the back door. Their faded Eiffel Tower pattern had grown on me.

Beyond the kitchen and the breakfast area was what could be called a minimalist living room but was mostly just me not having a lot of stuff. The couch was small and floral patterned. It had already lived a full life before I'd ever sat on it. The same could be said about the rest of the furniture in the house. Most of it was from the old owner, but a couple things I'd picked up at the nearest thrift store that benefited the local SPCA. It was mismatched and in decent shape, for the most part. Back when we'd moved around every semester, I'd slept on a blow-up mattress for years.

You didn't buy expensive things that might have to be left

behind if you had to take off on a moment's notice. It was why I had four plates, two bowls, four glasses, and two coffee cups total. There was no point in having more.

Pushing aside the loneliness that suddenly rose in my chest as he continued looking around, like the walls didn't matter—and maybe they didn't—I focused back on what we had been talking about. "I fed you while you were asleep. I'm trying not to move you around, even though I'm pretty sure you need to have someone take a look at you. Do you think something's broken?"

The Defender shifted his gaze back to me, the movement slow, almost too slow.

Fuck me then. "All right. Or you'll be totally fine on your own. What do I know?" I trailed off with a side-eye.

He didn't say a word.

A feeling of dread filled my throat, and my stomach went weird. Weren't superior beings supposed to be wise and well-balanced? Nice? If not happy, at least at peace with themselves and the world? I'd always thought they would be likable. Kind. Maybe serious because of all that pressure on them to save the world. I thought they would be charismatic.

That they would be as cool as they looked when they were in the air above a structure, looking down at the world like Mufasa in *The Lion King*.

But so far, that wasn't the vibe I was getting. That wasn't the vibe I was getting at all.

Because my gut said this man wasn't a ball of sunshine. I had a feeling he wasn't even a night-light.

What he was, was seeming like a pain in the ass, if I was going to be totally honest, and that made me feel like a criminal for thinking that of someone in the Trinity.

I was going to have to think about this.

For now . . . "I'll make you a sandwich, and if there's something else you might want, you can let me know. The grocery store isn't very big, and the selection isn't that great, but I might be able to order anything else; it'll just take a few days to arrive." More like a week, but . . . I wasn't even sure he'd be here that long. I wanted to ask if he was supposed to have some kind of crazy regeneration, but all I had to do was take in his expression and the question died in my mouth.

The less I asked, the better.

He was back to watching me like I had tied him to the chair and was holding him hostage.

I'd always thought The Primordial would have a queen-like disposition. She used intelligent words and concise sentences. She was the epitome of classy and dignified.

I highly doubted she grunted at people.

But this man . . .

Heading into the kitchen, I wondered for the twentieth time what in the hell I'd gotten myself into.

This whole situation was bad enough. I'd made promises—promises to people who mattered, to myself.

I couldn't let all my sacrifices—all their sacrifices either—be in vain. I just had to keep my shit together until this being was out of my life. Even if I felt about two wrong moves away from having life blow up in my face.

I could worry about that later. In the meantime, I made his damn sandwich, which looked really good, and once I was done, I headed over with a turkey BLT with avocado. I set the plate on the coffee table still there in front of him and sat on the chair that hadn't moved since he'd arrived either, planting my butt on it. Those dark, incredible eyes followed my movement.

I picked up the plate and held it up for him.

He stared.

God, I hoped his injury wasn't worse than it seemed, I thought as I took the sandwich and held it to his mouth.

The man's eyes bounced from the sandwich to my face and

back, but he opened his mouth, showing off those strong, white teeth, and took a neat bite, chewing slowly, that intense gaze still steady on me.

Maybe he was feeling me out.

Or maybe he was in a bad wittle mood over what had happened to him.

I'd agreed to help, and I would. Stomachache or not. Worst mistake of my life or not.

After he'd quietly demolished the sandwich and drank another two glasses of water, he seemed to melt back into the wheelchair while it groaned under his weight. He let out one of those deep, rattling breaths that told me there was something very wrong, and I had no medical background.

As I set the plate on his thigh so I could stand up, my knees already stiff, The Defender's voice rattled, all husky and irritated, "I want . . . to get out of this."

"Out of the chair or your suit?" I asked him as I straightened, trying not to think of how unreal this conversation was.

"Both," the man in the charcoal suit rumbled in the crabby tone I was starting to believe might be his usual one.

I blinked. "Are you sure it's okay?"

The fan on the ceiling spun once before coming to a sudden stop like when the lights turned off.

Except they hadn't.

I tensed. Was that a coincidence or . . . ?

It started spinning again.

"You think I don't know what I'm capable of?" The Defender whisper-hissed as he stared over at me.

Oh boy.

"I can get out of this chair," he said slowly, his nostrils flaring. "Every bone in my body could be broken . . . and I would still be stronger . . . than every human on this planet."

He'd said *human*, hadn't he?

With his gaze locked on mine, his fingers reached for the plate balanced on his leg. The Defender picked up the fork I had brought over to scoop up any food that fell out of the sandwich. Gaze on me, he set his thumb on one end, middle finger closer to the tines, and slowly folded it in half. Then, just as easily, he straightened it out and set it back.

It was hard to keep my face blank, but I did.

Because *really?* Suddenly his strength made up for the fact he hadn't even been able to feed himself? Or that I'd had to help him into the chair in the first place? I'd been sheltered most of my life, but I wasn't a fucking idiot.

I knew what he was capable of normally.

But he was starting to get on my nerves anyway.

I pressed my lips together and held up my hands. "All right, Hercules. You know your body better than I do. I can't carry you. You'll have to get up. There's the couch and my bed. Your choice."

Dark, curly lashes fell over his eyes. "Like you could carry me."

Well, this was going to go well, I could already tell.

This was a shitty idea, and I knew it. He should be in a hospital, or with other people who at least had a fragment of an idea what they were doing, not *me*. Someone who could actually lift him would be a better caretaker.

Just about anybody would.

"Do you want to go ahead and do it now?" I asked.

He grunted. Again.

All righty then.

The bed it was going to be because the couch wasn't big enough to spread out on, even for me. At least my room was clean, and I'd changed the sheets a few days ago. I didn't have another set to swap them out, so he was going to need to suck it up.

Silently moving around behind him, I grabbed the handles

on the back of the wheelchair and put my hamstrings into it as I started pushing, huffing and puffing as I turned it in the living room to go down the hall. And if he groaned under his breath more than once, I pretended I didn't hear it. He'd asked for this.

At the bedroom door, I put my back into it and pushed him the rest of the way in. The urge to ask him if he was sure this was a good idea was on the tip of my tongue, but his perfect pale face was so grouchy, I kept it to myself. But really, what the hell had I done for him to be this pissy? All I'd done was try to help him *because he'd asked*. I hadn't shot his ass out of the sky.

Bending down, I snuck my arm under his armpits. It took a while and a few groans before he managed to stand, his long legs shaking. This was such a shit idea, but this was what he wanted, so . . .

One step after another was difficult for him from the harsh way he started breathing, and we were both panting the three steps it took to get to the bed. Thankfully, I didn't live in a mansion and it didn't take long to turn him around. Then it was more struggling, and that too-tall body shook as he slowly lowered himself to sit on the edge.

"Suit's ruined. I want . . . to take it off," he huffed the second he was settled.

Off? As in off his body? It was a fucking miracle my eyebrows didn't jump off my face.

I'd helped my grandparents undress. This was nothing new. I could do this clinically.

I pushed the chair back and dropped to kneel in front of him, trying my hardest not to panic or let my heart start beating fast with nerves. "Where should I start?" I asked him in the fucking funniest voice of my whole life because . . . because . . .

I was going to undress The Defender.

Me. Gracie.

I gulped.

It was going to be a sacrifice in the name of humanity.

And it was the closest I'd been to a man in a really long time.

He wasn't just a man though, was he? He was all muscle and nice skin and a beautiful face that the world had no idea what it was missing out on, and . . . everything. And I was about to help him take off his suit. That world-renowned, charcoal suit and blue cape, or what was left of it.

Me.

"By my neck," he grumbled, raising a hand and pulling at the loop of material that barely managed to keep the cape on him. It ripped easily, way too easily, but he made a little sound like even that hurt.

Right, Mr. I Am Stronger Than Every Human On This Planet.

And really, maybe it was the pain—I hoped it was—but he was seeming like he really might be—I whispered it in my head just in case he could hear me—kind of a dickhead.

Thinking it felt like blasphemy, but also like the truth.

I nodded, side-eyeing him for clues he might have known what I'd just called him, as I reached for his face. He was back to staring-slash-glaring, so I ignored him. It didn't take long at all to pull the rest of the thick, heavy material off him. He'd done all the hard work ripping it, and I dropped it beside him on the bed. Most of the sleeves of the suit had gotten lost or burned at some point, so all I had to do was peel what was left down toward his middle section.

I kept my eyes glued to the dark material, making sure to pretend like stripping him wasn't blowing my mind. Like it was every day I got an up-close and personal view of a body I was trying my absolute hardest to pretend was nothing special when I 100 percent would have gotten a microscope and checked him out if I could've gotten away with it. Like I wouldn't have had a poster of him under a waterfall if my grandma would have let me get away with it as a teenager. Of course, this was a once-in-a-lifetime chance to see one of the most incredible bodies in the universe, and I couldn't even properly enjoy it.

What a fucking shame.

When I had the tatters down to his waist, I looked up at him. He was glowering, but he still asked, "Do you . . . have pants?"

I nodded.

Dark eyelashes swept over those incredible eyes. "Leave 'em. Turn around."

"You don't need help taking the rest of your suit off?" I croaked, hoping I didn't sound hysterical. Not because I wanted to help him take off his . . . bottoms but because he looked shaky sitting there.

But, obviously, that wasn't what he assumed, because somehow his expression got that much more irritated, which was a surprise because I hadn't thought that was fucking possible. "No," he snapped.

I'd go fuck myself then.

I *really* hoped it was pain making him this bitchy.

I peeked at his face to see if he'd read my mind, but he wasn't shooting daggers at me.

Whew.

Getting up, I went to my dresser and pulled out one of the pairs of men's sweatpants I wore sometimes when it was cold. They might be loose on him because his hips were narrower, but they'd fit. I also grabbed one of my biggest T-shirts, hesitating for a second when I noticed the design, but then I bit my lip and set the clothes beside him on the bed.

"Help me get up."

Whatever he wanted.

Back under his heavy arm, I helped him and his fucking concrete bones to stand up, and as soon as he was on his feet, he put his hand on the nightstand and shot me a dirty side-look that

I definitely didn't deserve. What was up his ass? Did I do something to him in a dream? "Turn around," he ordered in his crackly voice. "Close your eyes."

That's what I did, even though I wondered if he thought I was going to peek through my fingers.

I stood there, facing the wall, listening to soft groans that said he was definitely hurting. He hit something, then banged into something else. The sudden scent of something burning hit my nose at the same time a bright light flashed on the other side of my lids.

"Everything okay?" I asked, trying to imagine what the hell he was doing.

He gave me what I was starting to think was his typical answer as the burning smell peaked: The Defender grunted. Then he made the same noise as it sounded like he sat back down from the way the mattress creaked.

"Done," that exhausted voice huffed.

I pinched my lips together as I finally turned. He was on the edge of the bed. He'd managed to pull the gray sweatpants on, but the shirt I'd left for him had fallen to the floor beside his feet and the blanket.

Oh.

He was shirtless.

The Defender was basically half-naked.

And if I could've counted it discreetly, I was pretty sure there were eight little squares of muscle making up his abs.

But I couldn't actually confirm it.

I couldn't look at anything but his face, and I knew it. He would notice. And I had self-control. I really did. There was a box of cookies that I managed to only eat two of at a time.

I wasn't weak.

I had discipline.

I could do this. I could keep my eyes to myself. Above his

nipples. I could ignore his maybe-eight-pack and pretend I didn't see all that endless, dark-golden skin.

Keep it together. Keep it fucking together, Gracie. You can do it.

Compared to everything else I'd been through, that should be easy-peasy.

I'd almost convinced myself of it when I opened my mouth and croaked, "Do you need me to help you with the shirt?"

Yeah, I wasn't fooling fucking anybody.

The Defender's expression didn't change at all, and I didn't think I was imagining the ice in his voice when he answered. "Yes."

Oh boy.

Stepping close, I picked up the shirt and shook it out, keeping my eyes glued to the floor because I couldn't look at his chest, and I sure couldn't focus on the design either. Then, in a move I'd practiced so many times with my grandma, I tugged the biggest opening over his head, and then I picked up one wrist and paused.

His hands were red. Really, really red, like they'd been sunburnt to hell, even worse than his cheeks had been. Those were now a dark pink as well. His hands definitely hadn't been like that earlier.

Trying not to make a face or ask a fucking question, I lifted it carefully and put it through the armhole, then did the same for the other. He helped, but not much, and that said a hell of a lot.

There was something seriously wrong if he was struggling to lift his arms to get dressed and feed himself.

But that wasn't supposed to be any of my business. None of this was. Not his strength and not his suddenly red hands.

Much less the circumstances that had led up to him being here.

On my bed, about to give me a million-dollar view of his body.

I swallowed.

Dropping into a crouch, I tugged his shirt from where it was bunched up around muscular pecs—getting a good view of *two* brown nipples—down the most impressive stomach in the history of the world, and finally let it sit where the band of the sweatpants rested.

That memory was going to be burned into my brain for the rest of my life. The tight, hard muscles of his abs, on his obliques, along his ribs . . . all that smooth, tan skin . . .

I snapped out of it.

Where the hell had his suit gone?

Glancing up, he looked so . . . normal in my clothes. His dark hair was a tangled mess that was mostly tucked behind his ears. And there was the rest of that face and those roundish-shaped eyes . . .

The pants fortunately fit him fine, and then there was the shirt. I was pretty sure he hadn't noticed the white cat with a crooked pink bow on one pointed ear. It *was* one of my biggest shirts.

Lifting my gaze, I met those dark purple eyes, and a feeling of dread tickled me right between the shoulder blades. "If you're done . . . checking me out . . . can I get a wet towel to wipe off . . . with?"

The sound that gurgled in my throat reminded me of my old cat, Ryu, when he'd hack up a hairball.

Because . . .

Because . . .

Was he being *sarcastic*? Wasn't he supposed to be . . . I don't know . . . above that kind of thing?

Oh, God. Were they all like this in person? Were they all undercover smart-asses?

To be fair, I had been checking him out. I wasn't going to deny it, but he didn't need to call me out on it. I was sure everybody gawked at him. I pondered that unthinkable thought about the Trinity as I left the room and ducked into the bathroom for a couple washcloths that I held under the sink to wet and wring out.

Back in the room, I held them out to him.

He didn't take them.

Was he being for real?

Of course he was. *Don't check me out but give me a sponge bath.* Biting my cheek, I kneeled beside his leg and set one of the cloths on the bed. Then I took the other one and started from the top, just like I used to do with my grandparents. This sense of longing hit me full-strength in the heart right then.

I missed them.

They had been crazy strict and overprotective, but I missed them so much. Living with them, then eventually caring for them, hadn't been easy, but I had done it with love, and I would have kept doing it for years and years.

My eyes started to water as I swept the cloth over The Defender's forehead, then gently over his eyebrows and eyelids when he closed them, over one cheek then the other. I took my time with his chin and neck, going back up to wipe behind his ears. Folding the small towel, I moved it over his hair, noticing that it wasn't greasy at all considering he hadn't taken a shower since he'd landed here.

Literally landed.

How did this shit even happen to me? What were the chances?

Dropping it on the floor, I picked up the other towel and then started wiping at his upper arm, dragging it toward his wrist. I peeked up to find him sitting there, his eyes closed. His skin was smooth and golden in the dim overhead lighting. The shirt didn't do his body any favors, but now I knew what was under there, and my eyes were never going to be the same again.

In movies, actors had to wear padded suits to look the way The Defender did.

But there was no padding in what I'd just helped peel off. For the brief moment I'd touched his suit, it had felt . . . well, not like any material you could buy in a store. *And* I was pretty sure he'd just incinerated it somehow.

The Defender's throat bobbed as I kneeled there, wiping the towel over the tops of his hands and then his palms. His breathing seemed to still be a struggle, but other than that, it was steady. How did he get his skin so smooth under the sunburn? Or was it just the same shit that made him super strong that made his pores so tiny? Did he drink a lot of water? That's what all the models said was their secret, but I didn't believe that shit completely. I drank a bunch of water and still broke out from time to time.

"What day is this?" he asked suddenly.

That was a weird question, but I told him it was Friday.

The lean muscles on his face barely flexed, but they did. "What day and month?"

I told him.

I squeezed my hands between my thighs as I watched him take what seemed like another pained breath. I knew it was in my best interest to keep our conversations to a minimum, but . . . Clearing my throat, I picked my words as wisely as I could. "Why you don't know what day it is isn't technically my business, but it is at the same time. Is there something I need to worry about? I locked the gate to the property, but that won't actually stop anyone who's determined to come in. Is there . . . something else I should do?" I dropped my voice. "Did you change your mind about reaching out to someone more qualified?" I had pepper spray. I still had bear spray from a camping trip last summer in Montana that had been pretty fun and only a little bit lonely. It had been my first solo vacation.

Those lean cheeks did that flexing thing again.

I pressed my hands together tighter. "Look, I'm sure it's not every day someone like you needs help from someone like me. I don't know how to help you, how to keep you safe."

He opened his mouth, and I knew, I just *knew* something sarcastic was going to come out of his pretty pink mouth.

"Not that you can't keep yourself safe. Okay." Oh boy, someone was fucking touchy. "I can't even be a human shield because you're bulletproof—"

"Invulnerable," he corrected me.

I blinked. Oh boy. Excuse me. Maybe it was time I started playing *Call of Duty* again so I could get used to dealing with moody man-boys. "That. Sure. All I want to do is make sure that you're okay." I gave him another tight smile, ignoring the way my poor heart clenched. "That you're safe." It had been a long, long time since I had felt that way, but if I could make another person experience it, then I would do it in a heartbeat.

That got him to open his eyes and give me the most dubious expression I'd ever seen.

He probably didn't know what it was like to *not* feel secure. Must be nice.

Scratching the tip of my nose, I took a breath and tried to think of another way to approach this. To approach him. "Listen, I don't want someone showing up and accusing me of murder if you die. You're—" I gestured toward him. "—you. It's my moral obligation for the sake of the planet to help you, but I don't want to die. I don't want to be collateral damage if someone wants to take you out. No offense. If I had to be someone's martyr, you'd deserve it, but I still don't want to do it," I rambled on, figuring I had to be at least mostly honest with him. "No offense again. Thank you for everything you've done."

That sounded real sincere.

But somehow, I knew it worked because just a tiny bit of the wariness on his face disappeared, or at least I wanted to believe it did.

I tried again. "Is someone coming to get you? Is someone looking for you?"

He said nothing.

Dammit. "It isn't like I would tell anyone anything about you," I tried to reassure him. "But I need to know if there's something to be concerned about. You know, because I don't want to get ripped apart by The Centurion."

"Have your limbs rendered," he corrected.

I blinked.

He was in pain. In a stranger's house. Vulnerable as shit.

I couldn't imagine. Hadn't everything I'd done for my life been to not put myself into a vulnerable position? To not have to rely on other people more than necessary?

He still didn't say shit as I folded the towel and started wiping at his other arm, focusing on that as I thought about just how much I'd hate being in his position.

I opened my mouth just as he held up his index finger. "I don't . . . like interruptions."

I pressed my lips together and focused on the fact that he could barely talk without panting.

I would hate to be in the same position he was in.

"I got . . . hit. Hard," he continued, his words slow.

Something hit him? What in the hell was strong enough to *hit him*? Where had he been in the first place?

I shouldn't have asked. I wasn't sure I really wanted to know, especially if I wanted to actually sleep tonight or any night ever again.

"My back . . . hurts," he admitted so, so slowly, those cheeks flexing again.

Why was he saying it as if he thought it was my fault?

His eyes opened, and his gaze flicked toward me there on

my knees by his feet, his face wiped smooth of any expression, even the grumpy one. Those pale lavender lids fell over those dark purple eyes as he lifted his chin just a little bit and said—sounding . . . resentful?—"I'm . . . weak."

It was nothing I hadn't already figured out, but to hear him actually admit it?

I had to leave.

I was going to die. Whatever had done that to him was going to find him here.

We were dead, or at least I was.

I needed to go.

Oh shit, oh shit, oh shit.

"Stop . . . panicking . . ." The Defender breathed out.

Easier said than done. I tried to make myself calm down, but that wasn't the way this kind of shit worked. You didn't just tell your body to stop freaking out.

"Stop," he growled.

I'd get right on that. After I got my suitcase out, threw some clothes in, and drove as fast as I could away from here. Maybe I wouldn't even bother getting clothes and I'd go straight for my car. I'd have to live off-grid for a while, but I could drive to the nearest major town and do my lessons in my car. I had a translating job for a small publisher next month that would be enough money to hold me over for a while; I'd been trying to get into transcribing books to supplement my income, and I'd been excited to land it. I could figure it out.

I always did.

"If someone . . . comes . . . I'll sense it . . . first . . ." he struggled to say.

I wasn't feeling so optimistic about that, not when he'd been passed the hell out for three days straight.

But something must have been on my face because he narrowed those incredible purple eyes at me even more.

Was he . . . mean-mugging me? He was, wasn't he? Why? I was going to have to keep that knowledge to myself. I didn't want to ruin the dreams of millions of little kids around the world by being the one to tell everyone what his personality was really like. I could barely handle my own being crushed every time he glared at me.

I stared at him.

"I'm always . . . aware," he tried to claim.

I couldn't help it, I whispered, "Even when you're snoring?"

The glare I got . . .

"Kidding," I said, flipping his hand over to wipe the skin on his palm. I knew better. I needed to stop. "It's a joke. I had to check your wrist a few times to make sure you were still breathing, but I'm sure you're aware of that." *Lies.* "Look, I'm too young to die. That's all." At least that's what I wanted to believe.

"No dying," The Defender muttered.

I didn't believe him, not when he might be the one to wring my neck if I didn't get him his steak and chicken. I had other people to worry about doing the job too, but he didn't need to know that.

Just as I opened my mouth to reluctantly agree that I believed him, he started to strain on the bed like he wanted to lie down.

Catching him wincing, I helped him. His groans and low-key moans filled the room. There was something really wrong, and we both knew it, but he was in denial for whatever reason. I lifted one heavy leg after the other onto the mattress, helping him until he managed to lie flat on his back.

The Defender's face relaxed almost instantly, and a feeling of dread got to me again. My grandma used to say that I'd been born with a hint of intuition; then my grandpa would claim I'd gotten it from his side. He never really talked about his family, but when he did, he always brought up his own grandmother. According to him, she had known things that were going to happen before they did. Grandma had always made skeptical faces when she overheard him whispering about her to me, but I was pretty sure he believed what he'd seen and heard.

He had always loved telling me stories, and I'd loved listening to all of them.

He'd had countless stories about traveling through South America as a little boy. Looking back on it now, it was his way of taking me to all those places we couldn't visit together because he hadn't wanted me to get a passport. It would have been just one more thing in a system that someone might be able to track, so no passport for me.

It was such bullshit.

And I didn't want to think about it anymore.

For now, I wanted to get this guy better and out of here as quickly as possible. Then I could leave and start over again. By myself.

"Want some more water?" I asked him just as he let out a shallow breath.

"In a minute," he actually answered before leveling me with another long look out of the corner of his eye. "Have the . . ."

I waited.

"Rest of them been seen lately?"

"Them?"

"Like me."

All right, so they didn't call themselves the Trinity. Got it. "I haven't turned on the TV because I didn't want to wake you up. Do you want me to check?" It wasn't that they made regular appearances or anything like that, because they didn't. They didn't appear for petty, common shit. Just the big stuff and the rare appearance of The Primordial or The Centurion doing some kind of community-service-type project. Plus, I'd been so busy keeping him alive, researching them, and making three times the amount of food that I regularly did, that I hadn't kept up with the news. Stressing over him dying on me had been the only thing I'd been able to focus on lately.

That and the fact I was really, really worried I was making a mistake helping him.

Pulling my phone out of my pocket, I did a quick search before peeking at his tight face. Then I told him about how The Primordial had been seen just yesterday, and he grunted in reply. He might have relaxed just a little too, but I wasn't positive.

Regardless, it didn't put me at ease.

None of this was putting me at ease at all.

Chapter Four

His sleepy eyes started to drift closed.

I'd been reading him the articles I'd found about The Primordial for the last half-hour. He'd been paying attention at first, but after the fourth one, he'd either started zoning out or his thoughts had drifted elsewhere.

So that was cool.

Turning off my screen, I glanced at the superbeing on my bed, in my clothes, and before I could stop myself, I asked, "Can I call you Defender, or is there something else you would rather be referred to as?"

Dammit, I wasn't supposed to ask for more information than what I needed.

I couldn't backtrack now though, could I? That would be even more fishy. I made myself smile at him weakly. "I won't tell anyone. Promise." That sounded real believable. I needed to keep my mouth closed. I knew this. *I knew it.* I'd just . . . been alone for too long. Talking to my students wasn't the same as having a conversation with a friend.

Not that I'd had that many of those, or much less one in a long time, but . . .

One dark eyelid peeled back.

I looked at him.

He looked at me.

Then I gave him another weak smile even as I thought he was way too beautiful to be real, because he really was. I couldn't get over it. At least I wasn't stuttering or staring though. I wasn't gaping at being in his presence. I could be proud of myself later.

Not a single muscle in his features moved. Not a half smile or a quarter smile. I got nothing.

At least one of us had some fucking sense.

But The Defender stared in a way that might have made me nervous if I didn't know how injured he was. I was pretty sure, at this point, I could push him over and run if it came down to it. Not that I would.

Unless it was life or death. Then I'd be seeing his ass later.

"Call me . . . whatever you want," he muttered.

That was real helpful.

And friendly.

But it was a good thing he liked his secrets and knew how to keep them. I needed to take notes. Less talking, more grunting. Keep my mouth shut. Feed him, sponge bathe him, shut up.

He sniffed again as his eyes drifted closed. "I'll be going back to rest," he said quietly.

"Does that mean you're going to be out for a few days again?" I asked and got a peek of an eyeball before I raised my hands in defense. "Just asking so I'm not worried you're in a coma."

That got him to close his eye before finally sighing, "Yes." He settled deeper into the bed. His arms were at his sides, slightly away from his big, motionless body. He looked half-asleep when he whispered, "If you see . . . or hear of anything about . . . them . . . tell me."

Them? The Trinity? "Okay, sure."

But was it them we had to worry about? Why wasn't he trying to get in contact with them?

One purple eyeball opened yet again and peered at me, almost expectantly, like he knew something else was bouncing around in my head. I definitely needed to shut up, but I had to get this off my chest. I didn't want there to be any surprises and might as well do it now.

Might as well take my shot. "Can I tell you something real quick?" I croaked.

It took a moment—where he probably thought about telling me no—but he sighed.

Good enough for me.

"I promise I won't hurt you or put you at risk. I'll try my best to do what I can until you're ready to leave, and I'll do whatever I can to keep your presence a secret. But . . ." I swallowed hard. "Would you mind promising me that if anyone shows up here to try and finish whatever it was they did to you, that you won't kill me in retaliation if I run away? I know that makes me a coward, but there's nothing I would be able to do other than sacrifice my life in vain to help you, and I said, if anyone deserved a sacrifice, it's you and the other Trinity members, but I made a promise to someone that I would try my best to live a decent, long life, and I made that promise before I met you. I'm the last person alive in my family. I just don't want there to be any misunderstandings between us," I straight-up went on. "I don't want you to haunt me."

He didn't laugh.

And if my request surprised him or even irritated him in its honesty, it didn't reflect on his features. Not even a little bit. The Defender stared at me through that slit of his eye, probably weighing my cowardice, or the very value of my soul, who the fuck knew, before saying in a rough, tired voice, "Fine."

That easy, huh?

The Defender, The Primordial, and The Centurion were the three most important entities in the world. But at the same time, they'd only been around for twenty-something years. The world had been around before them, and it would be around after them—probably. The same as anyone else.

All life impacts the world, some lives just more directly than others. I knew that better than anyone.

I cleared my throat and squeezed my fingers. "One more question. Do you think it's safe for me to go for a run at night? Or do you think somebody's around here and they'll try and get me to get to you?"

He didn't even look at me as he closed his eyes and said, so quietly I had to strain, "Do whatever you want."

Wow, I thought, as his breath rattled and he fell back asleep that easily.

In midconversation.

If I had holy water, I would have put some in a spray bottle and squirted him with it, just to see what happened.

Was talking to me that much torture? I didn't think I was that awkward or annoying. If I'd been born to any other life, I might have had a lot of friends—if I hadn't grown up to be so paranoid and watch every word I spoke to strangers. When I tried, I got along with people pretty well. I was trying my best not to talk a lot so that I wouldn't say something I shouldn't. I was trying my best to take care of him, the ungrateful . . .

I peered at his sleeping face.

He wasn't at all what I'd expected. Not even a little bit. I doubt he was what anyone expected. A crabby, bossy, six-foot-something man. The thought felt like it should have been sacrilegious, but it was the truth.

He was pretty arrogant, and it wasn't as if he'd talked to me all that much in the first place.

For about the hundredth time, I wondered what exactly I'd gotten myself into.

Lifting my head, I looked around the small bedroom that had been part of my world for the last chunk of my life and remembered how the hell I'd ended up here. No knickknacks, just a single picture of me as a little girl with my grandparents at the park. The rest of my pictures were split between a box in the closet and my safe deposit box. I remembered what had been taken from me before I'd even had a choice.

Everything, that was what.

I would have done anything to be normal. For the chance to have an existence that wasn't built on so many fucking lies, on bone-softening loneliness that I called privacy to keep my sanity. To be able to totally be myself without fear of repercussion.

Unfortunately, I had to live with the fact that I wasn't sure that was ever going to be possible.

If I was lucky, dealing with him now might be the most stressful shit I ever went through.

If I wasn't lucky . . . I didn't want to know.

"*Boa noite*. Good night," I told my Brazilian student with a wave before logging out of the chat we'd been in for the last hour.

After rubbing my forehead for a second, I gently tugged my wig off and set it on the mannequin head next to my computer. It had been really expensive, and I babied the crap out of it. I'd underestimated how hard it would be to find a shade of blonde that complimented my skin tone. Then, just as carefully, I took the nylon hose that covered my hair and put it beside the wig so I could have everything ready for my next lesson later tonight; he was a nice man in Seoul who was brushing up on his conversational skills before his job transferred him.

Being an English teacher hadn't been my dream job, but I was really grateful that I'd grown into it so much. That I enjoyed it. It ate up the worst of my loneliness. Getting to talk to these people who paid to work with me was what kept me going. It was something to look forward to. I rarely got off a lesson with something other than a smile.

It wasn't like my grandpa had known all those language classes we had taken together, and the years I'd been babysat by the Park family that shared our duplex, would come in handy eventually. But it had. I was so grateful for everything he had done.

Running my fingers through my chin-length, straight black hair, I leaned backward in the chair and let my head drop so I could stare at the ceiling.

The last two weeks had been so tense, I'd started getting headaches every day, and today wasn't any different. I could already feel the pressure building in my temples. I was trying to be as careful with my words as I could with my guest in the other room, but it was really hard, even though I was a fucking expert at this point.

But I'd never had to be secretive at home before.

Twice, The Defender woke up randomly, always right around the three-day mark. Each time, he stayed up long enough to look pissed, grumble, and eat a meal while glowering at me like I was the reason why he was laid up in my bed. Like I loved sleeping on the lumpy couch and feeling awkward. Then, almost immediately after finishing eating, he fell back asleep.

Somehow, he'd managed to say about ten words in the whole week. I really tried not to talk more than I needed to, and if that was really fucking weird to me, I tried to be relieved that it didn't seem to bother him. It *was* for the best. For the most part, my sentences revolved around me reporting Trinity news to him. Nothing bad.

Well, nothing other than another article I'd come across about him and that fire from a year ago that people were still trying to bring up. I remembered enough to know that he had totally fallen off the radar after that—for about half a year, I was pretty sure.

So I wasn't about to bring that shit up.

While he was asleep, I tried to stick to my normal routine while avoiding the giant elephant in the room still sitting on the coffee table, reminding me that I needed to make some serious plans to leave. Every time I even started thinking about it, my stomach began hurting, which then led to me purposely trying to focus on anything other than moving. I started up my runs again, looking up at the sky every ten seconds, expecting to see something terrifying, but fortunately there hadn't been anything or anyone. I went grocery shopping and made sure not to make eye contact with anyone.

But I knew in my gut that I really did have to make a decision ASAP.

I had to quit being a chickenshit.

But maybe later, I told myself *again* before sitting up straight and rubbing my face some more. I'd get it sorted. I would figure it out as soon as the superbeing quit feeling like such a liability.

Opening the door to my office as quietly as possible, I headed back to the living room, trying to decide whether to read a book or fold my wrinkled laundry. I'd barely sat down on the couch when I heard a ringing sound from my room. I'd left a bell in there just a few hours ago.

I guess I was being summoned.

Getting back up, I headed to my room and, at the doorway, peeked in.

The Defender was on his back with the covers I'd pulled over him around his waist. Both of his hands were resting on his flat stomach, the bell back on the nightstand where I'd left it for him.

Oh, someone looked like a ray of fucking sunshine lying there. He was glaring at the ceiling. I think it said everything about what he was, that his eyes and cheeks weren't puffy and his mouth wasn't swollen, when I could take a thirty-minute nap and look like I'd gotten stung by wasps.

"Hey," I called out, hesitantly.

The reply I got was the usual—a grunt.

Everything about him screamed irritation, and he'd been up,

what? A minute? I'd just walked by the room a second ago. Every time I'd checked up on him, he'd been totally passed out.

Or not, according to Mr. I'm Totally Aware At All Times.

Bull*shit*.

I waited there, ready to help him as he kept glaring, his breathing about as even as it got.

I tried again. "Good morning to you. Are you okay? Do you need something?"

"It's dark outside," he replied in a deep, sleepy voice before blowing out a breath that was still too short for how incredible his lung capacity had to be.

I mean, he'd been filmed flying into space without an oxygen tank to repair a damaged satellite. I thought it was The Centurion who had plunged into the ocean, going thousands of feet down to do something to one of the tectonic plates there years back. It was nothing a machine could even handle.

But he hadn't had something wrong with him, with his back, when he'd done it. And if it still alarmed me that there was something wrong in the first place—my gut said he should have healed by now—I pushed the worry aside.

"Hungry?" I asked, preparing myself for more sarcasm since he already looked so crabby.

I almost rolled my eyes when he didn't respond.

If he wanted to keep being difficult, he could keep being difficult. I was going to choose to be nice to him, even if I really wanted to ask what had crawled up his ass and died there instead. "Do you finally feel like watching something?" I tried again. I'd asked before, in case he was bored, and he'd just ignored me.

Nothing new.

For once though, he blinked.

Was that a yes? I think it might have been. All right then.

It didn't take me more than a second to cross the hall, grab my tablet from the living room, and go back to my room. *His* room now. I held it toward him, but this time I wasn't surprised when he didn't take it. His loss. I logged in and opened the browser page to one of my streaming subscription services. Then I chose the first show under the Most Watched category instead of what I really wanted to pick to be ornery—the latest Electro-Man movie. I hadn't even watched it yet.

I genuinely wondered what he thought about all the Shinto Studios movies revolving around every superhero imaginable. Electro-Man had been around before The Primordial, and the similarities between the fictional character and the Trinity were close, but everyone had written it off as a coincidence. But now, I wondered . . .

What did superbeings watch anyway? *Did* they watch TV?

"I can set it on your lap if you want, so you can pick something else," I offered, trying to be hospitable.

Those dark purple eyes blinked at me.

All righty then. In that case, I set the tablet on the dresser across from the bed. "I'll go get you some food," I told him, before backing out of the room, waiting until I was in the hall to roll my eyes.

He'd graduated from being kind of a pain in the ass to full-on pain in the ass over the last week with that attitude. The guilt I'd felt for thinking that about him had slowly waned with each of our interactions. Now, I was at the point where there was no pretending he was something he wasn't.

And that was patient, friendly, and easygoing.

It didn't take me long to warm up the roast beef I'd made along with potatoes, throwing in some roasted carrots because everyone needed some lutein and fiber in their diet. Even big, bad superpeople who were currently out of commission, hanging out at the home of a stranger while they got better. Lucky fucking me.

Holding the plate in one hand and a glass of water in the other, I made my way back. The same show about kids and scary monsters from another realm was still playing. I'd already watched every episode twice. It was one of my favorites. In a weird way, they reminded me that if—fictional—kids could do the right thing, so could I. So could everyone, if they wanted.

That was the problem though, wasn't it? Most people rarely did the right thing. Which was exactly how I'd ended up here in the first place.

Resignation and determination and that same deep-rooted fucking anger and sense of how unfair things could be filled my chest again. I let it center me for a second; then I moved on. The Defender didn't need to pick up on it. Better not have something else to make him cautious. Fortunately, that intense gaze was on the tablet.

Sitting down on the edge of the bed, I cut up the meat with the plate on my lap. Spearing a piece, I pinched my lips together as I brought it up to his mouth, thinking about how I'd made choo-choo sounds at him under my breath the day before when I'd fed him because it made me cackle quietly. He didn't even look at me as he opened his mouth and bit in, chewing slowly.

I gave him mashed potatoes, and it was on the bite of carrots that he finally glanced over.

I gave him a level look and shoved another piece of meat into his face, taking in the brilliant purple in his eyes. I still couldn't get over the unreal shade of his pupils, and I didn't have anything to complain about. Mine were a clear, light brown that came across as hazel sometimes. I got them from my grandpa's side. His skin had been a deep reddish brown, a little darker than mine, and his almost-whiskey color had been incredible. What color were The Defender's parents' eyes like? I wondered. *Did he even have parents?* There was the chance he'd been made in a test tube after all.

"So . . . while you're awake, you might as well know, The Centurion was spotted in Bangladesh two days ago." I gave him some more mashed potatoes that he took without a glance. "A building collapsed, and he helped find the injured."

He didn't bother looking at me again, but I could tell he was listening from the way his cheek muscles moved as he ate.

I speared some carrots and brought them up to his mouth, earning myself a flash of a sharp canine before he ate it. "He seemed fine." More than fine, really. The Centurion had the tightest little butt. I couldn't help but look at it every time someone filmed it. Then again, that was probably half of humanity.

My answer was a side-look while he chewed.

"In one of the parts of footage I found, something about his face looked really . . . I don't know, concerned or something. I might be imagining it. Want to see?"

That got him to turn his head.

He had such a nice jawline, and that wasn't me thinking that because of a lack of handsome jaws I'd been in the presence of.

"Yes," he actually answered.

"Okay. When you finish eating, I'll show you."

He faced forward again, this time looking thoughtful even though his expression was still that normal, pissy, tight one that told me how he would rather be anywhere but here. *Same here, Sleeping Superhero Beauty.* He had no idea I hadn't been sleeping through the night from being worried about my stomachache, which had conveniently been coming and going since he'd gotten here.

Maybe it was because of him, but more than likely it was telling me that I needed to leave. Either way, they were both issues that were stressing me the fuck out. I was worried I was in danger having him here, but he hadn't brought up leaving yet, and I didn't want to be rude and bring it up. Staying wasn't an option, even though I wanted it to be.

You'd figure I would have been used to it by now though. Wanting things I couldn't have. Wanting things I had no control over.

Andddd I was depressing the shit out of myself for no reason.

I didn't waste time worrying about things I couldn't control anymore. At least for the most part. Most of the time.

Figuring that was all I was going to get, I fed him the rest of what was on the plate, content with being ignored while he kept watching television. But I kept thinking about all the things I wanted to ask him and couldn't. *Shouldn't.* Part of me still couldn't wrap my head around how he was here and injured so severely. He hadn't asked to move around since coming to the bed.

I really had to keep most of my curiosity to myself, as hard as it was.

I got up to rinse his plate, still thinking about my crabby, secretive guest, and tried to imagine life a month from now. When I was done, I made my way back to the bedroom, grabbing my laptop from my office, and took a seat on the floor beside the bed so that I wouldn't accidentally hurt him. His attention was still on the screen, so I was surprised when he asked, "Are you . . . going to show me . . . what you found?"

I slid him a side-look as I opened my computer.

He tipped his head down and gave me a side-look right back.

"Can you read my mind?" I whispered, instantly regretting it.

Fortunately, The Defender just did what I was beginning to think was one of the things he did best—stare.

"O-kay," I muttered. I was going to pretend I hadn't asked. The answer was a no. I'd just wanted to be sure. If it wasn't, he could only blame himself for being nosy.

But I really hoped he couldn't.

Chapter Five

I wasn't surprised when he slept another three days after that lovely interaction.

Honestly, it was a blessing.

I'd always thought I was pretty patient, that I was about as understanding as a person could be. I'd been a little kid when I'd mastered the perfect volume to speak to an older person. I walked really slow from all the years I had spent keeping pace with my grandparents.

As far back as I could remember, there had always been things that I'd had to quickly come to terms with. Thinking back on it now, it was more along the lines that I'd had shit I had to take with a smile on my face, and I had. Mostly because I had figured out really quick that I wasn't the only person who had to suffer due to the decisions that others had made.

I'd had to bounce from school to school, had to catch up with academics, start over, try and be friendly but not *too* friendly, but my grandparents had also had a cross to bear. Now I knew that it sure as hell couldn't have been easy for them either. Trying to find jobs that also didn't ask too many questions at their ages, finding somewhere to live that was cheap, starting over and starting over, and constantly living with the worst of the fear that we would be found.

I couldn't imagine, but just thinking about it made me love them even more.

I would have done anything for them, and that's why I had taken care of them as they'd gotten older. They had already been older parents when they'd had my mom. My grandma had been forty-two when she'd found out she was pregnant after a decade of trying. She had been in her late sixties when I'd been born. My grandpa had been even older. Once, when I'd been around five or six, he'd tried to tell me it was his hundredth birthday; he'd never actually admitted what his real age was, and if he had a birth certificate or passport, I'd never found it.

Together, we went through my puberty, and their diabetes, high blood pressure, and early stages of dementia. They took care of me in diapers, and I had taken care of them while they'd been the ones who needed them. I'd rubbed more swollen legs and feet than I could count. I had fed them when their hands had gotten too shaky to do it themselves.

Taking care of people wasn't something new for me.

But taking care of a cranky, irritable superbeing who seemed like he could barely deal with my presence for no good reason was a totally different fucking beast.

I might respect him, but I didn't love him, and with love, you could do anything.

But when you didn't love someone, it was harder not to want to wring their fucking necks when they got on your nerves.

And oh, the son of a bitch got on my nerves.

The other night, we had sat next to each other for hours, looking through every site with any detail of The Centurion's recent appearance. It was like he was hoping to find . . . something. Some mention. I wasn't positive of what, because he wouldn't tell me shit.

Was he worried about them? Did he think that what had

happened to him would happen to them? What was their relationship even like? Were they friends? Family? Had they been raised in a government facility together?

There were so many questions I wasn't going to ask but I wanted to. Oh, did I want to.

The problem was that I had the balls—mostly because I had the curiosity—but I had the brains to know that I better not.

Some people could handle the truth. I guess I wasn't one of them.

Anyway, I read him everything we came across. One article after another, even though most of them were the exact same with the difference of a sentence or two. Eventually, he'd finally fallen asleep without another word.

While he'd slept, I worked like I always did and, fortunately, none of my students mentioned me looking like I was on the verge of having a nervous breakdown. I'd gotten a small job translating a manual from English to Portuguese, and that had kept my thoughts on things other than superbeings and having my limbs rendered.

I'd also started eyeing my belongings so I could decide what to do with the few extra pieces of furniture I'd bought. It was a good thing I wasn't attached to anything. My grandma had taught me to use my sharpest imaginary scissors and cut the cords on the stuff I knew would be too big or too much trouble to take. At least that's what I was telling myself.

Because no matter how reasonable I tried to be, I still felt weird. My chest heavy. My stomach off.

My time was running out, and I was fed up with doing this shit.

It was days later, in the afternoon, that my temporary roommate who could snap my neck in half woke up while I was in the kitchen making lunch and rang the little bell again.

I fed him lying down and watched him carefully. No sooner

had he finished eating the olla de carne I'd made the night before, he'd leveled those unreal eyes at me—not glowing at least—and muttered, sounding pissy, "What?"

Was I that obvious?

I eyed the dark hair on the pillow as he lay there and let out another one of those shaky exhales that hurt my soul. Should I have lied? Should I have pretended like I didn't know he was picking up on my emotions? Probably but . . . "Not to sound rude, but how much longer do you think you're going to be here? Ballpark. No rush."

I'd totally failed on the not sounding rude part. Fantastic.

But being rude apparently didn't bother him too much because he didn't miss a single beat as he grumbled, "Do you think . . . I have a calendar?"

Did I? I blinked, more surprised than offended at his comeback. "Okay, I didn't mean to ask it like that. What I meant was, I'm worried about how much pain you're still in—"

"I'm . . . not," he cut me off.

I swear it took everything in me not to roll my eyes. Fucking liar, liar, pants on fire. What? Did he think I'd exploit him if he admitted it? That was dumb. *Patience, patienceee.* "Okay." I didn't sound patient at all, and I knew it. "I'm concerned you're not healing. That whatever your injury is, isn't getting better. I've seen The Centurion dive into the ocean from like miles high. If I fell from a hundred feet, I would die. He shot back out of the water like a missile. Whatever you are . . . is unreal, and from what you said when you did that Hercules shit, you should be better, shouldn't you?"

He didn't say anything for a minute. Then two. It didn't get awkward until the third. But that's when he said, in a grudging, tight voice that definitely sounded irritated as shit, "I should . . . be."

I knew it! Not that I was glad to hear that.

I waited, keeping my face even, like him actually talking to me wasn't still kind of a fucked-up miracle.

"I've never been . . . like this. Weak . . ." He trailed off and flicked those curly lashes at me. "This is . . . the longest it's ever . . . taken me to heal." His Adam's apple bobbed, and he gritted those pristine, white teeth. "I don't . . . like it."

It was just as bad, if not worse than I'd imagined.

I rubbed my face and tried to think. There was only one option. Two, but I really wouldn't leave him here alone while I ran away. "Are you sure I can't take you somewhere? Is there some place that can help you heal?" *Please say yes, please say yes.*

His "no" was instant and sharp enough that I knew for sure I shouldn't ask again.

Of course not. Why would he want to leave my double-sized bed in the middle of nowhere? I rubbed my face some more. "Okay, all right. No need to get your panties in a wad." I side-eyed him. Did he wear underwear?

The Defender glared like he knew I was thinking about his undies.

Which I was, but that was beside the point. This was where he wanted to stay while he recovered . . . because he would recover. I was getting his ass out of here, and he was going to go back to being the incredible being he was, saving the planet and people's lives. It was going to be my one amazing deed of my life. Sure, no one but us would ever know it had happened, but I would, and that was all that mattered. That I would know I had done something good.

That mattered to me. That mattered to me a hell of a lot more than I wanted it to, because I knew I needed to go and wouldn't. Not until he was ready.

So I told him the truth, or at least part of it. "I just want you to feel better. To get better. That's all."

That got me a grunt that had me eyeing his T-shirt.

I was so busy thinking about what he had on that I almost missed his grumbled-out question. "Why don't . . . you . . . have friends?"

Of all the things in the world I could have expected him to ask, that was the last.

How many words had he said to me in weeks? And now all of a sudden, here he was asking something personal. Not just a little personal either but really personal.

Or maybe I was just sensitive about it. Chances were that was it.

But honestly, it felt like a sucker punch with his strength right in the kidney.

Of all the things . . .

He didn't even know my name! I hadn't brought it up, and he hadn't asked. He had no clue what town we were even in.

"Shouldn't you . . . have friends? Family? . . . Boyfriend?" he asked, his face suddenly suspicious. "No one . . . ever calls you."

Yeah, a punch to the kidneys. Maybe the face too while we were at it.

How the hell did he know that?

He must have sensed the question I was shooting him because he said, "You think . . . I would leave . . . myself vulnerable? I'm not . . . completely . . . unaware of . . . my surroundings."

I bit my lip and couldn't help the snarky-ass comment that snuck out of my mouth. "Looked like you were passed out to me."

That got me a shot of those purple eyes. I even got a slight lift of his eyebrow.

I was pretty sure my kidney actually hurt though. "I have friends," I told him, keeping my voice low and steady even though I felt anything but.

His "Hm" dripped with sarcasm.

I tipped my chin up. This man had saved the world. He might be a grumpy, bossy shit, but he had done things for civilization that were . . . well, he'd never be paid back for it. It wasn't a surprise he wasn't some polite, courteous person. At this point, I was 99.9 percent certain he was missing those genes in his DNA.

But his comment really did hurt. Not just my kidney either, but my heart as well. Of all the things I'd ever been sensitive over, "friends" were at the top of the damn list.

"I do have friends," I whispered, my eyes suddenly stinging a little.

More than a little.

He made another one of those dismissive, rude sounds in his throat.

Why was he coming at me like this? Did I take a shit in his Lucky Charms? Had I stabbed him in another lifetime?

Couldn't he at least try and make decent conversation with me instead of this shit? Was that asking too much? If this was what having friends was like, I hadn't missed out on shit.

I was trying to be nice here. I'd *been* trying to be nice to him. It hadn't exactly been easy either, but I'd tried.

And sure, nice people probably didn't have to tell themselves to *be* nice, but too fucking bad.

I gritted my teeth. "It's true. What am I supposed to do? Invite people over when you're here?" Resentment stirred inside me. It wasn't exactly easy to make friends when I had so many things hanging over my head. So many lies I had to keep track of that I could forget what they were supposed to be.

Mostly though, even though I had too much experience with it, I hated lying. It had a spiderweb effect that leeched to everything, and eventually there was no freeing yourself from every fine string that clung to you. Once you started, there was no stopping, no telling what kind of design you'd end up covering yourself with.

So why would I want to waste someone else's time on lies? That wasn't fair. I didn't want to do it, I never had, but I didn't have a fucking choice. So, I opted for putting myself into the least amount of positions possible where I needed to. That was how I'd been raised. It was the best for everyone.

But it wasn't like I could explain *that* to him.

For once, it was my turn to grunt.

Plus, who the hell did he think he was judging me for not having friends? I didn't see anybody hanging up missing or wanted posters for him. I was just smart enough not to bring that shit up.

Fucking rude.

I shook my head. For the sake of both of us, and mostly out of respect, I forced myself to get up even though I really just wanted to flip him off instead. "On that note, I've got a few lessons scheduled. I'll come and check on you later," I managed to grind out.

Not that I was pissed at him or anything.

Unfortunately, I kept on thinking about his dumb insinuation as I worked.

He didn't know me. Didn't know my life. He didn't understand shit.

But his comments still made me pretty damn miserable anyway. I'd gone past being angry to just being hurt. I couldn't remember the last time anything had done that. It was one of the few benefits of not interacting with people. With not having friends or relationships, you didn't have people who could let you down.

He didn't know anything.

And that was why I found myself sulking in the shower later that evening, after I'd finished another two lessons and ignored Super Crabby, who also pretended not to see me when I walked by my room while he watched something.

When I heard, "Are you almost done?" I started to hold up my middle finger before remembering he might have X-ray vision and could see me—could he see me naked?—and grudgingly turned toward the shower curtain and tugged it back just enough to peek my head through so I could holler back.

But I didn't do anything more than squeak.

Leaning against the doorway, looking pale while holding my cell phone—the same cell phone I clearly remembered leaving plugged in to charge in my office—was my houseguest.

Who was currently pecking away at the screen.

He knew my password, which was something. But mostly, it was the *fact he was fucking standing up* that alarmed me. The urge to ask him if it was a smart idea for him to be up was right on the tip of my tongue.

But who the hell was I to say shit? I wasn't his babysitter. I was the lonely idiot who was taking care of him.

The man standing there in gray sweatpants and a white T-shirt looked a lot more awake than he had a few hours ago. Now that he was standing, his hair seemed longer than I'd thought. It was shorter than mine but not by more than a few inches.

And he was rude. He was so damn rude no matter how handsome he might be as he typed away on my phone's screen.

Would poison give him the shits? I wondered for a second.

I tugged the shower curtain closer to my neck, even though he wasn't even looking at me. "Dinner will be ready in about half an hour," I grumbled, figuring that's what he was bothering me over.

That got him to finally glance up from my phone, a slight wrinkle appearing between his dark eyebrows. "Where are we?"

Now he was wondering? "What town?" I asked him slowly, narrowing my eyes.

"No, what country," he shot back.

I swear my chin was *this* close to hitting the side of the bathtub. There was only enough room for one sarcastic person in this household, and that was me. But when I tried to move my mouth, when I tried to tell him that the last thing I needed was to take care of a man who didn't know my name, hadn't even asked for it, I just . . . choked on every word that flipped through my head.

Rude mother . . .

He was in pain. He was weak. Something was wrong with him.

All of which were totally foreign to him.

I had promised myself I was going to help him get better. He deserved it.

But oh my God, it was hard. So much harder than I ever could have expected.

Holding my breath, I tugged the curtain back into place, shoving my head under the shower spray as I pictured myself flipping that perfect fucking face off. "We're in Chama, New Mexico."

The Defender responded with his unique brand of silence, and I imagined another middle finger aimed right at him. I finished rinsing off, listening intently for him the whole time. Pulling the towel from where I had it over the curtain rod, I dried off and wrapped it around me under my armpits. Moving the curtain aside, I found him standing in the exact same place in the doorway, looking a little pale.

"Do you need something else?" I asked, my voice fucking flat.

Those purple eyes flicked up from my phone again.

All righty then.

Stepping out of the tub, I pretended like him standing there while I was naked except for a towel was no big deal. Like I'd done it before. He'd probably seen thousands of naked bodies. Women more than likely threw themselves at him regularly.

The poor, innocent fools didn't know any better.

I grabbed my comb and the bundle of clothes I'd taken into the bathroom with me and squeezed by him toward my office, purposely not looking at him even when I brushed my arm against his on the way out, ignoring that buzz that I'd almost gotten used to getting since being around him so much. Locking the door, I got dressed and wrung out the water in my hair into the towel.

I needed to keep my chin up. Get this done. Then I could move on.

I had this.

I tugged on socks and left my office, stopping in the empty bathroom to put some oil in my hair. I spotted him out of the corner of my eye on the couch as I headed straight into the kitchen. Someone was feeling a little better, I guess. I pulled out plates from the cabinet as I waited for the timer to go off.

I was so caught up in thinking about how much I needed to do, that I didn't hear him move into the kitchen until I heard, "Why . . . do you . . . live here . . . by yourself?"

Slowly, slowly, slowly, I glanced over my shoulder. He was shuffling toward the breakfast table, reminding me of how my grandma had tried to get around without her walker. Oh boy.

So, somebody wasn't as healed as he'd tried to make it seem.

I knew I hadn't imagined his face being pale in the bathroom.

"Well," I started to tell him as I turned off the oven and opened the drawer where I kept my oven mitts. How much could I say? The whole truth? Only part of it? Maybe he couldn't read my mind, but he might be able to hear if my heart started beating faster when I was nervous or lying. So where did that leave me? "I didn't always live by myself. I lived with my grandparents until they passed away. I moved here after that."

I knew he was asking because he didn't totally trust me not to backstab him, more than likely. He didn't worry about his food because he could smell if I put something weird in it. Could hear me if I spit in it. But he'd been here for about two weeks now, and he was finally becoming suspicious about my intentions?

I guess it had taken him this long to say more than three words to me at a time too.

"Explain."

I gave him a look.

If I'd wanted to try something, I already would have. He had to know that, so he was just being nosy, and that put me on edge. Putting on the mitts, I took the trays out of the oven. "My grandpa had a stroke about six years ago, and we didn't find him until it was too late, and my grandma got sick after that." That same lingering sadness started to rise inside of me, mixed with grief and anger. Anger at the lives that had been so altered for things none of us had asked for.

Grief at the love and the life that I'd missed out on.

They had been my whole world. The boulder onto which I'd built my life. My grandparents had been the one thing that had never changed when everything else had been so replaceable and temporary. They were the only people who had ever really known me. The only people who had ever loved *me*. And they were gone now.

My nose stung as I shrugged and set the pan on the top of the oven. "We moved around a lot," I offered up as another explanation because that part too was the truth.

Hopefully he wouldn't ask why or ask for specifics on just how much we had bounced around.

"What was your grandmother sick with?"

That was a weird question. "She had colon cancer." I didn't tell him that she had avoided going to the doctor for years, and how much it had haunted me that I hadn't forced her to go.

Not that you could have made her do anything she didn't want to do. And that was exactly what she'd told me too.

Fortunately, my answer must have satisfied him because he didn't say anything for a minute. It wasn't until I had grabbed tongs to get the veggies that shared the tray with the steaks I had broiled that he chose to say even more words. "What are you hiding then?"

Chapter Six

His eyes were locked on me as he sat at the table, one hand braced on the top, his other one gripping his thigh.

He looked ridiculous. Just . . . absolutely out of place at the little breakfast table that had to be older than he was. I could easily picture him at a giant dining room table with silver candlestick holders and a maid coming up behind him to serve his food. There was something about his energy, about the high tilt of his chin, that seemed so . . . arrogant.

But I guess when you were what he was, anybody would be. I'd probably be insufferable.

"What are you hiding?" he asked again, taking his time with every word, staring at me while he did.

I tried my best to look innocent. I couldn't get too riled up. "A lot of things, mostly stuff in my nightstand." I mean, there was truth in that. And if he hadn't already known what was in there, he would now, but I'd rather him focus on that than anything else. If it would distract him enough to change the subject, I would take out all my vibrators and give him a presentation on each one of their pros and cons.

He ticked his head to the side, not falling for my bullshit even a little bit. "You're hiding . . . something."

That wasn't a question.

I lifted a shoulder and tried my hardest to keep that easy expression on my face. "A lot of things, but isn't everyone?"

He didn't buy that either.

I had never done anything seriously wrong in my life. The shittiest thing I'd ever done was illegally download music during our dial-up internet days two decades ago. I was a perfect angel when I wasn't mad, and I was rarely mad. I didn't put myself into enough positions to get angry. At least that was the kind of energy I tried to put out in the universe.

He got squinty. "You live in . . . the middle of nowhere. You don't . . . have family or friends or hardly any belongings. You don't leave the house."

I held up my finger, telling myself I wasn't going to let his comment about friends get to me again. "It isn't like I'm going to leave the gate open for the FedEx driver to pull up and see you through the window."

Nothing I was saying was getting through to him though. "Who . . . are you hiding from?" he had the nerve to ask as he emotionally kicked my own feet out from under me once again.

For one split second, I thought about running out the kitchen door and toward my car. I kept a set of spare keys in the wheel well. There was a bag in the back seat with a couple thousand dollars hidden in a small safe under a blanket, a few changes of clothes, and a prepaid credit card—things that would hurt me if they were stolen but wouldn't kill me.

Maybe I could make it. Maybe I could beat The Defender to my car and drive away. Maybe he would never be able to find me. I'd had decades of experience staying under the radar. There were even more precautions I could take.

And maybe I was a fucking idiot if I thought for a second he wouldn't dig as deep into his reserve as he could and beat me to the fucking door, then . . . do something to me until I told him everything.

I was no criminal though. I needed to quit acting like I was. I'd never done anything. I didn't even speed.

I'd spent my whole life trying not to do anything so that I wouldn't bring attention to myself.

On the slimmest of slim chances that I made it out the door and managed to get away, did I really think he wouldn't eventually hunt me down? Because by trying not to be suspicious, I'd made myself more. Fucking great.

My feet stayed rooted exactly where they were, and it took everything in me to release the breath I was holding. He was on to too much. My voice wobbled, and I could hear how thin it sounded—nervous, I was nervous—but there was nothing to be scared of. And before I ran out of guts, I blurted out another slice of truth. "Hiding is a *very* strong word."

Not a single thing changed about his sharp features. His voice was deceptively steady as he asked in a mocking voice, the sarcastic son of a bitch, "Is it?"

I nodded slowly. "Yeah. I would rather not be found. That's not the same as hiding, if you want to get technical."

Those purple eyes were intense, and for one second, they glowed bright before dimming back to normal.

I pressed my lips together, and before he could ask something else, I rushed to change the subject and went with the first thing I could think of. "So . . . while we're on the topic of personal questions . . . do you know who or what did that to you? Because I've been losing sleep thinking about having my limbs rendered, as you called it, and I'm paranoid something is going to happen to me every time I go for a run."

The soft sound he made through his nose made the hairs on the back of my neck rise. Every time I got close to him, I'd noticed how he made my skin feel, and if I was beside him for too long, it made the rest of me feel weird too, but not in a bad way. But this? It was different.

And that was the wrong thing to fucking ask from how deep his growl had come out. Only he could have questions. Glad we had that sorted.

"Okay, we don't need to talk about that," I muttered under my breath.

I needed to stop asking questions. Stick to business. Dammit, I *knew* that. But he was talking more than before, and even though I wasn't sure how I felt about his sparkling personality, he was still someone in my presence, still someone I could talk to, and here we were.

I side-eyed him. "You know what? I'm going to go check my mailbox before it gets any later." I'd decided not to go for a run since he was awake. The last thing I needed was for him to fall and get hurt. Then he'd be here for longer. Neither one of us needed that. "If you can feed yourself, I'll leave your plate on the table right here. If not, I'll be right back," I told him before consciously walking toward the front door as calmly as possible and not like I was on the verge of throwing up from Mr. Observant over here.

Was I that obvious? Or did he pay that much attention? At this point, I was 99 percent sure he couldn't read minds.

On the other hand, maybe he was playing the long game and fooling me into *thinking* he couldn't.

I side-eyed him again.

He didn't say shit, but I could feel his gaze follow me out of the kitchen and through the living room. It wasn't until I was through the door, down the stairs, and halfway across the driveway that I happened to glance back toward the house.

The Defender was on the top step. His head was tossed slightly back, and a beam of moonlight brushed his perfect face. He almost looked like an angel.

An angel of death with that personality but an angel.

One who needed to get better so he could leave sooner than later, because I really did have to go.

But I *was* going to miss this place.

These five acres of land had kept me busy enough so that I didn't have a lot of time to sit around; that would have made me go crazy. There were thistles I had to dig out, a garden I'd taught myself how to care for, and countless little things that always needed to be worked on. I'd been at peace here.

After losing my grandparents, I had finished our rental agreement in Texas before I'd moved here; my grandma and I had picked it in advance. There had been a movie filmed close by, and that was how I had learned about it in the first place. It had fit all the criteria for every other location we'd ever stayed, so why not? We'd lived in New Mexico before, and it had been just fine, hot as balls and all.

Even though it had felt like cheating—living on without them—things had been okay. Hard but okay. The world had become bigger and smaller at the same time without their presence. I hadn't known what to do with myself, not having them to care for after so many years.

It had been the first time in my whole life I could almost do what I wanted. For so long, I had tried to be the person they wanted and needed me to be. I had followed most of their tight rules, rarely rebelling because I couldn't bear to talk back to them and hurt their feelings. I'd almost always done what I was told to because it was for the greater good.

And as much as I would have traded all of it to have them back, I had chugged along.

Loneliness was a hemorrhoid you couldn't see but could always feel was there.

Now, I was overwhelmed with the future, for the uncertainty, but I was still here, and I had enough work to pay my bills, and maybe, just maybe my situation would change. I had to hold on to that hope. I'd seen the news, even though I'd changed the channel as fast as possible.

I was going to do my best, and that meant I had to keep helping the fool who was clutching the post for dear life as he struggled to stand, all so he could soak up some moonlight.

He looked . . . *almost* happy.

Tenderness and what I was pretty sure was a protective instinct tickled me right between the shoulder blades.

There was only so much I could do for my own situation, and there was only so much I even understood about his, but what I could do, I would. Even if he was a bit of a shit. But there had to be a good heart in there somewhere for him to do what he did for this world.

Some people criticized the Trinity for not doing more, for not jumping into every situation that went haywire, for not saving every single person in every unfortunate incident. I understood though; there was only so much they could do. So many places they could be. I'd read someone's hypothesis on what they believed regarding their involvement—the Trinity didn't get involved in political affairs unless mass, innocent casualties were at stake. They helped in smaller situations if they were already in the area. Mostly though, they only stepped in if whatever was happening would cause mass damage to the planet. If crime had gone down over the last couple of decades, it was out of humanity's fear of the planet's powerful protectors.

Plus, there had been that phase for a couple of years where idiots had tried shooting them with guns and grenade launchers, and the world had learned real quick that weapons were nothing more than gnats to them.

Maybe not even that.

I figured we should all be grateful for their existence and quit expecting them to constantly save us. They did what they could. And that reason alone was why I was here.

Maybe he would never need help again in his life, so I had to make this count, I told myself again as I made it to the mailbox and opened it. There was nothing in there, as expected. Most of the little mail I got went to my PO Box. I'd just wanted an excuse to get out of the house for a minute, and this had been the first excuse I could think of. The house felt so small with him in it.

Then add him being a pain in the ass and the urge to talk to him but being fully aware I couldn't, and . . . here I was.

I rubbed my face.

Palming my phone, I pulled it out of my pocket and hit the buttons on the screen to call my voice mail. A few more touches started replaying my saved messages.

"Call me. I love you, bye" was the first simple message left by my grandpa in Spanish.

The second one was a butt dial where I could hear them talking in the background but couldn't actually tell what they were saying.

"Graciela," my grandmother's serious voice started to say in Spanish during the third message, using her nickname for me. *"Can you stop on the way home and bring some plantains and tortillas?"*

They were nothing special, but they were the last voice mails either of them had left me. I would never delete them.

I listened to them one more time, careful not to delete them, before slipping my cell back into my pocket.

Then I rubbed my face again.

I'd never had close friends because I'd been told it was a bad idea, that it put me at risk. My students didn't even know my real last name, and I'd known some of them for years.

And what did I have? I didn't even have the cat I'd always wanted to get after Ryu passed away. I didn't have a dog. I didn't have shit.

Should I have ignored every strict rule they had raised me with?

That same thought that occasionally popped in my head came back. What was the point of everything if I couldn't even enjoy my life the way I really wanted to? Surviving wasn't the same thing as living. Was it?

Maybe things weren't as dire as I'd always thought, as I'd been told. And maybe I was just desperate and lonely and a little scared about what these damn stomachaches meant and considering making stupid decisions because of it.

I started to make my way back toward my single-wide. The moon was just a sliver managing to slice across The Defender's face. His eyes were still closed.

He almost looked at peace.

Then again, so did Venus flytraps at a distance.

Walking slowly, I watched him the whole time . . . because he was doing the same to me, I realized. His eyes were narrowed, not closed.

Watching, always fucking watching. And judging. And more than likely thinking of what I was doing that was suspicious.

I couldn't say I blamed him either.

We're all products of our circumstances. I knew that better than anyone. Being nice, kissing ass, was so much fucking work.

When I was close enough, I held out my hand. "I'll help you back in," I offered.

This motherfucker didn't even think about it.

"Fuck no," he muttered before slowly turning on his own, going back inside in his pained, limping-shuffle, just leaving me there.

I blinked. Then I looked at my hand and gave myself a high-five with the other one before climbing up the steps and going inside too. I'd walked right into that.

Dealing with this man was going to be my good deed of the year. Maybe the century. It would be a thankless job, but somebody had to do it, and that person was me.

Because of all the millions of yards he could have landed in, it had been mine.

What were the fucking chances?

Chapter Seven

I was sitting on the edge of the couch, tugging my socks back on—I'd kicked them off in the middle of the night—when I heard sounds from down the hall.

Yawning, I got up and made my way toward my room, wondering what was going on. When I'd fallen asleep last night, he had still been up, watching the final season of *Stranger Things* on my tablet. Had he not been able to sleep?

I peeked into the room and blinked.

He was awake.

What shocked me the most was the fact he was wearing a hoodie that I knew without a doubt I'd left in the dryer last night, and beside him on the bed was an empty bag of Cheetos and the box of cookies I was carefully portioning out, and a bottle of my favorite beer was on the nightstand.

But Cheetos? Really?

And he liked peach beer?

After we'd gone back inside, he'd headed straight to the bedroom, making me think he'd overextended himself. Big surprise. I brought dinner over and fed him and gulped down my own portion afterward. Then I'd cleaned the kitchen, finished my last two lessons, and when it looked like he wasn't going to sleep anytime soon, I took the couch like usual and passed out there.

I didn't sleep that great, tossing and turning and having one crappy dream after another that I couldn't recall anymore. So when I'd woken up with a funny stomach, I didn't let myself think too much about it. Yesterday had been pretty weird after all, and I'd decided that today was going to be the day I finally picked a place to move.

I yawned, pushing that nagging worry in the pit of my stomach aside before fully stepping into the doorway. "Good morning."

Those purple eyes flicked over to me for a moment before going back to my tablet, which he'd plugged in at some point.

Good morning to me too.

I squeezed my eyes closed so that I wouldn't roll them and tried again. "What time did you wake up?" I asked, too tired to remember it was a waste of time asking him anything.

He didn't even bother glancing my way as he answered, his voice flat and either bored or irritated, probably both. "I haven't slept."

I eyed him. He'd stayed up all night? I glanced at the screen, and it took me a second to recognize that I'd watched the movie he had on.

Except I'd watched it with subtitles, and there wasn't any captioning now.

"Do you speak Japanese?" I blurted out in surprise.

"I speak . . . several languages," he replied, shocking me with just that. "I'm ready for breakfast."

He spoke *several* languages, excuse me. I spoke three fluently, another really well—well enough to teach students who spoke it; it just didn't come to me as naturally yet—and two others were a work in progress. Some people took dance classes; I had taken language classes. Whatever was offered, wherever we were, I'd taken with my grandpa. *For fun.* At one point, my grandpa had done nothing but speak to me in Portuguese for almost a year. *Just in case we ever went to Brazil.* After college, he'd spent a few years there before moving back to Costa Rica, where he'd met my grandma.

But I kept my mouth shut on that.

Because I was too focused on the fact that he thought I looked like a maid. Could he use the word "please" every once in a while? I tried to keep my nose from scrunching up and forced myself to clench my teeth so that I wouldn't open my mouth and say something I regretted.

He's a member of the Trinity, Gracie.

R-e-s-p-e-c-t and all that.

I could feed him. He already seemed to be doing a little better, which meant hopefully he'd be out of here soon. I could survive him and his fucking attitude a little while longer.

I kept on telling myself that as I walked out and headed toward the kitchen. I was only a little down the hall when I heard him get up and follow, shuffling and letting out these tiny groans that didn't sound much better than they had days ago. He took a seat at the table while I ducked into the refrigerator to see what I could make. I usually fasted a few more hours, but I could eat now so that I wouldn't have to waste more time later cooking again.

I opened the packet of bacon I'd pulled out of the fridge, put it on the skillet, and turned it on low. Then I asked, "Are you done sleeping for days at a time?"

He surprised me by actually answering. "Not yet."

What did that mean? I said "hmm" as I picked up the egg carton and thought about asking him how he liked them.

Then I decided he probably wouldn't give me that classified information either, so there was no point in even asking. I'd scramble them and make them sunny side up and eat whatever he didn't. Problem solved.

I'd barely cracked a couple into a bowl when my stomach clenched and my skin buzzed simultaneously, and he said, so rough it put every other one of his tones to shame, "I think someone is at your gate."

The thing was, I wasn't expecting anyone. I hadn't ordered anything either.

I turned toward The Defender and watched his shoulders tense as his nostrils flared. His gaze was fixed on the wall that was in the same direction the driveway was, and he was frowning.

The buzzing on my skin got stronger. Was that him doing it?

"What?" I asked him, confused.

He frowned even harder at the wall, his eyes narrowing even more. "Who is it?"

Was he serious? "I don't know. I don't have cameras." I'd thought about it, but they'd be too far away to reach my Wi-Fi.

Did that mean he couldn't see through walls?

His expression didn't change at all, but I could tell he was angry when he finally flicked his gaze over in my direction. "Who were you on the phone with yesterday?" he demanded.

There was no way I could have hidden the surprised expression that took over my features. He knew I'd been on the phone, but he hadn't heard through the receiver? The Trinity were supposed to have good hearing; they had rescued people buried under rubble.

"I didn't call anyone. I just checked my voice mail," I told him slowly, getting more and more irritated by the second. This shit was getting old real fast. What the hell must I have done in another lifetime to deserve it?

He narrowed his eyes, annoying me that much more.

I took a deep breath through my nose and tried to pick my words carefully. "All I did was listen to old voice mails from my grandparents. I was sad." He'd made me sad. "No one knows you're here. Look at my phone." It wasn't like he hadn't figured out the security code.

"Call logs can be deleted," Paranoid Pants tried to claim.

I lifted the flat of my palm against my forehead and let out another slow breath. I was patient, and I could be kind. I was a decent person. I was doing this for humanity. "Why would I give you away?"

He was dead-ass serious as he said, "For money."

I couldn't help it anymore, I rolled my eyes right then and there, then glared at his perfect, annoying face. "First of all, you're hobbling around, but I'm not stupid. I know you could kill me in the blink of an eye. You don't fool me. I see it in you; I hear it in your voice. The Primordial seems like she's an angel, but you don't. You guys don't have the same look in your eye. I thought maybe you're just crabby because you're in pain, but I don't really think that anymore. You're always grouchy. Or for some reason, it's just me you can't stand. I can't tell."

I'd said it. I'd fucking said it. I had stood up for myself to him.

Was it too much? Yeah, it was too much. This was why I didn't have friends. At least part of the reason. But I couldn't take it anymore. I couldn't keep my damn mouth shut and let him just keep being a butthole.

The Defender's eyebrows flicked up just a little. Such a small, small amount that I doubted he even realized he did it. But I'd been staring at his sleeping face for days, and I could see the subtle change.

"Look, I'm trying real hard to be nice here."

It was a small one, but his snicker made me blink.

Made me want to do a lot more than that, mostly including my hands and his neck, but I was going to let it go.

"Hear me out, all right? I'm not going to risk my life for money. What good would any amount mean if it ends with you—" I dragged my thumb across my throat "—doing that to me, huh? Anyway, you could probably hear me if I lied. I'm not a trained CIA agent; I can't control my pulse. You make me nervous, but it's because I know what I have living in my house. I don't want to be found by certain people, and that has nothing to do with you. I didn't give you away or invite anyone over. I don't know who is here, but I'll go out there and find out. Stay here and eavesdrop. You have my permission to use my body as a human shield if I'm gone. I won't care."

I wasn't as amusing as I thought I was, based on his expression.

But just as I was about to turn, I hesitated. We'd made it this far, and my stomach . . . wasn't right. And it more than likely meant nothing, but . . . "Look . . ." I started to say, knowing I was about to sound insane, but on the other hand, his entire existence was even more nuts. "I've got a little bit of ESP, and I woke up today with a stomachache, and the last times I woke up feeling like this, my grandma passed away and you showed up. Maybe it doesn't mean anything. I might just be gassy."

The Defender blinked.

I could have probably left the gassy part out. I shrugged to myself and scratched at the back of my neck. "Anyway . . . just . . . leave if anything happens, okay? If I scream or something, go out the back door. I've got a spare key for my car in the wheel well. The title is in a small safe in the back seat."

He said nothing as he kept staring at me.

Glad we got that sorted.

I gave him a long, irritated look as I turned the burners off and made my way to the living room. I rubbed my face and tried to think. There was nothing about me on social media. I had a website because you weren't legit with customers if you didn't have one, but it had the name of my LLC on it. I hadn't met anyone new in a long time. The only thing different about my life was my houseguest. Could it be someone for him?

Then again, if they could hurt him, what was a locked gate?

I tried to tell myself that everything was fine. I hadn't done anything to give myself away. Maybe I'd gotten a little lazy with carrying my pepper spray around and keeping the back dead bolt locked, but I hadn't slacked off with any of the other measures I'd always taken. Maybe they were lost.

Stomping down the dirt driveway, I slowed down as the gate came into view. He was right, there was a big box truck there. Putting my hand up over my eyes, I squinted and kept walking toward it. Who was it? My PO Box was in Albuquerque, and that was under my business too. I usually checked it every two weeks; I was already past due for a visit.

I forgot my wig. Dammit.

Through the windshield, I could see two figures sitting there. I was pretty sure they were wearing black too. Black hats, black long-sleeved shirts, and they both had sunglasses on. Why were they just watching? Why weren't they trying to come out and talk or going into the back to get a package? All my things were delivered under a made-up name. Pulling out my phone, I did a quick search in my email for orders I might have forgotten about.

But the closer I got to the gate, the more this odd feeling came over my arms and the back of my neck. When was the last time those had prickled? What I was pretty sure was The Defender's anger had made my skin react but in a totally different way.

My stomach cramped, hard. Nausea punched a path straight up my throat, so violent I almost stumbled.

Shit.

Shit, shit, *shit*.

No.

The hair on my arms rose, and so did every single other fine hair on my body. I shivered out in the morning sun, and I knew. I knew.

I turned, and I fucking *ran*.

And it was then, immediately right fucking then, three long strides in, that I saw that The Defender had followed me out. He was standing at the open doorway, one hand on each side of the railing, his body stooped. His nose in the air.

"Run!" I yelled at the top of my lungs. "Go!" I shouted like a fucking banshee. "Don't let them get you!" I screamed, my voice cracking in panic and worry and desperation.

Please, please, please, let him get away, I thought as I ran for my fucking life.

Because that was exactly what I was doing.

Just not in the direction I should have. Because I couldn't let them get him. That was what I'd understood. There was going to be no running away.

More of just trying to distract them away from him.

Fuckkkkk!

I'd remember for as long as I lived, that he stood there on the deck, barely able to stand just as a sound exploded across the sky at the same time something hit me in the back *hard*—so damn hard, oww, oww, *oww*—once, twice, three times, sending me flying forward.

Just like in the movies when a bomb exploded.

I went airborne for what felt like two minutes but was more than likely just a second before coming to crash, skidding across the hard ground.

My ears rang.

My mouth tasted like . . . iron. Like blood?

And oww, oww, oww, my ribs . . . my *back*. I tried to take a breath, but the pain was unreal. But somehow, even as my vision blurred and my back was on fire and hurt like the worst hell, I lifted my gaze and looked for him.

I found him.

Well, more like the mound of white and gray on the ground by the stairs to the deck.

Why hadn't he *run*? How the hell had they taken him down? Had they shot him too?

Out of the corner of my eye, I saw feet. One pair of black boots after another surrounded me, coming so close I thought for sure I was going to get stepped on if I could care about anything other than The Defender.

They couldn't take him.

No, *no, no.* "Run," I tried to say, even though I didn't actually hear my words because my ears were ringing. "Don't let them take you," my lips moved.

Something wet slipped down my cheek as more boots came forward. My back hurt so bad. All I could do was watch the figure on the ground get surrounded by those men wearing black too.

Tears poured down my cheeks, and I whimpered, at least it felt like I did it and—

My ears throbbed harder, and I slapped a palm over the one aching the worst, but I couldn't think.

I couldn't even see The Defender anymore, but I hoped more than anything he had managed to get away. He could, I knew he could. Lifting my gaze, I realized I was in the middle of what had to be . . . twenty . . . thirty men dressed in paramilitary-type outfits, holding guns all aimed at me.

I had to . . . I had to do . . . something . . .

I couldn't let them hurt him. How had they found me? I'd been so careful.

I struggled up to my least painful hand and balanced on my other forearm, trying to sit up. "He has nothing to do with this," I tried to say. "Leave him alone." I tasted even more blood. Why did my teeth hurt? "Let him go. I won't fight you. Please. I'll go with you."

I would. I'd go with them. Promise.

Everything hurt, everything hurt.

But I had to . . . I had to . . .

The sound of a gunshot cracked across the air at the same time something hit my back so hard, I screamed.

Had they shot me? Was I about to fucking *die*?

Sheer fear wrapped me up entirely at not knowing what was going on.

At failing him.

Failing myself.

My grandparents.

I felt the absolute terror of thinking this was going to be the end. After everything. Here. In the driveway, alone.

I had missed out on so much . . . and maybe that thought hurt more than the physical pain.

All I'd ever wanted was to be myself. To have a choice. To be valued. And now?

Then there was another crack, and I had to close my eyes.

Chapter Eight

It was the pounding in my head that woke me up.

Or maybe the fact that the pain coming from my back was almost unbearable.

The terrible taste in my mouth *might* have also been a factor.

More than likely, it was all of it.

I felt like I had gotten my ass whooped, and it had been a long, *long* time since that had happened. Back then too, it had been a bunch of people ganging up on me, except in this case it wasn't just because I was the new kid.

I wished it was that simple.

But the second I opened my eyes, the second my pupils adjusted enough to the blinding white bulbs installed in the ceiling, I realized *something was wrong*.

Really, *really* wrong.

Because daylight bulbs? I didn't have money for that. So what . . . ?

The shots. The men who looked like soldiers but weren't, at least not the good kind of soldiers. *The Defender sprawled on the ground in front of my trailer.*

I sat up so fast my head swam, and I had to squeeze my eyes closed when everything went white.

Holy fuck, my back. My fucking everything. Oww, oww, *oww*. Blindly reaching backward to try and touch it, I stopped at the weight on my wrist and forced myself to look. There was a band on my hand. One single, thick, heavy cuff.

Where the fuck was I?

There were white walls. The floor was a cold, pale gray concrete. There was a door that looked to be made of some kind of metal with no window of any sort. A toilet and a sink took up one corner.

But it was the figure on the ground to my right that shocked me the most.

It was The Defender.

On his side, in the hoodie he'd borrowed and gray sweatpants that were a lot dirtier than they had been the last time I'd seen them, he was there. Just within reaching distance.

I reached out, instantly going for his throat. Pressing my fingers against a spot on it, I waited, trying to ignore the painfully sharp silence from the plain, empty room that I'd wonder later whether it was soundproofed or not. A steady, ultra-slow beat pulsed against my fingers, and I let out a relieved breath.

He was alive.

He better fucking be.

Blowing out a breath, I pulled my hand back as I crossed my legs under me and pretty much wilted over.

I was alive, and he was alive, and those were both good things, I tried to reason.

But that was about as far as the "good things" here went, and I damn well knew it.

Maybe my head was still throbbing and every survival instinct in my body was going off, but I wasn't too out of it to not have a good idea of the situation we were in.

A fucked one, that was what.

Totally and completely *fucked*.

My throat suddenly squeezed in on itself, and when I tried to suck in a breath, my lungs decided otherwise. Tears filled my eyes, and everything went blurry. Panic didn't just rise in my chest, it tried to eat the whole damn thing in one bite.

I tried to suck in another breath through my nose, and that didn't work out either.

There was only one thing my body wanted to do, and it didn't include calming breaths. "Oh no, *no*—"

"Stop that."

I shut my mouth at the same time my eyes moved to the man who had rolled onto his back at some point over the last few seconds.

"Get yourself together," he rumbled in that rich, low voice, stretching his arms out across the floor, giving me a view of the cuff on his wrist too.

That grumpy face stared over at me, annoyed, impassive, and dirt-smudged.

But not actually seeming at all pissed off that we were *in a fucking room in God knew where after pretty much getting ambushed.*

I wanted to cry.

"*Do not* get . . . hysterical. I'm not . . . in the mood," The Defender grumbled.

I blinked.

He wasn't in the mood?

Him?

I took my time pressing my lips together, thinking, then asked so, so slowly, so quietly, "Are you shitting me right now?"

He yawned.

Yawned!

"I thought they hurt you!" I hissed, sounding 1,000 percent panicked. Because I was. I was scared on top of this. I was so, so scared.

"They used . . . beanbag rounds," he explained like he was telling me about the weather. Like we were on the couch at my trailer and not . . . not *here*. Having this conversation about being hit by beanbag rounds.

As tears filled my eyes and something terrible formed in my throat, he gave me another one of the irritated looks he'd been shooting my way since we'd met.

I stared at him. I stared at him in disbelief. In terror.

"They didn't . . . hurt me," he said, sounding almost dismissive even as his eyes narrowed. "You're the one who got hurt. Probably have . . . bruised ribs."

That explained a lot, but it didn't make me feel any better.

"How are you so calm?" I asked him, twisting my head to look around the room just in case I'd missed something a minute ago.

"Why shouldn't I be?" he asked in that grumbly, crabby voice that was the one I knew best.

"Is this not kind of a jail cell?"

"It is."

We were in a jail cell.

I'd been shot with beanbag rounds, which totally explained why my back and ribs ached so bad.

And now . . . now . . . he was choosing to talk to me.

Fuck.

Fuckkkkk.

I'd tried to live my life quietly. So small. *Don't draw attention. Don't become too attached to anything.* I had kept away from people for not just my own benefit but for theirs too. I tried to be decent. I believed in karma.

But I was still here.

Because I had been a stubborn motherfucker trying to do her best.

I'd ignored the signs like an idiot.

Resentment toward my parents stirred hard in my chest. In my entire soul if I was going to be honest. I didn't think it was possible to be so damn pissed off, but it was.

My eyes started to sting, and it took me a couple tries before I got my mouth to actually croak, "And you're okay with that?" Because I wasn't. This was my nightmare.

He huffed. "It's not convenient."

Convenience was a really loose word to describe this.

I slowly and very, very painfully rolled down, holding back whimpering until I was spread out on the floor too. I knit my hands together, ignoring the way they were shaking despite the weight of the cuff, and set them over my chest. I tried to take another breath and stopped when it felt like getting stabbed.

I had to think.

We'd been kidnapped for all intents and purposes. It hadn't been a dream, and I wasn't being pessimistic. This was reality.

It was also fucking freezing in here.

Squeezing my eyes closed, I tried to tell myself that this wasn't the end of the world.

I was still alive, so I was winning on that end. For a minute there, I'd thought it was all over. But it wasn't.

Once I'd managed to calm myself down as much as I was pretty sure I was capable of considering the situation, I asked in my most polite voice, which honestly sounded like I was deranged and not very polite at all because I was on the verge of panicking, "Are you not losing your shit because you know something I don't?"

"I know . . . a lot of things . . . you don't" was how he decided to reply, the ball of sunshine.

I gritted my teeth and tried to strangle my patience closer to my heart. I tried my best to calm down and put things into perspective. One step at a time. One minute at a time. I knew better than to freak out. You made mistakes when you acted impulsively, and I was in no position to make more.

First things first: "Do you know where we are?"

"No," he answered immediately.

Okay. Fortunately, he was responding. "Do you know if there are cameras in here? Microphones?" He had to be able to hear them or sense them or something, I was pretty sure considering he was the one who had known that they had been at the gate.

There was a beat of silence before he replied with "No." He lifted the cuff on his wrist like that explained everything.

It didn't, and I wasn't sure I trusted that there wasn't something in here that could communicate back to them somehow. We had to be careful with what we said. Another choke rose up in my throat, but I fought it down before trying to ask calmly, "You said you don't know where we are, but do you have *any* idea where we could be?"

I dropped my head to the side to focus on him. He still looked almost serene. But some tiny muscle in his cheek moved, and I could tell he thought about how to answer that. I'd known he was full of shit telling me he didn't know where we were. "I've got . . . a good idea."

I knew it! I opened my mouth, then closed it. Then I peeked around the room, thinking. Talking to him in Spanish was out of the question. Portuguese was a better choice, but a Spanish speaker could piece together some words.

"How?" I asked him in Korean.

His head slowly turned toward me.

"Do you understand me? I don't want them to know what we are talking about," I said, sticking to the language I'd learned from the family that had babysat me until we'd moved away for the first time. I was pretty sure that's how I'd picked it up so easily, my little brain had been a sponge back then. After we'd moved away, I'd had a Korean American teacher at one school who had worked with me a couple times a week. The rest I'd picked up by streaming every K-drama I could find and listening and reading subtitles over and over again, repeating everything to get the pronunciation right.

The Defender's gaze narrowed and then, in Korean, he replied, "I wasn't . . . sleeping when they . . . brought us here."

I rolled onto my side to get a better look at him. He was still on his back, his arms beside his body. His chest rose slowly before falling at the same pace.

Breathe. Calm down. I didn't need to panic.

Easier said than done though.

"You *let* them take you?" I had told him to leave. I knew I had. I'd fucking screamed it at the top of my lungs.

His purple eyes flashed for a brief moment before the bright color faded just as quickly as I'd seen it. I'd surprised him, and he'd surprised me by talking to me in flawless Korean right back. "I did not *let* them . . . take me. I would not have been . . . in a position . . . to be taken if I'd been . . . healing the way I should've. The only reason . . . you're here is because you kept this a secret."

Was he serious?

I switched back to English. "I told you to run!" I snapped at him in a hiss that surprised me. *Calm down.* But really, how could he turn this around on me? I had to calm down. Everything wasn't fine, but it wasn't crazy dire either unless there were vents I couldn't see that were eventually going to spew poisonous gases. "I thought something was off. I told you to go. Before I went outside, I warned you."

The stare he pinned me with was incredulous.

I knew in my heart this wasn't his fault.

None of this was.

I could own up to it. I could be the reasonable one between the two of us. So I was, even though it almost physically hurt me. "I'm sorry, okay. *I'm sorry.* I didn't know they were coming, and . . ." What was I supposed to do? Tell him everything? What a fucking mess. I wasn't supposed to tell anyone anything, ever. I wasn't supposed to even be here. I wanted to cry, and I could hear that urge in my voice as I murmured, "I told them to leave you alone."

That earned me an ice-cold glare and another dose of grouchy, as he switched back to English too. "The only person you can blame is yourself for being here."

Could I suffocate him? With my shirt? Would that work?

I was going to die here.

I was going to spend the rest of my short fucking life in this room with this man-being who had it out for me for reasons I couldn't understand. I was going to starve to death. That was how my life was going to end if I was lucky and my organs weren't removed from my body to be sold on the black market while I was still alive to keep them as fresh as possible. They'd harvest them for sure. They were good organs. I took my vitamins. I ate . . . maybe not great, but I ate food. I ran.

Tears sprang up in my eyes, and my heart started going even faster, and when I tried to breathe, it was hard as hell to because I was panting despite how much it made my back ache.

I was going to die in this place.

It didn't matter that I didn't have their money. That I had never done shit. They wouldn't believe me.

Everything had been for nothing.

I was going to be vulture food.

Virgin fucking vulture food.

Why hadn't I had sex when I had the chance?

"Are you crying?" the rich voice scoffed in disbelief.

Oh, my tears were there. They were fucking there. My heart was going to explode if it didn't just crack down the middle. I wasn't a stranger to being sad, but I didn't think I'd ever been this sad, and that said a lot because I'd cried every day for a year straight when my grandpa had passed away.

I was so stupid. So fucking stupid.

"I'm sorry," I whispered because I couldn't stop myself. I had no control over anything. Why had I ever convinced myself that I did? "But I'm going to beat myself up more than you ever could. I don't need you to be a butthole right now," I whispered, numb. Heartbroken.

My world was ending.

All my hope was dying.

I couldn't believe it.

It was over. It was all over, just like that. This was how my life ended.

Out of the corner of my eye, I saw that long body struggle to rise up onto an elbow. *"What did you say?"* The Defender sputtered in a voice that might have given me a nightmare if this whole situation wasn't already one.

A few more tears streamed down my cheeks.

Defeat beat at my chest. At my soul. My spirit. My brain.

My thirtieth birthday was in less than three months.

I had so many hopes, so many dreams. None of them were big. I didn't want to be rich or famous. Traveling would have been cool, but if I didn't get to visit every continent, I wouldn't have been upset.

All I'd ever wanted was to be loved, to have someone know me for *me*. To have more than just my grandparents, as ungrateful as that sounded. When I was young, I'd dreamed about having siblings. I'd dreamed about having my parents around to do things that they hadn't been able to. Then later on, I had wanted a partner in life.

I'd thought I'd have more time to meet someone I trusted enough to have sex with, and I hadn't even done that.

I could have settled for one real friend that I could tell everything to. Just one. I didn't need a girl gang or a squad. I wanted one person to share this burden with. That wasn't too much, was it?

A few more tears fell down my cheeks.

How was it possible that life could be this fucking unfair? What had I ever done except been born to the wrong people? I hadn't asked for any of this.

It was fucking *bullshit*.

All of it. All of this. Steaming *bullshit*.

I shrugged helplessly, training my eyes on the orbs of pure white light on the ceiling as my soul died a little. My vision blurred as I shook my head slowly, bitterly. "You heard me. What are you going to do? Kill me?" I asked before chuckling; it sounded as hollow and defeated as I felt. "Get in line. I'm dead in here anyway. You might as well finish the job and make it quick."

It would be better that way. It'd be less painful, I'd bet. Dying at The Defender's hand.

"Stop talking," he growled so fiercely I probably would have started shaking days ago, but right then, I didn't care. Not a little bit. Not any bit.

So this was what defeat felt like, huh?

I was Fucked. With a capital F.

More tears fell, and I chuckled, and it *hurt*. Life was over. It was fucking *over*. I couldn't believe it.

I wilted even more onto the floor, ready for it to suck me in and make me one with the earth. "For the record, I never wanted to drag you into this. It's why I kept asking you if you wanted to go somewhere else. I begged them to leave you alone." Not that it had done shit.

I was here after all.

There were so many things I still wanted to do. Things I felt like I'd been robbed of. Things that felt even more precious now that I understood the situation we were in.

I groaned and wiped my damp eyes with the meaty part of my palm as I shook my head in disbelief. *I'm sorry, Grandma and Grandpa. I'm so, so sorry.*

I shrugged at him, feeling more defeated than I had when I'd tried to play *Zelda* with a broken thumb.

Hope had lost its wings and needed some crutches now.

A picture of my grandma's face formed in my head right then though.

I couldn't let everything be in vain. There was no reason to think I was going to be dying anytime soon. Maybe they would drag this out and torture me for a long period of time. I had . . . I had ten toes. Ten fingers. Other body parts. You could still live a rich and fulfilling life without a tongue. I'd always planned on learning ASL.

I squeezed my hands into fists.

But I really liked my tongue and fingers.

Maybe I wasn't going to be keeping my shit together.

My chest bounced up and down as even more tears filled my eyes and nasal cavity. It was pure pride that kept me from melting straight into a panic attack. A straight-up shit attack. I couldn't. I shouldn't. I was still alive. *I was still fucking alive.*

"What does the Arenas gang want with you?" The Defender finally asked after I'd wiped at my eyes and tried calming the fuck down.

It didn't last.

Of course he'd figured that part out. I sniffed, suddenly feeling like a joke. "It doesn't matter, does it? I know you're feeling a little better, so I'll try and stay alive until you're strong enough to get out of here. Unless they straight up poison me or shoot me in the face, I'll try my best. I'm stubborn. I won't give up that easily."

Give up. Oh, I wanted to cry at the unfairness of all this shit. What had I ever done to deserve this?

There was a beat of silence as he probably realized how close I was to having a meltdown. I wouldn't have been surprised if he'd been able to smell it. But I was shocked when he very calmly said, "I wouldn't be asking . . . if it didn't matter."

"It doesn't matter. Trust me." I sighed, realizing how stupid that sounded. "Never mind. I forget you don't, but you can believe me, there's nothing that can affect you. Not anymore. I don't think they know who you are, so as long as you don't do anything to give yourself away, you'll be fine." I guess that was the only bright side.

Then I thought about it and lifted my head again to meet his gaze. I thought about it and said in Portuguese, assuming he understood it since he was Mr. I Know Several Languages. "Don't let them see your eyes. Please don't . . . do anything. I want you to make it out of here." All I had wanted was to try and help him, and it was part of the reason why I hadn't left my house despite all the warnings I'd ignored. I was such a stubborn fucking idiot.

I was going to be tortured one way or the other.

I wanted to laugh so I wouldn't cry.

From his facial expression, he'd understood what I said, but he still replied in English. "Why are you making those noises?" The Defender asked in an exasperated tone, still talking to me for some magical reason.

Dropping back down to the floor, I rubbed my hands over my face and laughed weakly some more. "This whole situation is just . . . wow. Literally, wow. I must have done something really fucked up in another lifetime for things to end up like this." Oh boy. "I wonder if it was in the same lifetime that I did something to you." I sighed. "All I ever wanted was just to have a choice," I mumbled to myself. It wasn't like it mattered.

Not anymore.

Why hadn't he tried to run? Or broken *their* backs? I was pretty sure if he'd really put his mind to it, he could have gotten away, or at least gotten some distance from the house so they couldn't find him.

But I guess I understood what he wasn't saying.

He still wasn't healing enough.

We were screwed.

At least it sure seemed that way.

But I had to stop feeling sorry for myself, and I had to think. I wasn't the smartest person in the world, but I had good problem-solving skills. I had always managed to figure everything out. We were short on money? *I had* this. I got my first job at fifteen despite my grandparents' protests. The car wouldn't start? Let me google it. I was lonely and bored? I was going to pack my days in so that I wouldn't have a chance to think about it.

Maybe we couldn't get out of here when he was in this condition, but on the other hand, there was the tiniest chance we could.

I had to try to get through this. If I couldn't, if I didn't, that would be one thing. At least I'd tried. At least I could look my grandpa and grandma in the eye when I saw them again. That was what they'd want.

I had to do this. For them.

First things first, I had to keep my shit together. We were in here, sure, but even if he wasn't running at 100 percent capacity, he was still more incredible than any other being on the planet. Or he would be with some more time. Maybe I wasn't remarkable at anything, but I paid attention, and my trusty gut—when I listened to it—had never steered me wrong. It was time I stopped ignoring it.

Breathe in, breathe out. Ignore the fact it felt like fire and it made me want to throw up because it was so painful.

Everything might be fine. It could be all right. No need to lose it. No need to fall apart. I was reasonable and practical.

Think, Gracie. How many shows and books had I read or watched with people who were trapped somewhere and they managed to escape? A fucking ton. I used to watch *MacGyver*. I just had to calm down and put one foot in front of the other.

One step at a time.

Propping myself up on a forearm and groaning while I did it, I looked around the room again to still find nothing but smooth white walls, flat light bulbs, a toilet, and sink. I didn't want to ask. I knew I shouldn't talk to him, but . . . "What do you think our chances are of starving in here?"

From the face he made, he seemed to actually think about it.

And I thought that said everything. Fuck. Oh fuck.

All right. How long would it take to starve? A month? How long until it really started to affect me? As long as the tap at the sink worked, at least there was water, or I'd be a goner a lot sooner than that.

I eyed him and wondered if he could rip out the sink, then the pipes from the walls, and get into the AC unit.

He could barely walk. How far would we really make it? There had to be some other plan. Maybe . . .

"You should know they went through your house," The Defender said abruptly. "They burned it down. Your car, the greenhouse, the building . . . everything."

My whole body went numb as I asked, "What?" thinking I hadn't heard him correctly.

I hadn't heard him right.

No.

I couldn't have.

"If you ask me," he said quietly and unexpectedly, "it was overkill."

No.

No.

They'd burned the trailer down? All my things?

There weren't a ton of them, but they were mine, and each one mattered.

My past and my present.

I wanted to ask if he was sure, but of course he fucking was.

He was sarcastic, bossy, and secretive, but he didn't hide being all those things. There was no reason he would make it up.

Everything was gone?

The place that had been my home for years. The remainder of my grandparents' belongings and our memories together. It was all . . . it was all . . .

Oh God, I had nothing left.

Nothing.

Not my cell phone, which had precious voice mails. Not an old blanket. Not the few family heirlooms that we had made room for no matter how little space there was in the car.

Nothing.

This was all because I hadn't fucking left when I should have.

My mouth filled with saliva, and those tears I'd been trying to keep control of poured out in the span of an exhale.

I slapped a hand over my mouth at the same time I drew my legs up and slouched forward, ignoring just how bad that hurt me everywhere.

Tears gushed over my fingers.

My home was gone.

Everything was fucking *gone*.

"Why are you crying?" the deep voice demanded from beyond my knees. "The house was small and smelled funny."

I cried. I cried harder than I'd thought I was capable of.

"I lost everything," I told him, my voice cracking. I mopped at my face with my wrist before even more came out. Losing my grandparents' things hurt worse than my own. My grandma's tablecloth. My grandpa's watch.

My hands shook.

A wail built up in my throat, and I clung to it for dear life. Threw a fucking lasso around it and gripped the end like I would get stomped to death if I didn't get it under control. It was stuff, yes, but . . .

"You still . . . have your life," The Defender said.

It didn't help. He was right, sure, but it didn't make me feel any better.

"Materialistic belongings don't mean anything."

I swallowed so, so hard.

He tried a different angle. "Could you . . . quit crying?"

I wiped at my eyes even harder.

"Anyone ever told you . . . that you cry ugly?" he fucking asked.

If I thought it would actually hurt him, I'd kick him in the nuts. Instead, I slouched forward even more, squeezed my hands into fists so tight my nails dug into my palms, and gritted out, "I. Know. That."

Good God, I didn't know it was possible to sound like I'd been a chain-smoker for half my life, but it was. "Believe me. I've moved more in my life and have had to leave so much shit behind every time, that *I know that.* That's why I don't keep that much stuff anymore. But there were still . . ." This was harder than I'd thought, and really, I was getting more and more pissed by the fucking second. Not just at him but at everything. "There were still a few things I was able to keep. A few things that really meant something to me. They were all I had left of the people I loved, okay? So please cut me some slack for being upset that I lost things that I can never replace." I choked every single word out so that I wouldn't scream. Or cry. I wasn't sure which was worse.

Then I made the mistake of glancing at him, there on the floor, his face dirty, and snapped, looking him right in the fucking purple eye, "And you're ugly when you cry."

Whether it was my words or tone or both, that got him to shut up.

It wasn't my best comeback. I was rusty. I hadn't talked shit back to anyone since my Xbox days, and I really had tried so hard to be nice to him.

But I didn't care anymore. My hands shook, and my breathing got choppy as I tried to tell myself that I had been planning on leaving and not taking 99 percent of the things in the mobile home with me.

But it didn't help.

It really didn't help.

Nothing did.

My life was fucking over, I thought sometime later.

But I guess it had been over since the day my parents had done the stupidest shit possible.

Most of my choices had been taken away from me before I'd even been born.

But now . . . now, it was official. Now it was real. It was *all* over.

I cried so much I was out of tears.

And energy.

Trying not to make a sound as your world imploded around you was a hell of a lot harder than making a big stink about it. That was for fucking sure. Staying positive? I might as well have convinced myself I was going to win a gold medal at the next Olympics.

I felt miserable in body and spirit when I finally rolled to face the ceiling. There was something almost therapeutic about lying on your stomach, crying into your stacked arms. Maybe it was just me though. I didn't cry often. I'd been dealing with a bad hand my whole fucking life. All I'd ever known was to keep going, even when it wasn't easy, and all I wanted to do was wallow.

But I didn't know how to do that with this.

I was alone, and I had no idea what I was doing, and I had no clue what was going to happen.

The truth was a fucking asshole that didn't wear a cape. It had a hammer like Thor, but it wasn't always used for good.

I felt beyond tapped out in the time after The Defender gave me the news about my things being lost as I tried to finally put myself back together and reason out the few options I had left. I told myself over and over and over again that stuff was just stuff and I would still have my loved ones with me always in my heart. After, I told myself that I still had a lot of pictures in my safe deposit box. You know, because of the paranoia of having to leave at a moment's notice.

What hurt the most was the possibility I might have lost the voice mails my grandparents had left me.

I wasn't ready to quit being upset, but I didn't have to totally waste my time either.

What I knew for sure was: There was a small chance I might starve to death. Maybe be tortured. I might be saying goodbye to my organs or a few digits, but I sure as hell hoped not.

Those fuckers had burned my house down. Even if we somehow got out of here, I had nowhere to go because I hadn't planned far enough ahead. A big chunk of my emergency cash was gone, and I had no access to my bank account.

Basically, I was in a worse situation than I ever could have imagined, and I was trying my best not to give up.

I still had my life. I could figure out the rest if I had a chance.

I sniffled once, then twice, and felt my face scrunching up again. My fucking lip was trembling. And everything *hurt*.

But if this *was* the end, at least . . . at least I wouldn't be alone—not that this pain in the ass was at the top of my list of people I would prefer to spend my last moments with, but he was still *someone*.

At least I'd had kind of a . . . kind of an adventure. A fucked-up one, sure, but *I'd* chosen it, and it had been with one of the Trinity. Who got to say that? I'd given my life to help someone who had done so much.

If it was going to be a sacrifice, at least it was an honorable one.

It would fucking suck, but it could be worse. Right?

I sniffled again and tried to ease my features into a calm expression but failed.

The house had things that had mattered, but my life still mattered more.

I wouldn't give up.

I hoped that every single person who had been at my house got hemorrhoids. Internal and external ones. If anything happened to me, I was going to come back from the dead and poltergeist every single one of their asses. None of them were ever going to have sex again if I had anything to say about it. They were never going to have a full night's rest either.

I didn't need to have super strength and speed to make someone regret being born.

So yeah, even if I didn't make it out of here, I was going to ignore that light at the end of the tunnel and haunt these motherfuckers for the rest of their lives. That would be my consolation prize. That would be my new purpose—haunting. I was going to find every person in the cartel and haunt them and their families. Maybe throw some things around. Pull on some feet from under the bed.

Pressing my fingers against my face, I dragged in a big, deep breath that hurt like hell before slowly letting it back out, ignoring the way my body wanted to shake at being so overwhelmed.

"Are you done . . . throwing a tantrum?" came the deep voice from its spot across the room.

He hadn't moved an inch since pretty much telling me that everything I knew was gone now.

Grief filled my throat, my soul again . . .

Then I thought about what had just come out of his mouth.

"I wasn't throwing a tantrum," I grumbled, rolling onto my side to find that he had moved. He was sitting up against the wall. His long legs were stretched out, and his arms were crossed on his chest. His breaths were deeper than they had been.

But he was still in pain. I could tell from the tightness at the corners of his mouth.

"You were throwing a tantrum," he insisted, sliding his gaze over to me.

"No, I wasn't," I muttered, grumpier than hell but trying to be decent. Because none of this was his fault. It really wasn't. I knew it.

"Yeah, you were. All that crying . . . and sniffling?" He made a dismissive sound. "Disgusting."

I swear . . . "There's nothing 'disgusting' about being upset."

He made a face. "You were wiping your nose with the back of your hand."

"Well, there isn't exactly tissue or toilet paper, is there?" I thought about it. Then I used my shoulder to wipe off my dry nose just to spite him. "I have a right to be upset. Everything I loved is gone. Maybe I'm never going to get out of here, and I've read about starvation; it's not a pleasant fucking way to go. *And I don't want to fucking die, okay?*"

Tears bubbled up in my eyes all over again, and I used the back of my hand to wipe them off, before sniffling so I could glare at him and look straight into those stupid purple eyes. "I'm scared, all right? And I won't let myself regret helping you, but I'm going to regret a whole lot of other things if this is going to be the end." Things like . . . things I couldn't control. Things like never having a real boyfriend, never having sex. Never leaving the country. Never doing a million other things I had hoped would be in my future. I'd never even had a girls' night out, for fuck's sakes. "You're not helping. At all."

Oh God, I was going to start crying again.

The silence in the room might have been stifling if I gave a shit. But I didn't.

I'd lost all my shits somewhere between being kidnapped and finding out my home had been burned down. I didn't deserve this. I had never done anything to deserve any of this. That was exactly what I was hung up on.

My whole life had revolved around decisions other people had made that affected me.

I'd had it. This could be it for me if I didn't think straight and take advantage of any and every opportunity I had. I'd drink my own pee if I had to, and that was just the tip of the iceberg in the shit I was pretty sure I was willing to do to survive. I'd made a promise after all.

Fuck it. Fuck everything. I already knew I had nothing left to lose.

"Are you done?" The Defender asked like I wasn't burning down my entire personality and life plans in the blink of an eye.

Was I? I stared at him and his crabby face, at the impatience stamped on his bone structure.

With a steady hand, I reached up, tugged the extra hair tie from my wrist—my faithful little black elastic that lived there—and in a way I'd practiced a hundred times out of boredom, I slingshot it across the room.

And I only felt a small, itty-bitty thrill when his eyebrows dropped right before he leaned out of the way and the tie hit the spot where his head had just been.

Those eyes stared at me just long enough for me to start to snort. Then he exploded from the floor.

One minute he was there, looking bored and hiding his pain as best as he could, and the next, he was lunging toward me so fast my eyes couldn't keep up with his movement. And in less than the blink of a fucking eye, that snort still halfway out of my nose and half inside of me, he was on top of me.

Holy shit. He was on his hands and knees over my body, his

fingers loose over my wrists. His calves pressed alongside the outside of my lower legs, careful to keep his weight off me.

I squeaked as his head dipped, those flaming purple eyes lighting up for one brief moment brighter than ever, his nostrils flaring wide as he growled, "*What in the fuck are you doing?*"

I squeaked. "It was just a hair tie." Plus, he was bulletproof. Give me a break.

I felt the growl that rose from his chest in the tips of my toes. In my inner thighs. Right at the juncture of my ribs.

His head tilted to the side, giving me a view of dark, wide pupils and honestly . . . honestly . . . I almost felt scared for a split second. He looked like a crazy person. And I understood then better than ever why crime had gone down. I wouldn't want to face this either. "Do you know . . . what happens . . . to people who . . . throw things at me?"

I stared.

Someone had thrown things at him? How stupid could you be? I wasn't going to count myself. I'd known what I was doing.

Maybe this had been my destiny all along—to get to this point with a savior of mankind and lose my life to him.

But I was fed up with him and his bad attitude, his ungratefulness, and mostly him just being mean to me *for no reason*.

So I couldn't help but try and growl right back at him just like he'd done to me. "I'm getting really tired of you being a butthole."

Oh shit.

My imaginary balls were the size of grapefruits now. I'd just called The Defender a butthole to his face. Literally inches from it.

I might just have the biggest fucking balls of all time. At least I thought so. You know who didn't?

The man who had saved a derailed train in Germany once, who was currently snarling down at me.

I just looked at him, my colossal imaginary balls heavy. "Jerk?" I offered with one of the first real smiles I'd given him.

He snarled even more. Ooh, somebody meant business.

"I'm not asking for comfort from you," I gritted out. "I know you're not here to do that. But you were being really insensitive and a—"

The growl was back, and I tried to huff.

"Jesus. I wasn't going to say butthole again, calm down. You made me mad, and it was just a hair tie. I didn't expect to hit you. Everyone knows how fast you are, even if you are . . . you know." *He knew.* Probably not the best idea to bring up his injuries, but I didn't have the patience or energy to tiptoe around him anymore. "But you've handled a lot worse than a little elastic. We both know it didn't do any real damage, all right," I told him, watching his eyes closely.

I'd tried to be nice to him. I'd sucked up all his comments, bitchy faces, and overall rudeness. But I was done with it. It was too hard. It was too much. I respected him, but that didn't mean I liked him.

The Defender kept staring at me, head still tilted to the side.

I glared right back, not about to apologize anymore.

"Why are you finally talking to me now?" I blurted out, knowing damn well how rude the question was.

He stared me right in the damn eye as he said, "I was in pain before. Everything makes sense now."

What made sense?

The Defender huffed, then rolled off me.

Fucking butthole.

And almost like he could read my mind, his head whipped back in my direction.

I looked at him, and then I sighed. "I'm scared, all right? Maybe you're used to high-stress situations, but I'm not. If something bad happens in here, it happens. But I don't want to die. I don't want to starve." My eyes helplessly filled with tears again that I could barely hold at bay, and I shrugged. "None of this is your fault. I'm sorry. I'm upset, and I'm taking it out on you. I'm sorry."

His brow went flat, but after a moment, he settled back against the floor. His head moved until he faced the ceiling, and his nostrils flared again.

I rubbed my face, angry and disappointed and genuinely scared.

"You're not going to die in here," he muttered after a moment.

That was easy for him to believe. He didn't know everything.

"We're going to get out," The Defender kept going . . . reassuring me?

I felt my lip wobble at the reminder of the maybe slim, maybe not slim, chance my life would end here in a brutal, painful way.

"Stop it."

I pursed my lips together.

"I'm healing," he said in Portuguese.

That got me to glance at him as even more tears filled my eyes. "I don't want to be rude, but I don't think you're healing enough," I told him in the same language.

His eyes popped open and slid toward me.

"You need to get better first." Whether I was going to be alive long enough for that was something I'd worry about later. Maybe I would have more time. Maybe they wouldn't come in here anytime soon. And maybe I'd magically grow six inches. "I want to get out of here more than anything, and I hope I can figure out how to get us both out. I know we aren't friends or anything, but . . ." I squeezed my hands together, desperation eating up my chest bite by bite. "Maybe we can be temporary friends. Until we get out of here." I sniffled. "We only have each other in here."

It wasn't like either one of us had more options.

Oh boy, I could feel the sweat on my forehead thinking about it.

Part of me expected him to go back to being that grumpy, quiet pain in the ass, but eventually, The Defender shocked me when he muttered in English, "Fuck. Fine."

Fine? *Fine?* All right. Someone was dying to be my friend. Oh boy. I almost laughed, but I did sigh.

"You need to get better, and in the meantime, I'll think about what we can do. You think about it too; you know what you're capable of and what you can handle. I'll try and buy us as much time as possible." And I wasn't going to say it out loud, but I could tell that movement a minute ago—him pinning me down—had cost him. I hadn't missed his flinch and the strain on his face. No matter how much more he was moving, there was still something wrong. He was getting better, but it wasn't some kind of miracle.

He wasn't that kind of superhero, I guess, who could regrow an arm in an hour.

Or at least not anymore for whatever terrifying reason.

I sighed and rubbed my face, wondering over that for a while until another familiar question popped into my head. I had nothing left to lose. Hadn't I already come to terms with that? Peeking over at him, I just went for it. Back to Korean. "Is there something I can call you other than Defender?" It felt awkward to call him that after I'd spoon-fed him and called him a butthole to his face. If that wasn't a solid foundation for friendship, what was?

I squeezed my hand into a fist, watching him lying there. "I promise not to tell anyone."

Like I even had people to tell in the first place.

Some muscle in his face moved *just* slightly. Just enough so that I noticed only because I'd spent so much time staring at his features while he'd slept at my house.

"I don't care," he grumbled.

I gritted my teeth.

We were definitely working on this "being temporary friends" thing.

Reality was though: I didn't trust him, and he didn't trust me, but we really were all each other had. He was my best shot of getting the hell out of here, so one of us had to start somewhere. I could . . . I could give an inch. Everything I had tried to prevent had come to fruition anyway. But my voice still sounded funny and a little high as I said, "My real name is Altagracia, but no one has ever called me that." It hit me then that he might be the last person to ever know my full, real name. My heart pounded a little bit; I was never supposed to tell anyone what it was, but I kept going anyway. "You can call me Gracie," I whispered.

Not even my students knew me by my name. Packages showed up to the house under the name Esther. When we'd lived in Texas, I ordered things under Lenore Castro. I was so many people, and yet no one at the same time.

It was all those damn lies after all.

"I don't . . . remember asking," the man across the room said.

And there he was.

I rolled my eyes and didn't even try to be discreet about it. He had his closed anyway.

I tried to take his comment about how we would get out of here to heart, but I wasn't going to hold my breath.

Not until we got the hell out of here. *If* we did.

I did the sign of the cross.

Chapter Nine

I tried my hardest to ignore my grumbling stomach, but it was like ignoring someone tapping on your forehead with a fingernail for hours nonstop.

But I couldn't complain, not when I knew I wasn't the only one hungry. Neither one of us had gotten breakfast. I'd finished eating dinner about fifteen minutes after he had.

I would have done some sketchy shit for a Klondike bar right about then.

On the other side of the room, the man-being had been asleep, or at least pretending to be, for hours. I'd tried my best to sit there quietly the whole time. Mostly because he needed to rest to get better, and our best chance of getting out of here was for that to happen, so it only made sense to do everything possible to accommodate him. That included creating the least stressful environment as possible, considering the circumstances. Whining wasn't going to help.

The problem was that my thoughts had been running in a circle of hope and despair, revolving around all the ways this couldn't end well.

Neither of us were beacons of hope, I guess.

If anything, I'd gotten angrier and more hopeless with every passing minute that really felt like a fucking hour. I was bored to death, worried to death, nervous, scared, and a whole lot of hangry.

He suddenly glared over at me. "I'm trying to rest . . . and your stomach won't quit making noise."

I just looked at him. "It didn't get my memo that it needed to be quiet. I'll let it know," I mumbled, dryly.

Oh, he didn't like that.

I didn't care.

Figuring I couldn't wake him up more than he already was, I got up and walked over to the sink, cupping my hands under the tap, to take enough sips to quench my thirst. I dreaded having to go pee in front of him—or pass gas—but it was going to have to happen sooner or later.

So was going number two, but I was going to cross that road when I came to it. It wasn't like I had his bowel system. If he had one of those.

"What did your family do to make a cartel come after you?"

I wasn't surprised he was asking again. How he knew I wasn't the one who did something was beyond me though. Plus, at this point, did being secretive even matter anymore? We were here. If our roles had been reversed, I would want to know too. I'd told him it didn't matter but . . .

One peek at The Defender's face told me he wasn't going to drop this.

Pressing my palms together, I tucked them into my lap and sucked in a breath I instantly regretted from the way it made my ribs and back feel. I hated every single one of those bastards who had brought us here. Those damn beanbag rounds had been unnecessary.

"I deserve to know," his rich, low voice reminded me.

Him deserving it didn't make it any easier though. It still felt wrong. It felt like writing with my left hand when I'd been a righty my whole life. *Tell no one. Keep your head down. Don't get too close to anyone.* Don't do this, don't do that.

But I was still *here*, and I had no idea what the future would hold.

"You do, but it's kind of a long story, so I'm trying to condense it." I might not have any loyalty to my parents, but it was still awkward to talk about their mistakes, if you could call the monumentally stupid shit they had done a "mistake." It was more like a disaster. Like walking in front of a moving bus thinking nothing would happen. That only worked for members of the Trinity.

"I don't need a short version."

How was it possible for someone so beautiful to have so much attitude? I side-eyed him. "You're not going to kill me or anything, are you?"

He side-eyed me right back. "If I wanted . . . I'd have done it already."

That was real comforting.

"I know enough about what I need to know." His eyes glowed briefly. "I won't use . . . what you tell me against you . . . Won't share it unless it's necessary."

It was so fucking weird to hear him talk.

But that was as good as I was going to get, wasn't it? I guess . . . I guess, I didn't see the harm in telling him. I guess I didn't want him to think I was a scumbag. I wanted to be sure he understood that, at its root, this wasn't my fault. That I had tried to avoid this.

I wished he hadn't gotten dragged into this. I pressed my lips together and sighed, then winced. "Okay. Let's see . . . I'll try and keep the story straight."

He stared.

I stared.

Then he grunted.

"My parents stole money from the cartel, and they want it back."

There. It was that easy, wasn't it?

The Defender's eyes had started narrowing from the moment I started talking and kept narrowing with every second that passed. Obviously, that wasn't enough information for him. I knew it wouldn't be, but I guess some itty-bitty part of me had hoped he'd accept that. That he wouldn't want to talk about it more.

But since when had I ever gotten what I wanted?

"Your parents? Not your grandparents?" he asked.

I nodded. "Right. Other than lying about our names sometimes, they were really good people. The best. They got dragged into this just for being related to my mom."

His face went thoughtful. "Do you have it?" he asked suddenly.

My body froze but I told him the truth. "No. My grandparents would have never taken a single penny even if it was the end of the world." I swallowed. "My grandpa used to say that even if the cartel got back the majority of the money, they would never let it go. They would never forgive or forget what was done."

Now that we were talking . . .

And what if this was the last conversation I'd ever have?

I guess that was the thing about feeling like you were running out of time—with every minute that went by, every second felt more and more precious. The things that had stopped you before suddenly didn't seem that important.

What was the worst he would do if I annoyed him? He'd ignore me? Talk to me all grouchy?

I'd tried being quiet around him for weeks. I'd always tried to keep my mouth shut so I wouldn't say anything I shouldn't by accident. And I might or might not be running out of time.

Fuck it.

"What's the longest you've gone being injured before?" I blurted out in Portuguese, not even realizing that's what I was going to ask until it was halfway out of my mouth, and at that point, I just had to roll with it.

Dark eyelids fell slowly over those incredible pupils. "This wasn't . . . a two-way road . . . with questions."

I knew that better than anybody, but we were past me catering to him to that extent. If this could be the end, I was getting all these fucking words out of my mouth. "But it could be." I thought about smiling at him, but I figured he'd see right through that. "I wouldn't tell anyone anything. I don't have any friends, remember?"

Something flickered in his eyes. "You said you did."

I snorted, and it was only about half bitter. "I was lying."

He blinked. Then he watched me for a long, long moment while I stared right back at him.

I didn't have friends. So what?

"Seconds," The Defender finally answered, totally grudgingly. But it was still a reply!

But seconds? It wasn't like I didn't know he was in deep shit. This wasn't news. It was what I'd expected.

Yet somehow, at the same time, it was devastating.

"Your parents . . ."—Did he say that sarcastically or was I imagining it?—"how much did they take from them?"

I tried to think about how to answer that without actually answering, but he must have seen how much I was overthinking it because his expression went wary.

"I want the truth," he demanded in that voice that still felt like a discovery.

I sighed, knowing there was no getting out of this shit. If I had any shot of getting out of here, as tiny as it might be, I needed him, and it was better to get this over with now than later. "My parents used to work for them. I don't know what they did, just that they worked for them. Fifteen years ago, for reasons I don't understand, they ran off with millions of dollars. I don't know how many millions, but I'd bet even a few hundred dollars would have been too much. Apparently, no one knows what they did with it, but some people in the group—the cartel, gang, whatever they are—think I have it, even though I haven't seen either of them since I was five."

That got him thinking some more. "Why?"

"Why did they steal the money? No clue. Why did they get involved with the cartel in the first place? My grandpa said they got involved with the wrong people and couldn't find a way out of it." I shrugged. "I don't know if that's the truth though. Part of me doesn't believe it. But that's why my grandparents raised me. Can't really raise a baby when you're doing illegal shit, I guess. My mom hid her pregnancy, dropped in on my grandparents randomly, had me, and she left me with them before she went back."

I really didn't want to get into all this, but I didn't see a point in leaving out pieces. According to my grandparents, my mom and dad had wanted me to "have a normal life," and that's why I'd been left. I called bullshit.

Over the years, as I learned more about my family—at least what they hadn't minded me learning—I'd decided my grandparents had done what they did to put distance between us and my parents. At first, maybe they'd been afraid they would change their minds and want me back. There was no other reason why we should have moved around as much as we did back when I'd been real young. No one had been after us at that point, but every few years, we'd picked up and gone somewhere else.

"I don't know anything about them." I shrugged. "Only what they did. I saw them only once. I don't remember what they looked like. Ten years ago, I read a letter my mom somehow got to them; it wasn't even addressed to me. It's just a DNA link between us. That's all. We changed our last names and started moving around a lot afterward." Might as well be honest about that. But that was all the truth for the most part. I figured he'd still have questions. It was more than I had ever admitted to anyone. It was also more than I should have shared. Dammit.

I wanted to change the subject though, and my curiosity was at its all-time high, especially since he wasn't ignoring me for the time being. So I went with the first thing that came into my head. "How old are you?" I asked. "I can keep a secret. If I tell anyone, you can . . . give me a wedgie."

His voice and expression were both flat. "A wedgie?" he muttered, sounding so not impressed.

"I don't deserve a death sentence for it. A wedgie is pretty fair. I'm not going to steal your personal information and get a credit card or take out a loan." I blinked and whispered, "If you forgot, I don't know your name."

The Defender blinked, and I almost didn't hear him as he said, "A thousand."

It was my turn to blink, and I swear I didn't mean to say it the way I did, but it came out dry anyway. "Bullshit."

His gaze narrowed.

"I'm twenty-nine," I offered, like he was curious about it when he hadn't even cared about my name.

Then he struck again. "Did I ask?"

Why did I even bother? Why was I still surprised when he talked to me like that? I glared at him. "I don't get why you have it out for me. Did I do something in another lifetime? Did I cut you off one day?"

Oh, the look. The fucking look he gave me. I must have done something fucking unforgivable. Maybe that's what had given me such terrible luck now. "Are you going to stop talking . . . anytime soon . . . or is this going to be my real torture, being stuck in a small space . . . with your mouth?"

With my mouth? Torture? I barely even spoke to him, so his words struck a chord deep in my chest.

Deep in my inner little asshole-self that I usually managed to keep in a nice, long nap.

I'd tried giving him his space, being understanding, but today was the wrong day to be a jerk.

I'd spent my life bouncing from one school to another. Some schools had nice kids, and others had little buttholes that loved to pick on the new kid. Twice I had gotten beat up. I had learned to stand up for myself when I didn't have a choice. And unfortunately for him, I had zero fucks left to give.

I heard once that some of the most dangerous people in the world were the ones who felt like they had nothing left to lose.

That was absolutely true.

And that's how I managed to smile at him and say, dead serious, absolutely meaning it, switching back to Portuguese, "I get it now. I know why they don't let you talk on TV."

He laughed.

The son of a bitch who didn't care what my name was, what my age was, and was annoyed by my hunger, fear, and mouth *laughed*.

I almost fell backward from how unexpected the sound of it was. Because it wasn't a chuckle. It was a straight-up *laugh*. Round and free and not the evil cackle I would have imagined if I'd ever thought about it. Or no laugh at all.

I had to slap a hand behind me to prop myself up, because just like his face, it was fucking stunning.

How was it possible for someone to have an incredible laugh?

Sure, my back and ribs hurt from the movement, but it was almost worth it.

Narrowing my eyes, part of me expected the world to end suddenly. A meteor would strike, or a volcano would suddenly erupt. Maybe The Primordial would smash through the ceiling and end me.

I mean, I thought I was funny. Back when I talked to people at school and work, I'd made them laugh too, but the most I'd gotten out of him so far was a stare or a grunt.

But as much as my body recognized the fact I should be alarmed, and I *was*, curiosity got the best of me. Like it always did. Part of it might be because I still couldn't wrap my head around being around him, going through this together, the fact that he was talking to me in the first place or *laughing* period.

More than likely though, I missed having someone to talk to, and this grumpy ass was better than nothing.

I had always gotten a sick enjoyment from bickering with people.

So the question came out of me faster than I could stop it. "Is that why you don't talk?"

If his laugh hadn't been bad enough, his actual answer was a fucking bomb that shook the pilings I'd built my life on. His "yeah" set off another explosion I hadn't been able to prepare for.

The fingernails on the hand I had propped behind me curled into the hard concrete-like floor beneath us, and I wouldn't have been surprised if my eyes had bugged out. But I still had no control over my body, because I snorted without meaning to. Because I'd *known it*.

"I don't see a point . . . in spewing off bullshit . . . I don't mean," he admitted.

Bullshit? I knew that was exactly how he'd felt too. I knew it! Dammit, I loved it when I was right.

I eyed him and thought about staying quiet, but what if this was the last conversation I ever had? I changed the language again. "The Centurion said recently that he wished for world peace, and I was sitting there thinking about how you can't get people to agree on apples or oranges. That's never going to happen."

He made a soft sound of continued amusement before replying in my third most familiar language. "We know better than most that . . . that's never going to happen . . . but he still . . . hopes."

What all did they talk about? I wondered in the silence afterward as I eyed him and thought about his laugh some more.

"This isn't . . . the end," The Defender added.

Was he trying to assure me? The smallest amount of hope bloomed in my chest, and I swallowed hard before asking quietly, "You think so?"

A dark eye settled right on me. "We'll get out of here . . . long before you have to suffer . . . too much."

Before *I* had to suffer. I didn't miss that part. And how could he sound so certain? I wasn't exactly a fan of suffering, period, but a little bit was better than a lot?

I wanted to point out his health again but didn't want to shit on his parade when he was in a relatively good mood for once. I mean, he'd fucking *laughed* and was actually being talkative after all the time he'd spent with me. It made no sense, and I was suspicious about his reasons, but I wasn't going to waste my time overthinking it right then.

I was desperate.

"Why do you think that?" I asked him.

"Because there is nothing . . . on this planet that can contain me."

Big fucking words from someone still struggling to sit up. It was hard to reconcile him with the force of nature that he was in that incredible charcoal suit performing some kind of miracle.

Now, I just saw him more as the grouch who had laid in my bed and eaten a whole big bag of Cheetos.

And like he sensed my negativity, he narrowed *both* eyes at me. "There isn't," he insisted.

He closed his eyes, and his features eased, and I sat there and thought about his words for a while. For enough time that I was pretty sure he'd fallen asleep from the steady rhythm of his breathing, but then he made the mistake of cracking an eye open . . . and caught me staring at him.

"What are you . . . doing?" The Defender deadpanned, back to irritated.

I shrugged, crawling over to sit on the opposite side of the room against the wall. I'd already tried lying on my back and on my side, and both positions were uncomfortable. Every way was going to be uncomfortable on this floor with my ribs bruised, but there was no use crying over it.

"I'm trying to figure out just how the hell we're going to get out of here before I end up with brain damage or long-term physical illness from starvation." I wasn't going to tell him how slim my hopes of that were regardless of his assurances.

He huffed and closed his eyes again, dismissing me. "We're getting out."

So he said. I pressed my lips together.

The Defender took a short sniff as he settled against the floor like it wasn't hard as a rock. "Don't start snotting up. I don't like the way . . . your tears smell."

"I'm not going to cry," I muttered in English.

Those bright purple eyes flashed briefly before he sighed. "Thirty-five."

He was thirty-five? "Huh," I muttered in pure surprise. I really wanted to ask why he was talking to me all of a sudden, but I didn't want to ruin it. "You look younger." Maybe it had been the sunburn on his face before, because now that his skin was less red, it was hard to believe he was thirty-five.

The Defender made a face that said he knew he did. A minute or two later, he spoke up again. "Your parents . . . that's why you don't have friends?"

We were still talking about this? I was already tired of talking of it, but fine, if we were actually being truthful, I could play, even if it felt so, so wrong. "Yeah. What kind of life would I be able to live if anyone found out? I told people my parents died in a car accident, and even then, it brought way too much attention. Even before they took the money, my grandparents didn't want anyone to know the truth." That was one of my oldest memories, them telling me to keep it a secret. To tell people that my mom and dad had died. We'd practiced. I hadn't even known back then what death was.

I got a sniff and a very thoughtful expression that honestly surprised me.

"Are you and The Primordial together?" I asked him in a rush in Korean, without thinking.

The look of absolute disgust that came over his features would follow me for the rest of my life. "Fuck no."

That was almost disappointing. And him using the f-word was still surprising. Double standards were real.

Then it was his turn to change the subject. "What happened to them?"

"I have no idea."

He didn't believe me. "You don't know?"

"Not for sure. I didn't really get a chance to ask them when they ignored my existence. I know they ran away, and every time we watched the news and body parts were found, I thought that maybe that was them. I'm pretty sure they aren't alive anymore. I told you, I read a letter that my mom somehow got to them. I think through an aunt or something. We always had PO Boxes at post offices hours away from every place we lived; that had been my grandpa's idea. Anyway, my mom thought they were going to be found and she was scared. She didn't apologize, but it was written in a way that made me feel like she wanted them to help her or something. They didn't. I think they didn't want to put me at risk." For one split second, I did what I never allowed

myself to, and thought about what else I'd read in that short letter. Then I wiped it from my mind like I had every time before,
and went on with my life.

"One day, a couple months after the letter arrived, I overheard
my grandparents cry like someone had broken their hearts, all
night, every night for weeks. They tried to hide it from me, but I
knew they were upset about something and wouldn't tell me
what. I'm pretty sure they somehow found out something had
happened, but I don't know for sure." I understood that some
part of me should have been devastated—they were the reason I
was alive in the first place—but I didn't remember anything
about them. It was like hearing a celebrity had passed away. I had
no emotional connection to the two people who had only caused
so much heartache in my life. I'd used those super-sharp imaginary scissors a long time ago and cut them out of my life.

It was complicated.

And I didn't want to talk about them anymore, so my brain
went for the next logical question it could possibly come up with.
"Do you have a partner? A wife?" All right, I'd gone there. Too
late now. I made the shape of a cross over my heart. "Our secret.
Promise. Or if you'd like the reminder, chances are I'm really
not getting out of here."

The son of a bitch growled.

I stared at him for a moment, then somehow managed to
smile a little. It really was kind of nice to not tiptoe around his
ass so much anymore. "As good-looking as you are, it would take
a very special person to deal with you, huh?"

That got me another world-class glare.

I smiled a little more.

"If I wanted a partner, I could find a partner," he grumbled.

My nod was so serious, even I almost bought it. "I'm sure."
He was gorgeous after all. "As long as you didn't actually open
your mouth."

The Defender blinked, then dropped his voice. "You know from experience?"

Oh boy.

Who was this man and where did the quiet, grumpy being go? *And why was I eating this shit up?* Was I that starved for attention? "I don't know why you think I talk a lot, because I really don't."

Did he snicker?

"I'm only talking now because you deserve to know why we're here, and I can't stop worrying about the fact you might be the last person I ever talk to."

The Defender raised an eyebrow slowly.

"So, are you rich?" I went for it again. "What? I don't want your money. I'm being nosy, and you've been sharing more than I thought you would for some reason, so I'm going to take advantage of it since you ignored me for weeks." I paused and changed the language again. "Do you like being . . . who you are?"

His face instantly went tight, and I could definitely tell I'd really gotten under his skin with that question. Part of me was shocked I had gone there. But I wasn't sure who was more surprised when he actually answered. "Sometimes."

Wasn't that vague?

I had always thought the Trinity were some kind of superior species—smarter, faster, stronger, better than everyone else. I guess I'd expected them to be on another level emotionally and mentally too, like spiritually enlightened people.

But all I had to do was take one look at the man on the floor by me and see that *nope, I was wrong.* There was a living, breathing man with an attitude like nobody's business. He had opinions. He was judgmental. He sure as shit had bad moods and a smart mouth.

For all his other talents, he was . . . I wasn't sure I was ready to use the word I was thinking of. It was disturbing.

I couldn't say I was surprised that he felt a certain kind of way about what he did and who he was, though. All it took was for me to remember how people called him the Antichrist, how he'd mentioned people throwing things at him. That fire that had hurt a lot of people before he'd gotten there to help save so many lives, some people even managed to blame him for it. Once I thought about it, I could see him waiting a second or two to save someone if they'd pissed him off.

I could totally see him being petty enough.

Those purple eyes met mine, and we stared at each other for a second.

He'd regretted his answer.

He confirmed it when he closed his eyes and turned his chin away.

I shrugged and settled against the wall, rubbing my arms at the cold. Had they turned down the air? Were they going to try and test to see at what temperature I got hypothermia? Brr.

I hoped he was right about getting out of here sooner than later.

I hoped . . . I hoped he would talk to me a little more too, just in case.

I pressed my hand flat against my stomach and tried to ignore how hungry I was.

Then I tried not to think about my parents, grandparents, or just how much worse things could get.

A loud bang scared the hell out of me. I hadn't even realized I'd fallen asleep, and it took me a second to remember where I was.

Where *we* were.

I looked around to spot The Defender still lying flat on the ground, eyes closed.

But it was the multiple packets on the floor between us that had me squinting.

Crawling over and ignoring the way pain shot through my poor kneecaps, I picked up one bar and then the other. There were six of them, all the same. Granola bars. They were granola bars.

Were they poisoned?

Standing up with one in my hand, I ripped the wrapper off and took a sniff. It smelled like cranberries and some kind of nut butter. Breaking off a small part of an end, I smelled it again.

I still didn't trust it. There were some poisons you couldn't smell or detect—at least on TV there were.

I spit on the end I'd broken off, but nothing happened.

I went to the sink, dropped half the piece I'd broken off into it and ran water over it. Nothing.

Hmm.

Maybe their plan was to keep me alive, be decent, and politely worm their way into making me feel safe-ish so I would think they were doing me a favor by asking me about the money.

Or maybe they wanted me desperate and scared, and then they'd try and torture me into telling them things I didn't know. It was a good plan. Fuckers.

"If you want to keep going with your science experiments, go for it, but there's nothing in there but oats, almond butter, cashews, cranberries, and preservatives," The Defender said, startling the shit out of me even more than the door banging had.

I'd thought he was asleep.

Turning around, I held it toward him to get a better sniff. "Are you sure?"

"No," he replied sarcastically.

Good enough for me. I dropped the rest of the piece into my mouth and ate it with sheer *glee*. It was so bad it was good.

But would it be better to eat it all at once or split it up? Was this a one-time thing, or could we expect more? The fact I had no idea was answer enough.

Kneeling beside the small pile of nutritional bars, I eyed one of them and picked it up before stacking the other four in my other hand and making my way over to Mr. Crabby Pants. I set them down about a foot beside him, ignoring that incredible gaze until I pulled my arm back.

Those purple eyes were steady on my face, his expression leery. "What are you doing?"

"Bringing you some of the bars that someone threw in here?"

He narrowed his eyes.

Was he mad? "I'm sorry for taking a bite out of one, but I thought we'd share. I was planning on giving you the majority, no need to get pissed off." But really?

He kept on staring at me.

"Do you want me to throw up what I just ate?" I asked in disbelief.

His features said he was skeptical. "You were trying . . . to share?"

Now it was my turn to not believe what the hell he was implying. "Did you think I wasn't going to share with you? You need the calories more than I do. I've got more body fat to keep me going than you." I sniffed, switching to Portuguese. "Here's four of them, but I can give you one more if you're going to throw a hissy fit. The faster you get better, the faster we get out of here."

At least I hoped. Dreamed, more like it. Unless I could think of something, but I wasn't holding my breath. Nothing was happening. I'd thought maybe there would be guards who would go on duty and have some kind of shift change, leaving an opening we could exploit, like in movies.

But there hadn't been anyone or any kind of change other than this.

Had he been able to hear them coming? He hadn't said anything or tried to take advantage of the opportunity, so more than likely, he still wasn't in a position to get us the fuck out of here yet.

Dammit.

His eyes bounced from one of mine to the other before he reached toward the granola bars and pushed them over. "Take them," he grumbled.

I pushed them back. "No, you need them."

He shoved them again. "I don't like . . . repeating myself. Take them."

"I don't like you telling me what to do. You need them. We need to get out of here, temporary friend," I tried to remind him. And if we both couldn't escape, then at least he needed to survive. I shivered. "Is it cold in here, or is it just me?"

"I don't feel cold the way you do," he muttered in Korean, looking at me sideways, almost warily.

Rubbing my arms up and down for a second, I met his gaze before scooting closer and timidly pressing my fingertip against the back of his hand.

He didn't move.

I pressed the rest of my fingertips against the skin on the top of his hand and raised my eyebrows. It was second nature to switch to Portuguese. "Does your body regulate itself or—oh, forget it." He wasn't going to admit shit; I'd barely gotten his age. We weren't on a first-name basis yet. What was the point in asking?

The Defender stared at me in a way that confirmed exactly what I thought.

I kept on eyeing him as I pressed my back against the wall, about a foot away from him, and waited to make sure he didn't tell me to get away.

He must have decided to be in his version of a good mood again because he didn't say a word. That, or he felt like shit and didn't have the energy, which wasn't a good thing either, but

I'd deal with that concern later. He was talking more, so that had to mean something good.

Drawing my knees in to my chest, I tucked my arms in and set my chin on them.

A few minutes had to have passed before he said roughly, "Eat more of the bar. I want to rest . . . and can't when your stomach . . . is making a racket."

I nodded at him but didn't move.

"Now," the bossy bitch said.

I frowned at him. "I will in a second."

"You will . . . when I tell you to."

Really? "Do people usually do what you tell them to?"

He didn't even think about it. "Yes."

The snort that shot out of my nose surprised me, in pain and entertainment.

Just when I thought my life couldn't get any more ridiculous, I was proven wrong. I was arguing with The Defender.

He gave me a long look before saying, "That's not funny."

"It kind of is."

"It's not."

"It is, but it's okay. Not everyone has a sense of humor. It's no big deal." I was doing this. My balls were regaining their size and shape, I guess.

His side-look would have killed me if he had lasers that could shoot out of his eyes. Luckily that was The Centurion. From the expression he was making, I wouldn't be surprised if he was wishing he did.

"I have . . . a sense of humor," he tried to claim, actually looking and sounding serious.

I pressed my lips together. "If you say so."

"I do," he insisted.

"O-kay."

That got me an icy glare. "I don't like . . . your tone of voice."

I really got way too much of a kick out of this. "I don't really like yours either, if I'm going to be honest." I paused. "You probably think *Halloween* is a comedy."

There went another glare. "I watch comedies."

I looked at him.

"When I have time."

I kept looking at him.

His jaw worked. "It's not often . . . what with saving you idiots from yourselves five times a day."

It took everything in me not to scoff at his still-perfect Portuguese. "You should really look into a job change with that kind of attitude."

He shot another burning look my way. "Do you . . . know what I am? Who I am?"

"I know. I've fed you by hand while making airplane noises. Almost broke my back helping move you. I almost went bankrupt feeding you. Do I need to keep going or . . . ?"

I got the longest side-eye in the history of side-eyes.

Then, *then*, The Defender tore his gaze away, going back to being grouchy. "I'm going to rest. Leave me one of the bars and eat the rest."

And before I could open my mouth to argue with him more, he was out.

Again.

Leaving me with my thoughts. And all my fears. And with my assumptions about why he was finally talking to me.

Then I took a long look around the empty, quiet room, and I sighed.

Chapter Ten

I was bored out of my fucking mind.

And hungry.

I would have thought I'd be prepared to be locked into a smallish room with another person because I had experience being at home, alone, but I was so wrong. At home, I could still go outside. I had the internet. Television. Work. Chores. Projects. Arts and crafts. Books.

I had *something* to do, even if I was bored there too. But this was a different kind of boredom.

This one felt straight from hell.

But in those hours of staring blankly at the walls and wishing I could sleep more to make the time go by faster, I thought about stuff.

Some of those thoughts revolved around how I was jealous the superbeing across the room managed to sleep so much. Or at least pretended to. Most of my thoughts were mean, ugly ones that had me questioning what kind of parents would put their children at risk like mine had; it wouldn't be the first time I'd pondered that. A few centered around the choices my grandparents had made too.

When I got tired of that, I stared at The Defender a lot because it wasn't like there was much else to do. There weren't tiles on the walls to count. Or ants. There wasn't anything to focus on.

And it was so, so cold.

I spent a lot of time focusing on my hands, counting the fine lines on each of my fingers. Wondering if that freckle had always been there. Trying to bite off the small callus I had on my palm from the garden spade. I'd hummed quietly under my breath. I had made up a lot of scenarios in my head about how we could get out of here. I thought about what I would have to do if we ever did get out of here.

I cried a couple times too.

For the most part, they were tiny tears that had me holding my breath to keep from making a sound. Tears for the home I no longer had, for the things I'd lost, and especially for the possibility that this place would be the end of me.

And a few times, I cried like a fucking drama queen, these big, hiccupping gasps into my palms.

Then I got pissed off over being upset and started thinking about other ways to hopefully one day bring down the fucking cartel.

That was the only way I was ever going to have a normal life—if they were gone.

I'd been content just getting by, trying to do everything possible to not catch their attention. For so long, they were the bogeyman living under so many of the beds I'd slept in, the monster in every closet my clothes had been in.

Was I totally unprepared to bring down a multimillion-dollar operation that had withstood other cartels and whole government interventions? Absolutely. But it wasn't fair. I hadn't done anything to them. I'd never done anything to anyone.

And they now knew without a doubt that I was alive.

It was then that I thought about the one idea I'd brought up to my grandma right after my grandpa had passed away. The idea she had shot down immediately because it required too much trust in people who could be paid off and in people we had no reason to believe wouldn't backstab us to make a point. The idea that was way too risky.

So I stopped thinking about it.

I didn't know what the cartel's game was drawing this shit out, but I had to stay on my toes. It wasn't like they'd brought me here for shits and giggles. For whatever reason, they weren't jumping straight into pulling out my fingernails, but I wasn't going to hold out hope that it wouldn't eventually happen.

The anticipation was the fucking worst.

I drew invisible patterns and designs on the floor. I cracked my knuckles and spent a lot of time doing breathing exercises. Just doing those hurt; my ribs were so achy, but if there was a chance I might need to run in the near future, I had to keep my lungs in shape.

And like I said, I spent a lot of time looking at the man seemingly sleeping like a baby and wondering what in the hell was going on with him and if he was going to get better anytime soon.

Sometimes I went and sat closer to him. I made sure he was still breathing. And maybe once or twice I sat by his head and pictured myself choking him out for showing up and putting me into this situation, even though I knew I should have moved away months ago.

And that was when he woke up.

With me sitting by his head, in the middle of glaring at him.

"What are you doing?" The Defender asked, scaring the shit out of me. "Why are you on top of me?"

For the record, I wasn't *on top of him*. I was next to him.

And I'd thought about it, sure, but for heat purposes. It was still freezing, and that was part of the reason why I couldn't sleep that well. I'd tried tucking my arms into my shirt to stay warm, but it didn't help enough. Neither did curling into a ball.

"Why are you looking at me so much?" the most beautiful

man I'd ever seen asked, somehow still looking amazing even though he'd been asleep for days and hadn't showered in who knows how long. He didn't even smell. How unfair was that?

I eyed him, taking in the fact he was still speaking to me. "I don't look at you that much."

The expression on his face said he disagreed.

I blinked. "I don't, and you've been sleeping so . . ."

He yawned, flashing me those bright white teeth. "My eyes are closed, but I'm aware."

I scoffed. Yeah, all right.

He caught me. "You used the bathroom eight times, hummed the Electro-Man theme song about a hundred times, hummed other songs completely off-key."

I stopped moving.

"Cried too much," he had the nerve to add.

I don't know what it said about me that I wasn't sure if I would rather him go back to ignoring me again or if I enjoyed him being a shit-talker.

"You—" He winced. His gaze flicked toward the wall by the door. "Be quiet. Pretend you're asleep!"

The hell was that tone for? "What? Why?"

"Shut up and pretend you're asleep!" he hissed before struggling to roll onto his stomach with a low groan that reminded me he still wasn't doing well.

My heart started pounding. "Is someone coming?" I just about shouted.

My stomach did a sudden, funny, little thing.

But I knew what it meant—nothing fucking good.

I threw myself on top of The Defender a second before the door flew open.

His body went stiff.

My heart was pounding too quickly, and I squeezed my eyes closed and tried my best to pretend to be asleep. Would they not take me if I was unconscious? Did he know something I didn't? Why had it taken him so long to hear them coming? *Should I have laid down beside him?* I'd just wanted to protect him . . .

Shit, shit, *shit*.

"Remember, Boss said not to hurt her," a voice spoke up from the direction of the door.

If anything, The Defender's body went even harder under me. I was literally sprawled on top of him. Covering him like a pitiful blanket.

I squeezed my eyes closed and tried not to pant from how nauseous I suddenly felt. My poor fucking stomach did a barrel roll, trying to warn me again. Too late though. Way too late. Why hadn't it acted up before?

Footsteps squeaked across the floor. "If you know what's good for you, stay right where you are," the same voice said. I was pretty sure they were talking to The Defender. I hoped he kept his eyes shut. I hoped he didn't do anything to bring attention to himself until he could get out of here. "Shoot him if he moves. Take her."

Oh shit, oh shit, oh—

Please don't move, buddy. Stay where you are.

Hands clamped down on my wrists and ankles.

I wanted to move; I really did. I was ready to claw some eyeballs out, maybe bite a few fingers off. But I wouldn't, and I knew that instantly too. Because maybe if I didn't do anything, they would leave him alone.

That was enough to keep me immobile.

For him.

So that they wouldn't try and hurt him, then figure out who he was.

Oh God.

Terror like I didn't know gripped my entire body as I was lifted. He'd said to pretend to be asleep. He'd said to be quiet, but the second I was up, my weight focusing on the joints of my wrists and ankles, which was pretty fucking painful, totally fucking vulnerable . . .

I opened my eyes and locked onto the long body belly-down on the floor.

Fear wrapped its brittle, too-hot wings around me right then.

Not the kind of fear like when I'd watch a scary movie or when I heard a strange sound in the middle of the night. It was pure, genuine terror. Like what I'd felt immediately after my grandma had passed away and I'd thought there was a good chance I was going to be alone for the rest of my life.

Some people say that the opposite of love is fear. But the truth was, without fear, there can't be love. If you can't worry about losing something you find precious, it probably isn't all that valuable to you in the first place.

And I had already lost the two people in the world who meant everything to me. Now everything else was gone too. I was going to lose my job after this shit too, but that was at the bottom of my list of concerns at the moment.

But to lose my life? Maybe it wasn't perfect, and I had road-blocks set up at every corner preventing me from living it the way I dreamed or at least would have settled for, but it was some-thing. It was mine.

I didn't want to lose it. Not my life. Not my future.

I was *scared*.

I was scared they were taking me. I was scared my life was really going to be over before it had even really begun. I was just . . . plain terrified.

And reason didn't exist when terror was present. I suddenly understood why people did such stupid fucking things in horror movies that got them killed. I would have been one of those dumbasses, and I wasn't fucking proud of it.

But I still did it.

I tilted my head just enough so I could spot him still flat on his stomach, his eyes closed. I was pretty sure his features might have been strained, but I didn't know for sure. My vision was too blurry.

"I'm sorry!" I cried out, just in case . . .

I hoped he knew. I hoped he understood I hadn't meant for this to happen. That if I could have chosen, he wouldn't have been involved.

I was going to hold on to my word if that was the last thing I did.

If I was going to die—and that thought made me whimper—I had to make this right. I had to try. He didn't deserve this.

"Please leave him alone! We barely know each other! He was a one-night stand!" I wailed, sounding like a fucking crazy person, but . . . but . . . I was.

What if this was the end?

"I'm sorry!" I shrieked, my voice breaking as I tried to move my arm, tried to reach for him, for something . . . but nothing budged.

Oh my God, I was so scared.

But he had to get out of here. He had to survive. "I'm sorry! Live a long life!" My voice just . . . broke, and I gasped for a breath that hurt so bad my eyes watered even as my ribs, back, and all my joints cried out in protest from how roughly I was being carried. "Be safe!"

I was on my own.

Like I'd always known I would be.

I screamed.

I screamed for help. For my future. Like my grandma had told me to if a stranger ever tried to abduct me.

I screamed for them to please let me go.

Please and please and *please*.

I didn't want to die. I wasn't sorry, and I didn't say I was sorry.

And I didn't say I would do anything to keep on living, because that wasn't true either. I wouldn't betray him. I had nothing left but my honor.

I screamed, hoping for mercy maybe. For my life.

I wished I could have done the sign of the cross. I tried to remember the prayers I'd said thousands of times. *Our father, who art in heaven . . .*

Big, fat tears pooled in my eyes and onto the floor. No one listened as they carried me down a hall with more concrete floors and through another heavy door. I was pretty sure I heard someone laugh, maybe more than just a single someone.

My shoulders and hips hurt as blood rushed to my face and into my nose, making it hard to breathe. Eventually, they stopped in front of another door. Then, just like that, these fuckers let me go, dropping me onto the hard floor. For some reason, my eyes instantly went to the sink in the corner, to a hose attached to it and dangling to the floor.

A moment later, my arms were grabbed again and tucked behind my back, and something sharp bit into my wrists.

I cried out as they tugged them up, forcing me to sit up, jerking even more at my shoulders.

I dipped my head back to find the faces of two men looking at me with hard, solemn expressions before a voice said, "That was a lot more dramatic than I'd expected."

It was a woman. She had dark brown hair and was dressed in gray slacks and a black button-down shirt. She looked just like a person who worked in an office. And she was short. She could have been anywhere between her thirties and fifties. Pretty.

She looked fucking bored. This bad energy came from her as well. My stomach didn't like it.

I pressed my lips together to keep from making another peep.

"Don't waste my time. You know what we want. Make this easier on both of us and just tell me where it is," the woman straight-up said as I sat there, sniffling because my nose was burning from all the blood that had rushed to my head. "Don't make me ask you again."

So this was how they were going to do this. No beating around the bush. I didn't know what to do.

I swallowed hard before tipping my chin up and flicking my gaze from her to the two men looking down at me. I hated all three of them. I really did. "I don't have the money, and I know you aren't going to believe me anyway, but it's the truth," I replied slowly, sniffling, knowing I needed to buy The Defender time, and pissing her off wasn't the right way to do it, but . . .

She stared at me for a long time with dark brown eyes, and I just stared back.

I hadn't taken the money from her. From them. I hadn't asked for any of this shit.

Eventually, the woman ticked her head to the side as she flicked her index finger just enough for me to barely notice. "Are you sure that's what you want your answer to be?"

There was something about her tone that didn't sit well with me, not at all.

But I had to do this for The Defender. This wasn't about me. "I'm sorry they stole from you." That was a lie. I was sorry that this had trickled down to me. If anybody deserved to have money stolen, it would have been them. I'd done my research. I knew what kind of drugs they produced. What kind of crimes they were guilty of. But as much as I wanted to give her—give all of them—the middle finger, I had someone to protect. Someone worth keeping my mouth shut for. "I don't have the money, and that's what I'm going to tell you now, what I'm going to tell you six months from now. *I don't have it.*"

The woman's expression went carefully blank in this creepy way before she smiled, and it wasn't a nice one. Just from the look in her eye, I knew there was nothing behind it. "Everyone always starts by saying they don't know, and most of them change their mind after a while, Altagracia."

I shivered at her use of my name, and if I had some sense, I might have shivered at her low-key threat too.

My sense had walked out the door the second a member of the Trinity had landed in my yard. And that's why I shrugged at her, holding back a groan at the discomfort. "I don't have it, and I don't deserve this."

I hated her fucking smile.

"So be it." She turned to one of the men who had tied me up, still looking so amused. "Boss said not to hurt her yet, so don't leave any bruises. I don't know when he's going to come by, and I don't feel like listening to a lecture from him."

I'd watched a lot of action movies in my life.

Maybe it was because I'd liked the characters' strength or their sense of adventure, or more than likely, I just liked revenge.

And in those action movies, a lot of them included torture in some way. There was always some information that needed to be taken by force. But everyone knew that once you ratted something or someone out, you were dead. The "bad guys" were never going to free you. They were never going to let you live no matter what they promised.

And that's why I kept my mouth closed.

Because I *knew*.

I'd made my decision. And I especially wasn't going to give this motherfucker who had *burned my house down* shit. Even if she was giving me granola bars to keep me alive.

So I wasn't surprised.

Heartbroken and scared, definitely, but not surprised.

What felt like some kind of cloth was put over my face. A familiar, faint sound I wouldn't recognize until later came from somewhere in the room, and in the time it took me to take a deep breath that had the material getting sucked into my mouth, the water was there. Rushing over my mouth and fore-head and chin.

The water came again and again.

The sound of the door opening had me glancing up from the cocoon my arms had formed around my head. I was huddled into the corner, shivering and miserable. I was fucking scared too. I hadn't stopped being scared. But if I'd thought I was mad before, it was nothing compared to now.

If someone examined my cells under a microscope right now, they'd probably discover they were shaped like middle fingers at this point.

And they would have been aimed at this asshole. At the men doing what she asked them to do. At everything.

This was all her fucking fault, whoever the hell she was.

And it was her who appeared at the door, hands casually inside the front pockets of her now-blue slacks, the expression on her face so blasé, so I-don't-have-a-worry-in-the-world, I wished there was a zombie apocalypse so somebody could eat her face.

Hell, I wished I was The Defender and could drop an airplane on her ass.

I wished I could give her a yeast infection. I'd settle for that, no problem.

"Are you ready to talk now?" the woman asked so casually it was like she was asking what time it was. Like she hadn't asked these other motherfuckers to drown me.

I'd thought about it a lot honestly. Over the last few hours, while I'd been sitting there, alone, wet, and cold, with a head-ache that put every migraine I'd ever had to shame and my nose and throat almost unbearable from being forced to feel like I was on the verge of drowning for what felt like hours, I'd thought a lot about how I could have handled this differently. If I should have. And no matter what way I looked at it, I kept reaching the same conclusion.

No.

I wasn't going to beg them, and I wouldn't give anybody up, no matter what they promised—and nobody had promised anything.

Fuck this whole shit.

So that's why I lifted my gaze, hoping like hell I wasn't making anything close to the expressions that The Defender had shot my way at any point.

I'd choked and coughed for hours thanks to this asshole.

My whole face, every nook and cranny in my head, was on fire thanks to this asshole.

She sighed again, but it seemed superficial to me, like she was putting on an act. "I don't enjoy doing this, you know."

I bet she didn't.

Liar.

I lifted my eyes and focused on the two men standing in the corners of the cell. Even if she didn't, they did. I was going to remember the way they laughed after I'd thrown up all over myself. It was why I'd taken my shirt off when they'd removed the zip ties on my wrists to give me a break and tossed it in the corner.

I was going to remember their faces.

I was going to remember all of this.

Maybe they were just employees doing what they had to do to pay their bills. Who was I to talk? But I'd heard them. Seen their sly smiles. They'd enjoyed what they had done.

That had made it personal.

And I wouldn't forget.

That became the second reason why I decided I was going to make it through this and out of here, some way, somehow. So that one day, even if it was in the afterlife, I could pay these two a little visit. Just a little one. If I was still alive, I'd have to spend the rest of my life amending for what I would do, but that was something I could live with. And if I was a ghost, they were fucked because I wasn't going *anywhere*.

The woman put her hands on her hips, everything about her just so irritating. "All you have to do is talk. I'd like for you to tell me a few things, that's all." She slipped her hands in her pockets and aimed for another fake smile. "I know you didn't take the money yourself, but make this easier on all of us and tell me where it is."

I clenched my teeth together.

"Tell me what you know."

Fat fucking chance. How stupid did she think I was?

"At least tell me what you think you might know about it."

Rubbing my hands up and down my arms, I just kept looking at her.

After a moment, she raised an eyebrow and her chin a little. "How about a little more water?"

Oh, she'd gone there.

"I get nothing from hurting you, Altagracia. All I want, all my family wants, is their money back. It was ours. Help me, and you can go home."

The money was theirs. Give me a break. And home? Really?

I rubbed at my arms as I shivered and told her so, so quietly, mostly because with every word out of my mouth, my throat hurt worse, "Then don't and let me and the man leave. He doesn't know anything. He doesn't even know my last name. We had just messed around. He doesn't deserve this."

The woman came forward and crouched. Out of the corner of my eye, behind her, I saw my torturers step forward too. "Why won't you tell me what I want to know?" she asked deceptively sweetly.

"Why won't you believe me when I tell you that I don't have it? I haven't seen or spoken to my parents since I was five years old."

An edge came over her sharp features. She was pretty fair-skinned, a lot lighter than me. A little older too, I was pretty sure now that I'd had time to think about it, even though my head hurt so bad it was hard to think or focus on anything. "You expect us to believe that you don't know where the money is, but you've been trying to hide from us for years. Innocent people don't hide."

I kept my mouth shut. Was there a point in explaining that innocent people understood that they were going to be blamed for something regardless of what they did and said? Wasn't that exactly why I was here?

"Maybe you think you'll escape somehow and run and hide, and we'll never find you again. But we'll always find you. We're never going to quit looking for you. Twenty million dollars can pay for a lot. Your cousin sold you out for a ten-thousand-dollar debt."

My *cousin*? I didn't have a cousin. Maybe a second one in Costa Rica I'd never met before.

But as far as I knew, no one had kept in touch with my grand-parents since that letter had arrived from my mom.

"Tell me a little something. I'll even tell you who gave us your new name, and you can do with that what you will. Family should always take care of family."

My eyes wanted to widen. I didn't want to believe that that was how they'd found me, but . . . what? Before we'd changed our last name, my grandma used to talk to someone on the phone. Her sister maybe? Niece? I knew there had been someone obviously, since my mom had found a way to get in contact with them the one time. I hadn't thought about that in forever. And if someone in the family knew something, why had they waited so long to rat us out? Rat me out? Because of desperation? Because of a debt?

Ice snaked its way down my spine.

"I'm ready when you are," she said with a mocking smile.

I knew in my heart that there was a good chance I wasn't getting out of here alive. Maybe The Defender wouldn't be able to get us out. Maybe this raging asshole would really drown me or cause me some kind of brain damage and life as I knew it would end.

My life had been so small for so long, I hadn't had a whole lot of opportunities to prove to myself who I was. But I did know who I'd always wanted to be. Someone I could or would admire.

And being a snitch to save myself some pain—or a whole lot of it—wasn't worth it. Not when I would be betraying someone who might not exactly be the person I'd thought he was but still did the right thing. And maybe that was more impressive than if he did what he did because of some altruistic gene in his body.

She could eat shit.

All of it. She could eat all the shit in the world. Her and her whole fucking family and every person she knew and every person she would ever know.

I hoped she got a kidney stone.

I hoped it hurt when she passed it too.

But the most important thing at this point was to buy The Defender time. As much as I wanted to tell her to fuck herself, I had to do what I had to do, and that was be a bigger person. For him. For the rest of humanity.

So I ducked my head back down and planted it on my stacked arms.

She was probably going to kill me and harvest my organs, but I hadn't been joking. If I saw a white light, I was going the other way. Grandma used to say that her grandma had stuck around after she had passed away, until her husband eventually died. Apparently, he'd cheated on her and she had taken revenge in her own way.

I think I would have liked her.

If this was the end, it was the end. I didn't want it to be, but I wasn't willing to give up on the only person who might someday make this fucker pay for what she had done to me. Sure, it wouldn't be in my honor, but that didn't mean I couldn't enjoy it.

Fear and misery fought a battle in my heart as I pretended she wasn't there. I shivered and then shivered some more before the sound of the door opening cut through the quietness in the room. "All right," she said in that bored, flat voice. "Remember you asked for this."

And I wasn't surprised when the two assholes moved toward me, grabbing my arms and lifting me. There were more zip ties. Another cloth. One of them was already holding the spewing hose. They aimed it at my face.

Then they did it again.

Chapter Eleven

I flinched at the sound of the door opening and tucked my arms into my sides even closer, like my body had any heat left to make a difference.

It didn't.

I'd tried thinking about all the hot afternoons working in my garden that had been almost unbearable.

I'd tried remembering how warm it had gotten in the houses we'd always lived in because none of them had had efficient air conditioners.

None of that worked either.

I was cold down to my damn bones. My jaw hurt from how hard and long my teeth had rattled.

Plus, my head hurt like hell, my throat felt like it was battling a mutant strain of strep throat, and basically every single inch of my body hurt too from how hard I'd been shaking for hours. Or had it been days? Everything seemed so blurry now, so I had no idea. I felt straight awful as I lifted my head and peered at the doorway, expecting the worst.

Two men were there, dressed in the same black clothes as the last shitheads, but they weren't the same people.

I didn't move, mostly because I didn't have the energy to.

"Are you getting up or do you need to be carried back?" the one on the left asked, his tone bland.

I hoped their significant others cheated on them.

I sniffled and instantly regretted it when it felt like a knife being shoved up my nostrils, straight into my brain. The sarcasm I kept wrapped up so tight in me loosened, even though every word hurt on the way out. "Depends. Are we going somewhere fun for me or fun for you?"

That got me two glares.

Stupid asses.

They deserved the surprise they were going to find behind the toilet eventually. I had taken advantage of the moments of privacy I'd gotten when they weren't on the brink of drowning me. I wasn't about to shit my pants in front of them if I could help it.

"I can walk. I don't want you guys ruining my dreams of being in the Little League World Series by tearing my rotator cuffs," I told them sarcastically, my throat filled with glass.

"Get up," the other man demanded with a flat tone that made me think none of this was new to him. Did they do this a lot?

I thought about putting up a fight, but honestly, I had nothing left but my pride. I could barely talk. I was beyond exhausted. I'd pulled muscles I didn't know existed. And literally, I never would have thought that it was possible for my sinus cavity to feel the way it did.

Whatever was going to happen . . . needed to just happen.

I had told them I didn't have the money. We all knew no one was going to believe that though. They were going to wait me out until I begged, or I'd be back in here for more.

I would take the break they were offering, just like I'd taken every other one.

Gingerly getting up, my knees cracked and my tailbone ached like hell from the hard floor. Even my wrists creaked as I planted my hands to help me up. They'd taken the zip ties off after the last time, and my skin was bruised and tender. The cuff felt twice as heavy. Once I was finally on my feet, I stumbled forward, debating whether to ask where they were taking me, but then I decided it didn't matter. What was I going to do? Fight them and run away? I'd played a ton of *Street Fighter*, but that wasn't exactly going to help me. Plus, I hadn't been paying enough attention when they had brought me in here. I had no idea where to go, and I knew I'd only have one chance to escape, if I even had that much. I wasn't going to waste it. Not in this condition.

Hunching my shoulders, I watched as one of them opened the door. Only then did I take a step, every movement so stiff I felt terrible for how much pain my grandparents had to have been in at the end of their lives because of their arthritis.

And it was with just thinking about them that I remembered again why I couldn't give up. Why I had to pay attention and do whatever I could to get the hell out of here.

How the hell could I have forgotten?

If not for me, for them. To make their sacrifice worth it. I had to try my best.

Fuck all these motherfuckers.

I wasn't going to die in here.

Tipping my chin down, I flicked my gaze up and took everything in as discreetly as possible. The walls were white and smooth, and we went by one heavy, metal door before walking farther and passing by another. None of them had keyholes, I noticed, but there was a knob of sorts on each so they could only be opened from the outside. Sneaky.

I'd tried pushing on the door to our cell, but nothing had happened, so I knew they had some kind of mechanism to lock them.

Not that that should matter to one of the strongest people on the planet.

Once he was feeling well.

I hadn't let my brain wander too far in his direction. He had to be fine. They weren't desperate enough to hurt him yet, but at some point, they'd bring his head to me on a silver platter or some shit—or at least they would try, and surprise!

I didn't see that really happening. But I needed him to get out before then at least.

"Walk faster," the man behind me barked.

I would have turned to give him an ugly look, but I didn't want to push my luck anymore. Being a smart-ass had been enough, and I was just so tired.

I kept going, trying not to move my head from side to side as I watched. We went through one door that led out to a long hallway. How big was this place? The guard in front of me stopped suddenly beside another nondescript door and moved his hand quickly across it.

That's when the guard behind me grabbed my ponytail and shoved me so hard I went stumbling through the opened doorway.

I crashed in on hands and knees, sprawling on the floor as the door slammed shut.

"Oww," I moaned. Really? Did they have to be so rough?

It took me a second to lift my head. I moved to sit on my hip and butt cheek and flipped the door off. Then I stopped and tensed.

Because sprawled on his back with his head drooped to the side was Sleeping Superhero Beauty.

But the alarming part was the way his chest rose and fell way too slowly. Slower than ever.

Oh shit.

Oh *shit*.

"Hey?" I whispered, my throat aching with just that single word.

He didn't react.

I tried again, my voice weak. "Yoo-hoo?"

Nothing.

With a groan, I crawled over, ignoring the shooting pain through my knees, wrists, and shoulders. At his side, I put my fingers against his mouth and cursed. His lips were cold. Why were his lips so cold?

Falling down to my stomach, I pressed my cheek against his chest and listened. His heart . . . his heart wasn't right. I'd counted the beats. They were slow but they weren't this slow.

"Hey?"

Nothing.

Sitting back on my hip, I set my palm on his cheek. That was cold too. I pressed my hand over his heart again, counting those too-slow beats like I hadn't done it right before.

"Temporary friend?" I tried again, attempting to ignore the panic rising in my chest.

Nothing.

"Wake up." My voice cracked. "Hercules, wake up."

Nothing.

Tears popped up in my eyes, and I wiped them off with the back of my hand. I shook his shoulder, squeezed his biceps, and even grabbed his cold hand. Nothing.

"You can't do this to me," I whispered. *What the hell had they done to him?* How could they have hurt him? He'd said he was invulnerable.

More tears formed in my eyes as I lifted his arm and let it fall, not getting a single response from that either.

Lowering my head, I pressed my ear against his chest and listened once more.

Was it even slower now?

Was he . . . dying?

He couldn't just . . . he couldn't just go down like that. Not after everything he'd been through. After everything he'd done.

Not here, like this.

FUCK!

I closed my eyes and took his hand, tight.

What should I do?

Before I could think too hard about it, I sat right by his head and pushed him onto his side, propping his back on my knees. Then I pressed on the hinges of his jaw to open it and shoved my fingers as far down his throat as possible, fast. I was pretty sure I touched his tonsils.

I wiggled my fingers in there, and I gagged. I had no clue what I was doing. Not even a little bit but . . .

His body jerked. His back arched. And The Defender retched. Literally gagged so hard his whole body nearly convulsed.

The muscles in his throat spasmed.

I didn't move my fingers out fast enough.

The vomit . . .

I gagged just as something warm and liquid-like shot out of his mouth and over my retreating fingers, landing all over the floor.

It was clear and not much of it, but . . .

I gagged again as I slapped his back while he coughed and coughed.

Oh God, he'd thrown up.

I watched him as he coughed, as he rolled onto his back, partway on my knees, with a ragged groan.

Those purple eyes opened, but it wasn't the color that caught me off guard that time. It was his mean-ass scowl.

"Are you going to be okay?" I hissed at him, ignoring how fast my fucking heart was beating.

"*What the fuck are you doing?*" he snapped, coughing. Going up to an elbow, he grabbed his throat, eyes wide. "You trying to make sure I have tonsils?"

Some part of my brain recognized the fact that he looked shocked. Like I'd really surprised the hell out of him. But the rest of my brain didn't understand what the fuck he was yelling over.

I'd thought . . . I'd thought . . .

"I thought that maybe they'd poisoned you! Or you were choking! Your lips were blue," I grumbled back, a ball forming in my throat almost instantly. Even my eyes got watery all over again as I took him in, on his side, massaging his throat as a pool of clear vomit lay beside him.

"What the hell would I be choking on? I was resting!" The Defender gave me the ugliest fucking look I'd ever seen.

But I couldn't even find it in me to care.

Mostly because *he was fine.* He wasn't dying. Why'd he have to scare the shit out of me like that?

"Your lips were blue," I explained, hearing how funny my voice sounded and not sure how to stop it. Slowly, I got up, numb. "I thought you were dying," I managed to whisper, each word softer than the last as I made my way to the sink and rinsed my hand off. "Your heart was beating even slower than before, and you were cold, and your lips were blue . . ."

Tears pooled over my eyes and down my cheeks, and I didn't even bother wiping them off as I let more water stream over my fingers and palm. When it was as good as it was going to get, I shook the water from my hand and finally turned to glare at him. Getting angry all over again. "Why the fuck would you do that? Why didn't you open your eyes when I came in? I tried talking to you," I cried. "I thought you were dying, and I thought it was my fault, and . . ." Slapping a hand over the center of my chest, I shook my head.

I'd felt like I was about to have a heart attack there.

"You scared the shit out of me," I croaked as even more tears came over my eyes. "You never did that before." I sniffled and wiped at my eyes. "Fuck you, dammit."

His eyes almost bulged out. "Fuck me?"

I nodded, ignoring my poor bruised brain. "Yeah." Fuck him. "Fuck you," I repeated so there was no misunderstanding what I said.

He narrowed his eyes as he watched me, and I was pretty sure I saw some muscle in his face relax a little bit. "Were you . . . crying for me?" he asked almost warily.

Why did he sound so surprised? "Yeah, and?" I winced, palming my chest. I'd forgotten about my shirt. About being in a sports bra in the first place. But I couldn't muster up half a shit. Mostly because even more tears poured out of my eyes from relief. "Why were you like that?"

He narrowed his eyes even more as he switched languages. "I was in deep rest."

"You didn't look like a corpse when you were in deep rest before," I answered him right back in Korean. Legs weak, I eased to the ground.

"That wasn't a deep rest; that was a normal rest. I knew they weren't going to come back until they brought you, and I knew they weren't going to kill you or do anything to me yet. I took advantage of the time." A little growl formed in his throat. "I didn't think you were going to stick your whole hand down my damn throat."

The hand I didn't have against my chest, the one he'd thrown up on, I set on the ground so I wouldn't be tempted to use it. "How the hell was I supposed to know?" I wiped at my face again. "You scared the shit out of me. That's what you get for ignoring me." And that was what I got for jumping to conclusions.

Son of a bitch.

He gave me a terrible glare before his eyes finally flicked down, as if noticing that I wasn't wearing a shirt.

Or maybe he was finally noticing that I had boobs.

The Defender's gaze moved back up toward my face.

He stared at me.

I stared back.

Then he grunted something under his breath before slowly sitting up, wincing as he did. But once he was in a seated position, his gaze was steady on mine as his hands went to his hoodie and he unzipped it.

Part of me expected him to hand it over once he'd peeled it off, but he set it aside and let his hands drop back toward his waist.

And that's when he pulled the shirt up over his head and tossed it.

It hit me in the face.

By the time I pulled it off, he was pulling the hoodie back on, zipping it up over his abs, then the rest of him.

Even with my head on the verge of bursting, I'd gotten a good look at *everything*.

Including his chest.

The chest.

The chest to end all chests.

I'd noticed it was a nice one before, but I hadn't appreciated just how magnificent it really was.

His shoulders were just as broad as they looked in the unforgivable suit that I had a feeling he'd completely eviscerated since there hadn't even been ashes anywhere after he'd taken it off. The amount of muscle mass—all defined and impressive—shouldn't have been surprising. Because again, the suit hugged everything. But it still caught me off guard. He was shredded. Striations lined his shoulders, his biceps were a work of art, even his forearms deserved a symphony for how perfectly they were covered with hair.

There were also his pectorals and thick, solid abs, which were also covered with a sprinkling of dark hair.

He glared at me for about the millionth time. "Would you close your mouth?"

I closed it and glared right back. "Nobody told you to strip, *Magic Mike*, and I didn't say anything when you were looking at my boobs a second ago. You could've just given me the hoodie instead of getting naked."

He finished raising the zipper as high as it would go, right between the notches of his collarbones, giving me a long, long look as he did it. "It's easier for me to hide my eyes with the hoodie, if I have to," he grumbled in Portuguese.

Oh.

That made sense.

He switched back to English. "Are you done crying now?"

I shrugged.

"You done fingering my throat?"

My face burned. "You can only blame yourself for that. I was trying to save your life."

His snort shocked me.

"You should have woken up, and I shouldn't have jumped to conclusions. We're both idiots, all right?" I tried to compromise.

"Speak for yourself." Those purple eyes narrowed even as he pushed himself back against the wall, watching me the whole time.

I shivered just as another throb came from my head, reminding me of just how bad I felt. My arms were clumsy as I pulled the shirt on slowly, careful not to jostle my shoulder or the other million body parts that were achy. It wasn't *warm*, but it was a hell of a lot better than nothing. I would rather have the hoodie, but fine. He needed to hide his eyes.

And why was I so dizzy all of a sudden?

Breathing in deeply through my nose even though it triggered that pain from my ribs, I pushed backward until my back touched the opposite wall and I groaned. I tipped my head to rest against it too. Then I watched as The Defender eyed my every move.

My vision went blurry again, this time without the help of water being poured into my eyeballs, and I swallowed hard, scrubbing at the back of my neck with my clean hand.

I wanted to ask him what his deep rest meant and just how much better he was feeling, but my head . . .

"What is it?" the grumpy voice asked, reminding me he was observant even if he was mad.

I closed my eyes as a shiver snaked down my frame. Then I told him the truth. "I don't feel so good."

Chapter Twelve

"What's wrong with you?" a familiar, rich voice asked as I cracked my eyes open.

I moaned. *Oh shit*. Had someone beat me up and then run me over with a Humvee while I'd been sleeping?

I tried to take a breath, instantly realizing just how hard that was. If I'd thought I'd felt like hell before, it was nothing compared to right then. It was like something heavy was sitting on my chest. My mouth was dry, and my head was still pounding as hard as ever. Basically, I felt like fucking shit as my eyes focused on the face peering down at me.

I recognized it, but it still managed to look different.

It was a smooth face with golden tan skin, beautiful and dewy; elegant features were framed by brown hair that hit almost at a jawline that would make a sculptor cry. But it was the roundish-shaped eyes that I focused on next, with their dark purple irises framed by thick, black lashes.

They were glowing.

I shivered.

I tried to swallow, but that was even more painful than before. My *head*. How was it possible to be this nauseous too? I moaned.

"What's wrong with you?" the beautiful man looking at me demanded. "Are you *sick*?" he asked in what sounded an awful lot like disgust.

I raised my hand and moaned more before touching my forehead. "You haven't brushed your teeth in I don't know how long, back up," I managed to whisper, annoyed with him for being irritated with me while I already felt like poo. The truth was, I couldn't really smell his breath, but that was my secret. He wasn't going to be the only one to talk trash, even if I felt like a steaming pile of it.

The familiar-unfamiliar face dropped closer to mine, giving me a good view of those definitely familiar eyes and that scowl I'd seen way too much of. His dark eyebrows were knitted together. "Why?" he asked almost cautiously.

Why was I sick?

Closing an eye, I tried to think, but all I could do was stare at his smooth skin. It was the stuff Photoshop and beauty product commercials tried their hardest to emulate.

"Because I am," I whispered. "And lower your voice, my head hurts." I wanted to throw up, but I kept that to myself. No need to remind him of what I'd done with my fingers.

He growled so loud, I felt it in my bones and temples.

"Please?" I tried.

That only earned me another growl that might have been slightly quieter. Or it might have been my imagination. "Your body temperature is higher than it should be," he told me in that bossy-britches voice.

"Wow, you're a breathing thermometer."

He blinked.

And it made me feel bad. "I'm sorry." I swallowed. "I feel like shit, and I'm grouchy."

Curly eyelashes fell over those glowing, amazing eyes.

I winced through a swallow. My hands weren't cold, but they were slightly less warm than the rest of me. A memory of water flowing into my mouth, of the sensation that I was going to fucking drown, had me holding my breath for a second before

I realized it and let it back out. And if it was shaky, I tried my best to pretend that it wasn't.

"What happened?" he asked after a while.

I guess I'd been far enough away that he hadn't heard what was going on? "They took me into another room," I told him, keeping my eyes closed. "They asked where the money was."

"And?"

"She said they would let me out if I told her what she wanted to know, and I told her I didn't have it, and then they . . ."

I was going to set them on fire.

No, no, that was too easy. I was going to find a way to freeze their pipes at home and make them explode. You wanted a real nightmare? A financial one was terrifying, and not having water really, really sucked.

"They put a rag over my mouth and poured water over my face," I explained, taking my time with each word. "I threw up. That's why my shirt is gone, because I puked all over it. I got it all off, I think." I sniffed, terror rising inside of me for a second, making my nose sting even more than it already did.

I wasn't sure why I said it, why I would admit it to him especially, but maybe I just needed to get it off my chest. I'd heard somewhere that admitting something gave it less power. I hoped that was the fucking case. There were so many things I'd never talked about that kept me up at night. Maybe there was some merit to it. "I was so scared the whole time, but I didn't tell them anything." I sniffled. "I hope they all eat shit."

"What else happened?" he asked quietly, surprising me even more.

"They did it again and again," I told him. "I asked them to let you go. I told them you didn't know anything. Promise."

He didn't say a word.

I kept going. "Then they left me in that freezing room until they brought me here." I winced as I tried to swallow what felt like a cup of glass shards. "She didn't do it to be nice. I think they're going to start starving us, or maybe they're going to come in here and try and torture you next to get me to break."

Reality was, I was going to fucking die if we didn't get out of here soon.

I tried sniffling and failed because I'd swear even my hair follicles were bruised. My head was pounding so much it took me a second to switch to Portuguese. "You need to get out of here. You look better, and I think you're feeling better—"

"I am," he cut me off.

I opened my eyes. "Is that why your eyes are glowing so bright now?" I struggled to ask, a language I'd known for most of my life suddenly feeling brand-new in my mouth. Was that why his skin was almost luminous too?

His nod was severe.

Oh, that was good. That was great.

But . . .

My head throbbed so bad I whimpered. The urge to throw up was *right there*, but I'd already thrown up everything I had in me. I couldn't even summon tears now, I was so dehydrated. But the part that concerned me the most was that I wasn't hungry or thirsty either.

"Tell me something," The Defender said quietly.

I made a noise to tell him to go ahead.

It seemed like it took him a second to pick out his words. "Why would you risk your life to save me? Why didn't you leave like you said you would?"

Oh. He remembered. I tried to shrug but closed my eyes instead. "I only said I'd leave if someone was coming for you. I've never wanted anyone to get hurt because of me. I'm not going to let you suffer for it." It was that easy.

There was a huff, and if I hadn't been so tired, I might have peeked at him.

"Go back to sleep. Stop being sick," he demanded after a moment in that gruff, bossy voice that still hinted at irritation.

Oh how the tables had turned.

I needed to stop feeling so bad, sure, but I had a feeling I was running out of time.

We both were.

Chapter Thirteen

I groaned at the feel of something damp touching my forehead.

More than touching it, pressing down on it.

Moaning, I peered up at the frown hovering above me. I must have fallen asleep at some point. The last thing I remembered was gagging after telling him I wasn't feeling well.

"What are you doing?" I whispered, my voice hoarse as hell. Just when I'd thought I couldn't possibly feel worse, my body said *check this shit out*.

And I was checking it out. I was checking it out big-time.

The superbeing rolled his eyes. "Trying to cool you down. What does it look like?"

If I'd been worried he'd been body snatched, I could live at peace now.

"I don't know. It isn't every day I wake up to someone in my face." Honestly though, for one microsecond, I'd thought he was planning on playing tonsil hockey in revenge.

The gorgeous man still hovering over me huffed. "I'm trying to keep you alive."

When he put it like that, I felt like a jerk. "Thank you." I winced at how much my swallow burned. "I'm not trying to be ungrateful. I just feel so shitty, and you surprised me." I sniffled. "You keep surprising me." That was the understatement of the century.

That perfect face went a little funny.

I tried to smile at him, but my cheeks felt like they'd been pinched to hell. "Thank you," I repeated, "for trying to help me."

He blinked. His gaze moved from my eyes to my chin and lingered on my shirt. On the shirt I'd given him, the one with Hello Kitty on it. Then, just as slowly, those purple eyes swept their way back up, and I don't think I imagined that his voice got a little quieter as he said, totally serious, "I've never taken care of anything."

Oh.

"I've never been around anyone this sick," he admitted just as low.

But here he was.

Moving my hand from where I'd had it on my stomach, I set it between my breasts. The shirt was damp. I was sticky.

"You're still running a fever." The Defender kept staring at me with those intense, incredible eyes. "Is this the right thing to do to bring it down?"

"Mm-hmm," I answered with a wince.

A notch formed between two thick, dark eyebrows. "How do you feel?"

I tried to laugh and automatically regretted it. "Like shit."

The Defender sighed and got up, walking . . . normal.

He'd gotten up effortlessly, no huffing, no puffing, no struggling at all. I kept watching as he headed to the sink and turned it on. I was only a little surprised when he turned around, hands cupped together, and made his way back, pausing right beside me. He raised an eyebrow, and somehow, I knew exactly what he wanted.

I opened my mouth, and he poured the small amount of water into it.

I licked my lips, my mouth so damn dry.

He blinked, and I watched his lips go tight before he bent over and . . .

"What are you doing?" I croaked just as he slipped an arm under my knees and another across my shoulder blades, lifting me effortlessly. "Don't hurt your back!"

The Defender didn't look at me as he said, "It's fine now."

It was?

He walked us over to the sink, the side of my body pressed against the front of his, and slowly lowered me to my feet, keeping an arm around my lower back as he turned the tap on with his other hand. "Drink," he ordered. "I've got you."

He . . . did?

I coughed and ducked down, sticking my mouth right beside the sink. I ignored the way my heart started beating faster at the idea of that water touching more than just my mouth and how bad my legs were shaking. I drank as much as I could, until my throat hurt even more than it already did.

I'd kill for some honey. For something warm and soothing. To be back home, in my bed.

A cough shot through me, and my ribs ached in response.

A wet hand rubbed over my forehead and the back of my neck as I dragged a ragged, painful breath in. Tilting my head, I peered up at him. His features were smooth, and he was staring again, being so, so watchful, like he really was weighing some part of my soul in his invisible scales, seeing if I was worthy or not.

I wasn't sure I was, but I'd like to hope so.

And that's when he picked me up, pressing me against him and his buzzing skin and the presence I was getting used to. So, so easily.

"You're sure?" I whispered. "Your back is okay?" I checked, taking in the immaculate line of his jaw.

"It's fine."

For some damn reason I didn't understand, I said, "You can call me Gracie," ignoring just how strange it felt to say my name out loud to another person after so long.

His glance was so quick I almost missed it. "Gracie," he actually said.

A sinking sensation suddenly socked me in the gut, and I flinched up at him. "Why are you being so nice to me?"

"Because I don't want to smell your rotting corpse."

My whole body jerked. "Am I dying? Is that why you're finally talking to me?" I just about shrieked, or tried to.

It didn't feel like I was. Dying, I meant. Wouldn't my stomach hurt if I was on my deathbed? I felt like shit, but I couldn't be dying. I couldn't . . .

The way he looked at me made me instantly stop panicking. "*No.* You're not dying. Your heartbeat is normal; you don't smell poisoned. You . . . smell like you haven't showered in days." He made a noise in his throat. "You smell ill."

Uh, rude. And maybe I felt like hell and smelled like it, but not bad enough to keep my trap shut. "You haven't showered either," I reminded him, each syllable costing me but totally worth it.

He huffed. "I don't sweat the way you do."

Maybe he had a point there.

Then he added, "It's fine. I've smelled worse."

He'd smelled worse. Oh, I would have laughed if I had the energy. "Is that supposed to make me feel better? Because it does a little," I admitted.

He sighed and carried me back toward the wall. "I thought people stopped talking when they don't feel well," he said under his breath.

Someone wasn't just trying to be nice; he was back to being sarcastic too. "I'm not sick enough, I guess," I said under my breath right back, letting out a tiny, dry laugh that cost me a fortune of discomfort. Oh boy. It wasn't going to be the cartel that got me; it was going to be pneumonia or whatever this shit was. That would be my luck.

He grunted as he set me down so, so gently, surprising me for about the millionth time by that point. Maybe he was going to make up for all the lack of surprises I'd missed out on over my life by keeping my circle so small. I eyed him as I leaned back against the wall, closing one eye as my head throbbed worse. "Are you sure you're okay?"

The Defender balanced on the balls of his feet. His grouchy face there, totally focused on me. "I'm fine."

I hoped he was. I sighed. "You're sure I'm not dying?"

"Unless you die from talking too much, no." His eyes narrowed. "You're tough. You'll be fine."

It wouldn't sink in until way later that he'd said I was tough. That he thought that about me. All I managed to do was swallow. "I hope you're right. I've got a lot left I'd like to do someday." I sniffled. "I haven't even learned how to swim yet," I told him for some fucking reason, probably because after this shit, I wasn't sure I'd ever be able to stick my face under water ever again, much less swim.

He stared.

And I just frowned at that beautiful face. "Really though. Why are you being so nice? Why are you doing this?"

His eyebrows arched. "I'm not being nice." The rest of his face caught up in an expression that fell somewhere between a frown and confusion. "You did the same for me."

He had a point. That didn't mean I trusted him all that much though, even with how kind he was trying to be . . . or how nice he *was* being. It made more sense that he didn't want to have to deal with my smelly, dead body. I was sick, and my brain wasn't running on all cylinders, but I was still going to accept anything he was willing to throw my way.

I smiled weakly. At least I tried to. I probably just looked dehydrated. "You look a lot better," I told him quietly.

"I am."

"I'm really glad you are."

Rubbing a hand against my forehead, I was attempting to hold back a moan at the pain radiating from my head when I heard him sigh and say, "Come here."

"Come where?" I asked, rubbing more. I hated this. I hated this so much. How could I feel so bad? I would do some sketchy shit for a painkiller right about now. If I got out of here, I was never taking one of those for granted ever again. I might kiss the next bottle I bought. I'd dress it up for Halloween, maybe take it for a daily walk. Might stuff one into my bra in case of emergencies.

"Here," he replied, sighing again, sounding only a little exasperated. "Come here." He crisscrossed those long legs and tilted his head back, raising dark eyebrows at me. Then he opened his arms wide, stretching the material clinging to his shoulders and biceps for dear life. "Come on," he demanded.

Where? There? *By him?*

I looked at the hard, concrete floor, then at his crabby, little eyes.

The thing was, I knew who I was and what I'd been through. What I'd experienced. I understood exactly what kind of quicksand I was in.

And I was pretty sure I understood exactly what he was offering, even if it didn't feel real.

Did I get why he was doing it? No. Should I question it? Probably. Was I going to?

It only took a second for me to decide.

I'd played it safe my whole life, and look where it had landed me.

He'd offered. It was his idea, I justified to myself about a split second before scooting over then scooting over some more, right into the gap between his legs. Then I scooched down right in there. On top of him. My butt cradled right in the nook The Defender's knees created.

Slowly, so cautiously, my giant, imaginary balls swelling in size, I stretched my legs out and draped them over his thigh, part of me expecting him to suddenly change his mind and tell me to fuck off.

To tell me to get off his lap.

It didn't happen though, and I took my time leaning against him about a second after I settled on him, letting the side of my forehead slowly rest against his chest, right at the base of his throat. It made the most sense to put it there. The zipper on the hoodie wasn't annoying, or maybe the rest of me hurt so bad it was easy to ignore it being pressed against my cheek.

And damn near instantly, at least ten of my muscles, muscles that had been strained so tight, relaxed.

Because he wasn't warm, but he wasn't cold. And he was more comfortable than the floor. So much more comfortable than the floor.

And let it be said, I knew I missed touch. Missed hugs. Affection in general. But the feel of his body brought a comfort that I was desperate enough to suck up with a straw.

Right then it didn't matter that he was The Defender. He could have been anybody, and I would've appreciated it. It was one of the nicest things anyone had ever done for me.

And sure, it was because I'd done the same for him, but it wasn't like I'd done it expecting anything in return.

While we were there . . . while he was being so willing . . .

His inhale of surprise was the only noise he made after I reached behind me, picked up his arm, and wrapped it around my side. I even set his hand in my lap. Like we weren't damn near strangers. Like he hadn't spent weeks glaring at me for some reason, and he wasn't one of the most special people in the world, and I was . . . not.

Like I had any right to demand anything of him.

I didn't. Nobody did.

But he still felt pretty fucking amazing.

If I had any body fluids left, I might have cried.

"I know this is probably hell for you, but you can count to three hundred and then push me off," I whispered, feeling a violent shake go through me.

I was freezing.

He moved the arm I'd draped around my hip a little higher.

Maybe this was the end. Maybe this would be the last nice moment I'd ever have with another human being. I'd made my choice. If I could have had more of them, life could have been so different. But that wasn't the case.

It never had been.

Life was what you made out of it, and I'd tried my damn best.

If I was going to die, it would be nice to not go alone. It wasn't sex, but I'd bet it was just as good. And it made me regret so much that I'd never experienced this before. If this was half as nice as snuggling with a loved one, I totally understood why people who were happy lived longer.

At least I would have gotten to experience something like this once in my life.

At least someone other than my grandparents had cared about me for at least a little bit.

That was something.

I tried to hold back a groan as a wave of nausea rolled straight through me.

"What hurts?" he asked after a moment.

"Everything." I tried to laugh but coughed instead, and damn, my lungs weren't right. Since when had breathing been so hard? "Thank you . . . for this."

"You're not dying, but you are really sick," that almost comforting voice said against my ear, his words slow and steady.

"I know. I've never been this sick before."

The arm around my hip moved just a little.

I squeezed my eyes closed and took another painful swallow, trying to put my thoughts in order. "Hey . . . if something happens to me, if I don't make it out of here . . ." I could barely say it. I could barely fucking think it, but I had to. It had been on my mind since I'd been in that room with those assholes.

His body tightened, and I didn't imagine how gruff his voice came out. "Nothing is going to happen. You're sick and you're puny. That's all."

I let out a slow breath through my mouth. Me? Puny? "Says the man who couldn't feed himself," I mumbled, half expecting him to make a smart-ass comment in reply.

What I got was a chuff.

Did that count as a laugh? Had I made him laugh again? "I'm serious though," I whispered. "Tell everyone I saved the world. Make it up. Let me at least go down a hero."

His muscles stayed hard. "You're not going to die," The Defender grunted.

I pressed my forehead a little more against the column of his neck. "My last name is Castro. You can tell them my real name if you want, or Gracie, I don't care. I wouldn't be able to." I shivered. "My grandparents never called me Gracie anyway, only people I met did. They usually called me *mi amor*, that means—"

"I know what it means," he cut me off. His chest rose and fell slowly against my cheek. "You talk in Spanish in your sleep."

I did? "I do?"

"Yeah." Neither one of us said anything for a moment until he asked, "Why do you pretend like you don't know Spanish?"

"I don't pretend. I'm just not speaking it now just in case

they're listening. I'm paranoid. And why would I have said any-thing to you when you barely talked to me in English?" I thought about it. "We, my family, never spoke it in public, just at home." That was why I had never been allowed to call my grandma Abuela. So that no one could pinpoint their accents.

He made a sound in his chest that I was going to hope was acceptance.

"You smell nice for having not showered," I mumbled.

"I told you, I don't need to sweat as much as you do, and it doesn't have an odor."

"Lucky," I muttered.

His head tipped down, his chin brushing my temple. He sighed right before he lifted his arm, moving it to the side and—

I heard the zipper, then felt him shift a bit before he tugged the opened sides of the hoodie wide and wrapped them around me. Like a taco, and I was the filling.

I blinked.

Oh shit.

I was T-shirt on skin with a beautiful man.

And not just any beautiful man, but The Defender. The fuck-ing *Defender.* A gorgeous pain in the fucking ass. One who was taking care of *me.*

People would pay millions for this. If I had them and I hadn't gotten to know his real personality, I would too.

Could he really be such a dickhead when he went to this extent?

I dropped my head and even caught my breath . . . until my teeth chattered and I shivered again. I swallowed, deciding to try and get my mind off this, so I asked the first thing I thought of. "Are you a cyborg?"

I felt his huff more than heard it. "No."

Turning my head a little, I lifted my hand—and I was going to blame the fever on messing around with the hormones controlling my brain—and with the tip of my index finger, I lifted his lip a little. It was firm and soft at the same time.

I tapped his canine tooth with my fingernail. It felt . . . normalish. It wasn't like I ever poked at my own teeth.

Moving my hand, I nudged at a spot on his jaw with the pad of my finger, and still, he let me.

Then I gently knocked on the part of his collarbone that was exposed from his unzipped hoodie.

"What are you doing?" The Defender asked slowly.

"I don't know, making sure you're not."

I heard the deep breath he let out from his nostrils. I felt the shift of his muscles beneath my legs and beside my arm. I barely heard him say, "You can call me Alexander."

I tipped my head back. If my eyeballs weren't so dry, I was pretty sure they might have bugged out.

Those bright eyes went squinty. "Tell anybody and—"

Oh shit, oh shit, *oh shit*. "You'll render my limbs, I know," I whispered, stunned.

I sounded his name out on my tongue. A-l-e-x-a-n-d-e-r. Huh.

It was so . . . so . . . normal.

"It's a nice name. Very solid, very fitting," I whispered, wondering now if this was some kind of delusion or something.

Maybe I was dead. Or I was dreaming.

"Not Alex. Not Xander. Alexander," he muttered, already sounding like he was regretting his decision to give me that much.

Maybe it wasn't a dream.

"Alexander, got it," I confirmed weakly, reeling and trying to play it cool.

He had a name. Like everybody. And it wasn't Goliath or Stormkiller or something that sounded like a mathematical equation.

It was Alexander. Not Xander. And even though he said not Alex, I already saw him as that more.

This felt monumental.

The question spilled from my mouth before I could stop it. "Do you have a last name too?"

"What do you think?"

"That you do." I swallowed and gave him a little more information. Just a little. Just in case this was the end, I wanted him to know the truth. "My real last name is Castro, but we legally changed it when I was fifteen to Garcia. I've never felt like a Garcia though. It was just more common."

His thighs bunched under mine, and his breathing was slow as he said quietly, "I know what it is. I know your middle name too."

It was my muscles that tensed then. "You . . . found my birth certificate?" Other than the paperwork from when we legally changed our names—which I knew for a fact I didn't have at the house—that was the only thing in the world that had my full, real name on it. My original birth certificate before my mom had signed her rights over to my grandparents. I thought I had stored it in my safe deposit box along with that letter I should have burned a decade ago but hadn't. I really needed to stop thinking about it.

He didn't reply.

When the hell had he had time to snoop and find it? I couldn't believe I'd gotten so sloppy that I'd had it at the house. Fortunately, all he would have seen was my last name. And my real middle name: Ximena. He-men-ah. For my grandpa's mom. I had kept that too throughout my life. It was the Altagracia that I'd had to dump when we'd changed our last name after my parents had done what they did. I had gone from Altagracia Castro to Gracie Garcia.

I guess it wasn't that big of a deal that he knew that. What did it really matter at this point?

Turning my cheek, I buried my face a little closer into his firm chest. I had no energy. I wasn't hungry either, and I was always hungry.

The arm that had been resting beside his body shifted, and before I knew it, those long fingers were grazing my cheek.

If I could have sucked in a surprised breath, I would have. "Your hand feels nice," I told him honestly.

"It's only a hand. Your face turned red. I thought your fever might be spiking."

"No, I just miss human contact," I admitted, stopping myself from leaning into his touch more than necessary. I'd already put his arm around me. Sure, it was for warmth and because I didn't feel good, and even though he hadn't done anything to save me from those assholes because he couldn't, his presence still made me feel safer than when I'd been alone.

And that was something.

It was a hell of a lot.

"You sound like Cookie Monster."

I wanted to laugh, because he was right, but all I did was kind of puff a little bit of breath out.

"Did they leave you alone after they took me?" I asked quietly.

His body tensed, and I knew that was all I was going to get.

Nausea rolled through me, and I needed to focus on something else instead. "I asked them to," I told him, feeling bile rising in my throat.

"I know you did. Two of them kicked me. That's all," he answered surprisingly fast, his breath a warm puff against my hair.

I nodded, thinking about how I'd yelled out of desperation. I swallowed the memory and the hurt down. The shame too. Because anybody would have yelled for help, right?

Except maybe not him.

But he wasn't here to save me.

I wasn't his responsibility.

Even he'd said he wasn't being nice. He was being decent. To not smell my stinky decaying corpse.

That was why he cared.

Setting his arm onto his thigh, I forced myself to slide over onto the floor beside him. With a sigh, I sprawled out right there, slipping my hand under my head and closing my eyes.

"Eat some of your bar. They're in my pocket," the man named Alexander said steadily.

"My head hurts too bad right now. I might throw up," I told him.

"You haven't eaten since they took you."

He was right, but it didn't change anything. "Give me a minute and I will," I lied, dead serious about throwing up. Draping my other arm across my eyes, I sighed, way more reassured than I should have been by knowing he was two feet away from me. That if I reached out, I could poke him.

I really was glad he was here, even though the only thing that mattered at this point was him getting out. I couldn't forget that.

I was a fucking liar.

And that was exactly what he said at some point later on.

"You said you were going to eat."

Palming my head with both hands, I could hear how nasally my voice was as I muttered, "I will."

He huffed.

I pressed my lips together and bottled the moan in my throat. It felt like my nose was made of ground beef. I squeezed my face between my hands like that would help my headache. It didn't.

What could have been two minutes or twenty later, I heard the crinkle of a wrapper and opened an eye to find one of the nutrition bars a few inches away from my hip.

"Eat it," he growled.

I tried to growl back, but it came out as a cough. "I'm not hungry."

"I don't care if you're hungry. Eat it," he demanded.

The urge to argue with him was right there, but so was the pounding in my head. Instead, I flicked my fingers weakly in his direction. "Later. Let me try and take another nap first."

"You need more water."

I covered my eyes with the inside of my elbow. "In a minute."

"You need water," he repeated, his tone gruff.

"I know."

Alexander sighed. "Fine. Be dehydrated."

I'd forgotten he'd given me a real name to call him. It almost made me feel better. Almost.

Restless, I rubbed my face and shifted my legs around, shivering hard. "Did they lower the temperature in here more or am I imagining it?" I pretty much whimpered.

"They did."

They were trying to kill me. That shouldn't have been a surprise. Fuck. I needed . . . to stay up a little bit.

And I needed to bring up the elephant in the room.

Him. His health. That was the elephant in the room.

"Are you . . . feeling even better?" I managed to whisper.

"I am."

Lord, he could toss a dog a bone here. "Back to normal?"

There was a brief pause. "I've regained a significant amount of my energy and . . . everything else."

Everything else?

My heart started pounding even harder. Reality settling in. I knew what was going to happen. We both did. They were going to come for him. There was a reason he was here.

But I didn't want to be left behind. I didn't . . .

If I could have mustered up a tear or two, I would have, but I knew what I was doing. At least, I understood why I had to do what was necessary. "Hey?"

"Shut up and rest," he grumbled, pretty half-assed.

"But—"

His sigh was long and clear. "Whatever energy you're about to waste, save it."

Did he sound less grouchy or was the fever messing with my ears?

I squeezed my eyes closed as my head swam, and I tried out his name with my lips and tongue. "Alexander?"

"Yeah?"

I rubbed my face. "I think you need to—"

The Defender groaned. "Don't bother finishing that sentence. I'm already regretting telling you my name."

This butthole. "I regret opening my door. I guess we're even," I told him quietly, joking. Mostly.

And I thought . . . I thought I imagined it . . . but I didn't.

The crazy bastard huffed. A little. But it was pretty damn close to a chuckle.

It was the warm touch on my face that was my silent alarm clock.

But it was the sight of a big palm retreating that had me flinching.

I opened my mouth to make a sound, to say a word, but everything crusted in my throat and dried out before I could even squeak.

Alexander's face moved into my line of sight. The line was back between his eyebrows, his mouth flat. "Your fever is higher."

No surprise. My brain felt like it was going to explode. I shivered and tried to find the words, pushing them through lips that felt too dry. "If something happens to me . . . I hope every person in this building gets a paper cut on their tongue. I'm going to poltergeist them, don't try and talk me out of it."

He ignored me. "You need water."

I did need water, some antibiotics too. I needed to move. I knew I needed to. When my grandma had gotten sick, her not wanting to move around had been the source of a lot of our arguments, if you could call them that.

"Get up, Gracie."

I had no energy, but I needed water . . . and movement . . . and food, even if I didn't want it.

It took a second for me to get to my side and then another few seconds to pull my hands and knees under me before pushing up onto them. For a split second, I thought about trying to stand but realized almost immediately that wasn't going to happen.

I thought about asking him for help, but if he'd wanted to, he would have already. Just like he'd done last time. Was he testing me? I wasn't going to ask. He was already doing so much.

I could do it.

It took too long to crawl toward the sink, then even longer to actually manage to stand up. My legs shook as I leaned against the wall and tried to catch my breath. It took a long time to cup water under the running tap and bring it to my mouth. I didn't drink enough, I knew it wasn't enough, but when my legs shook too bad to keep me up, I pretty much slid back down onto the floor and spread out on it.

"Eat the nutrition bar," a bossy voice said from somewhere close by.

I closed my eyes instead.

I was shaking so hard my teeth rattled.

I had to be morphing into a literal pile of shit. I was turning into the poo emoji on my phone.

I slept but didn't. I rested, but I stayed awake too, so uncomfortable—that word was the understatement of the century. I would have sold my soul to feel better.

But it was during one of those times that I opened my eyes when I felt myself being moved. Being lifted just a bit. My head drooped for a second before . . .

Prying an eyelid open even more, I found a leg stretched out in front of me. I was still on my side. Rolling onto my back and ignoring the ache in all my bones, I found The Defender's face looking down at me. All smooth, unreal skin. All that perfect bone structure. Those beautifully shaped and colored eyes. All that wrapped into one being.

And he was letting me use his leg as a pillow? Why did that suddenly seem like the nicest thing in the whole world? And why did it make me want to cry?

I sniffled, and that unbelievable face tipped down, his gaze moving over me.

I think my heart broke a little bit. "Why are you so beautiful?" I whispered.

He didn't even sound sarcastic as he answered, "Superior genetics. Go back to sleep."

I tried to laugh, but it just hurt.

He made a tight, tight, tight noise in his throat as those dark purple eyes moved over me again, the corners of his mouth going flat. "Your fever is worse," he said. "Get better."

"I can't . . ." Why was I so out of breath? "Just get better."

"Wrong. Make it happen."

Even snorting hurt.

"Stop it."

I sniffled some more.

"Get better," he insisted in that familiar, rich voice.

I groaned some more and rolled onto my side again, still on his leg. On his thigh.

"Gracie . . ."

I closed my eyes.

My fever *was* getting worse—or was already there. I could feel how hard my body was fighting. How even my spine hurt. My throat felt like I'd swallowed a couple hundred rocks with no water.

I burned up while I slept.

I remembered reading about how some people had vivid, crazy dreams when they had a fever. I didn't dream of shit. I slept and I slept, fitful and restless, remembering every turn and roll, and forcing my brain back to sleep because my head couldn't handle how bad it hurt and needed the escape.

And in one of those rare times that I did wake up, my back on fire, I found myself in a seated position.

Sort of.

I was shivering, and I frowned at how dry my throat was. And it was that distraction that had me noticing that I wasn't just *sitting* up, my back was propped up against something that wasn't the wall. What . . . ?

There was a thigh on either side of me, two big feet planted flat on the floor. It was on those raised knees that a wrist was propped up on each of them. It was the full-looking forearms covered in a familiar, gray-colored material that had me blinking. They were connected to sturdy elbows and full, strong biceps bracketing my shoulders.

I was wrapped up in the hoodie. Buzzing bare skin was touching parts of me.

Oh.

Scrunching up my face, I licked my lips and tried to tilt my head back and to the side.

He didn't make it easy for me either, not moving at all. It wasn't until the back of my head touched what had to be his shoulder, my cheek to his bare chest, that I finally got a good look at the face above and behind me.

Like I didn't already have every inch of it memorized.

Smooth, healthy cheeks. A mouth with two full, dark pink lips. Brilliant purple eyes that flashed from beneath dark eyebrows.

I blew out a breath slowly, confused and miserable.

Then, tucking in my chin and dropping my eyes, I took in the definite fullness at the shoulder in my view.

At the bicep muscles that had been personal pillows.

The thigh at my hip seemed to bulge at the seams of the sweatpants he had on. He'd put my head on it. More than once, I was pretty positive.

Tipping my head, my eyes stung, and those dark eyelashes dropped, and the man who looked an awful lot like The Defender, but better, scowled.

"What are you crying for?" He frowned.

I felt one little tear slide down my cheek a moment before I whispered, "Am I . . . dead?"

His snicker caught me off guard. "You're not fucking dead."

His chest was almost warm, and my skin tingled just a little bit where it touched his. "Are you sure?"

"Yes." The handsome face hovering above me dipped, and his nostrils flared before he frowned. It looked like someone had lit a flashlight beneath his skin, making him damn near practically glow with health or power, or maybe even both. "Your fever is still high but not high enough for you to be delusional."

I reached up with an arm that felt too heavy and touched his cheek lightly, taking in the firmness.

He felt real.

I couldn't help it. I was too focused on the perfect planes and the magical muscles. And there was the fever. And that's what I was going to blame for moving my finger to touch the corner of his mouth as I whispered, "You really are pretty."

"And you're sick and could use mouthwash," the grump replied.

It was so mean, but I still snorted weakly, and the familiar-unfamiliar face scowled down at me even more.

"Stop it."

"You keep saying that like I have a choice," I croaked.

The thigh on my right pressed closer to my hip.

"Why are you still here?" I asked before I could stop myself and really think about what I was pointing out to him. "Can't you leave already?"

Those purple eyes bored into me, and his brows dropped on his high forehead. "Yeah."

So then why?

And again, he must have been able to tell what was on my mind because he blinked, and his tone went totally exasperated. "You want me to leave you?"

My neck felt too weak to shake my head. "No." I swallowed, regretting waking up. "But I'm surprised you didn't. This isn't your business."

His expression darkened. "I don't go back on my word."

I closed my eyes and leaned even more against him, totally fucking wiped out. "I wouldn't want to be here without you." I swallowed, flicking my finger against the soft material of the hoodie. "It makes me feel better that we're both miserable."

His chest made a strange motion against my cheek. "You like me being miserable?" he asked, his voice funny.

I liked him talking to me, even if it was sarcasm that came out of his mouth half the time. I still didn't get why he was doing any of this—I *didn't*—but I appreciated it. So much more than he'd ever understand.

I tried to nod, and his chest did that same thing again that damn near felt like a hiccup. "I would be so scared here alone, but I don't want them to get you."

"They won't."

"How do you know?"

"Because there's no one in the facility but a couple guards, and they don't have any plans to come over here," he said, almost quietly. "They're waiting for someone to arrive. There was a problem with a shipment. The woman is gone too."

I tried to think about that. "How . . . do you know? Super hearing?"

"And vision."

I huffed, even though I wasn't surprised. It took me a second to get my throat in shape to keep talking. "Were your hearing and vision messed up while you were injured?"

"Yes."

That explained a lot, yet at the same time only left me with more questions about why there had been something seriously wrong with him in so many different ways. "That's why . . . you're still here?" I asked instead.

"You're too sick to move," he said, like that explained everything. "I'm not going to risk it when we have time."

How much time though?

As if he could read my mind, he said, "They come in shifts between this facility and others spread out over a couple hundred miles. Those guards are hired help to protect the family, not to chop off a finger or two. We've got some time left. That missing shipment is worth a lot of money."

I hadn't been the only one concerned about me losing a digit. That was nice. Scary but nice. "But . . . you can't wait too long because then you won't be able to get out."

He made a noise that almost sounded like a snort. "We're getting the fuck out of here."

It took too much of my energy to tilt my head and peer up at him. He was already focused down, and his expression said he was dead serious. Confident beyond belief.

"We are," he insisted gravely. "I told you, nothing made on

this planet can hold me back. Not once I've regained what was taken from me."

I lifted my weak hand and touched the manacle on his thick left wrist. What the hell had been taken from him? His health? His power? I guess he had just brought up the hearing and vision thing, but the way he worded that . . .

He held his wrist closer to me. "This is nothing."

"You can take it off?" That was dumb, of course he could.

"What do you think?" he confirmed. "But there's a device in here that might go off once I remove it, and I'm not going to risk it until we're ready to get out of here."

"Oh." That sounded so easy, but it couldn't be.

"I'll hear them before they come. We'll leave then," the man known as The Defender said, steadily.

I sighed, weakly, exhausted and feeling like total shit. "I'm sorry I'm holding you back."

His broad chest did that funny almost-hiccupping sound. "You should be; it's annoying."

Surprised, I glanced up at him.

The son of a bitch blinked.

"You're . . . annoying," I whispered. Rude.

His gaze ran over my face for what felt like a long time. The muscles at his cheeks flexed, and even his throat bobbed. He didn't exactly sound happy about it, but he still said it. "I owe you my life, Gracie."

I shivered. He didn't. He really didn't, but I couldn't get the words out.

Those eyes glowed for a second. "I take it seriously." He sounded like it. "You could have told them who I was, and that might have made them stop what they did to you." He took a deep breath that I felt more than heard. "You tried to protect me."

All I could do was look at him.

"We're going to get out of here," he claimed, sounding for

once exactly how I'd imagined The Defender talking—serious and powerful with just a hint of arrogance. "I promise."

What a promise that was.

I nodded, my chest feeling heavy, my soul too. But I wanted to believe him. I really did. Part of me didn't, but I wanted to. So I nodded again, my head against his chest. That nice, not warm but not cool, yet very comfortable chest. "Thank you."

He grunted.

"Want to know a secret?" I whispered.

I felt his "hmm" more than heard it.

"I used my underwear as toilet paper in the other room and hid it. I hope they throw up when they find it."

Alexander—The Defender's—chest puffed again, and I could tell his chin dropped to look at me.

I smiled, and the last thing I remembered hearing was his slow, slow heartbeat in my ear.

Chapter Fourteen

I sensed my body being moved once or twice in the time that came afterward, and I definitely felt my cheek and head resting on what felt like a leg or something else hard but more comfortable than the floor. Warmish liquid was fed into my mouth in streams, and I was pretty sure I heard a voice coaxing me to swallow each time.

More than once, I felt something that wasn't exactly cool being brushed across my face, but it still felt so nice. Soft, mushy food was slipped into my mouth, that same voice urging me to chew, to swallow again.

I had a weird memory that almost felt like a dream of sitting on what felt like a toilet seat and being told to pee. I was pretty positive I did it too. That was what being delusional must be like.

I was hot. I was cold. Hot, cold, hot, cold. It was a never-ending flip-flop of misery.

But at some point, while my brain was at its fuzziest, hurting so bad I wasn't sure how I could still think, while total darkness enveloped my consciousness, while I felt like I cried and could have sworn I felt a hand wipe my face, all of a sudden, the shitty-ness lessened. The worst of the shivering tapered off, and eventually my brain didn't hurt so bad. And when I finally opened my eyes, weak and still with the remnants of a headache straight from Satan, I was surprised to realize that my side was plastered against a body.

Not just a body, I found. Alexander's chest again. I spotted the flat plane of his stomach first. Then the hint of a muscular arm.

I was on his lap. Not between his thighs, but on *him*.

The side of my face was sealed up against his chest.

He smelled spicy and dark, and for a brief moment, I wondered how bad I had to smell. I hadn't put deodorant on in . . . I didn't even know how long it had been since we'd gotten here. I'd sweated. I hadn't showered. My skin was grimy and oily, and now that I thought about it, my head itched like hell. Then there was everything else wrong with me.

But I was on top of him.

Lifting my head was hard, and speaking was too. Tilting it, I met the smooth skin on his neck and cheeks and pushed the words out, ignoring the dryness and the burn in my throat as I said, "Did I die?"

"No." His head dropped into my view, eyes on me. "Your fever is lower," he said in almost a whisper. "You still sound like the Cookie Monster."

"I know."

Those dark purple eyes narrowed, and I didn't want to imagine what I looked like right then, especially so close. "I've waited long enough," he told me solemnly.

He'd waited long enough? To what? Leave? He was leaving me here *now*?

Before I could say a word, *Alexander* shook his head.

I was never going to get over knowing his real name. Never.

"No," he grumbled almost gently, so different from the way he'd been talking to me before. "I'm not leaving you, Gracie. Stop doing that. If you'd listen—"

"I'm listening," I tried to say.

He scowled. "If you would *listen*, I can explain our plan."

Our plan?

Almost like he could read my mind, he barreled for-ward. "Drink water and eat a nutrition bar. We're leaving after that."

I opened my mouth to tell him I really didn't think I was going to be able to follow, at least not any time this year, but he raised his eyebrows and somehow told me to shush without actually saying it out loud.

"We're going together." His face was oddly even, gaze intense. "I'll carry you."

He would? I gulped, and somehow his scowl got worse.

"Why are you doing that?"

"Doing what?" I could barely get out.

Those purple eyes zeroed in, and I didn't even realize my bot-tom lip had started trembling, like I was getting ready to cry.

Oh. "Because."

"No 'because'. *No.*" A grumble built in his throat that I felt along my head. "Don't do it."

I turned my cheek into his shoulder, like I had a right to. Like I wasn't being a complete inconvenience and this shit wasn't tot-ally my fault. It was needy and unnecessary, but he was being *so nice*—in his own way—and it'd been a long, long time since I'd been held.

If I hadn't used up my one tear already, I would have cried.

What might have been a few minutes later, a big hand nudged at my knee. "Get up, eat your bar, drink water, and use the bath-room," he said above my head. "We need to go."

We need to go.

Because he hadn't left me even though he easily could have.

I wouldn't forget this. I would never forget this. I took in the crabby man's jaw and swore to myself right then that I owed him my life. That I would stand by him for the rest of mine in any way I could.

Slowly, I rolled off his thighs, accidentally balancing myself on one of them, noticing just how hard it was. I counted to three, then tucked my feet under me and tried to get up.

My thighs said no.

Taking a deep breath, I planted my feet and tried again.

A push on my butt had me standing up straight.

My legs shook, everything hurt, and suddenly the urge to pee was a punch to my stomach that had me waddling straight for the toilet, ignoring every urge in my body that had me wanting to be shy about going in front of him now that he was awake. But what the hell did I have to be embarrassed about? He'd already seen everything, hadn't he? And that's why I dropped my pants and took the absolute longest pee of my life.

And I was in the middle of releasing half my bodyweight in fluid when a huff had me lifting my gaze to the man still up against the wall. He was focused on the ceiling.

Was he smirking?

"What?" I asked as loudly as I could, in basically still a whisper.

Alexander started shaking his head slowly, looking . . . amazed? "How do you still have anything left in you?"

I was still going. I tried to smile. "At least my organs aren't failing."

A solid five seconds more had my body continuing to release at least another half-gallon of pee before it was finally over.

With a sigh, I winced at the lack of toilet paper and waited before pulling up my sleep pants.

With any luck, we'd be out of here soon, and I'd have access to a shower and toilet paper. Real food and—

"Would you hurry up?" the impatient voice across the room asked.

I guess some things hadn't changed.

I was weak, and we both knew it.

But I'd done the best I could and eaten a nutrition bar slowly and drank as much water as possible despite my wrecked throat.

I could tell he was antsy to get out of there, and I was too. He knew things I didn't and didn't feel up to asking about.

The truth was, I was nervous. Or more like practically scared shitless. But I hoped like hell everything went smoothly. It was some kind of miracle that those people hadn't come back, and I knew it. Despite everything else wrong, my stomachache hadn't started up again, but I couldn't trust that to be enough of a warning sign that something bad was about to happen.

If I had ever needed to keep my shit together, it was now, and I would put one foot in front of the next for a thousand miles if I had to.

And that was how I struggled to my feet too when he finally stood and gave me a serious nod. The man who had joked with me about stinky breath and not talking because of his bad mood was gone. It was time to fucking go.

Gathering all my will, I followed him stiffly to the big, metal door.

He turned to me, dropping his voice. "Wait here. Let me deal with the guards, and I'll come back."

I blinked, my chest going instantly tighter than it already was. "Can I come with you?"

He started to shake his head before his gaze swept over my face, maybe sensing my fucking panic at the idea of him leaving me behind. "It's safer for you to stay," he explained slowly.

I understood, but I really, really didn't want to get left. "I'll stay out of the way. Promise."

Alexander, The Defender, hesitated, really not looking all that happy about it, but after a second, he nodded reluctantly. "Let me see your wrist. I don't know what these will do, but I don't want to risk it."

I held it out to him. He took it carefully, and in the blink of an eye, I watched his fingers curl a millimeter closer around the band on my wrist. It cracked into three pieces and fell to the floor, and in the time it took me to blink again, he'd ripped the ones on his wrists off and threw them beside mine. Only then did he place his hand in the corner where the door met the frame, and he pushed. The door popped open like it was nothing.

Like taking candy from an ant. Not even a baby, an ant.

Then he reached over, wrapped his fingers around my forearm, and started pulling me behind him.

If he felt the way I started shaking at the thought of being left, he didn't react.

The hallway was exactly the way I remembered it. Long and straight, reminding me of a storage facility except for the normal-sized doors instead of the big, garage-style ones. My brain had been too busy panicking before, and I hadn't paid enough attention.

And that's when I thought about something.

"Psst?"

He turned to look over his shoulder, giving me a hard glare as he let go of my arm to press his index finger to his lips.

I mouthed, *Is there anyone else here?*

No, he mouthed back instantly.

That was a relief. If I didn't have him, I would have wanted someone to think of me. To save me.

I was so lucky he was here. This whole situation was so fucked, but it could have been a million times worse, and I was grateful, so damn grateful, even though none of this should have happened.

And it must have been the emotion, or the remnants of being sick, that made me reach out and grab the first thing I could— his pinkie finger. I gave it a light squeeze, half expecting him to shake me off. To ask me if my hand had gotten lost.

He didn't.

All he did was turn and lead us forward. He didn't make a single peep even on those big, bare feet. I hadn't noticed or processed until now that he didn't have shoes.

We moved, going in the same direction they had taken me. Suddenly, he stopped, and I barely managed not to bump into him. The Defender glanced at me over his shoulder and put his index finger against his mouth again.

I nodded.

A lot more gently than I would have expected, he slipped out of my hold, set his hands on my shoulders, and moved me to the side, halfway between two doors. He gestured for me to stay where I was, and I nodded again. *Cover your ears and don't move*, he mouthed.

I gave him a thumbs-up, wondering what the hell was about to happen, then put my palms over my ears.

He pressed those same big hands against what seemed like a heavy door and pushed it.

I was too far off to the side to see what was in there, who was in there, but one second he was there, and in the next he was inside.

A loud crack made me flinch a moment before the wall by my shoulder shook. There was a thud and an even louder crack that had me jerking in place. He was fine. He had to be fine. Maybe a minute later, the door opened and Alex came out, a backpack over his shoulder. I dropped my hands.

"Are you okay?" I asked him, my eyes landing on the hole in the hoodie by his shoulder. A hole that hadn't been there before he'd gone in.

Now I knew what that crack had been about.

He didn't even glance at what should have been a gunshot wound . . . if his body couldn't repel bullets. "Fine."

What in the hell had happened in there? I wondered before

deciding it didn't fucking matter. Not when he held his hand out, a small white bottle in his palm. "Take two."

I read the label. Generic painkillers. He'd gotten me painkillers.

I grabbed them and shook two out, swallowing them dry with a wince. Alexander watched me slip the bottle into my pocket before waving me to follow him again.

I did, turning down a hall I hadn't seen before, then another. He'd said there were only two guards, but was that really it? Had both of them been in that other room? It was so quiet; I kept my eye on the walls, looking for cameras. Maybe some trapdoors or booby traps.

But there weren't any. I guess everything could be hacked into, including security footage. Maybe that's why they didn't have any security?

The hallway abruptly ended at another heavy-looking door. Alexander did the same thing, placing his hand at the intersection where it met the frame and slowly pushed it. There was a sound right before it popped, and a sliver of weak light came in through the crack.

I tapped him on the shoulder. "Are you going to blow it up?"

Those purple eyes flicked toward me. "Blow what up?"

I tipped my head to the side. "The building," I whispered.

His blink was so slow. "We don't . . . do that."

Oh. Duh.

He gave me another look out of the corner of his eye as he held out the backpack he'd taken from the office. "Get on my back. I bought us time, but we need to run," he said, already moving on to the next step.

I hesitated as I slid my arms through the straps, holding back a groan at the weight and the feel against me once it was on. Running was what I'd been training for, for years. What I'd

expected, but . . . there was no way. Not right now. Not any time
this decade from the way my lungs were acting.

I was out of breath just walking, and this damn backpack felt
like it was loaded up with bricks instead of whatever was inside
of it. Fuck. "Are you sure your back is okay?" I asked him, ready
to . . . ready to tell him to leave me behind. That I'd figure it out.
He had already done more than enough.

But his tense look turned into a dirty one.

Okay then.

"Get on my back," Alexander ordered, his tone almost urgent.

I don't know about this, but at the same time, my gut said this
was our best shot. As long as he was okay, which he claimed to
be, we could get so much farther away. We could hobble together,
I guess, if he ended up hurting.

He gave me his back and I jumped, at least I tried to jump
considering how weak I was. It was more like a bunny hop. Fortunately, those big hands caught me by the backs of my thighs
and hoisted me high along his spine. Wrapping my arms around
his neck, I squeezed my thighs around his ribs—or at least I
tried to, they were so weak—and just barely heard him say over
his shoulder, "If you fall off, I'm not stopping."

This mother . . .

All those supple, hard muscles bunched under my legs, arms,
and chest. He threw the door open just as I did the sign of the
cross and put my arm back around him.

Where the hell were we? I blinked, taking in the dark gray
sky. *Those clouds don't look good*, I thought as he walked toward
two SUVS parked right beside the dark gray building. I stayed
quiet as he went to the first one and lifted the hood—it popped
as he did it—and he reached inside and . . .

Something crushed in his hand like a fucking eggshell.

Then he moved to the next car, lifted its hood with another

ominous pop, and grabbed something, and I watched it literally break into pieces and dust in that strong hand.

A big fucking crack of thunder exploded somewhere in the distance.

It was one thing to see his strength on television, but it was a totally different thing to watch him crumble metal in his hand like it was paper.

It's incredible, I thought, as Alexander, the man known as The Defender, broke into a run, taking us away from there.

Turning my head, I finally let myself focus in on the landscape. There was so much *rock* everywhere. It was a sea of orange and brown formations, of rocks, sparse bushes, and trees. So much desert-like landscape, I noticed as my breasts, ribs, and stomach constantly bounced against the muscular back I was clinging to like a spider monkey.

Where the hell were we? Arizona? Utah? Did it matter? We were in the middle of nowhere, and from the way the skies were looking and the air was smelling, it was going to start pouring soon.

I didn't give *a fuck*. We were leaving, *alive*, and I had all my toes. I hugged him even tighter.

He was fast, but not as fast as I'd seen The Primordial or even The Centurion move; they weren't even blurs when they tried. It was like they could teleport. Was he not going full speed because of me? My head started hurting almost instantly from the bouncing, feeling so bruised, and I decided that was probably it.

I didn't make a single sound as those long legs led us away. I didn't dare open my mouth and distract him. What I did do was look behind us a few times to make sure no one was coming.

The coast seemed clear.

Thunder crackled again in the distance, contradicting that thought.

Please, please, please, I begged in my head, squeezing my eyes closed. *Let us get somewhere safe and far away from these fuckers.*

Sometime later, too many hours later, with my thighs weak from clenching around his hips, my arms exhausted from pretty much choking him out, my brain and sinuses on fire, and soaked to the fucking bone, my superhuman transportation finally started to slow down.

The hands that had been clutching my legs for so long widened and moved, letting me slide down his back. My thighs shook as I got my legs under me, and it took me way too long to stand up straight. He wandered off, hands going to his waist.

Maybe someone wasn't feeling as great as he'd thought.

Then again, I had no clue how far we'd traveled. Even if I'd been healthy, my limit would have been five miles. With adrenaline pumping through me, I might have been able to do a little more. Who was I to talk shit?

I waddled toward one of the same kinds of thousands of trees he'd run by after we'd finished crossing through the craggy landscape, and I clung to the trunk, trying to steady my breathing like I had actually done something. *Oh, I felt like shit.* Breathing through my nose was a nope; breathing through my mouth was a nope. My lungs were struggling. My ribs hurt.

More than once, I'd wanted to cry and tell him to leave me.

But neither one of us had said a word in the hours we'd traveled. Not a single complaint had been made, and I intended to keep it that way. I wasn't the one who had run like our lives had depended on it . . . because they had. At least mine had.

At first, I think we were both too focused on getting away from the building as fast as we could. My nausea had gotten worse with each uneven, bumpy step, and eventually he'd slowed down a little. Still going faster than I could ever run but not at the speed he might have gone if I'd been feeling better. Or if he'd been feeling better.

And then the rain had started.

Huge, cold drops had hit us with a vengeance, and at some point, I'd had to close my eyes. For one second, my heart started to beat faster, a knot just beginning to form in my throat at the water hitting my face, but I squashed it down. The fear, I mean. The panic. It was only rain. And maybe it was the feel of his body pressed up against mine, that helped remind me I wasn't alone. That I wasn't back in that damn room. Just maybe, the smell of the rain grounded my thoughts too.

Fortunately, he could see just fine because he went through it effortlessly, or at least he made it seem that way. Lightning had streaked across the sky, and the thunder had been so profound it made me flinch. But on the few occasions I'd cracked my eyes open, I'd seen that there wasn't anywhere safe for us to stop. Not with the possibility of flash floods in these super-dry areas.

So we'd kept going. And going. Through the rain stopping. Through some hail. Through it starting over again and vice versa. Until now.

"There's water here," Alex spoke up, straightening and casting a long look around the damp wooded field. Orange-and-tan-colored mud was splashed all the way up to nearly his waist, the sweatpants clinging to his thighs like a second skin. Even the hoodie, with me having been a human shield, was totally wet. His hair was plastered to that perfectly shaped head.

I didn't want to know what I looked like. I was just as wet, if not more, than he was. There were scratches all over my arms from the branches we'd gone through. The skin on my legs stung too from the same. My sleep pants were heavy with water, and I had to retie them to keep them from slipping off my hips.

I was so thirsty.

Nodding at him even though I didn't think he was even

looking at me, I limped in the direction of where I was pretty sure the sound of water was coming from. When Alexander didn't tell me I was going the wrong way, I kept going, finding the stream close by on a downward slope. The ground was mushy with wet needles, and another round of thunder echoed through the forest just as my head swam.

Nausea rode me like a professional cowboy, but I wasn't going to let it win, not after this many hours.

I hadn't wussed out yet, and I wasn't going to start now.

With a sigh, like it weighed a ton, I dropped the backpack in an area that looked slightly less wet than everywhere else. Remembering this thing I'd read before about surviving around water when you weren't sure whether it was good to drink or not, I carved out a shallow pool off to the side of the bank and waited for the rocks to purify it. If I was going to get diarrhea, I was going to get diarrhea. It would be better than being dehydrated, which I was pretty sure I was on the brink of.

I drank until my stomach hurt, and when I was done, I rolled over onto my back. Stretching my legs, I spread my arms too and felt my spine slowly curve into the cool, damp ground under me. The worst of my fever might have been over, but parts of it were still hanging around. I shivered, closed my eyes, and sighed.

"We have to keep moving," Alexander said, walking so quietly I could barely hear him moving. "It's going to rain again soon."

"Are you okay?" I asked him, even though my vocal cords felt like they were swollen to twice the size they should have been.

He kept coming, his steps long and steady, and I rolled my head to the side to find him. His gaze flicked to mine briefly before he came to a stop a few feet to my right, crouched, and quickly scooped water into those big hands, not worrying about bacteria or parasites from the looks of it. "I'm fine," he said after taking a few sips.

I had to swallow a few times before I could get out, "Do you . . . want me to run for a little while?" It hurt me to offer it, but I had to. He'd already taken care of me and gotten us this far, and I couldn't just force him to do it all, even though I wanted to.

I had my eyes squeezed closed when he said, "No. What I want is for you to catch your fucking breath. You'll just be slowing us down. Drink more."

Oh, thank you, thank you. I took my time doing what he said, drinking more and taking some deep breaths that felt like a knife in the back. "Thank you for carrying me."

He grunted, still taking his time to drink too.

"Are your feet okay?"

"Fine," he answered dismissively. "My skin can take it."

Of course it could, he was fire and bulletproof.

"Do you know where we are?" I asked him a couple sips later. I hadn't paid enough attention with my eyes being closed so much thanks to the rain, but I'd taken in some of the trees we'd reached. They were pines, but I didn't know more than that, at least not enough to tell me where we were because of what was native in these areas.

We could have been in Kentucky, Montana, or Colorado.

Shit, we could have been in New Hampshire if we hadn't just been in the desert not too long ago.

"I have an idea," he answered a moment later, finally sitting on his butt. His elbows went to his knees, and he cupped one wrist with his other hand. His eyes slid over, and I didn't miss the way those eyebrows hiked up just a little bit. His nostrils flared. "You look like shit."

I gave him a long fucking look. He'd just finished taking care of me. Carrying me on his back for hours upon hours. But all the gratitude in the world wasn't enough to stop me from muttering, dry as hell, "Oh, thanks." *Fucker.*

I tried not to roll my eyes as I focused on the stuff that

mattered. I'd spent a lot of time thinking about things so that I would have something to focus on that wasn't throwing up. "*Anyway*, not to be the bearer of bad news, but we don't have money, a phone, or even ID, and we need to find somewhere to rest."

At least I did. I didn't know how much more I could handle. I really had thought about asking him to leave me, but just the idea of being by myself in the middle of nowhere with only basic survival skills, considering we had *nothing* to help us, had made me shut the hell up instantly.

I didn't want him to leave me. Not yet.

So in truth, as much as I needed a break, I wouldn't admit it. Who knew how far we were from a town, or at least a house. I would take a tree house. A cave. Anything.

And that was when the reality of our situation really hit me.

Not only was my home gone, but so was my wallet. I had no money. No computer. No key to my safe deposit box.

I was missing so much work. Everyone was going to fire me, if they hadn't already. What day was it? How long had it been?

I fisted my hand as my eyes filled with tears *again*. I dug my fingernails into my palm just enough to cause pain, to ground me. Another choke hiccupped in my chest, and I dug my nails in just a little harder.

What the hell am I going to do when this is over?

I had no one.

No place to live and be safe in.

No money. No identification.

I might have ruined a career that I'd carefully crafted and enjoyed.

How the hell would I even start going about getting anything back in the first place?

I had nothing.

Just about nothing.

I had this being who was suddenly stuck with me but not by choice. Eventually he was going to dump me somewhere, and I wouldn't be ungrateful because he'd already done so much. But . . .

"Stop it, Gracie," the stern, demanding voice called out.

Another sound cramped in my throat, and I pinched my nose to keep it inside.

"Stop it," he repeated.

I was trying.

"Stop," The Defender insisted.

Tears wet my fingers, and I ground down hard on my molars, keeping the breath in my lungs so that I wouldn't make a peep. It was the same way I'd cried in that damn cell when he'd first told me about the trailer being burned down. The tiniest little sound slipped through my hand though.

"Stop."

I sucked in a breath, pinched my nose, and tried to remind myself . . . tried to remind myself that this wasn't the end of the world.

Things were just things.

Maybe I could explain and beg for forgiveness so that my students would come back.

I was free, and I had no reason to think I wouldn't have a long life ahead of me. I could hide again. So what if I was technically broke and had no identity?

Home could be anywhere.

The sob exploded out of my mouth.

I was full of shit.

If they had found me once, they could find me again. My cover was blown. What the hell was I going to *do*? This wasn't the eighties or the nineties. You couldn't even rent a hotel room without a credit card.

I cried.

I cried and I cried, silently at least, and my chest shook as even more tears came out of my eyes and out of my soul.

I had nothing, and they had almost killed me in there. I'd thought I was going to die. I really had.

My brain hurt. My nose hurt. My throat felt like it was never going to be the same again because of what they had done. I was so fucking mad at being so damn helpless, my brain instantly hurt even more.

Deep in the back of my head, I heard a growl, and at some point, there was a poke at my side.

Then I heard a super-serious voice ask, "Why are you crying?"

I didn't answer. I was too busy pressing my hands to my eyes harder.

"Why are you crying?" he asked again, that time in an almost gentle voice that was hard to ignore.

"I'm s-sc . . . I'm . . . *scared*." Oh shit, my voice broke. In half. In pieces. I was *blubbering*.

Another poke came at my side, followed by a "Gracie" that was so deep I couldn't ignore it. "There's nothing for you to be afraid of."

He was right. I knew he was fucking right, but . . . but . . .

No. No, I didn't know that. I was full of shit.

There was another poke to my shoulder, and I wept even more. Wept for the last few weeks. For the last few months, for the last few years since my grandma had died. For the last six since my grandpa had passed away.

I was so alone—so goddamn alone—and so overwhelmed, and I wasn't sure how the hell I was going to get through this next chapter in my life. I would. I had to, I knew that, but *how?*

After what might have been a few minutes, but might have been longer than that, there was another poke so hard that I had to lift my head because *oww.*

Long fingers curled under my chin, and the next thing I knew, he was tilting my face up and Alexander was dipping his. Right there, he was right there. "No one is close by. They won't find us."

"Okay," I said as I cried even harder and it *hurt*. It fucking *hurt*.

"What are you worried about?" he asked after a long moment.

I told him the truth. "Everything." My bottom lip was trembling. I could feel my chest shaking too if I was going to be honest. But I couldn't summon a lie, even a half-assed one. It felt too big for that. I blubbered out, "I . . . don't . . . have . . . a . . . *home*."

He blinked. "This again?"

Again? I gasped and felt even more tears slip down my cheeks. "It's not a little thing!" I didn't have multiple ones sitting around, dammit. "I don't . . . I don't have *anything*. No money. No ID. No home. No computer. No job. No nothing. I'm really worried I lost my voice mails. *They know my name. They found me.* I got waterboarded. I'm sweating it just thinking about taking a shower. What if they find us? I don't want to die. I don't want to die *alone*. Not like this. I've got no loved ones, no one who gives a shit, no one to—"

Alexander tilted my head just a little bit farther back, and his face got that much closer. So close I could feel the heat of his forehead just shy of mine. "Stop." His bossy voice was back.

"No." I shook my head and then instantly froze. "Why? Am I being too loud? Is someone *coming*?"

His breath brushed against my mouth. "No one's coming."

My relief was out of this world, at least until he opened his mouth next.

"You're right about some of that." He paused. "You are fucked."

No shit.

I just about snorted at the oversimplification before really taking in the sober expression on his face.

Then he kept talking. "Part of what happened is my fault." Something moved across his features that might have been guilt. Maybe? "The life you knew is over, you're right."

I knew it was bad when he was telling me it was bad.

I whimpered. Dammit, he didn't have to rub it in. I bent over and slapped my hands against my knees as my head swam, and I suddenly felt dizzy all over again. Nauseous. Oh boy, I was going to fucking throw up.

"Not again. Calm down," he told me in his bossy-britches tone.

But I didn't care. I was going to have a panic attack.

No, scratch that, it was going to be a straight-up shit attack.

I gagged.

He cursed. "*Stop.*"

Was this what a panic attack felt like? An imaginary elephant sitting on your chest? "I can't breathe. I can't breathe." I was human. I should be proud of myself for keeping it together in the first place. Shouldn't I? Shouldn't I?

"You're so dramatic," he had the nerve to say because *his* life wasn't over. Everything he had tried to keep a secret for, oh, his entire life, hadn't just gone into the shitter.

Mine had.

Literally every precaution I'd ever taken, every sacrifice my grandparents had ever made, had gotten blown up with C4 and then lit on fire all over again.

It was all for nothing now.

I didn't have the money, resources, and sure as fuck didn't have the *power* to protect myself.

My whole body started shaking.

The man cursed again, dropping an f-bomb, then another, and a third, and out of the corner of my eye, I saw he dropped to a squat beside me and sighed just as he moved his head to meet my eyes. "Calm down," he ordered in what was definitely his superhero voice.

I didn't give a fuck. I shook my head. "No!"

He groaned. "*Please.*"

That got me to peek at him.

"You haven't been thinking things through, but I have."

He had?

"Take a damn breath and listen." He almost sounded patient.

But my body shook again anyway.

"*Gracie,*" he enunciated my name in a way I'd never heard before.

I tried, opening my other eye to look at him. His face was smooth, and considering how the day had gone, he didn't look tired. He still looked pretty damn good despite the clay-like mud all over him.

But his features were serious, not grouchy, not irritated, just absolutely solemn.

He looked like he was about to give me bad news, and I braced myself.

"My people . . . we take life debts seriously." He didn't exactly sound happy about that. "That's what I owe you. My life. Time and time again."

I sniffled, wanting to tell him that he didn't, that that wasn't true, but . . .

"Your life is over—stop it and *listen*. You might be the most hardheaded person I've ever met," he grumbled, peering at me with those purple eyes. "The life you knew *is* over. Any alias you've lived under or were planning on living in the future, isn't an option anymore. They went through your whole house. They opened and looked at everything. You're good at erasing your browser history and keeping your tracks covered, but they took your laptop. You have to expect them to find something. They are going to go to the ends of the earth to find you."

I started panting again, ignoring my back and rib pain. "If you're trying to help, you're doing a really shitty job at it."

That got me a glare. "I'm not done talking," he went on. "You need to understand what's going to happen. They are going to look for you. Even if their operation were to shut down tomorrow, it wouldn't matter because someone else will come looking for you and the money, and you'll never be safe."

I choked.

He whacked me in the back almost too softly. "I'm not done. What I was saying is that when we get through this, when we get to where we need to go—" The lean muscles in his cheeks flexed, and his voice went slightly tight, it wasn't anger but maybe resignation? "—you can live with me until we can figure out a safe, long-term solution."

I hadn't heard him correctly, had I?

My cheeks started to tingle, and more tears bubbled up in my eyes as I stared at him. Mostly in disbelief. Maybe a little bit in shock.

"You can interrupt me now," The Defender said.

"But . . . you don't even like me." There, I'd said it. It wasn't like that was anything new.

There was literally no hesitation in his response. The son of a bitch even shrugged a little bit. "You're all right."

I was all right.

Me. Gracie Castro was all right.

Half the shit that came out of his mouth was rude, and he had the patience of a toddler, but *I was all right*? "I don't understand why you're doing this." Was this the dumbest thing to argue over? Yeah, it was, but it was the truth.

Then he gave me more of that personality, that reminder of

who he genuinely seemed to be. A grumpy man who saved people. "I told you already. I owe you."

I held back tears, trying to pick my words carefully, even though most of them escaped me.

I had to think about this rationally.

He was right. I understood that, even if I didn't want to. Even if it felt like the end of the world, which it kind of was.

The end of my world at least.

But it was what it was, and I couldn't rewind time.

He was doing this out of pity. No shit he was. Neither one of us had known what was going to happen on the day he'd landed in my yard. I'd done what I had to do. I'd known it was going to be complicated.

The idea of relying on someone went against every instinct in my body.

But I *was*, and I didn't have anyone who could actually help, and the idea of having something to fall back on, somewhere to actually *go* . . .

To not be alone, at least for a little while longer . . .

Especially in this shit storm of a situation.

"Maybe you could make it a month, maybe a year, but eventually, they would find you," he said quietly, stressing his point.

It was a good point.

"I know," I muttered, still trying to convince my body that I didn't have another choice.

Because I didn't.

Of all the things my grandparents had taught me, of all the things they had asked of me, there was one that rang the brightest and the truest: survive. It was all they'd ever wanted. I was the one who had wanted more than just that.

But all I'd wanted was something. A little something more than I already had. Which was a whole lot of not enough.

I needed to survive any way I could.

This would be the same as lying to protect other people. As keeping to myself. As wearing my wig and carrying pepper spray and religiously clearing my browser and cookies every single day.

Forcing myself to stand up straight, I rubbed my face with my palms and tried to calm down. Dropping them, I lifted my head and wiped under my eyes before nodding as another roll of thunder pierced the forest we were in, and I shivered. We were so vulnerable here.

I was going to be vulnerable everywhere now though, wasn't I? That was the whole point. Everything had changed, and I either rolled with it or I let it roll over me.

If my life was a comic book, if I was Mistress Mayhem, I'd do what I had to do. She was my favorite antihero. She did what she had to do, even if she bitched and complained the whole time.

I fisted my hands. "You're right," I told him weakly. "Neither one of us chose this, and I don't have any other options. And I'm sorry I don't. Other than just being able to protect me if someone came to kidnap me and giving me some ideas for how to figure out some other way to hide, I don't know how else you'd be able to help, but . . . I'll take it until I can figure something out." I shrugged my shoulders as much as my poor body would let me. "I don't have anyone else I can ask to help me." My voice wobbled. "I don't have anyone period."

It felt so wrong. Not in my stomach but in my head. I wasn't supposed to get other people involved, but I was never supposed to be in this position, so where did that leave me?

Having to rely on someone with no allegiance to me other than a debt he really didn't owe me, if he put his mind to it.

On the flipside, he had no reason to believe I would be true to him either, especially with the amount of information he'd willingly shared with me, which I was still suspicious about.

Then again, I was suspicious about everything with him. Why he had suddenly started to talk to me. Why he had gone out of his way to hold me while I'd been sick when he could have easily just let me lay there, miserable.

But my paranoia hadn't gotten me anywhere in life. Not really. And if he could go out on a limb and tell me things about himself, then I could do the same.

For the first time in my life.

Watching him carefully, I slowly lifted my hand and held it out toward him. "Friends?" I offered slowly, expecting him to laugh or scoff or something.

Those incredible eyes moved from my hand to my face and back.

"We were temporary friends before. I want you to know that I don't have any plans to backstab you or sell you out. Friends don't do that kind of shit to each other, right?" I asked him, holding my palm out mostly steady. "You saved my life, and I want you to know that whatever I can ever do for you, I will. You can use me as a human shield, really, even if I'm not dead. But I hope you won't. Because that would kill me."

His face was remarkably calm.

Then those long, almost cool fingers and that big, smooth palm met mine. Alexander shook my hand as his eyebrows rose . . . and was that amusement on his face? A little bit of it? Then he let go just as fast. "That was easy," he said in a funny voice. "Good."

I lowered my arm, rubbing my fingers against my palm. I'd felt a light zap on my skin from the contact. "You're ruining it by being smug."

He lifted a shoulder, and his amusement disappeared. "You'll stay with me. You agree?"

I nodded. I didn't have a choice. Not a smart one at least. "I agree," I said, ignoring the slight panic.

Alexander dipped his own chin, and those damn purple eyes burned over my face one more time, making me wonder again just how rough of shape I had to be in. His voice was low, serious. "You'll be under my protection for the rest of your life. You understand?"

The rest of my life? "You mean until we figure things out?"

He shook his head, gaze intent. "They're never going to stop looking for you, Gracie." He nailed that coffin shut. "You laid on top of me to save me, even though you knew nothing they could have done would hurt me. For. The. Rest. Of. Your. Life."

The urge to cry was so strong, it took everything in me to keep it together. "Okay. I promise not to take advantage. I'll try and get something figured out as soon as I can," I swore, trying to hold on to my sanity as thunder cracked overhead, sounding closer.

I had no choice. I was out of them. Again.

But—I swallowed hard—I was alive, and I'd agreed to this. That was my choice.

I wasn't alone either.

I had this butthole. My new friend.

Life was never going to be the same again, and I just had to deal with it.

I wasn't sure how any of this had happened. How he'd landed in my yard of all places. How exactly the cartel had found me after I'd been so, so careful. But all of this had occurred, and there was nothing I could do about it.

Nothing but figure out everything as it came.

And it just so happened my only ally was a member of the Trinity. A man who could crush part of an engine into dust effortlessly. Who had been shot in the shoulder and only gotten a hole in the hoodie he had on. A being who could run barefoot over rough terrain and pine needles for days without a single scratch or complaint.

It could have been a hell of a lot worse to have someone else feel like they owed me.

It definitely could have.

I didn't want to live with him. I didn't want to take advantage. I definitely didn't want to owe anybody.

But there were a hell of a lot of things I'd had a lot of time to think about while I'd been freezing my ass off, thinking my life was over. There was so much I wanted. And all of it outweighed what I didn't.

I could be reasonable.

He already knew too much.

It didn't make sense to be stubborn in this situation.

So . . .

One step at a time. For now. Even if it was scary.

But that was fucking life, wasn't it?

Chapter Fifteen

"Fuck," Alexander cursed as his steps slowed, and he lifted his chin up toward the sky.

I'd been watching it for the last . . . however long we'd been going. It had been hours since we'd last stopped. The sun had stayed sleepy and hidden the whole day, the clouds being a bunch of dramatic pains in the asses that had only gotten darker and darker. Thunder had been crackling for hours nonstop, like it was following us.

He was probably thinking the same thing I was—the rain was coming, and it was coming soon.

Again.

Fortunately and unfortunately, we hadn't found anything other than some game trails. We were nowhere near shit. I hadn't seen a house or even some kind of hunting cabin, and I doubted he had either with how focused he'd been on keeping his run steady.

I'd swallowed more vomit and thick saliva than I'd want to admit.

"We need to take shelter," he said, coming to a complete stop. His hands went to his hips and grazed my thighs for a second before he dropped them. An eye peeked at me from over his shoulder. "It smells like it might hail."

The Defender raised his gaze again at the same time thunder

and lightning shook the trees and lit up the sky directly over our heads.

I jumped, or more like I squeezed the shit out of him. One of us could handle getting struck by lightning, and that person wasn't me. I wasn't the only one who had the same thought when he glanced over his shoulder again.

I smiled at him. Weak. Tired but relieved enough that it almost made up for it.

He focused forward again and started to move, glancing up over and over again. Then his head swung from side to side, from tree to tree, like he was trying to find something. Not too long later, three more way-too-close rolls of thunder and streaks of lightning above our heads, he suddenly stopped under a big tree with wide, spanning branches. One hand brushed my calf, and I took that as my sign to jump down—or slide down more like it, wincing in fucking soreness as my legs wobbled.

Honestly, I had a newfound respect for cowboys. Alex was no damn horse, but I still had no idea how the hell those men and women could ride all day. They were my new heroes.

I swallowed hard, trying my best to ignore my headache and everything else wrong with me—which was fucking everything—as he gestured me to follow. Eventually we stopped at a decent-sized creek as the trees swayed and the faint tinkling of raindrops hitting the branches and the leaves warned us it had started again. I almost fell on my face as I kneeled. I wanted to massage my ass, but I didn't want him to know it was bothering me. His shoulders might ache from holding me.

We both drank quietly, and I was beyond worrying about dysentery or whatever other fucked-up illness I could get from contaminated water. Pulling the bottle of pills he'd given me earlier out of my pocket, I shook two out, then swallowed them with a handful of water.

As I wiped at my mouth with my shoulder, a shiver raced from my shoulders down to my thighs.

A big hand gripped my elbow, and I looked up as Alexander helped me stand. "Come on before it starts pouring."

He let go, but side by side we so, so slowly walked back in the direction we'd come, a few drops making it through the canopy and onto us.

"Under here," he said, ducking beneath the same tree I was pretty sure we'd stopped at. It was a huge one.

At the base, he kneeled and rolled onto his butt, pushing back against the trunk before stretching his legs straight out in front of him.

Don't mind if I do. This might as well be the Ritz. Taking the backpack off, I crawled after him under there, doing the same, but beside him, so close his arm pressed against mine. The ground was hard, but not as bad thanks to the bed of pine needles. I sighed just as more thunder and lightning struck even closer, heavy rain making the branches ring right before drops hit the ground around us. A few landed on my arms and legs, but he must have chosen a good tree because what fell on us was only a fraction of what was falling around.

"How are you feeling?" he asked out of the blue after a long while, his voice steady like the countless hours of running with a full-sized human hadn't worn him down.

Here I was exhausted, and I hadn't done shit. "I'm feeling much better," I croaked, not just full of shit but bursting with it.

And I knew he knew that when he glanced over. "You know I can tell when you're lying?"

I sniffled. "Yeah, I figured. Do you know where we are?" I changed the subject, a lump in my throat.

He leaned his head back against the trunk, his jaw a hard line in the darkness as he faced forward, out to the forest. "I have an idea, but my senses aren't fully back yet. I can't get my bearings like usual," he said just loud enough for me to hear him. "I thought we would've come across a town or a house by now. They drove us farther out than I had thought, and we're going slow."

Slow? My brain didn't think so. Neither did my nausea, but I appreciated his sacrifice.

The wind picked up even more, the sound of the rain getting harder with more drops sneaking their way through our natural canopy. Drawing my legs up closer to my body, I held back a groan at my exhausted hip flexors as I curled my arms around my knees and set my chin on top of them. Part of me wanted to sprawl out, but I was over being rained on if I could help it.

"We're going to keep going northeast until we find somewhere to stay," the man beside me said as he crossed his arms over his chest.

"Okay," I agreed, even though I had no idea what direction northeast was or why we would be going there. Reaching down, I wrung some water out of my sleep pants before sighing. "Maybe we can steal someone's horse."

His low chuckle was the last thing I expected, and I rolled my head to the side to see him. He wasn't smiling, but he looked . . . I didn't know what he looked like. "You know how to ride a horse?" he asked, like he knew as well as I did that I damn well didn't. "Do you want to steal people's laundry from a clothesline too?"

I groaned, even though it hurt, then laughed just a little bit. "I didn't realize how stupid it was going to sound until after I said it. I used to watch a lot of Westerns with my grandpa."

His snicker made me peek at him.

Lifting my hand, I put my cool palm on my forehead. "I was thinking . . . why didn't we take one of their cars?"

"Why didn't I think of that?" Sarcasm dripped from the son of a bitch's voice.

I blinked, turning my head slowly in his direction.

"They were new cars. The last thing we need is to risk getting tracked. I wasn't willing to chance it."

Ohhhh. That made sense.

Out of the corner of my eye, I could tell he glanced at me.

A strong breeze blew through, and I shivered again, tucking my arms between my legs even though I'd already learned that wouldn't really keep me warm. "Since I'm on a roll with the dumb questions, I was wondering if maybe there was some kind of call or noise or something you could make to get The Primordial or The Centurion's attention."

His laugh was louder than the rain. "What do you think we are? Orcas?"

I snorted again, instantly regretting it. "I figured it was a long shot, but I had to ask," I told him with a little laugh.

Alexander snickered. "No, there's no 'call.'"

A few drops of rain fell through the branches, hitting my arms, and I shivered again.

A nudge had me peeking over at him again. He'd spread his legs a little. His head tipped to the side. Toward him?

Was he gesturing me to . . . ?

I raised my eyebrows.

"I can hear your teeth chattering," he grumbled. "Are you going to come over here or are you planning on getting pneumonia again?"

"I had pneumonia?"

"I can't tell if you're trying me or being genuine."

I smiled, not needing him to tell me twice to get on him.

I sniffled as I turned, ready to crawl onto his lap when his arm slipped around my lower back and he scooped me up and onto him. He'd raised his knees a little as he lowered my butt onto one thigh and hip, my own legs still curled up so that one side was tucked against his stomach. On my back, I felt him reach to the side and lift the backpack over my head before handing it to me.

I peeked up at him and he lifted his chin.

Was he tired?

My fingers were shaky as I undid the zipper and opened it. Inside there was a small first aid kit, three cans of tuna, two things of canned chicken, one can of pears, a box of crackers, and a Snickers. I looked at him again, and I smiled.

He didn't smile back, but he did tip his head toward the bag, telling me to keep going.

He didn't need to tell me twice.

I took out a can of tuna, peeled back the lid, and handed it to him. He took it, and I grabbed another one and did the same, balancing it on my knee, before I opened the box of crackers— which was halfway full—and shook some out onto my leg. I handed him one before taking my own.

Then, we ate. Tuna and crackers. I'd been so stressed out the whole day, I hadn't let myself feel hungry, until now, and it hit me with a vengeance.

I sighed with fucking pure contentment as I scraped the bottom of the can for the juices just as he set his can aside and tucked his arm low around my back, giving it some support.

"Crack open that Snickers," he murmured, his voice gruff, almost tired.

I wasn't the only one still healing. I couldn't forget that.

I tried to whistle, but it made my throat hurt too much so it sounded like a choke instead. I grabbed that Snickers bar, tore part of the wrapper off, and held it out.

But he didn't take it.

Alex—Alexander—leaned forward, took a bite, then gestured for me to take one too. Over his. And I did.

Then I held it up for him and watched as he took another bite.

I wanted to talk to him, to ask him more questions, but my throat was so raw, I stayed quiet instead.

And we sat there, with the wind howling, both of us still wet, rain falling around us, covered in dirt and mud, in the middle of nowhere.

We finished that Snickers bar.

When the hail started to fall, when I was half asleep from exhaustion, Alex raised his other arm and wrapped that one around me too.

I wanted to crawl into a hole, close my eyes, and sleep for a year.

We'd been following the same creek for the last two days, but it had felt a hell of a lot longer than that.

That first night, the unrelenting rain kept us under the tree. I woke up with my head half on Alexander's chest and shoulder and crawled off him enough so I could curl into a ball, setting my head on his thigh, hoping an ant didn't crawl into my mouth. When he shook me awake with the tiniest bit of light creeping through the trees, we drank more water, and then I climbed onto his back. My whole damn body was so stiff, it took everything in me not to flinch. Then we took off again, fast but not so fast that my brain jiggled.

He was a machine. If he was tired, I didn't see it, as those long legs pumped us forward and onward, effortless, unwavering, and incredible. I remembered seeing a show about how some athletes did these intense 100-mile races through the mountains over the course of sixty hours. I had no idea how far we had gone, the two of us, but none of them were carrying a Gracie-sized backpack and running off almost no food.

I didn't just owe him a little; I owed him big time, I'd decided.

And he wasn't the only one who repaid their debts.

More rain sidelined us, and we had to hide under one tree after another when lightning got close. We stopped and took water breaks—and I peed—when it was necessary, which wasn't often enough, but we weren't drinking a ton of water either. That second night, with me back on his lap, he used his *fingernail* to open two cans of chicken that we ate with more crackers. I was pretty sure we both looked longingly at the backpack, hoping a bar of Snickers magically appeared.

On that third night, we shared the last can of tuna, ate the best pears I'd ever had, and shook cracker crumbs into our mouths. Fortunately, it didn't rain, and it wasn't too windy or cold, and I fell asleep with my side pressed up against him. Early in the morning, he patted my thigh to wake me up. Then we left again.

We probably said thirty words to each other every day. My throat hurt so bad, I didn't want to talk, but more than anything, I didn't want to irritate him. Not when I was at his mercy, and I could tell that even though it seemed like his strength and stamina were back, there was still something off about him.

And if he wasn't talking to me because he had other things on his mind, I had no idea.

I was in the middle of thinking about how I was never going to take being healthy for granted when the man I was clinging to suddenly said, "There's a house up ahead. Let's scope it out."

Lifting my head to peek over his shoulder, I saw that sure enough, just like he'd said, there *was* a building settled on a tiny clearing ahead.

A house. Oh, *a house.* I felt like Goldilocks all of a sudden, the trespassing asshole.

But that was going to be me now: the trespassing asshole, and I didn't care. I couldn't. *I was so happy.*

Alex's strides slowed as he approached it, and when we got to a deck around the back, he crouched to let me slide off. We'd nailed that shit down over the last few days. My legs hadn't gotten any steadier, but by now, he didn't even give me a side-look when I had to cling to his forearm so I wouldn't fall on my face.

I wasn't even a little surprised either when he slipped a hand around my elbow and helped me up the porch stairs. He'd done that a lot lately, leading me places. To the creek. To a comfy tree.

He hadn't asked again how I was feeling, but I was pretty positive he knew I felt like absolute shit. I'd wanted to throw up every single moment I was on his back, but I'd sucked it up through sheer will. I would've been damned if I'd complained. He didn't, and I wouldn't either. I had one job, and that was to not make a shitty situation a shittier one.

When we were at the door, he put his hand on the knob and twisted his wrist slowly. Something popped, and a second later, the door opened. All righty, he'd broken the knob like it was nothing. I still hadn't moved past him crushing an engine part and opening a can with his fingernail.

He went in first, flipping the light switch. Dark yellow light bulbs instantly turned on overhead, giving us a good view of a small, single area cabin. There was a leather couch, a fireplace surrounded by dark brown bricks, a table with two chairs, and a kitchen that was more like a kitchenette. There were even two bunk beds built into the wall. It was all clean, and there wasn't anything worse than some dust it looked like, but not even much of it.

I looked over at Alexander, who had already done his own inspection from the ease of his body.

He was fucking filthy, and if I had any fucks left, I would have been scared to see what I looked like. But despite having a layer of dirt and mud covering him, his eyes were bright and clear, and he looked better than he had any right to, considering what we'd been through.

You couldn't have paid me to sniff my armpits or breath.

"I'm never going to take having a roof over my head for granted again," I whispered for the first time since last night when I'd told him "thank you" for handing over the last half can of tuna we'd split evenly.

Even he sighed as he looked around the cabin again.

"Are we . . . staying here tonight?" I asked to be sure.

I'd learned how to speak Alex grunts, and I knew the one he'd let out was a "yes."

I wanted to fucking hug him.

Because the truth was, I didn't think I could handle getting on his back again anytime soon. My groin had gone past sore and around the corner. My thighs and butt were bruised, but not as bad as I would have expected, and I highly doubted I could hold a fork right now.

I realized in that moment, somewhere in the back of my brain, that this stop was more than likely for me.

Or maybe not.

Toeing off my shoes, I rubbed my face with the backs of my hands and tried to decide what was the most important thing to do. And that was taking a shower. There had to be one here. There just had to.

I peeked at the man who had saved me, and figured now was just as good a time as any. Holding back a wince, I trudged toward one of the closed doors and found a small bathroom. I could have cried . . . if I wasn't dehydrated again.

Purposely not looking at the tiny mirror over the sink, I went straight for the stall tucked into the corner. Turning the tap, I almost squealed when water shot out of the head, sputtering from how calcified it had to be, but who gave a shit? It worked! I was never taking running water for granted. Never, ever. From the smell, it had to be on a well, which then made me wonder about the electricity and how I hadn't seen any solar panels, so we couldn't be too far away from civilization. There was a bottle of shampoo and a single bar of dry soap on a rack hanging from the showerhead.

If I didn't need to wash my hair so bad, I might have put off taking one a little longer. I'd been eyeballing the creek every time we stopped, thinking about washing my face at least, but I was already so cold, so wet.

Stripping off my crusty clothes, I waited until the water was warm enough and ignored the almost furious pounding in my chest as I eyed the spray. Carefully, so, so carefully, I made sure not to let it stream over my face. Just my chest and below at first.

My heart was beating so fast.

I cupped water with my trembling hands and scrubbed at my neck. I washed my face by wetting my palms and scrubbing my cheeks and forehead, trying not to hyperventilate. Trying to appreciate having hot fucking water and a safe place for the first time in what felt like a fucking month.

It might have been for all I knew.

A lot quicker than I would have imagined, considering I'd been dreaming about being clean, I soaped up the rest of my body twice then washed my torn, filthy clothes under the spray with the soap too. So much black, brown, and gray swirled around my feet that I washed them again. I was basically panting by the time I got out. The urge to sit down on the floor was strong, but I had a feeling that if I did, I wasn't getting back up anytime soon.

The towels were musky, and my hair was tangled to shit, but I brushed it out with my fingers as I got my breathing under control. Only then did I finally look at myself in the mirror. I had to lean forward to make sure I wasn't imagining it.

My face was a little sunburnt, and there were a few scratches on my temples and cheeks—on my arms and legs too, I'd felt and noticed while I'd been soaping up—but my skin looked nicer than it ever had. I actually didn't look half bad. There weren't even bags under my eyes.

That was . . . weird.

I thought about that as I used a tube of toothpaste that was expired, then borrowed a cracked deodorant I found under the sink. With the towel wrapped under my armpits and my wet clothes in my arms, I opened the door and stood there. We were past me being shy about shit now. Earlier today I'd peed with him standing three feet away from me while he pretended not to see and hear me.

There was nothing but silence in the cabin though.

Stiff as hell, I headed straight for the dresser. I opened the first few drawers and found a pair of flannel pajama pants and a dark brown flannel that looked baggy enough to hide most of my boobs. With my back to the rest of the room, I tugged the pants on under the towel and then buttoned the shirt up.

Eyeing the couch, I had to fight the urge to plop onto it and fall asleep. I was running on fumes, and I needed to focus. Needed to dig up the rest of my energy.

It didn't take me long to drape my wet clothes over different places to dry, and with a grumbling stomach and a headache that was going to need more painkillers soon, I found cans of beans, a couple cans of Spam, and pancake mix that only required water. The mix was expired but only by a couple months. But it could have been a couple years and I would have eaten it. Alex would have done the same. I'd caught him licking the lid for the pears last night.

After gulping down a couple more painkillers, I found a pot. I boiled water and poured it into a pitcher to cool. Then I found some salt and oil and cooked the meat in it before adding the beans. In an old skillet, I made as many pancakes as I could without finishing the box.

I had no clue where Alexander was, but I wasn't about to panic over that shit.

If he'd finally decided to leave me, I couldn't hold it against him. I was too tired to worry about it that much.

I sat down on the tiny couch and ate beans with a slice of Spam, surprised by how good it was. Then I finished off a pancake, adding a little bit of honey I'd found in a glass jar because I remembered reading somewhere that honey lasted forever. And at this point, if something was going to kill me, as long as it tasted good, there were worst ways to go. I'd already gotten lucky to not be crapping my brains out from drinking creek water.

There was a radio that looked to be from the eighties sitting on the side table, and I reached over and fiddled with the knobs, getting a pop before staticky voices filled the air. "... *they're monsters. The government needs to do something about them before it's too late. I don't care what anybody says about those three. They aren't human. Why would they watch out for us? We need to put them down before they put us down!*" the angry voice shouted.

I rolled my eyes as I turned the knob back in the direction it had been, turning that shit off.

I rolled my eyes again as I got up. *What is wrong with people? He's a pain in the ass sometimes, but he isn't a monster*, I thought while I cleaned up, then walked over to the door and cracked it open.

Lying in the clearing of grass and what I was pretty sure were pine needles, a few feet away from the porch, was one of the strongest people on the planet. Arms spread wide, eyes closed, his chest rose and fell slowly and steadily. He was still dressed in those dirty sweatpants and hoodie that were a mix of orange and brown-black mud.

But I'd watched him enough to recognize the depth of his breathing and what it meant.

The fucker wasn't asleep.

Were his lips moving?

Knowing damn well he'd heard me and knew exactly where I was, I went back in to get him a plate. Carefully, so that I wouldn't step on anything pokey, I crept outside. Everything shook while I crouched and set the plate of food beside him.

One eye opened. Both his nostrils flared.

I pushed the plate a little closer as I pretty much plopped onto my butt.

His other eye opened too, right before he knifed up and reached for the plate. Placing it on his lap, he started shoveling the Spam and beans into his mouth, peeking at me once or twice while he pretty much inhaled it. After that, he started in on the pancakes that were half covered in bean and meat juice, carefully cutting a little piece with the edge of his fork and taking a tentative bite.

Those dark eyes flicked toward me as he took a bite and then another, spreading the honey around the top of the three pancakes I'd stacked.

"There are two more if you want them," I offered when he set his fork down and folded them in half, finishing them in three bites.

He got up with a nod in my direction and disappeared into the house.

I tipped my head back, sucked in a small breath of the clean, cool air, and blew out a slow, slow breath just as the door opened. It smelled better now that I knew we weren't going to have to sleep outside. *We'd gotten away.*

We were . . . safe.

Even if they found search dogs to locate us, it would take them twice as long to follow. That reality was the only reason I'd probably been able to sleep.

I had to strain to hear his steps on the deck, then on the grass before he took a seat beside me again. I kept my gaze upward on the little bit of sky visible through the trees. I'd seen so much of it over the last few nights, but somehow it still looked totally different each time. When it seemed like it had been long enough for him to finish eating, I looked over at him, the plate on his lap. A single pancake remained.

He held it out toward me.

I shook my head.

"Eat it," he said in that rich voice I'd barely heard any part of for the last few days.

"I don't want to eat it," I argued, or at least I tried to. It didn't sound all that effective when I was still whispering and my voice was so hoarse.

"You need the calories. Eat it."

I opened my mouth and closed it. "Half and half?" I croaked.

He gave me his look. The annoying one.

"Please?" I compromised. "My stomach is all off. It's pathetic. I know."

His gaze narrowed, but he seemed to think about it for a moment before eventually nodding.

Taking his fork, I ate half and then handed him the plate.

It wasn't until sometime later, when my butt was numb and the temperature started to drop so quickly that I was considering going inside, that he said, "I'm going to spend the night out here."

Really? Even after we'd done the same for the last three nights?

"I've had enough of enclosed spaces for now," he explained, like he knew what I'd been thinking.

Oh. "Is that . . . was that . . . your first time, you know, being captured?"

Alex had leaned back on his palms, head tipped back and aimed up toward the darkening sky. "Yes and it'll be the last."

I "hmmed" and nodded. That was good.

"I told you, there's nothing that can hurt me," he explained.

Other than what already had, I thought.

Did he know what had happened to him, then? He didn't seem all that concerned about it anymore. He wasn't focusing on the sky like he was scared of something in it. If it had been me who had gotten hurt the way he had, I'd be fucking terrified. So why would he be so nonchalant about it?

And why was he admitting this to me? Because he knew we were stuck together? At least until we figured out some way of hiding my identity. Or was I going to have to live in a house within hearing distance so I could shout if anyone ever showed up again? I guess that wouldn't be so bad. There could be worse things than living close to someone who *could* protect me against just about anything.

You know, I could have water poured down my face and into my mouth again.

Fuck.

Just thinking about it made my throat tighter than it already was.

I had to think about something else. "I'd give a year of my life for a bag of Cheetos right now," I told him. "What about you? What would you want?"

"I could go for a fucking cookie."

I snorted, surprised. Him having a sweet tooth was the last thing I would have expected.

We sat there quietly for a while before I thought about something that had crawled into my head while I'd been trying to distract myself. "Say, Alexander . . ."

I peeked at him to see what he thought about me saying his name.

The side of his mouth might have tweaked a little.

"You don't happen to live near a beach, do you?" I asked him.

"No." There was a pause. "Why?"

I took a shallow breath through my nose. "A couple nights ago, I had a dream about a beach, and it just reminded me that I've always wanted to go to a real one."

Out of the corner of my eye, I saw him turn to me. "You've never seen the ocean?" he asked, like I'd told him electricity was witchcraft.

I shook my head and decided I wasn't going to feel any shame about how little I'd seen and done. "No. We've always lived in small towns in the middle of nowhere."

"Why?"

"It's easier to rent a house in places people don't want to live. Cheaper too. There are always job openings."

"I thought you were a translator."

He'd been paying attention. "But only for a few years, since I graduated."

"They have colleges in small towns?"

I tried to groan but coughed. "*No.* You can get a perfectly good college degree online. I did." My grandfather had told me it would be safe to do it under my legal name, and it had. We had been so lucky that the cartel hadn't figured out we had changed our last names until now.

His voice was low. "First job?"

Was he really asking me questions about myself? "Not even close. I started working when I was fifteen to help my grandparents out. Their savings and social security benefits really weren't that much."

I saw him glance at me.

"Anyway, it doesn't matter where you live. I was just wondering." I pursed my lips and focused on the bright stars over our heads. So free. So beautiful.

If I could have felt envy toward a star, I would have.

"Hey," I said, "I wanted to tell you thank you for everything. Whatever happens from now on, even if I die tomorrow from some freak accident, or if I get that sick again, thank you for this. I used to dream about doing something fun, whatever the hell that really means. It's been a fucked-up one, but it's still been an adventure. I got mystery, drama, angst, explosions, kidnapping, and a grand escape . . . Anyway, I just wanted to tell you thanks." I'd almost had a panic attack taking a shower, but every great adventure left some scars. I had a bunch of scratches that I was pretty sure were going to leave their mark too.

So there was that.

I'd raced for my life with *The Defender*. We'd agreed to be *friends*. Who else could say that?

"You're not going to die," he snapped.

"You don't know that. I could get bit by a black mamba while I sleep. That would be my luck." Which reminded me that I should check under the covers to make sure there wasn't some hidden scorpion in them.

"There's no black mambas here, and nothing is going to happen to you," he said, and I could tell without looking at him that he was rolling his eyes.

It was almost enough to make me smile. He really wasn't heartless, was he? "I hope you're right." But I still wasn't holding my breath.

"Of course I'm right."

"So you think." I sighed. I wasn't sure how much worse things could get. We were already starting off in the shitter. Hopefully it would be the good kind that composted and made things better though.

He turned toward me. "How many times have I told you nothing is going to happen?"

"A lot?" I rubbed my throat with a wince as I glanced at him. His look was dirty.

I couldn't help it. "Are you sure we're safe here? That we've gotten far enough away?"

I got another dirty look.

It almost made me smile, and even though I felt like garbage, the urge to mess with him rode me hard. "Why are you in such a good mood now anyway? Because we're somewhere?"

"What makes you think I'm in a good mood?"

"Because you're talking to me."

He grunted. "Why are you asking me that like it's a bad thing then?"

"It's not, but it's just weird."

His next grunt was even deeper.

All right then. I smiled weakly as I rolled onto my hip and got to my feet slowly. "Do you need me to stay up? Because I'm falling asleep . . . We weren't leaving, right?"

Alexander's eyes glowed. "No. Go inside and rest. You still look like shit."

I tried not to laugh because I knew it was going to hurt, but it happened anyway, just a little one. "And here I thought I didn't look as bad as I thought I would. Thank you. Don't let the Candyman come in through the door to get me, okay?"

He sighed. "Go to sleep. Nothing is going to happen unless you keep annoying me."

I was stumbling toward the door when I rolled my eyes. He might be a protector of mankind, and he might have a heart under that prickly exterior, but he was a pain in the ass too.

"Wake me up in a few hours, and I'll keep watch so you can get some sleep too, all right?" I told him.

I was pretty sure I heard him huff, but I was too tired to care.

My hand was on the doorknob when he called out, "Gracie."

I glanced over my shoulder.

His eyes were closed again, and his voice was just as steady as the rest of him. "You went through something traumatizing, but you're going to be fine, you hear me?"

That was the last thought in my head as I laid down that night.

Chapter Sixteen

Rolling over the next morning, I groaned as I draped my arm over my eyes. I was going to need a readjustment, a massage, and whatever shot athletes got when they were in pain. I might need a hip replacement too.

"Do you always snore, or is there something wrong with your sinuses?" a familiar voice called out.

I hadn't even realized my mouth had been cracked, but at his words, I pressed my lips together and dragged my hand off my face. It only took a second for me to lift my head and find the body on the couch across from the bed. Alexander was sitting up, elbow on the armrest, a hand on the side of his head, looking like a fully clothed Rose from *Titanic*, minus the come-hither expression.

His was smooth and even, but the sarcasm in his tone said everything.

Somebody was back.

From the sound of it, I must have not been the only one who had been feeling rough around the edges, if he'd contained the crabbiness until now. Was it the meal? Was it actually getting sleep?

I was almost impressed.

And I guess it was nice that some things were back to normal. Normal for us. Even though I hadn't exactly been in a talkative mood the last few days, it had been weird to say so little to each other considering we were joined at the fucking hip.

But we'd had bigger things to worry about. Like getting away, trying not to be hungry, staying warmish.

Which reminded me, had I felt the mattress shift while I'd been asleep? I'd swear I had. But maybe I had imagined it. I had passed out almost instantly the second my head had hit the pillow last night.

I didn't even bother scowling; I was glad he was feeling better and wasn't hangry. "Water getting poured down my mouth and nose fucked up my sinuses, thank you for reminding me," I muttered before noticing how much less my throat hurt. It wasn't back to normal, but it was better. "Was I really snoring though? You didn't complain the other nights."

He didn't reply.

The fucking liar.

Scrubbing my hand across my face, I rolled to a sitting position, my stomach growling. "Did you sleep?" I asked him as I eyed the tiny couch with a yawn.

"No," he actually answered.

So was it just the food that made him feel better? That made sense, I guess.

Slipping my legs over the side of the bottom bunk bed, I arched my back and heard half my bones crack. It was so hard to get up, and I found myself out of breath just sitting there.

I had to keep it together. I'd been doing a decent job at trying to hide just how awful I felt. How I was pretty sure my fever was back, and my headache was better but not by a lot.

I'd been sucking shit up my whole life, and now wasn't any different.

It would be nice to stay another day or two, but I already knew we couldn't. "We can stay if you want, but we ate all their food, except for maybe a pancake or two worth of mix, and I think we should find a phone." To call who, I had no clue, but there had to be someone who could help us.

Then I thought about his sparkling personality.

Or not.

He'd either come to the same conclusion already or going another day without food was too much because he pushed himself up almost instantly. "I'm ready when you are."

All right then.

I tried my best to clean up around the house and make sure things were as close to how they had been before we got there. I triple bagged the trash and wiped the counters down. I promised myself that I would send the owners some money to pay them back for their unwilling help. I didn't want to be a total freeloader, and I'd found a couple of bills in a drawer with an address in Nevada—there was no way we were there—and I memorized the names so I could look them up later.

Alex wedged a rock behind the door to keep it closed; then I climbed up on that broad back, and we made our way . . . somewhere.

Again.

I did the sign of the cross in gratitude.

"Any idea where to go?" I whispered a few minutes later.

"North. There are a few communities we should be able to reach today."

Oh, please, please, please, let us be able to make it somewhere today.

Luckily, for the first time in a while, something actually managed to work out, because not too long after, we made it to a real road—not the pothole landmine mess that we'd come across at the other house—and he purposely turned onto it.

Like he knew exactly where we were going, I noticed.

Soon after that, I started spotting houses in the distance

spread out among trees that might have been different kinds of pines. Most of the driveways were empty and overgrown with long-dead weeds. I'd bet that these houses were vacation or rental properties, maybe.

Alexander led us down a rutted dirt road that wasn't as nice as the one we'd been on a minute ago. His muscles bunched, and his breathing was nice and even as he turned down another deserted, muddy path.

"You know where we are?" I asked him.

"Yes."

I waited for him to tell me something else, but he didn't say shit.

We were back to that, I guess.

I rolled my eyes. It wasn't like it mattered. He hadn't left me behind, and he could've been leading us straight into hell, and I would have gone just so that I wouldn't have to walk on my own. That was the important part. He didn't need to be my best friend or anything. Being regular friends was good enough, even though we were more like "friends."

It was still more than I'd had before he'd come into my life.

Tipping my head back, I soaked up the bright sun hitting the road and sighed. I really was glad to be alive. Like I'd told him, regardless of whatever else happened, at least we'd made it out.

At least, I'd finally had a choice, which was all I'd ever wanted in the first place. Then I'd gone and bitten off all this shit. Taking care of one of the most famous people on the planet, getting kidnapped, waterboarded, getting sick, and now extreme camping with no money or IDs or friends to call for help.

Oh boy, if I could have snorted without it feeling like an icepick to my brain, I would have.

If this shit wasn't totally my luck, I didn't know what was.

Alex stopped suddenly.

Perching my chin on his shoulder, I saw him peek at me out of the corner of his eye for a moment before we suddenly started walking again. "There's a car coming," he warned.

Not two minutes later, an engine grumbled from the direction we'd just come, and he moved off to the side where the gravel was lighter.

Just as it was right behind us, someone yelled, "Get a car, assholes!"

The driver had rolled the passenger window down, and I got a real clear view of a middle finger being shot at us from a lifted, older-model pickup with a small, blue flag mounted to the rear window. With another bark of the muffler, the truck picked up even more speed as it shot down the road, leaving us in a big cloud of dust that had me closing my eyes and holding my breath.

I hadn't even realized that Alex had stopped walking, but the second the dust settled, he started moving again.

I glared at the taillights way up ahead. "Is it hard not to destroy people like that?"

He sounded dead serious as he replied, "It makes me feel better to know I can."

"Did you see the Trinity flag?"

Alexander huffed.

Fucking hypocrites.

I hoped he got a flat tire.

We made it down the road; then his body tensed beneath mine. "Someone is up ahead."

I tensed too, squeezing his throat with my forearm before I realized I was choking him and loosened my hold. "Someone bad?" I whispered like they could hear me.

His gaze was focused straight ahead. "No, a couple in their driveway," he explained quietly. "Don't say anything."

I pressed my lips together and clung to him, knowing what

came out of our mouths wasn't going to be the problem. He was still barefoot and covered in three different shades of earth. I was in sleep pants and a flannel, with a dirty backpack perched on my shoulders that was filled with my damp clothes and a slightly expired can of beans I'd ended up taking from the last house.

We were a fucking mess.

I hugged him a little tighter.

"What are you shivering for? It's not that cold," he grumbled.

Now he wanted to get chatty again? I glared at him out of the corner of my eye. "Says the guy who doesn't feel cold and is wearing a sweater."

"I can take it off if you want. It hasn't been washed in weeks."

I eyed the side of his deceiving, perfect face, wondering again if it was the food alone that had revived his grouchy ass. "Do you just like to argue for the sake of arguing, or did I do something to you in another lifetime that I don't remember?"

I wasn't much better than him in the first place, I knew it. Hadn't I been giving it back to him just as much as he'd been dishing it? Hadn't it made me secretly smile too?

A purple eye peered at me a moment before we made it to a deep driveway with a huge, downed tree across it. Beside it was a woman who had to be in her seventies or eighties, along with a man around the same age, holding a chain. A chain that was connected to an all-terrain vehicle parked beside it.

"Don't say anything," he repeated under his breath.

I watched the man move around the side of the trunk, like he was trying to find something. Where to hook it to? "We're supposed to ignore them?" I whispered.

"Yes."

"What if they try to talk to us first?"

"I don't care. Ignore them."

He was serious.

"Don't," Alexander hissed.

I gulped.

Sugary-white hair crowned the woman's head. Her neck and most of her face were covered by a colorful, red scarf. She waved as soon as she spotted us. I tensed.

"Gracie, don't," he repeated under his breath.

The man with the chain raised his free hand and waved it too. He was smiling.

Shit.

I tensed even more.

The muscles pressed against my chest did too.

And maybe I hesitated for about two seconds before I quickly lifted my hand and waved back.

Alex growled.

I ignored him.

"How is your day going?" the woman called out as we approached their property.

Alexander grunted, irritation vibrating through his skin and straight into me.

I still ignored him.

"Fine, ma'am, how is yours?" I hollered back, knowing he wanted to kill me, but I couldn't stop myself.

They seemed so nice, and they were older. I was a sucker for older people.

"I'm letting the Bogeyman in tonight," he threatened just loud enough for me to hear him.

Was that . . . a joke?

Was he fucking *joking*?

I leaned forward to peek at his face.

He was already shooting me a dirty look that made me really, really grateful we'd agreed to be friends. Or "friends."

Friends didn't kill friends.

"Dandy. Here dealing with this old stump," she said with a

shake of her head and another bright smile. "Are you staying at the Akita place?"

"Yes, ma'am." It was Alexander who replied easily, his own tone almost as friendly, and not like he'd been shooting me imaginary murder daggers a second ago.

She smiled like that explained everything. "Y'all be safe now. Make sure your car is in four-wheel drive if that storm comes down this weekend. Those ditches have gotten us all," the woman said.

"Yes, ma'am, I'll be sure to keep that in mind," the man I was clinging to replied.

I glanced at the back of his head, at all that dark hair that I'd had my cheek pressed against for countless hours, surprised at his acting skills.

"Someone I know has driven into it once or twice," the man said with the most adorable chuckle.

The woman gasped. "You said you would stop telling everyone about that!"

"It's nothing to be ashamed of, sweetheart."

She muttered something I couldn't hear that made him chuckle. He smiled back at her with so much affection, it made my little heart yearn. My grandparents had loved each other, but they hadn't been too playful. Every once in a while, I'd gotten a glimpse of a sweet, wonderful relationship, but more often than not, things had been quiet, but I'd always thought it was more that they were just tired.

But they'd had a lot hanging in the balance.

I think in a different lifetime, before I'd been born, they had to have been a lot different.

Before me.

Or more like, before my parents had lost their minds.

"Have a nice day!" the man called out.

"You too!" I hollered back, snapping out of it, trying not to feel guilty over things I hadn't asked for.

I waited until we'd gotten farther down the road before I sighed.

"I thought I told you not to talk?" the man carrying me muttered.

"They were so polite. We couldn't just ignore them."

He snickered. "Yes, we could have."

I swear . . . "Do you not have any manners?"

"I have manners."

"In your dreams maybe," I muttered.

That got me another murder-glare that wasn't all that scary.

Neither one of us said anything else as he kept going, until he stopped in front of a mailbox on the road. It was black and heavy-duty just like all the rest we'd gone past. But he peered down the overgrown driveway with two huge, downed trees across it.

Was there a house back there? If there was, it had to be set pretty far back.

Alexander looked down one side of the road, then the other, and started walking again. We'd made it about thirty feet away from the abandoned driveway before he turned right and started trekking his way back toward the house. To hide our trail?

Soon enough, we were going around the back of a small, dark house, and he was going up the steps of a well-maintained deck. Alexander patted my calf, and I slid off before he suddenly bent over. He flipped a rock upside down and plucked a key from what was apparently not a rock but a hide-a-key. Then, easy-peasy, he unlocked the door and took a step back, gesturing me in.

That was . . . convenient.

Breaking into someone's home. Again.

I went in, looking around for cameras but not seeing any. The house was cold. I could instantly tell it was bigger than the place we'd been in last night. He stomped in too, flipping on lights and locking the door.

It was really nice, and bigger than I'd first thought.

I toed off my shoes, rubbing my arms as I wobbled into the kitchen.

I yelled, or I tried to. It came out like more of a squeak.

"There's a phone!" I croaked.

A real house phone!

I picked it up from where it was set beside a black refrigerator and paused as something bitter set up shop in my throat.

It wasn't like he hadn't figured it out already. He already knew all the worst, saddest parts of me, didn't he?

I thrust the phone toward him, trying to keep my voice steady as I forced myself to meet his eyes instead of his chin. "Are you done pretending you don't have someone we can call for help, or are you finally going to give me a number we can call?"

His bottom lip dropped maybe a millimeter, but I noticed it.

And if I hadn't felt like shit and been so sad about the fact I had no one to reach out to, I might have enjoyed it.

He wasn't the only observant one. Sucker.

"You know a bunch of different languages, you remember everything, and you pay attention. I wouldn't be surprised if you have an eidetic memory. There's no way you forget phone numbers. Something broke your back, not your brain."

To give him credit, his lip snapped back into place instantly. But it was his glowing eyes that almost made me smile as he narrowed them at me. "Yes, I know a fucking phone number."

Aha! *I'd known* it. The idea had been in my head since before I'd gotten sick. But the thing was, it made no sense. If he had someone to call, why hadn't he from the beginning? Why had he stayed with me instead?

Those questions led to an even bigger one that I hadn't been willing to poke at more than I already had—what was strong enough to hurt him? He'd said nothing on this planet, so . . . There was only one answer that I'd come to, and it was a terrifying one.

And also possibly the reason why I didn't want to think about it too much.

I was scared to.

Alexander flicked his gaze toward the phone. "Are you going to dial the number next week or . . . ?" He trailed off.

I blinked. "Did God give you strong bones because he knew you were going to have a personality people wanted to hurt?" I snapped. "What's the number?"

He huffed.

Did his lip tilt up a little?

It might have, but he read a number off the top of his head, just like I'd expected, the son of a bitch. I dialed it, and once it started ringing, I tried handing him the receiver.

He didn't take it.

He lifted that snobby, perfect nose at me. "You talk to them."

"I don't even know who we're calling," I whispered, gesturing toward my throat, reminding him that there was a reason we barely talked for *three* days.

His expression said more than any words ever could: *tough shit.*

Oh boy, this man tried my patience. I put my hand over the receiver. "You want me to talk to them because you might say something that makes them not want to help us, huh?"

The fucking look on his face was classic.

I snorted—and instantly regretted it when fire leaped up my nostrils and straight into my skull—just as a deep voice answered, "This is Hephaestus speaking. How may I help you?"

I looked at Alexander, who mouthed instructions out.

All right, he could only blame himself.

I cleared my throat and winced. "Hi . . . Hephaestus. Can I please speak with Agatha?"

"Hold, please."

There was a click, and I watched Alexander's even features for a moment before someone picked up. "Yes?"

Yes? That was . . . weird.

"Hi. My name is Gracie. I'm hoping you might be able to help me, or at least point me in the right direction . . . ?"

Silence.

The jackass in front of me made a circle with his hand, gesturing me to keep going.

I held the phone out to him, but he shook his head.

I huffed and brought it back to my face. Fuck it. Hopefully I wouldn't be sticking my foot in my mouth. "I have . . . Alexander here with me"—whoa, that felt weird saying it out loud like that to someone—"and he asked me to call you. We're in a bit of a, uh, pickle."

Crickets chirped in the background.

Not really, but they should have.

Peeking at the man in front of me, I was surprised to see him looking oddly calm. Apparently, his name wasn't a secret to whoever Agatha was. Then it hit me. Was this someone special? He'd said he wasn't married, but . . .

"Alexander?" the woman asked after a moment, his name coming out clean and way too crisp.

She knew exactly who I was talking about.

"Yep. Tall, his favorite color is, uh, blue. He thinks the f-word is an adjective and has an attitude . . . *I'm kidding*," I said when he gave me a dirty look. I wrinkled my nose and whispered to him, "She won't believe me if I tell her you're nice," I teased him, trying to get back at him for all those dirty looks and tones.

Whether he was more surprised over my description or she was, I would never know. What I did know was that there was another long beat of dead silence before she coughed, and it almost sounded like she snickered there for a second. Then she replied, "Can I speak to him?"

The man in question shook his head. I lifted my shoulders and mouthed, *Why?*

Alexander shook his head some more and replied, *I don't want to.*

Oh boy. I threw him under the bus. "He says he doesn't want to."

That was definitely a snicker, and I highly doubted it was in surprise. "We've been concerned about him for a few days now," she replied, still sounding cryptic.

A few days? It had been at least a month.

"What's going on?" the woman on the line asked slowly.

I was watching that imperial-like face and tried not to show surprise on mine when he mouthed another sentence out. "He says he was the victim of a hit and run," I said, still looking at him closely. Because what the hell kind of code words were those? A hit and run? What'd he get hit by? A fighter jet?

"I see," she replied. "What's your location?"

Before I could say that I didn't know, I read his lips and repeated the address he mouthed.

How did he already know it though? I'd thought there was something fishy about him earlier, but . . .

"What kind of assistance do you need?"

Apparently, we were playing charades because he used both hands to make a driving gesture. "A car?" I guessed.

He shook his head. A ride?

"A car?" the Agatha woman repeated in confusion.

"Yes. A ride. Some kind of transportation? Back . . . ?" I said, trying to guess why that's what he would ask for when he could . . .

Oh.

For . . . me? Where the hell were we going?

"For me," I told her. "I'm sick. I've been sick." She had to hear it in my voice. Just because my throat hurt less didn't mean it sounded that way.

"I see," she said, sounding even more perplexed. "I think I understand. I'll make a few calls, check on who can get out there. It might take me a few hours."

I gave him a thumbs-up and got a nod in reply. "Okay," I confirmed.

"I'll call back once I get it sorted. Call me if you need something else," Agatha said, her voice getting odder by the second.

I said bye, got one in return, and then we hung up.

The deep sigh that left Alex's chest had me instantly glancing toward him in surprise. "You okay?" I asked. "Relieved?"

"I won't be relieved until I'm home."

Home.

It was the fact he wanted to feel relief that got under my skin, but I wasn't about to ask over it.

"Where is home?" I asked. After all, his home was going to be my home, at least for a little while. All I knew was that it wasn't close to a beach.

"Does it matter?"

Could he give me one straight answer? "Are there trees? Or is it in a city?"

He tipped his head back, giving me a good view of his muscular throat. "Do you care?"

"I get to choose?"

"No."

That's what I thought. Pressing my lips together, I thought about things for a second. "Are you sure you'll be okay with me staying with you until we figure out plan B?" I asked before I could stop myself.

He tipped his head to the side. "Do I look like the kind of man who would go back on his word?"

I mean . . .

"I'm sure, Gracie."

So he said now, but things changed. One minute I'd been pretty comfortable in a home I liked, and now I had jack shit. Now, I was doing exactly what I'd been raised to avoid—depending on someone, telling them the truth, just fucking talking to them in the first place. My brain wanted to protest it, but my stomach wasn't exactly protesting it, which was confusing. I balled one of my hands into a fist. "If you get tired of having me around, you'll tell me? With time, so I can make other plans?"

His nostrils flared before his eyelids dropped over those incredible eyes. "Why do you ask so many questions?"

I narrowed my eyes right back at him. "I just want to make sure."

"We don't need to talk about it anymore. I told you the plan."

I eyed him, telling myself that I could do this. That I could rely on him for a little while. I knew who he was. I knew his name. I knew he wasn't as invulnerable as he'd seemed.

I knew secrets about The Defender, that I doubted 99.9999999 percent of people would ever know.

That meant something. It had to.

I could trust him. Some. Couldn't I? I had no choice but to try. "Let me see if they have anything in here to make for breakfast, and hopefully someone will get here soon." Which then reminded me . . .

He didn't move as I brushed by him and started digging through the cabinets like this wasn't some stranger's house we had snuck into. Like I wouldn't go to jail if we were caught. We were criminals now, technically.

But I was also a hungry one and a sick one, and one day I'd just have to pay these people back somehow too. Like the last ones. That should be the least of my worries right now though. I just wanted some food so I could take more painkillers.

It didn't take me long to rifle through what turned out to be well-stocked cabinets. The freezer was packed too. For a moment, I'd thought about looking through drawers for cash, but I really, really didn't want to do that. It was one thing to steal food but a totally different thing to take actual money.

But if whoever this Agatha person was could pull through

and get us a car . . . and cash, then we would be fine. At least he had one person he could rely on for help. Maybe he had more.

I could feel his gaze on me as I grabbed four cans and a box of biscuit mix from the cabinet. So many questions rolled around in my head as I prepped the food that the silence wasn't awkward. *I was going to be living with him. Or near him.* That was still a pill to swallow.

It made me want to sweat.

"Are you having another meltdown?"

That snapped me out of it. "No."

The look he gave me said he didn't believe me. Not at all.

And there must have been something in the expression I gave him right back because he blinked.

"Don't start," he grunted.

I stared at him.

He pointed at me. "No."

I kept staring at him.

Alex narrowed his eyes even more. "Think of something else."

"What?" I whispered.

"Anything."

Anything?

Pressing my lips together, I tried. I really did, but my thoughts only went to one place. The same place they always did—to the three hundred questions that lived on my tongue at any given point. So really, it was his fault for why I asked, "Did you want to do something else? When you were little?" I thought about it. "If you were ever little." I really, really didn't think he'd been grown in a test tube at this point, but you never knew.

"I grew the same as you," he told me with . . . was that a smirk?

And why was he giving me so much information? Because now he knew I wouldn't be able to get away from him? "I wanted to be a fighter pilot like in *Top Gun*," I blurted out, like he cared.

He grunted. What might have been a minute later, he said, "The only thing I remember ever wanting to be was a firefighter."

"Really?" I asked, surprised.

"Yeah," he answered, giving me only that.

I didn't mean to say it. I really didn't, but it still came out of my mouth, probably because I was stunned. "The more time we spend together, the more you talk to me, the more I realize you are . . . you're so much more than the spandex you put on. It's weird."

"It's not spandex."

Yeah, but it wasn't like he was going to tell me what it actually was, was he?

But of all the jobs in the world, he'd picked one that helped people.

Was it really just me he had beef with? *Had* I done something in another lifetime? Maybe I had a doppelgänger who broke his heart?

I was thinking about that as I opened and dumped the cans of chili I'd found into a clean, newish pot when *he* asked, out of the blue, turning everything I thought about him upside down one more time, "What else do you want from your life?"

"Huh?" I asked, stirring the beans and meat.

He repeated his question word for word.

Was he really asking about *me*? "In the future?"

"No, right this second."

I groaned a little. He hadn't moved from his spot against the cabinets. The rest of him was still mud-splattered vogue. His arms were crossed over his chest, and his expression was a different one.

I already knew he was being ornery, but was he really just trying to mess with me?

Did he . . . want me to mess with him back?

He was so complicated.

"You know," I said cautiously, trying to read him, "I think I liked you more when you grunted at me all the time."

He didn't miss a beat. "And I liked you when you didn't talk back. What happened to her?"

Fucker. I smiled at him. "She was just being nice because she was scared you or someone else would kill her if you didn't get better."

A little huff snuck out of his nose.

I shrugged. "It's true. I don't want to die."

"You keep saying that."

"I've got a few things I want to do before I do," I told him.

I was giving the premade chili a stir when he spoke up again. "Well? What things?"

He wanted to know? I peeked at him, more shocked over that than I probably was when he'd given me his name. "It isn't like they're five-year goals or anything. Just random stuff."

Out of the corner of my eye, The Defender tilted his head to the side, saying everything with just that little gesture.

I added some salt to the pot, trying not to feel uncomfortable. Or vulnerable. "Just . . . stuff that will probably sound dumb to you. You can just make fun of me now and save me my breath."

He didn't say anything for so long, I looked at him.

Alexander looked stunned. "I wouldn't make fun of your dreams."

It was my turn to tip my head to the side, like *come on.* "You make fun of everything else. Why are you making that face? You do. I know I'm more your frenemy than your friend, and that's okay, even if I don't get why I get on your nerves so much. But I meant what I told you when I said we should be friends. I want to be yours, even if you get on my nerves when you're rude."

His face . . .

"It's okay, you're not the first person to ever not like me. There was always at least one person at every school I ever went to that wanted to pick on me for no reason, and at least you tell me things to my face instead of behind my back. And you saved my life. It's okay."

His mouth moved. "I . . ." His jaw went hard, and his eyes glowed for a moment. "I wouldn't make fun of the things you want to do with your life, Gracie. I'm . . . I'm only messing with you."

I narrowed my eyes, not trusting him.

"I am," he insisted so seriously, I couldn't help but believe him.

But it still felt like too much. Telling him my name or what my grandparents called me was one thing, but sharing other stuff? Being vulnerable was fucking hard. I eyed him again.

His features were blank, but there was something in his eyes that seemed a little different.

I sighed. "I don't know, okay? Not really. What's the point in planning if I didn't know whether I'd ever have to up and leave unexpectedly? There are things I'd like to see with my own eyes. I'd like to do some of the things I've seen people do on television. Little stuff, you know? I've always wanted to go skydiving or wear one of those squirrel suits and go paragliding. But at the same time, honestly, little things would be great. I'd like to get a pet. I've always wanted an Oriental Shorthair cat, or a Peterbald. I'd love a dog too. Any dog, but I'd really love a corgi or a dachshund since they have little legs like me." I gave the pot another stir, ignoring the tightness in my chest. "Sex. A relationship. I've probably thought about that the most, honestly."

I'd just said "sex" in front of him of all people.

And I'd also done more than pee in front of him. We were way past that point. Down the block, around the corner, and in a totally different neighborhood. He was an adult. I was an adult. We both damn well knew what sex was.

I peeked at him to find him leaning against the counter again, arms still crossed, biceps bulging beneath the hoodie. He didn't *seem* interested, but I could tell he was listening.

"Anyway, I want what everyone else wants. Love, happiness, traveling. Not to be alone." I snorted, thinking about how I wanted my job back too. "It's not that original. I don't want to climb Mount Everest. But when you're too busy hiding, you don't really have that many options. You can't really get to know people too well because it's too hard to lie all the time."

Oh boy, that was more than I'd ever told anyone, even my grandparents. At some point, when I started talking about my hopes and dreams as a teenager, they had started making these sympathetic faces that took me a while to process. They had known what my future would hold, and that was none of what I used to go on about.

I gave the pot another stir, a slightly harder one, and forced myself to change the subject. "Why did you want to be a fireman?"

Again, he surprised me by actually answering quickly. "I wanted to help people."

Huh. *Huh.* But he didn't always like being a superhero. That was . . . interesting. It was what I had thought too.

He made a grumbling sound deep in the back of his throat. "Where were you going to move? You sighed over that atlas on your coffee table a lot."

Was he trying to distract me too now? "I hadn't decided." My snicker was bittersweet but not bad. "I didn't want to leave. Every time I started making plans, I started doing something else so I wouldn't. I bet you've been able to go a lot of places. Maybe you can make me a list for the future. Maybe I can see how much rentals go for in those areas. The cheaper the better."

There was a weird, weird look on his face, I noticed. I bet he was probably thinking I was stupid to think I would ever be able to live far away from where he was, if I was going to be in danger. And I guess I was.

But that didn't change anything.

I wanted to find happiness.

And keep it.

And have a life.

That wasn't too much to ask for, was it?

Friends? A loved one or two? A furred one and one that could talk back to me?

Some people wanted to cure cancer, fly to the moon, go to every country.

And me? I just wanted to go to a beach for once. Have *one* friend. Be loved at least once. I would love to one day maybe have a kid or two that I could love just as much as my grandparents had cared about me, but minus the extreme strictness.

Most of all, when it came down to it, I didn't want to be alone.

If I had to pick, that's what it would be: to not be alone anymore.

Oh boy, I was depressing, and I needed to steer away from that shit.

And that was probably why I decided to piss him off. "Say . . . Alexander." I put emphasis on his name and tried not to gulp. It felt so *weird* to call him that. Part of me still expected it to be some kind of trap. I peered real hard at the beans before I asked, "Why can't you fly?"

Chapter Seventeen

"What are you nervous over?"

I froze and slowly turned to look at him. At the man who had finally showered an inch of dirt off and changed into sweatpants and a pullover hoodie that fit him surprisingly well. The same man I was having a harder and harder time picturing in a charcoal, skintight suit that hugged his body better than a glove. It was strange, to be honest.

A lot of things seemed to make me feel that way now.

Everything was different, and it was all going to keep on being different for probably the rest of my life.

That was a hard, hard pill to swallow and accept. I'd always been pretty good about going with the flow. When you fell out of a moving car, you tucked, rolled, and hoped you didn't get hit by another car. But I was starting to think that was only the case when I knew in advance that flow was changing and when I picked the direction of it.

I was not going to have a shit attack. I was going to handle this future with dignity and grace. Or something like that.

In the meantime, I'd been sitting on the sofa, staring out the windows of the cabin, waiting. And coughing. It had been two long hours of mostly silence.

The only thing Alexander had said in a long time was "next door" and "yes" after I'd asked him where he was going and if

I could go with him while he'd headed for the door after we'd eaten in silence.

I'd followed, figuring I needed to stretch my legs and do more than be a human backpack. The day had gotten a lot cooler, I'd noticed as I trailed behind him while he went the long way around the back again before turning toward the road. I took my time, wondering what he was up to.

But he'd surprised the hell out of me for about the hundredth time when he'd gone for the house where we'd talked to the elderly couple. The ATV was gone, but the tree was still in the same spot it had been in. Alexander had gone straight for the big trunk in the yard, circling around it carefully, like he was watching his steps. Eventually, he took a long look at our surroundings— ignoring me while he did it—and like it was nothing, put both hands on a random spot on the bark, then pushed the tree over to the side in less than two seconds. It might have even been faster than that.

That thing had to weigh . . . a lot. Hundreds of pounds? It was a big fucking tree, and he'd pushed it over like it was a twig.

I'd wanted to ask him why he didn't lift it, but as I watched, it made sense. If it looked like it had been dragged, there would be less questions than if it was carried. How the hell would you explain that without a crane? Then I'd kept watching as he picked up a few massive branches and dropped them beside the downed trunk in the middle of the yard. I picked up a couple too but got out of breath almost immediately, then got dizzy, and that's when he'd looked over, gave me dirty look number three hundred and fifty, and I stopped.

When he must have been content with his good deed, I'd followed him back to the house, thinking a lot about stuff. Especially the question I'd dropped on him that had suddenly turned his mute button on. When I wasn't pondering that, I was trying not to dread the future. The danger we were still in.

The danger I was going to be in until . . . who the hell knew when.

It felt so real now when before it had been more like E.coli. Something I knew could happen, that could kill me, but chances were, it never would.

Realistically, there wasn't a whole lot to be worried over. He could hear who was coming, smell them too. If someone approached that wasn't trusted, he would know well in advance, and we'd be able to get away.

What he had just done with that tree . . .

Maybe he wasn't back to 100 percent, but he was closer than he'd been a month ago.

And I couldn't stop thinking about that when we got back to the house. All that power, that strength. Could you imagine?

I ended up playing solitaire a little while with a deck of cards that were sitting on the coffee table but kept glancing out the window. After that, I set up shop where I currently was, on the couch, with a magazine. I'd poked around the cabin while Alexander had pretended to rest on the biggest of the two couches.

It was a really nice house, about the same size as most of the ones I'd lived in. It was cozy and cleaner than the last place had been, not that I was complaining. I'd felt his eyes on me while I'd picked through the cabinets in the kitchen and the bathroom.

I'd gotten this strange feeling going through the single, small bedroom, opening the closet and finding men's clothes and a couple pairs of boots and worn sneakers inside. Part of me had been tempted to take another shower, but once I saw that neither bathroom had a tub, I decided I could wait.

He didn't tell me not to snoop, but I could have almost felt his urge to tell me to sit down when I'd squatted by a bookshelf to read the titles on the spines. There were a lot of hardbacks on Roman history and a few thrillers with titles that had been adapted into movies. There had been a big stack of *National*

Geographic magazines and paperbacks on cinema history and screenwriting. It was a magazine that I'd sat with while he ignored me.

He was really good at it too.

And it was when my stomach growled again, hours after we'd already eaten, that I started to think about how much money I should send the owners to make up for the food and utilities we were stealing.

Which then made me freak out because I didn't know how I was going to get access to my money.

How the hell did you even get an ID when you had no proof that you'd existed in the first place?

That was exactly when he asked about me being nervous.

Not that I'd wanted to admit it, and that's why I looked at him and tried to give the crabby man a blank expression before I lied. "I'm fine."

"I can hear your heartbeat, liar."

Dammit. "I'm just nervous about what's going to happen." I tapped my finger against the page I'd been trying to read. "About the future." I was shaking my foot, and I hadn't noticed. I stopped. Forming my hand into a fist, I lifted my chin. "Okay, part of me keeps expecting the cartel to show up, and I'm worried."

At some point, his head had drooped to one side, and I'd swear one of his eyes got squinty.

"I'm sorry, am I boring you?"

"Yes."

I scoffed, but his head lifted, and he gave me another long look with that elegant face.

"You know I'll be able to hear someone coming," he said, his voice flat.

"I know, but I still don't trust it."

His face . . .

"Don't take it personally. I have trust issues. It has nothing to do with you."

Mr. I Don't Want to Talk About Why I Can't Fly Anymore glared, and I thought I might have insulted him. "I'm listening. I'm paying attention. No one is going to randomly show up. We're not being tracked."

I tried not to give him a dubious expression, but . . . "Are you *sure*?"

"*Yes*. You're safe."

I pressed my lips together. "Am I safe from you?"

He blinked.

"I'm kidding," I whispered, feeling insecure and shy and nervous. "We're friends, right? Friends aren't scared of each other."

That got me one big grunt.

I guess that was as good as I was going to get. "Do you know who might be coming? With the car or whatever?"

"I have an idea."

So helpful and informative.

I bit my lip, noting how he wasn't really easing my worry over anything. Honestly, it kind of helped. We weren't sure how we were going to make this work, how I was going to get my life back, but . . . I knew he would help me any way he could. At least I was pretty sure. It was what he'd promised. He might be a rude, big turd, but . . . there was a good heart in there. Or at least a reasonable one. A prideful one.

You didn't do what he did for money. You didn't think about being a firefighter for recognition.

I started shaking my leg. "Do you have any siblings?" I asked him in a rush.

He blew out a breath that made his lips make a raspberry sound. "Is talking going to make you quit shaking and being nervous?" he grumbled.

I nodded seriously.

His gaze slid up toward the ceiling. "Yes."

Yes? "I can't see you having siblings." I still couldn't picture him taking a poop. Had he snuck one in? He had to have gone at some point, but when? I had finally caught him peeing. "A brother or a sister?"

"Both."

Oh, he'd let me ask *two* questions. So much information. I wanted to ask where they were, what their names were, if they were close, but maybe I shouldn't push too much. I should keep it vague and maybe later on ask him more personal stuff before he shut down. Quantity over quality.

I scratched my nose.

"What happened the last time you saw your parents?"

I wasn't the only one with questions, I guess. He kept catching me off guard with what he paid attention to, too. Which seemed to be everything. "I don't remember, but from the way my grandparents reacted afterward, I think they got a vibe from my parents that they might have been interested in taking me with them, wherever they were living. The first time we moved was right after that," I answered. All that had been blurry. I didn't know for sure that had been the case, but that was right around the time when my grandparents had stopped talking to me about them unless I brought them up. I flexed my hand, then closed it again. "Do you have kids?"

His nose literally scrunched up before he answered with a definite "No."

Touchy much?

"Why haven't you had a boyfriend?" he shot back without missing a beat.

I hadn't seen that shit coming, but okay. "It's too hard to lie to people you barely care about, much less people you do care about." Now I sounded like a pathological liar, but that was me. "Do you really not have a girlfriend?"

His eyes narrowed. "No."

"Huh," I said, surprised and not surprised at the same time.

That got me a face.

I didn't mean to smile, but I did.

"What?"

"You're a very handsome man. I'm sure you know that."

A muscle in one of his cheeks flexed.

"It's just—" I sniffled and got myself together. "—when you open your mouth, people realize beauty is only skin deep." I smiled sweetly at him. "You didn't get to choose your face. You just got lucky to have your . . . what did you call them? Superior genes." I shrugged. "You have no idea how lucky you are to be so special."

"It's not all it's cracked up to be."

I eyed him, wanting to ask what exactly was so hard about being super-fast, strong, having superior hearing and vision, and being badass. He could fly . . . or he used to be able to. That was my dream. A dream I would never be able to enjoy because people couldn't just . . . fly. If only it was that easy.

Plus, he had almost nothing to be scared of other than what had broken his back, and I wasn't about to bring that shit up, ever.

I cleared my throat gently. "Can I ask you something else?"

One side of his mouth went flat. "If I say no, you're still going to ask anyway, aren't you?"

I nodded.

His whole mouth went flat, and I took that as permission. More like resignation, but same thing.

"Do you age?"

His blink was the same speed as his answer. "Slowly."

So vague. Fine. "What's your favorite power?" I asked.

"Telepathy," he answered immediately.

My eyes went wide in disbelief. "Fuck off." *He couldn't be.* Could he?

His eyebrows rose a little. "Do you know how many people tell me to fuck off?"

"Not enough?" I whispered sarcastically, but actually really relieved. Son of a bitch, I knew he'd been lying. He'd almost gotten me. "No, seriously. What is it?"

"Fl—" he started to say before cutting himself off.

But I knew. We both did. The elephant in the room.

Better yet, the spaceship in the room.

I pressed my lips together. *Shut the hell up, Gracie. He might leave you here if you annoy him enough.*

"Telekinesis," he offered after a moment.

That was enough to make me forget about the f-word. "You're telekinetic? As in, *you can move things with your mind*?" I had no idea it was possible to be this jealous.

It was, apparently.

"That's what telekinesis means."

"I didn't know you could do that."

"On a low scale, and it isn't something we've chosen to advertise."

"We?" I gasped. This almost felt like learning Area 51 was real.

He blinked. He wasn't joking. Oh *shit*.

"How many times have you changed your name?" he asked suddenly.

Okay, that was going to be something to think about for a while. "Legally, just the once. I lied about my other ones. Some places where we lived, no one asked for identification, so it was easy to lie. Why don't you have a significant other?" I asked, on a roll, taking advantage of this. Maybe tomorrow he would wake up in a bad mood and never answer another one of my questions. Who knew?

That got me a long, *long* glare, and that said a lot because he'd given me some impressive ones already.

I tried to look innocent.

It didn't work.

Alexander's head suddenly tilted up, and his eyes flicked to the door before he shot to his feet so fast that I didn't actually see the process. "Wait here." There was something off, something wrong. "I think everything is fine, but if it's not . . ." He shook his head. "There's nothing you'd be able to do anyway."

"Someone's here?" I squawked.

"My sister."

His sister?

And why the hell was he telling me this? Was I suddenly not the bad guy? Was his sister the bad guy? Was she who had hurt him? How the hell had anyone gotten here so quickly?

He moved toward the door so fast, I didn't see it open, but I did hear it slam shut behind him.

I didn't want to eavesdrop, but . . .

Let's get real. I loved secrets. Not having to keep my own, but I loved hearing other people's. I knew things about some of my students that had almost made my jaw drop.

Anyway, if she was like him, she'd be able to tell I was inside even if I didn't go out there. And he'd basically said there was nothing I could do to protect myself against her, hadn't he?

Did that mean she was strong?

A sinking feeling suddenly took over my stomach. Not a nauseous, squeezing one like when something bad was going to happen but a different one. A knowing one, maybe?

Moving toward the window beside the door, I pulled the curtain aside.

And I *gasped*.

Because I must have been a fucking idiot to not put the pieces together. How the hell hadn't I? My skin prickled, my armpits got damp. Even my heart fluttered. A few people in forums had guessed, but . . .

I squeaked.

Because standing directly in front of Alex, who was in the yard just a few feet away from the porch, was none other than THE FUCKING PRIMORDIAL.

OHHH SHIT.

I made an unholy noise in my throat, and I really, really hoped they couldn't—

Alexander glanced over his shoulder, giving me that familiar, exasperated face, confirming that my hopes were in vain.

But I was so excited and overwhelmed and in awe over the woman in the yard, that my shame had packed up and moved away. Somewhere very, very far, from the shit-eating grin on my face that made my cheeks hurt.

It was her!

The most legendary woman on the planet. The dark red suit she had on could only be pulled off by her statuesque form. Anyone else would look like a giant spicy Cheeto wearing it.

THE PRIMORDIAL WAS HIS SISTER.

My knees went weak.

I squawked again, and I guess at some point, he must have turned back toward her, because he glanced over his shoulder one more time, holding his arms out at his sides in a "what the fuck" expression aimed at me. I shrugged at him, surprised out of my mind.

His sister!

They didn't even . . . they didn't even look alike!

Well . . .

I squinted, trying to take in their opposing bodies. They were both tall. He had to be a little over six feet tall, and she was just about the same. They both had wide shoulders and athletic, muscular frames that were graceful and long. Their cheekbones were kind of similar, so were their eyes: at a slight angle and roundish-shaped. They both had straight, brown hair.

His skin was a luminous gold, and hers was a bronzy brown. On second thought, they had the same jawline too.

Now that I paid attention, The Centurion looked the least like them. His skin color was the lightest, and he wasn't built as muscularly as they were. I didn't think he was as tall as they were either, and his hair was short and dark blond. They were spread across the rainbow.

HE WAS THEIR BROTHER. I just knew it. Alex had said he had *siblings*. Plural. He had to be. Oh shit, oh shit, oh shit.

I was going to faint.

There *were* people who believed they were related, but most thought that they couldn't be because of their varying skin colors, like genetics didn't do what genetics wanted to do.

Like their existence even made sense in the first place.

But they *were*. If you looked hard enough. They had never appeared at the same place and time, for a reason, I was pretty sure now.

And my mouth was open in surprise right when the woman, *The* Woman, looked over in my direction at the same time that Alex did. They were talking about me, or about the situation, that was for sure. But *she* was looking at *me*.

I lifted my hand and waved.

The Primordial—THE PRIMORDIAL—waved back. She didn't hesitate. And it wasn't a half-assed wave either. It was a *real one*.

She was waving at *me*.

Oh man. *Play it cool, play it cool, play it cool.*

The Defender shook his head and rolled his eyes before his mouth started moving and he said who knew what to *his sister*.

I couldn't believe it. If I asked about The Centurion would he tell me the truth? Why was he telling me all this in the first place?

She turned her attention back to Alexander and said a few more things, crossing her arms over her chest.

She really was magnificent. I wanted to be her when I grew up.

I kept watching as Alex talked, and they went back and forth, a frown forming as she listened and staying there even as she spoke. At one point, she put her hand on his shoulder, then around the back of his neck, her expression growing more distressed.

Standing there like a fucking creeper, I witnessed them talk a little more, seeing them both glance toward me again too.

And in a move that would haunt me for probably the rest of my life, I gave them a peace sign.

I wasn't sure I'd ever done a peace sign before.

And I knew I was going to regret it when he blinked and stared.

The Primordial smiled at least.

I thought about letting the curtain drop back in place, but I kept standing there. Unfortunately, a moment later, they nodded at each other, and he stepped forward and they hugged. *They hugged.* Like normal people. And in the blink of an eye, she shot straight into the sky like a missile.

Alex turned slowly back toward the house and met my gaze. He shook his head.

Shit.

He was still shaking it as he came in and stopped just over the threshold, so unbelievably handsome it was a little irritating. How the hell had he gotten through life without someone looking at him and knowing he was different than the rest of us normals?

"What the hell was that?" he asked.

Yeah, he'd brought it up. "I panicked," I muttered.

He pressed his lips together, blinking slowly.

This was going to haunt me for the rest of my life. Even if

I never saw him again after this, I was never going to forget. I blinked right back at him, my soul shriveling up by the millisecond.

I'd given The Primordial a peace sign.

Some people could pull them off, and I wasn't one of them, and we all knew it.

My voice was the size of a Smurf. "She's like a god, okay?"

This motherfucker was still blinking at me. His voice sounded funny as he said, "We're basically the same."

"Not really."

Another blink. "Yes, really."

I closed one eye. "No, I don't think so."

That finally got me the stink eye.

"She's Earth's Champion," I kept going.

Those purple eyes settled on me, glowing faintly. "And I'm . . . what?"

"You're cool too, but everyone feels like they know her. She's the face of the Trinity. You're the one who, well, no one even really knows what your face looks like because it's never been captured that well. Twenty percent more of the population started recycling and reusing after that speech she gave about climate change. I compost because of her." I *used* to compost because of her. Oh, that made my heart hurt. I held my breath so I wouldn't make a peep at the reminder of what had happened. I couldn't change anything about it. I couldn't magically get my things back.

But I was alive.

And I still wanted to cry. And knowing and accepting both was fine.

He crossed his arms over his impressive chest. "I like the anonymity."

Oh. "But how do you do that? I mean, do that thing so nothing can get a shot of your face?"

He made a smug expression I didn't like. Someone was back to his secrets, I guess.

But while we were on the topic of things he might not want to talk about . . . "Is The Centurion your brother?" I blurted out.

"Yes."

I almost fainted again.

What did his parents look like? Genetics were pretty amazing, and it did make sense. This was a State secret. More than that.

A thought came to me out of nowhere.

It made my throat start hurting even more as I flipped the thought one way and then another, looking at it at every angle.

And it only made it worse.

If I'd thought my voice had been small before, it was Hobbit-sized as I said, "Are you telling me this because you're planning on killing me before I tell anyone?"

No. *No.* He wouldn't have kept me alive this long just to kill me.

Would he?

His mouth opened just a little bit.

Then he blinked. I blinked. And his voice was totally flat as he asked, "What is wrong with you?"

Did he have to sound so serious?

I tried to smile but was pretty sure it was a total fail. "Are . . . you? Going to kill me?"

He gave me a look that seemed to last an eternity. "No." He squinted. "I promised to keep an eye on you for the rest of your life. How does that make any sense?"

"It wouldn't be a lie if it was a short life."

A funny expression came over that handsome face. "That's a good point."

He sounded almost impressed. I wasn't the only one who had something wrong with me.

"I'm telling you these things because you're going to find them out soon anyway," Alexander went on.

It was my turn to watch him dubiously. "Why?" It had seemed so suspicious when he'd gone from purposely ignoring me and glaring, to talking a little more, then a little more when we'd ended up in that cell, and now here we were, with him being willing to tell me a few things. With his sneaky, under-cover kindnesses.

Why was he doing it?

"Because we're going back to where I live." His biceps bunched beneath the worn material of the clean hoodie. "You're going to be involved in my life, and I'm not going to waste my time hiding the truth from you. It's too much effort, and you're going to find out anyway." His eyes glowed that brilliant purple for a moment before his voice dropped. "And I'll know if you tell someone."

All right, that just made me think of at least ten more questions. "I see," I mumbled, trying to put them in order of importance. "Was everything okay with your . . . sister?"

His sister! They were siblings! I was never getting over it.

"Yes," he confirmed. "She spoke to Agatha and came to see what the problem was."

I pressed my lips together and went for the next question, as carefully as possible, wearing imaginary white gloves and every-thing. "Is there? A problem?"

"You're too weak to travel on my back anymore. That's our biggest problem right now."

Ooh, he'd hedged that well, but I was on to him.

She could have carried us both easily. Or he could have asked her to fly me back. She could fly faster than he could run, at least I was pretty sure that was the case.

There was more to this than he wanted me to see, but I was aware of it.

And I had a feeling it had to do with his flying. Or more.

I scratched my chin. "Did you tell her about me?"

That beautiful gaze settled heavily on me. "I didn't need to. She figured things out."

Okay, this mystery was starting to get way too big. "So, that's not the first time you've said something that sounds really, really loaded. You just said something about me learning the truth, and you've made hints that you know things that you couldn't have learned snooping through my mail. I really don't think I had my birth certificate at my house. And now you just said that. About her figuring things out." I paused. "What did she figure out?"

Someone went broody, and he huffed.

I waited, getting more and more wary by the second. I'd been dealing with lies my entire life. I'd weaved a thousand of them myself, as much as I'd tried to avoid them. I was a fucking pro. I was Gracie by day and the Sorceress of Secrets by night.

But I knew . . . I knew . . .

Alexander crossed his arms, confirming just what I'd thought.

I was on to something.

What the hell was going on?

He shook his head, his gaze narrowing again. "I thought you were being oblivious and secretive, but you aren't, are you?"

I made a face. Secretive was one thing.

"What do you know about your family?" he asked with his bossy, no-nonsense voice.

I wanted to go back to the oblivious talk because *rude*, but I wanted to know where the hell he was going with this more. "What do I know about them?" I parroted back.

"That's what I asked, isn't it?"

"Your tone sometimes, boy . . ." I shook my head. "I keep asking if I did something in another lifetime to make you dislike me, and you keep not answering. You know that?"

That dark gaze moved over my face, and he scrunched his nose just a little bit. "It's not your fault I don't want to like you. What do you know about your family?"

He didn't want to like me? What did that mean? Why? It made no sense, but . . . I shrugged. "Okay. That's a broad question. I don't know anything about my dad's side of the family."

He waved me off. "They're irrelevant. What do you know about your mother's side?"

"Those grandparents are the ones who raised me, I told you that. Her mom and dad."

Alexander made a circle with his hand, telling me to keep talking.

"Okay. My grandma was Costa Rican, but her parents were originally from Spain. My grandpa, his dad was Costa Rican, but he was vague about where his mom's family was from."

Something moved across his face. "What else do you know about your great-grandmother? That one?"

"Not much. My grandpa loved her. He talked about her, but not really anything that I think you'd care to hear."

"You'd be surprised what I want to hear."

This man-being-person. Wow. No wonder they didn't let him talk in public. I rattled off some information about her, her first name, that she'd had three children, one who had passed away as a baby. Alexander didn't exactly look all that interested so much in that, but then my mind trailed to the other thing my grandfather had always said about her. "He told me she had these premonitions sometimes. How she sometimes knew things were going to happen before they did. He said she called herself a *bruja*, a witch, and would laugh about it." His grandmother had been the same. He had spoken about her in awe, but I didn't think he wanted to hear that.

Nothing on his face changed exactly, but something in his eyes did.

"Sometimes I get these stomachaches when something bad is going to happen or when something important is, and he told me I got that from her. Remember? I told you that day when the cartel showed up that I had a little bit of ESP? Why are you looking at me like that?"

The man raised his eyebrows. "That's even less than I thought you knew."

"What does that mean?"

"Your great-grandmother wasn't a witch."

It was my turn to roll my eyes. "I know that."

He crossed his arms over his chest. "She was a fourth Atraxian."

The urge to reaffirm she had moved to Costa Rica as a little girl was on the tip of my tongue, but it dried up real quick. Because somehow, I knew we weren't talking about nationalities. My heart started beating really quick as I asked slowly, "What does that mean exactly?"

Those bright purple eyes powered up, and I know I didn't imagine that his voice went deeper and so, so serious. "That she was from Atraxia. That means you're one of the few people on this planet with Atraxian blood."

My stomach did a little tap dance, not in alarm, not in warning, but like I had figured being on a roller coaster would feel like. Like the world was about to change. "I still don't know what that's supposed to mean. I wanted to take one of those DNA tests, but it was just one more way someone one day might find me, so I didn't do it." Why was my hand shaking? Why did my voice sound so weird? "Where is that? Atraxia? It sounds like a moon or . . ." I trailed off, my stomach doing another quick jig.

He tipped his head to the side, his face unreal and handsome. Almost angelic. Those eyes of his were grave, and his voice was very, very even. "Atraxia is a planet in a solar system with a lot of syllables that I don't feel like pronouncing."

I looked at him.

I thought about what in the fuck he'd just said.

And then . . . then I fainted.

Chapter Eighteen

"Damn, you're dramatic," Alexander said.

I groaned up at him, blinking slowly.

It wasn't the fact I'd fainted that surprised me the most, but the fact I wasn't sprawled out on the floor with a big knot on my head. It had taken me a second to realize that I was on the couch with my head propped on the armrest as he looked down at me in exasperation.

He hadn't let me bust my ass.

"You done?" he asked, sounding bored.

"Fainting?"

The Defender gave me a face that said "duh."

"I hope so."

He sighed as he glanced at the sliver of couch at my hip, and I scooted over an inch before he slid onto the spot. His hip pressed against most of my stomach as he focused down on me. "I might as well take a seat because I can tell you're going to have at least a hundred questions."

He wasn't wrong there, but I didn't appreciate how well he thought he knew me already.

"Go ahead."

I tried to put my thoughts and questions together so that I wouldn't talk more than I needed to. I didn't need to sound like a crazy person. I could handle this conversation. Once I was ready, I kept my voice steady, though the rest of me felt anything but, and said, not sounding like I was insane, "So you're telling me that my great-grandmother was this . . . Atraxian person, and that's why she had these . . . premonitions my grandpa knew about."

"Not 'Atraxian person.' Atraxian. From Atraxia."

He was correcting me about a planet in another solar system.

I wanted to laugh hysterically, I really did, but all right. I could keep my shit together for a minute. I could wander down this road with an open mind. "From a planet called . . . Atraxia?"

He gave me another expression like being from another fucking planet was a normal thing and he had no idea why I was struggling to comprehend what he was implying.

I pressed my lips together and clung to my sanity. "How do you know about it?"

He almost looked disappointed. "Really? You haven't put it together?"

He had a point, so I told him the truth. "This doesn't feel real, and I want to hear you say it."

He blinked. "I know about this 'place' because my family is from there too. Only our line isn't as diluted as yours is," he answered.

Open mind, Gracie. Open mind.

I wasn't dreaming. If this was a dream, he would probably be shirtless. And so would I.

If this was a dream, my lungs wouldn't feel like I had a hippo sitting on my chest.

This was real. It 100 percent was.

"Okay. I see." I didn't. Not really. "How . . . do you know about my great-grandmother? That she . . . was that?"

"Because my grandmother knew her."

He had a *grandma*? I had to keep my shit together. He wouldn't be lying to me. Why would he? *Rational, practical, open-minded.*

That could be me. Rational, practical, open-minded, and maybe a little bit of this Atraxian thing.

Oh God.

My heart was beating like crazy, but I could go along with this story. Stories were great. I read them all the time. "So her . . . family . . . was from the same place as yours? As you? And The Primordial? And The Centurion?" The fact that I was saying these words out loud was blowing my fucking mind.

"I told you they're my brother and sister."

I made this terrible sound in my throat of pure disbelief that hurt like fucking hell, and it wasn't rational at all when I squeaked, "So you're telling me that I'm a little bit of an alien?"

Alexander rolled his eyes. "That's a simple term for it."

My brain was fucking spinning. "And you're an alien?"

He gave me a really hard, almost disgusted look. "We don't do rectal probes, if that's what you're thinking."

"But you look human." The words, the comments were about to just flow out of my mouth. I could tell. *"Are you shapeshifters?"*

He was trying to fight an eye roll, some part of me could feel it. "No. Why would we . . . ?" He blinked. "What's your definition of a human? Being bipedal? Having two eyes and two hands? Having hair? Or being born on this planet?"

Oh boy.

"We're humanoid, if you feel more comfortable with that term. That's why we came here, where we could fit in." He blinked. "Atraxia is an older, bigger 'cousin' to Earth. It's what scientists here would consider a twin planet."

"Like in the Galaxy Battles movies, where there are human-looking people on a bunch of different planets but there's also all kinds of alien-looking people too?" I whispered in shock. Even in some books I read, they didn't call people *humans* when they were from Earth. They called them Terrans sometimes.

"Oversimplified but yes."

"So you aren't cloaking yourself to hide the fact that you have four eyes and your skin is green? *Is being Atraxian why I can memorize some things so easily?*"

His groan was enough of an answer at least for part of my questions.

"Is there an Atraxian language?"

"Yes, but I wasn't taught it. Neither of my parents saw a point in speaking it around us. There are eight tones to it, so a single word can be pronounced in eight different ways, and each one would have a different meaning."

Fuck. "How did the first people to come communicate then?"

Alex's face went a little smug. "We learn fast."

"How come no one ever noticed anything different when I've had bloodwork done?"

"Because you've descended from enough humans, and you've more than likely not been to the doctor enough for them to see certain markers."

That made so much sense. The questions just kept building up in my head. "So our ancestors came here on a spaceship?"

"From what I was told, the ship only made it as far as Mars, and they 'flew' the rest of the way here. Later on, my great-grandmother went back and destroyed it to remove the evidence."

"Why did they come here?" I asked.

"Why do people leave their homes?" he asked right back.

I had to think about it. "Religious persecution? Colonization? Just to explore? Because their lands are dying?"

His eyebrows slowly rose. "If they wanted to colonize, they would have."

He was right. That would have been the easiest shit in the world for them. If he wasn't making this whole thing up.

"One of your ancestors had a vision that war was coming. She predicted that it wouldn't be in her generation or the next but sometime in the distant future. The majority of the population refused to listen—Atraxians are a peaceful people by nature, they rarely leave their planet—but a small percentage understood the magnitude of what would eventually come. Those who didn't want to stay were granted permission to leave; they even gave them four ships to travel, but on the condition that they could never return. That they could never reach out to the people who stayed behind or tell anyone where they were going. All I know is that each one went in a different direction, they were led by members of your family and another family's visions. From what I understand, they were seen as traitors for leaving. Our civilization was advanced, but they were much more traditional with their views."

"But . . . how? What does all of this even mean?" I dropped my voice. "Why are you telling me this?" I asked him, scooting up a little higher along the couch so I was in the corner. "My grandfather didn't know. He never said anything."

Alex was watching me so, so closely. "There is no way he didn't know. My best guess is he knew not to say anything. He was aware that your family's gifts would weaken with time, that his child and every generation afterward would have so much human DNA their abilities would be almost nonexistent. Your line also isn't one that is remarkably strong physically, it makes it easier for you to fit in. His ESP had to be what kept you hidden and alive for so many years."

I thought about my grandpa and how every time he'd told me about them—his grandmother and mother—it had been without my grandma around.

I thought about how he had surprised us with the random locations he picked for us to move to sometimes after everything had gone to hell and relocating had quit being fun. Places he had seemed so confident in. Towns there was no way he'd ever heard about in the news or in the paper.

I shrugged, feeling a little helpless, a little confused and overwhelmed. I was a little in shock. A lot in shock.

"It's safer for everyone the less people know. It was the agreement when the families came here and some of them married humans."

Married humans.

Abilities.

Agreement.

The world rocked under the couch like we were in the middle of an earthquake. "Families?" I squeaked.

"Twelve of them."

Oh boy. Oh boy, oh boy, oh boy. There were twelve fucking families that came from another planet? And this son of a bitch was telling me I descended from one of them and that explained my Nostradamus stomachaches?

How the hell was that possible? Was *this* the greatest secret of all time?

"One family died off soon after they arrived, four others have so much human DNA now in their lines that their abilities don't exist or are mostly latent, six still have some, and then there is my family," he explained, those purple eyes totally focused on me.

I could barely get the words out of my throat. "Mine is one of those?"

"One of the four with hardly any abilities. Your great-great-great-grandmother married a normal man. So did her daughter and her daughter. Your grandfather married a normal woman. Your mother the same."

"How many Atraxians came here?"

"I'm not positive. I know your great-great-great-grandmother wasn't married; she was the only member of your line that came here. She did tell me that."

My ears started ringing. "I think I need to lie down."

His snicker was soft. "You are lying down."

"I need to lie down more," I warned him, sinking back into the couch, tilting my head up to focus on the wood-paneled ceiling and not on the fact that I wanted to start panting but I might pass out for sure again if I did. "I don't understand," I told him in a tiny voice.

"I explained it as simply as I could. Need me to try again?"

Man, fuck this guy. Pushing my elbow into the couch, I knifed up to stare at him. "Didn't anyone ever tell you that if you don't have anything nice to say not to say anything at all?" I asked him flatly, the room centering again as I focused on him and that pain-in-the-ass beautiful face.

"A few times."

Really? He was joking now? I pressed my lips together and tried to focus on the important shit. "I just . . . I can't . . . believe what you're saying." I pulled the pillow out from behind my back and hugged it. "Why are you telling me this? Why did you wait so long to tell me this? You knew all along?"

Those big hands went to his knees as he twisted his body even more to really watch me. "I already told you: because you're going to find out eventually."

"Why? From who?"

"When you meet the rest of my family."

How many more of them were there?

But most importantly . . .

That same thought I'd been babying for weeks now came back ferociously. What *were* the chances that he would have landed in my yard of all places? That had to be . . . a one-in-seven-billion chance. Wouldn't it?

It wouldn't be a chance at all.

The expression on his face gave me the feeling he knew exactly what I was pondering and was telling me to hurry and catch up.

"Alex . . . ander." I squeezed the pillow even tighter. "It wasn't a coincidence, was it? That you landed in my yard?"

He shook his head.

The ground rocked under me again. "But how . . . ? You didn't . . . ? You said someone or something did that to you. Did you make that up?" I hadn't taken him to actually be a liar. He seemed too blunt for that. Secretive? Absolutely. But not untruthful. "You were so mad for weeks after you got there. After we met. Like I did something, and now you're saying it didn't 'just' happen."

"You think I broke my own back, landed in your yard, drained of all of my power on purpose? Really?" he deadpanned.

Okay, that was stupid, but it still didn't make sense. "So then how . . . ?"

"I was left there for a reason."

Left? What kind of conspiracy theory crap was this? "By who?" I gasped.

"What's that you like saying? 'Does it matter?'" he grumbled. I guess he'd put this together already and none of this was news.

"Yeah, it matters to me. Why are you telling me this now? Why didn't you say anything before?"

"Because I didn't trust you."

No shit.

He made a sniffing sound. "I didn't want to know you."

That was honesty at least.

He gave me a side-look as he leaned forward to put his elbows on his thighs. His attention strayed to a spot straight ahead on the mantel. It was a plain brick one that was nice. "I was in a lot of pain the first few days I was there. It was hard to think about anything but my back and being in that condition."

He meant weak and drained.

"Then everything happened, and now I can't walk away from you, can I?"

I squeezed the pillow a little tighter. "You could. I wouldn't blame you." I dropped my face to just let my eyes peek over the edge of it. "If we're going to be totally honest here, I thought about leaving you at my house a few times. I knew I should leave, and I'd been having those stomachaches. If you hadn't been in such bad shape, I might have."

Nothing about his features changed.

"But I couldn't just leave you there. Not after everything you've done. I know that's not very nice, and I'm not a good person, but I made my grandparents a promise that I would try to live a nice, long life, and I can't do that if I'm dead. Which, thank you again for not leaving me in there or along the way. You didn't have to, and I appreciate it."

The fucking Defender looked uncomfortable. "You didn't give me up either. That's why we're here. That's why we're stuck together. It's why I'm telling you all this."

This was too much to keep track of, and I struggled to get more of my thoughts straight. I was apparently this Atraxian . . . person in mostly name. It didn't seem real. It didn't seem possible. He was Atraxian and just *look* at him. Look at him. It was like comparing a watermelon to a bruised-up apple. The only obvious thing they had in common was that they were both fruits.

I rubbed my lips together and tried to take a breath through my nose. "Were you sent to find me then? Is that why you were in the area?"

"No, I've known about you for years."

That got me to lower the pillow and stare over at him. "Then what?"

His nose scrunched. "I didn't want to meet you now, and I didn't want to years ago. I almost started looking for you once but I changed my mind." He focused on the fireplace again. "No offense."

Yeah, like that was going to be easy.

He'd known about me for years?

He hadn't wanted to meet me?

But I couldn't move past him *knowing I existed in the first place.*

How?

I didn't need to flip out. None of this even seemed believable, but *open mind.* Open heart. At this point nothing should be a surprise. The Defender had been carrying me around for days. He'd let me sleep on him. We'd shared a Snickers. Anything was possible. I could be rational. Rational was my middle name. I sniffled. "You weren't sent to find me, you didn't want to meet me but you were left at my house on purpose. That doesn't make sense."

For the first time since he'd come into my life, he looked uncomfortable. "Someone has been keeping track of the Atraxians left." His expression went even more ornery and troubled. "This person . . . told me about you."

Who? I wondered as I put together the clues he'd given me. "Was it your grandmother?" I asked, my voice funny. He had brought up her knowing about my family after all. "Is she trying to find people with . . . this Atraxian blood? Why? To update the family tree?" I realized he was skipping around with answering my questions, but I could worry about that later.

He watched me closely. More closely than I was comfortable with. "You were handling this pretty shitty at first, but you're coming to terms with it faster. Good."

He had no idea how close I was to laughing hysterically. "Oh, I'm not coming to terms with shit. I want to throw up, and part of me doesn't believe you, but it's almost so outrageous I have to," I admitted. "Because of the stomach stuff, I mean. The ESP. And comments my grandfather said that I don't think he thought twice about but made more sense than my great-grandmother being a witch." I pressed my lips together. "I always did think you three had to be from another planet. I never really thought you were government experiments."

He snickered. "We're not."

"This is a lot to process."

He rubbed his chin and gave me an expression that was *almost* sympathetic. Maybe he wasn't used to rocking people's worlds on a regular basis. Maybe it *was* rare that you were told that somewhere down the line some ancestor was . . . maybe . . . more than likely . . . not from . . . Earth.

I had a special tool to help me open tight cans, for fuck's sake.

But hadn't I dreamed about this my whole life? Being special? Didn't everybody? Sure, all I had were stomachaches, but . . .

I blew out a breath that hurt and stared at the small coffee table right in front of his knees, still in shock.

Lifting my gaze, I eyed the almost normal-looking man sitting at my hip. He still hadn't grown a third eye. There weren't gills along his ribs, even though that might have been cool. Other than being too beautiful, his skin too smooth, he was . . . just like everyone else. At least on the outside.

Was it possible? That a great-grandparent had been like him? Was that really why my grandpa had been so secretive about his family?

I let out a shaky breath before wiping at my face, exhaustion suddenly hitting me. Recovering from being sick, not eating or drinking well, and getting an emotional bomb dropped on my ass would do that. At least I was pretty sure. "I need to lie down here for a minute, maybe have a quiet meltdown. Maybe cry a little. Will you let me know when whoever is coming gets here?" I asked him weakly.

His eyebrows rose, and he looked amused? "As long as you're quiet."

I gave him a dirty look.

His amusement didn't go anywhere. "They'll be here soon."

Training my gaze on the ceiling, I hugged the pillow a little closer to my chest. "How do you know that?"

"Because I'm listening," he answered.

Right. Because he was an alien. Or at least part of one? Enough of one to be so special?

Oh boy, this was going to take me a while to process and accept. Not that it changed my life or anything. If it was true, it didn't do shit. All it did was explain a couple things.

I'd been trying not to think about how scary the future was going to be. I had no idea if I still had a job. Where was I going to sleep? How was I going to be able to eat? How much had the cartel found out about me?

I needed a cell phone.

My laptop.

And now this?

Keep it together, Gracie.

He'd said he'd help me. That he would keep an eye on me. To what extent would he be in my life?

I had no fucking clue, and my spiritual balls must have dried up since I wasn't willing to ask.

We were moving on, and the world was still going to be a scary place regardless of who I was with and who my great-grandparents and great-great grandparents were. That didn't change anything.

The point was, I couldn't totally entrust my safety to another person, no matter how strong or special they were. I couldn't forget that. He hadn't told me exactly why his grandmother was looking for other Atraxians, and he'd sure been weird about that. Maybe she wanted to harvest my organs, who the hell knew.

I needed to keep my ears peeled and my senses on high alert in the meantime. There was no better time to start than now. I had a lot to think about.

Maybe I would need that little cry after all.

I'd think about it.

My body was stiff as I set my hand on his thigh to push myself up to standing. Figuring I already owed this family enough, I made my way into the kitchen and plucked a small knife I'd had my eye on from a butcher block. I found a clean-looking rag under the sink and wrapped it around the blade for protection. Then I slipped it into the pocket of the pajama pants I'd permanently borrowed, hoping I wouldn't forget it was there and cut myself later. But it instantly made me feel better.

A snicker came from the living room.

I looked over.

"What's that for?" he asked almost casually.

I patted my pocket. "I don't know where we're going. I don't know who's coming." And I'd already told him I was scared. I shrugged. He could figure it out.

Alexander's head tipped to the side.

"I know you said you'd protect me, but you can't be too safe, you know?"

His eyes got squinty, and his tone was still low as he said, "You don't have anything to be worried about."

That was really easy for him to say. "I almost had a panic attack yesterday while I showered. I thought about asking you to come and sit on the toilet. That whole incident could have been a lot worse, and I know that, but that doesn't really help me much." I shrugged. "It makes me feel better to know I could jab someone in the eye if I had to."

Because I would.

I'd lost almost everything. I'd been sicker than every other time in my life combined and multiplied times one hundred. Never in a million years would I have imagined sleeping out in the woods with almost no supplies, but I'd survived that too.

With Alex.

And if I could get through all this shit, I could get through just about anything else.

And maybe that was the best thing I'd learned from all of this. I wanted to live, and I wouldn't go back on my morals. Regardless of what happened, I had that.

Alexander patted the cushion beside him on the couch with a put-out sigh. "Come here."

Okay . . . I didn't drag my feet on the way back, but I almost did. I sat down right on the edge of the seat and raised my eyebrows at him. "Yes?"

He raised his right back. "I don't need you fainting again."

"I fainted *one* time."

"You still did it," he replied, the corners of his mouth twitching.

I swear . . .

"Gracie."

I focused on him, on that serious face and tone.

"You understand what's happened, right?"

I didn't like the sound of that or his grave, nonsarcastic tone. "What do you mean?"

His eyes glowed as he tilted his head a little, that gaze of his intent. "Your situation."

My face must have expressed just how fucking confused I was by his comment and by his expression because he said, "That's what I thought." The muscles beneath his clean sweatshirt bunched. "The cartel might not figure out how you got out of there, but they might."

I blinked.

"I disabled the cameras in the facility, but the guards might remember they shot me and there was no blood left behind. If anything, you might be in more danger now than you were before. You understand that? Because I don't feel like you do, and we might as well get all this out on the table so there aren't surprises later on."

I swallowed. There was a lot we'd already put out on the table, and I wasn't sure how strong the legs were in the first place.

"You'll be fine," he told me, sounding so confident, so absolutely serious I wanted to believe him.

Oh, how I wanted to believe him.

I hadn't thought about that *at all*.

A nudge at my leg had me glancing down. He pressed the side of his knee against mine as he leaned forward, and he said the second to last thing I would have expected. "Friends don't let friends die. Everything's gonna be fine. You've got something better than that knife. You've got me."

Chapter Nineteen

The honk came in the middle of the night.

I'd taken a nap in the bedroom on a queen-sized bed—on top of the sheets—and had only been a little surprised when I'd come out to find Alexander sprawled on the couch, those long legs propped on the coffee table, a notepad on his lap. He hadn't made a peep while I'd slept, or maybe he had and I'd been too tired to notice or care.

I almost choked on my yawn when I noticed he'd showered and changed again. His hair was damp and down, tucked behind his ears. Instead of the sweatpants and a Hello Kitty shirt with a dirty hoodie that I'd gotten used to seeing him in, he'd put on a nice navy pullover sweater and sweatpants that hugged his muscular legs even more than the previous pants had. He even had sneakers on.

He looked brand-new.

And extra, extra handsome.

Stupid handsome.

"It's time to leave," Alex said, his attention still down on the notepad that looked like it had a lot of writing on it.

I nodded. It didn't take me long to go back in the room and straighten the bedding. Squinting around the cabin, I picked up the backpack, went back into the kitchen, and managed to put one can of beans inside before he called out, "You don't need to do that."

I already had my hand on another can, a tomato soup one, and I hesitated, staring at the label, remembering just how hungry we'd been. Maybe his stomach hadn't growled like mine had, but I'd seen the way he'd pretty much licked every can clean. I hadn't been the only one.

"Gracie." His voice went remarkably soft, almost a sigh. "You won't go hungry again. I promise."

Lifting my head, I found him on the couch, a notch between his eyebrows. "I was going to pay them back."

Something else in his features changed. "We're fine now. You don't need to worry about food anymore." His throat bobbed. "Or paying anyone back."

He'd promised? It took me a second to let go of the can and set it back in the pantry, but I couldn't get myself to take the other one out. I'd send them money. I closed the bag, and when I peeked up, Alexander was still looking at me.

He knew.

And that hitched something tight in my chest for a moment before I shook it off and turned around to make sure we hadn't left a mess. I tied up the garbage bag and then put it into another. We hadn't left anything that would go bad, other than the cans I'd rinsed out.

I was going to find a way to pay the family that owned the cabin back too. Some way. Some time.

Alex was at the door by the time I came up behind him, headlight beams shining through the windows. I slipped my hand into my pocket and touched the small knife just as my eyes focused on the faint shape of the idling car outside.

"You really don't need that either," he claimed, his purple eyes glowing before he opened the door and gestured me to go through first.

I took a single step forward onto the deck and stopped as I eyed the car. He locked the door and tucked the key in a little gray box hidden in a corner beside some shrubs . . . not the same fake rock where he'd originally gotten it. I could tell he was side-eyeing me as he turned and stopped beside me, those dark eyebrows slowly rising upward.

My heart started beating extra fast.

And before I thought twice about it, before I could remind myself that I wasn't his responsibility, that he was only here because someone had dumped him into my life, I reached out and grabbed the first thing I could: his pinkie.

His eyes met mine.

Just for a split second, every one of his muscles tensed. His fingers were cool and stiff as I clutched the one. But as I started to let go, with his other hand, he folded my fingers back around his, pinning me quietly with his bossy gaze.

Then he started moving, going down the steps of the deck. My fingers still wrapped around his pinkie. Just his rock-hard finger strong enough to crush metal.

I followed him. "You don't have to," I whispered because I didn't want to make him do something he didn't want to. "Just so you know, Alex . . . ander . . . thank you. For everything." I clutched his finger tighter, and then I blurted out, "You're my first friend in a really long time, and I know you said you don't want to like me, which means you don't want to be my friend either, and I get it, but it still means so much to me."

He didn't nod, didn't even blink, but I didn't take it personally that he didn't respond. After a moment, he faced forward again and led me across the lawn, toward the car parked on the overgrown driveway that I was surprised they'd even found in the first place. It was pulled up right against the downed trees.

Gravel crunched under my still soggy sneakers; I'd been trying to ignore the fact they hadn't gotten a chance to dry. I was almost used to the squishing by that point. I had to close my eyes against the bright lights, sticking as close to his side as

I could without seeming too clingy. Or at least clingier than I already was.

Someone was reclining against the hood of the car.

The sound of a door opening and closing had me tensing just as I spotted another figure coming out from the passenger door. Both bodies seemed long as they moved toward us, one slightly taller than the other.

I let go of his finger at the same time a voice—a masculine one—said, "Told you. You owe me fifty bucks, Selene."

A feminine voice replied, "At least one of us isn't going to die sad and alone."

But then the strangers surged forward, and a split second later, most of Alex's body disappeared in a cocoon of bodies.

I slipped my hand into my pocket and clutched the knife handle, watching the three of them. I couldn't see much because the lights made my eyes water—but hey, at least I wasn't totally dehydrated anymore—and I was groggy and still felt like crap, but I paid as much attention as I could. Their hands. Their arms. They were high around his shoulders, around his ribs, and I made sure they weren't holding anything.

I peeked through the windshield to make sure no one was in there. I didn't see any movement.

For what seemed like minutes, the three hugged.

Alexander was hugging people. I knew he wasn't some heartless monster, but it was still fucking shocking. Just as quickly as I thought that, I realized a hug sounded nice.

It had been a long time since I'd had one of those. Sitting on his lap while I was sick didn't count. Did it?

I crossed my arms over my chest and let that sink in for a minute, feeling so alone it almost hurt. You would have figured I was used to it by now.

No sooner had I thought that than those purple eyes I could have found in a dark room with a thousand other glowing eyeballs in it moved to me. I couldn't see his mouth at all, but his words were clear. "Gracie, put the knife back in your pocket and come here. They can't hurt me, and they aren't going to hurt you." His eyes glowed even brighter. "I promise."

I held it a little tighter just to spite him telling me what to do, but I didn't move.

"Tell her you're not going to hurt her," he demanded.

I could see both heads move from him to me and back again.

"Tell her," he repeated. "She's been itching to stab someone for a couple weeks now."

He wasn't wrong, but he almost embarrassed me saying that out loud.

"We would never hurt each other or you," a male and female voice said at the same time, their words layered on top of each other.

But that didn't really make me feel any better.

"Come here," The Defender said after a moment.

I hesitated before taking a step forward and then another.

I didn't trust him-trust him, but I didn't *not* trust him either. At the same time, he hadn't let me down yet, had he? As long as I didn't forget that no one would ever take care of me better than me, that was what would keep me alive.

I couldn't forget that.

I wouldn't.

But it still didn't mean I couldn't do this one small thing. For one of the rare times I could have someone to have my back at least a little bit, I would.

He'd let me hold his finger because I needed it.

If I had to choose anyone to trust . . . if I could, it would be him.

He was the closest thing I had to someone who cared about me. And if that was sad, it was what it was.

So I took it. I took his fingers, then skimmed mine until I touched his palm.

Slowly, he pulled me toward him, toward *them*. Then he did the last thing I ever would have expected.

Alexander, The Defender, the hero, the icon who dropped f-bombs, hugged *me*.

His chin went to the top of my head as he pulled me into him. One arm went around my shoulders, the other around the middle of my back, and he hugged me tighter than I'd ever been hugged before. Plastering my front to his. Folding me up in those strong limbs.

It shocked the hell out of me more than his admission about having some alien ancestor had.

He was hugging me.

And nobody was threatening him to do it.

Maybe it was because he knew I was terrified or because I'd almost died or because he felt bad for me.

But I didn't give a shit.

With a deep breath, knowing what I was being given and wanting it so bad it should have made me feel guilty, I snuck my arms up and wrapped them around his waist. We weren't really, really friends, I was aware of it. We were strangers stuck together by circumstances and genetics. We'd become acquaintances due to necessity. Friends to form a bond that made us both slightly more trusting.

We'd survived this with each other's help. We had almost died together, or at least I had.

I owed him. I owed him big-time. Especially more after this.

I tucked my forehead into his neck, closed my fingers to grip the clean sweater he'd put on, and let out an exhale so shaky that I was pretty sure a bone might have rattled itself loose somewhere in my chest.

"No one is going to get you," he said straight into my ear, his voice that low grumble.

I wanted to believe him. I wanted to believe him so bad.

One hand slid off my back, and the next thing I knew, he was gently prying the knife away. I let him. And he was still holding me, hugging *me*, as he slipped it back into my pocket and gave it a pat. He dropped his voice again and said so quietly I barely heard him, "You're safe."

My limbs locked up.

"Say it."

I swallowed the knot I hadn't even realized had formed in my throat. "I'm safe," I muttered, my voice raspy and low.

His breath brushed my ear. "I won't let anything happen to you."

I didn't even mean to, but I balled up his sweater in my hand.

"Say it, Gracie."

Squeezing my eyes closed, I said it, "You won't let anything happen to me."

He hugged me closer. Even tighter. I'd be a lying son of a bitch if I didn't admit that it touched me more than anything else he'd ever done.

Plus, this wasn't about me. This was about him. He was back with his . . . whatever they were. He'd recuperated, or at least mostly. This whole experience had been something for him too—his injury, his weakness.

It was that, that was enough for me. That had me taking a step back to give him some space, and I lifted my chin. I focused on the strangers, telling myself that everything was going to be okay. That I was safe, at least for the time being.

I made myself focus on the bigger one first.

Even in the night, I could tell his hair was short, thick, and dark. His cheekbones were sharp, lips full. He was handsome.

And I mean very, very handsome.

So handsome it took me a second to realize he looked almost identical to Captain Not-So Crabby Pants over here.

The corners of the man's mouth twitched, his eyebrows

shooting up his forehead, just as I held out my shaky hand. He took it instantly. His palm was cool too, just like Alex's.

"Hey," he said, that twitch of his mouth turning into a straight-up smile. "Leon."

I looked back and forth between Alexander and this Leon person, realizing they were . . . were they fraternal twins? Just enough was different about them to not be identical, but it was close. Really, really close.

What the hell?

"Hi," I greeted him back, suddenly feeling shy—and still cautious no matter what anybody said—as I pulled my hand away and fought the urge to palm the knife again.

"I'm Selene," the voice to my left spoke up, pulling my attention toward the woman just an inch or two shorter than Alexander. Her hair was a lighter color, maybe blonde, and she was really pretty.

Her hand was already extended.

I took it too and said, all shy, "Hi."

A huff had me snapping my head toward Alex, who . . . why the hell was he side-eyeing me like that?

"What?" I blurted out like I hadn't just been on the verge of hiding behind his indestructible ass.

The son of a bitch smirked. "That's all you have? 'Hi'? After you were ready to gut them?"

Oh hell. "I wasn't ready to 'gut' anyone. I just wanted to . . . protect myself. Protect you," I hissed at him in a whisper, embarrassed. To be fair, I was ready to shank people, but he didn't need to say anything about it. He knew what we'd been through. They didn't. "Just in case," I insisted, barely loud enough for him to hear.

He didn't believe me. "We talked about this already."

"We did, and remember what I said about trust issues?" I asked.

That got me a sigh before he shook his head and focused on Selene and his almost doppelgänger, Leon.

Who were these people?

"Can we go?" he asked them. "We've got a long drive."

Long drive? How long?

It didn't matter, did it?

This was the start of the next phase in my life.

Homeless. Penniless. Exposed.

But it was a new chapter. Maybe even a new book.

I had no idea where we were going, and I couldn't find the right time to ask.

We'd been in the car for hours, and I'd spent most of the time staring out the window pretending to think . . . but really, I was listening.

Alex had caught everyone off guard when he'd gotten into the back passenger seat. I'd seen their faces; I knew they hadn't expected it. I got into the back seat before either of them beat me to it. The man named Leon shot the woman a look, and they'd both smiled before she got behind the wheel and he took the front passenger seat.

Alex hadn't exactly talked nonstop, but he had told them a lot more than I'd expected. From what I was starting to pick up, it was only me he was hesitant to talk to. That, or he was in a really, really good mood. I wasn't sure which, but since I was curious about everything, I wasn't going to complain about him being a chatter bug.

He told the strangers about being "hit in the back" and finding himself in my yard. I didn't miss the tension in the car or the looks that all three of them shot one another through the rearview mirror. He told them about how I'd helped him, about how weak and injured he'd been the whole time. Selene and Leon asked questions, and I could tell that they knew . . . well, everything it seemed like. About him, I meant.

Neither of the strangers made a peep about how he had waited to contact them. No one touched on the topic of what might have possibly been able to hurt him, which just told me they knew exactly what or even who had done it. The fact none of them seemed overly alarmed about the injury calmed me down some.

Alexander had continued with the story, talking about the cartel showing up and taking us. When he skated over what they had done to me in the other room and about his back finally healing, you could tell they were surprised. He even mentioned how sick I'd been afterward. How sick I still was, as if they couldn't hear the coughs I was still trying to muffle or how even though my throat hurt less, I still sounded like a cartoon character.

Except when he told the story, I realized just *how* sick I had been. *He hadn't wanted me to know*, I figured out real quick, which I appreciated.

Alexander continued recalling the rest of our adventure, about us escaping and him running for days until we came across the first cabin, then how we had trekked the rest of the distance to the house.

They had put together the rest, I figured, because there weren't questions after that.

We were safe now, I tried to convince myself again. He'd said so.

Closing my eyes, I exhaled and wondered, not for the first time, where we were going. It could be anywhere. The car was a rental; they had said that much when Alex had asked why they'd brought such a small car. We could be going to Chicago, or we could be going to New York. Maybe they were working on a fake passport.

Maybe one day . . .

"Gracie?"

I held my breath and looked at the pretty woman driving.

"Do you want us to take you somewhere?" the blonde asked carefully. I'd caught her looking at me a bunch of times. Not in a mean way, but more like when I saw someone wearing a shirt with a movie or a book I really liked. I couldn't get a good idea on her age, but I was pretty sure she might have been in her early twenties. I'd been peeking at her right back too, but more to make sure she wasn't going to pull over and throw me in the trunk when I was least expecting it.

But *take me somewhere*?

Before I could open my mouth, Alex answered for me. "She's going back home with us."

Leon's head swiveled toward his maybe-brother, or maybe those superior genetics made him a cousin. At the same time, Selene's facial expression went straight surprised in the rearview mirror.

He'd glossed over that little fact.

"She's staying with me."

"I thought you had said you weren't . . ." she started to say.

They knew he hadn't wanted to meet me, huh? I gave her a weak smile. "I don't have anywhere to go," I tried to explain vaguely, not sure if I should bring up other stuff. I sure as hell didn't want to, but reality was reality. There was only so far you could run from it.

The blonde woman blinked. Her head turned to the right, to Leon who was already looking at her. Even in the darkness, I could tell his mouth was formed into the shape of an O.

They both burst out laughing.

Why was that so funny?

"Both of you can fuck off," Alexander muttered, shaking his head as he shifted beside me.

"I'm not trying to take advantage of him or anything." Sure, this whole thing was ridiculous. Who was I to live with him? A member of the Trinity?

But I wasn't chump meat.

And neither was he.

"He asked me to stay with him since the cartel might figure out who he is and come after me," I explained, trying not to get irritated at them for laughing. Maybe being rude ran in their family? "It was his idea."

That instantly got both of them to sober up. It was Leon who said, "We're not laughing at you. We're laughing at Alex." I met his eyes when he glanced over his shoulder.

I held my breath. Did his eyes just glow blue? And had he really told me to call him Alexander to be more formal with me? To keep a distance between us?

"It isn't you," he tried to assure me.

I wasn't sure I believed him. I also wasn't sure I'd just seen two bright blue globes where his eyeballs were. But if I hadn't imagined it, did that mean . . . ?

The woman sat up straight behind the wheel and smiled at me through the mirror. She *was* beautiful. Something about her seemed so familiar too . . .

Huh. My stomach relaxed.

"Really," she said sweetly, "we aren't."

She seemed . . . earnest. I snuck my hands between my thighs. "Is it because he didn't want to meet me and now he's stuck with me?"

The man, Leon, snickered before fully turning around in his seat to look at Alexander. "What's wrong with you? Why would you tell her that?"

"What? Was I supposed to lie?"

Leon shook his head at the same time Selene did. "Ignore him. He's lucky you're so pretty," she said.

I blinked at her random compliment, but beside me, the son of a bitch snorted. "She's all right looking."

I scoffed. He wasn't wrong, and part of me couldn't believe he'd noticed what I looked like, but . . . "I can hear you," I griped.

"I wasn't trying to be discreet," he shot back.

Oh boy. "I thought we were friends now!" I said softly, feeling betrayed.

"Friends don't lie to each other." He sounded so damn serious too as he lowered his voice and said, "I made sure you didn't pee on yourself. You're welcome."

He'd gone there.

Why did that surprise me? "Well, thank you very much for that, much appreciated, but I fed you after you hadn't brushed your teeth in who knows how long, so I'd say we're almost even." I'd meant to whisper it, but it came out louder than I expected. Plus, I was still in his debt. We weren't even at all, but with that "all right looking" comment . . .

Alex blinked, then he spoke a little louder too. "My body doesn't excrete fluids the way yours does. My nose is more sensitive than yours is."

Really? "Maybe your sweat isn't stinky, but I think you're overestimating the freshness of your mouth."

"I didn't hear you complaining when you slept on top of me for days."

"You put me there."

"Exactly. I didn't see you crawling away from my breath then," he said, sounding fucking smug.

I swear . . .

I almost laughed.

What was wrong with me? How the hell had I ended up here? I was *arguing* with one of the Trinity about body odor. I couldn't have even dreamed this shit up; it was so ridiculous.

What had the world come to?

But that was the thing, wasn't it? He wasn't just The Defender. He was . . . Alexander. He was a crabby, sarcastic little shit who wasn't actually little. He liked arguing.

And for some fucked-up reason, I liked arguing with him.

And I refused to fucking admit it.

"They're bickering like little kids, and I am here for it," Selene whispered.

"How has no one suffocated you in your sleep?" I growled.

It was his maybe-brother but maybe-close-relative Leon who muttered, "We've tried."

"I wish you would have tried harder."

Selene's laugh made me smile, and the funny expression on Alex's face made me smile even wider.

I smiled at her a little through the mirror, my stomach loosening just a tiny bit more, giving me the tiniest hope that maybe this was all going to be okay. "Can I ask you both something?"

Beside me, Alex's eyes glowed, but I ignored him.

"Is he always this mean, or is it just me that brings out the best in him?" I asked them, not totally sure which answer I wanted to hear.

They both laughed, these nice, bright, friendly laughs, but it wouldn't be until hours later that I realized neither one of them actually answered me.

Chapter Twenty

"This is your *house*?" I gasped.

Alex grumbled as I stumbled after him in front of the modern Tudor-style building that may or may not be his home.

It was massive.

I'd passed out at some point in the car ride after listening to Selene and Leon explain just how they had gotten to us. They had flown to the nearest major city—Denver, apparently, we'd been in a town two hours north of there—and they had rented a car and driven over. Something had been off in their tones while they explained, and I wondered if even they were wondering why we hadn't flown back. And I didn't mean in an airplane. I had no ID.

Their words had gotten soft as I'd fallen asleep, the nerves, not feeling well, all of it hitting me hard. I'd woken up a few times, thanks to a shake of my shoulder to use the bathroom or to eat fast food they'd gotten through the drive-through. The sun rose and fell, then rose again in the longest road trip of all time. But I must have really needed the rest because I'd fallen back asleep almost instantly each time.

Until now. A strong nudge at my knee had had me lifting my head off the middle of the seat and blinking at the darkening rays coming through the car windows. And it was while I'd been processing that we'd arrived somewhere that I'd opened the door and taken in the home we were parked outside of.

What a home it was too.

My mouth was open, and I stared at the grandeur of what was pretty much an estate. Not a house. An *estate*. Or at least very, very close to one. Trees flanked it like something out of a movie or a storybook.

A fly was going to fall into my mouth, but it didn't even matter. I couldn't close it. Not when this was where Alex might call home.

"Is this how rich people live?" I counted the floors. There had to be . . . three. Maybe four?

I was pretty sure I whispered, "Wow." The house didn't even have normal windows. They were huge and paneled with black trim. The whole place, with its trees and wide property line and what seemed like it might be a giant garage behind the house, it was incredible.

"What else have you been hiding? Five kids?" I asked him in awe.

His growl was everything I would have expected it to be. "I liked it more when you were trying to keep secrets from me," he grumbled.

I almost smiled and tipped my head back even more, whistling short and shrill when it made my throat hurt. Were those vines growing over some of the walls and windows? I started to gasp and coughed instead. I'd been trying my best not to in the car, and it was getting harder and harder. "You sure you don't have a crazy wife locked in the attic?"

"She's in a locked room next to mine," Alex answered as Leon circled around the car and went to stand beside him.

Damn, they had to be closely related. With better lighting, I'd been instantly able to tell that they weren't twins. I had done my fair share of staring each time we'd stopped for gas and food. Leon seemed to be a little older, his features broader, eyes deeper set, and more blue than indigo.

I'd had to blink a couple times just to absorb and comprehend the sheer magnitude of beauty radiating from both of them when they'd happened to stand close beneath the bright lights at the gas station pumps.

It was too much, the two of them together, side by side. I'd caught a couple of cashiers staring at them too through the windows, overheard them being extra nice when they'd happened to come inside, even though that wasn't as often as Selene and I did. Neither one of them had bladders apparently.

"She used to be in the dungeon." Leon chuckled as he leaned against the car, looking just as tired as I felt. He and Selene had taken turns driving the whole time, while I hadn't done more than offer once.

"You've got a dungeon?" I reached over and poked at the hand closest to me to get his attention. "Can I see it?"

Alexander growled half-heartedly. "Not in this house, but if I did, maybe. Come on. We could both use soap, you could definitely use a toothbrush and toothpaste, and I'm ready to stop hearing your stomach grumbling. It's been more talkative than you. I didn't think that was possible."

Oh boy. "I said like five words in the car . . ." I trailed off with another whistle as he started moving toward big, double front doors that looked like they belonged in some architectural digest magazine. The sensation of being overwhelmed filled my soul for a moment, but I tamped it down and focused on just being . . . relieved.

Maybe everything in my life was a total shit storm, a complete and total mess that I had no idea what to think of or where to start dissecting or fixing it, but . . .

I was alive and I was free, and with time, I would get better, and that would be more than enough to make me happy for now.

Alexander opened the unlocked door, and I followed him in as Leon and Selene hung back. They'd been making faces at each other and whispering to one another a lot, but I didn't have Alex's hearing, so I had no clue what was being said. The entrance highlighted tall ceilings, and it was instantly noticeable that the home wasn't just beautiful, it was *rich*. There was so much wood everywhere; not the paneling I was used to either.

He stopped inside, his gaze eating up the view while he took off his borrowed shoes. Someone was glad to be back. Had he genuinely been worried that he wouldn't make it home?

Some weird sense of tenderness filled my heart, to think he might have something in the world to be concerned over.

Then that thought led me to think about all the stuff he probably did have to worry about. Big stuff. Huge stuff. Things I would never have to comprehend.

That suddenly made me feel guilty. Who got to go through life without worries? Nobody did.

I took my sneakers off and set them next to his. Then I followed him as we went through a spacious, beautiful living room. The furniture seemed timeless but new. It wasn't like I knew that much about interior design or trends, but I liked everything.

I spotted a few built-in bookshelves with brass or maybe bronze knickknacks. Delicate crystal things. There were even some gold-plated eggs that had gems in them that looked real. Through an impressive kitchen with pots and pans hooked over the range, sunlight spilled into the area and over late-model appliances. There was even a staircase that wasn't the same one I'd seen when we had first come in tucked into a back corner.

Upstairs held more dark woods that somehow managed to seem as cheery as the downstairs had. There was a *library* with potted plants; he pointed at a closed door that he called his office— an office for what, I had no clue, but I really wanted to know. We passed one bedroom after another that had to have been decorated by a professional from how nice they were. There was a huge room with a big bed that I'd bet had to be his from the way he stood at the doorway and sighed, blocking me from looking in.

So this was where he lived.

I hadn't seen that shit coming.

A brush at my elbow had me glancing toward the blonde woman right behind me, Leon just to her side. She tipped her head toward the hallway with a small, sweet smile that made my chest feel okay. I couldn't kick the feeling that something about her seemed really, really familiar.

Was she related to Alex too?

We backed out and headed in the direction we'd come. They stopped in front of a room down the hall beside the epic library I was already hoping I could snoop around in at some point.

"If you want to shower and settle in, we can stick a couple pizzas in the oven," Selene said, her sky-blue eyes crinkling. What was with these people and their amazing eyeballs?

I nodded and then hesitated, patting the sleep pants I hadn't mustered up any embarrassment over at any of the gas stations we'd stopped at. Someone had covered me with a clean hoodie at some point, and I'd put it on, but . . . "I don't have any clothes. Is there anything I can borrow?"

She nodded, and I purposely focused on her instead of the one who looked almost too much like Alex. "I'll find something, and tomorrow, I'll see what else we can do."

"Whatever you can get me. I don't mean to be an inconvenience," I agreed, giving her my best smile and trying not to feel awkward about having to rely on her generosity.

Her smile was bright and warm. "You're not."

"I need to leave, but Selene is gonna stay," Leon said, finally giving me a reason to glance in his direction.

He had his hands in the pockets of his jeans, his eyes set on me like he was inspecting me. Not mean, not judgy, just curiously. And if he knew about the Atraxia thing, that would explain it. It was obvious he knew about Alex, so why wouldn't he know about me?

Speaking of him, Alex wasn't necessarily better looking, but I liked the shape of his face more than his maybe-brother's.

I wasn't sure why the hell I thought about that randomly.

"Thank you both for everything. For coming to get us, for driving us . . . everything. If there's something I can do to help, please tell me," I offered, even though I didn't know what I could give them or much less what I could do. My pride made me try though.

They'd gone above and beyond for a stranger. For me. These special people whose presence made my skin tingle on a lower scale than Alex's did.

Why hadn't my grandpa told me about his mom and where she'd come from? I wondered again, wishing so much I could ask him.

As if sensing my mind was on other things, they both gave me these watchful smiles before turning toward the staircase and disappearing downstairs.

They were at least a little like Alex. I could just *feel* it. How they were related to him though, I didn't know for sure yet.

I headed into the bedroom that was heavy with blue accents as I thought about whether or not he would tell me more about his family. The room was pretty. The prettiest room I'd ever been in. A queen-sized bed sat up against the back wall with a beautiful but simple headboard. There was an opened door that led into a bathroom two times bigger than any bedroom I'd ever had. The shower stall had an intricate tile pattern, but it was the claw-foot tub next to it that stole my attention.

I found a couple of clean towels under the sink and hesitated when I didn't see any shampoo or conditioner but didn't want to bother anybody. The idea of getting my hair wet made a knot form in my throat as I stood there.

I could do this. I could use the tub. I was safe here.

I told myself that again, then again, and one more time, even as my skin prickled. I hadn't been this worried about it at the first house we'd stayed, but I'd been desperate then. Filthy.

Now though, I wasn't that dirty, maybe I could wait. I couldn't smell half as bad as I had before, and he'd put up with me.

"Gracie?" a familiar, rich voice called out from the bedroom.

I held my breath and tried not to sound deranged. "Yeah?"

"You good?" Alex asked from what was definitely the other side of the bathroom door.

Slowly, I lowered myself to sit on the edge of the tub and squeezed my kneecaps. "I'm great."

There was a pause. "I can hear your heart, liar. We already went over this," he huffed.

Dammit.

"You're fine. Nothing's going to happen to you here," The Defender assured me steadily.

I was fine. He was right. How much safer could I get than being in his home? I couldn't even let my blood pressure go up without him sensing it. Why did that make me feel so much better too? "Yeah, you're right," I agreed, squeezing my kneecaps again. "I forgot."

He didn't say anything for so long that I thought he'd left the room, but suddenly he said, "I don't want to smell your tears."

It hurt, but I snorted. "Then hold your breath."

Did he laugh? I think he might have. "Need me to sit out here until you're done?"

I was starting to think he might be the nicest rude person in the world. I let go of my knees. "It's okay. I was going to take a bath if that's all right. I won't fill up the tub or anything."

"Do whatever you want." There was another pause. "You're safe though."

I was safe, he'd said, and even though I hadn't relied on anyone or trusted anyone other than my grandparents, it was hard not to listen to him and that bossy-ass superhero voice he wielded too perfectly for someone who never talked in public.

"Gracie, say it."

I sighed. "Alex . . . ander?"

I was pretty sure I heard him sigh from the other side before he said, "You're not saying it."

I pretended like I didn't hear him. "Do you think I'm ever actually going to be safe? Do you think they'll stop looking for me someday?"

There was a thump at the door that made me wish I had X-ray vision to see through it. It sounded like he was on the other side. "I don't want to smell your tears," he started.

"I won't cry."

"You're lying, but no, I don't think you ever will be. If the cartel were to disband, there would still be someone who would remember."

I couldn't have felt any lower than I already did, at least, because I'd already known that was the case, but hearing him say it too, made it that much more real.

"I'm not going to let anything happen to you," he told me in his Super voice, sounding so certain.

I nodded to myself. "Okay."

"Are you going to be fine?" he asked after a long while.

I stared at my hands. "Yeah, I will."

I'd make it that way.

My heart didn't beat that hard while I filled the tub up halfway as I undressed. I didn't have anything close to a panic attack as I climbed in with the hand soap dispenser either.

I was safe. I could do this.

Settling for just soaping up the important parts, I lingered in the murky water before rinsing off, using my hands as a cup to get my neck and shoulders, then doing the same for my face. I would have rather taken a shower, but I could wait a little longer for it.

A creaking noise outside the bathroom door had me staring at it, but no one called out. I doubted Alex was waiting around. It was ghosts, probably.

Oh boy, with my luck it probably was. *I'm just kidding.*

I took my time drying off, taking in all the luxury fixtures one more time as I wrapped the towel under my armpits and headed into the bedroom, deciding whether I should wait around in the room until someone brought clothes or if I should try to find Alex to raid his dresser. He'd already seen me looking my absolute best in Mud Couture, and the only way to go was up.

Everything is going to be okay, I reminded myself, feeling my eyes start to water.

I stopped just on the other side of the doorway.

On the bed was a small pile of clothing and a plate with pizza and two glass water bottles.

There was no underwear and still no sign of a bra, but I pulled on the loose navy sleeping pants and the black T-shirt, that I bet had to be his. I didn't really like not wearing a bra. My boobs were too big to go without one, but mine was still wet and balled up in the backpack sitting on the floor. Everybody had already seen me swinging around for days at this point, what was one more? This whole adventure had changed a hell of a lot about my priorities, and I didn't think they had been that messed up in the first place.

I sat on the bed for a minute and listened.

Damn, this place was quiet. I was used to silence, but my house hadn't been huge, and the TV was always on.

Were there ghosts?

Nah. No way.

I ate my pizza standing up, chugged one bottle of water, and then sat there a little longer. The sun must have totally set because it looked pitch-black outside through the windows. Tired but restless and antsy from being in the car and on the run for so long, I did some stretches for my back and neck that I hadn't done since before everything. Once I was finished, I sat on the edge of the bed again and looked around the room, hoping to think of something to do instead of just sitting here, on the verge of contemplating all the ways my life had gone to shit.

If I went down that rabbit hole, I might never get out.

There was a library next door. There had been a big chair in there that looked kind of comfy. Maybe I could hang out in there? There had to be at least one book I could read. This room was nice and all, but by myself, it reminded me of that cell. And where was Grumpy Goose at? I needed to talk to him, but I could put it off until tomorrow, or whenever he had time. He probably had a million things to catch up on.

Who was I kidding? He was The Defender. Was he ever going to have time to deal with me? Chances were, he was going to forget all about me even if I lived at his house.

Rubbing at my face, I got up and headed in the direction of the library. I hadn't been in all that many houses, but this one reminded me of one in a gothic movie. I just hoped there weren't ghosts or wives with psychological issues.

On second thought, I went back into the bathroom, picked up my knife from the counter, and put it in my pocket.

He'd said I was safe, and part of me believed him, but . . . better safe than sorry.

Carrying a blanket I'd found in the closet, I made it to the door of the library and stopped right there. Someone had beat me to it. Alex was on one chair, Selene on another, and there was a small worn, leather love seat between them. A pizza was on a coffee table in the center, a few bottles of beers surrounding it.

The Defender looked up at me and raised those dark eyebrows even though I knew he had to have heard me coming.

I clutched the blanket closer. This was his house. I'd tried to make him feel welcome in mine, and he'd invited me to stay, but . . .

Awkward.

For a moment, I thought he was going to tell me to beat it.

But just like he'd surprised me when he'd knocked on the bathroom door, he did it again. "Over here, Cookie," he said.

I didn't hesitate. I made my way over, flashing the pretty blonde a little smile. I shook out the blanket before moving a small throw pillow to the side. Pretending like they weren't watching me, I laid down on the compact couch, my knees practically to my chest, and pulled the blanket over me, making myself at home.

Why I felt instantly more at peace, I didn't really want to think about too much.

I peeked over at Alex.

He was watching me, a bottle of beer hanging loosely in his fingers. Those eyebrows were still up, and his expression was . . . Why was he amused?

I blinked at him and pulled the blanket up to my chin. "I don't want to be in this haunted mansion by myself, bu—no, don't give me that face. I was going to call you buster, not . . . you know what."

Oh, he knew what. "Sure you were."

"I was," I told him quietly, peeking at the blonde who had the brightest smile on her face. Thinking about it for a second, I wiggled my finger at her in greeting before focusing back on Alex. "Just in case you forgot though, you threw up on me. I can probably call you whatever I want for a while."

Those purple eyes glowed on and off instantly as he scowled. "You can only blame yourself for that shit."

"That's debatable," I whispered.

He glared for a moment.

I glared back at him.

That sneaky corner of his mouth curved, and he held the bottle out.

I reached over and took it, taking a long drink of what tasted like . . . what was that? Raspberry? I passed it back over to him.

I was sharing a bottle of beer with The Defender. In his house. I was on his couch.

While my life was falling apart.

"You're really going to sleep in here?" he asked as he took a sip.

I froze. "If it's okay?" I debated whether or not to tell him the truth for a second but then remembered all the shit we'd been through. We were past that. Weren't we? "I don't really want to be alone, and that room is beautiful, but . . ."

He'd understand. I knew he would.

Or not.

There was another long moment of silence, and I wondered if I should have just sucked it up and gone somewhere else in this big-ass house. There was a living room downstairs. I could hang out on the steps outside.

"I can go somewhere else."

I was the stranger here after all.

His silence had me sitting back up and grabbing the blanket, but a big hand landed on my shoulder and pushed me down toward the couch.

"Lie down," he huffed. "You can be wherever you want."

I rubbed at my throat and asked, dead serious, "Are there ghosts?"

The son of a bitch didn't even blink. "Only Myrtle."

I rose up on an elbow. "Seriously, is that a no, or do I need to make a salt circle around the bed?"

"What's a salt circle supposed to do?"

"Repel ghosts, everyone knows that." It was Selene who answered.

I looked at her and smiled. She looked at me and smiled right back. Right then and there, I decided I liked her. I got a good feeling about her.

"Everyone knows," I agreed.

He just looked at me.

"Except you, I guess." I couldn't help it, I laughed. Selene did too. My throat hurt, but I couldn't stop. Closing my eyes, I settled in, wanting to give them some space before they regretted letting me hang out with them.

But to my surprise, they didn't wait for me to fall asleep before they started talking again.

It was Selene who spoke first. "Did you make a decision then?"

"No," Alex replied, "especially not after this shit."

"I can't believe it, Lexi. You think Mom knows? Do you remember how pissed she was when she did it to Achilles? I thought there was going to be an earthquake that day."

His huff wasn't a normal one; it was an irritated one. "Who the fuck knows, Selene."

Who was "she" and what had she done?

I tried to keep my eyelids loose so that it wasn't totally obvious that I was forcing them closed.

"I bet she didn't tell Grandpa."

So they *were* related somehow. Was it just her grandpa? Did they share a grandpa?

Had she said "Mom" earlier?

"Doubt it. I've done everything else they've ever told me to do. She crossed the fucking line, and she knows it," Alexander said in a voice so controlled I knew he was actually really pissed off. "What she did doesn't make up for it."

"I get it. You know I get it."

I wished one of them would drop a clue or three.

"I haven't talked to Mom yet, but I will. You might as well let her deal with it," Selene kept going with a little cackle at the end. "I'm going to get my popcorn ready."

Alex's answering grunt was low, maybe irritated too, the sound of glass on glass clinking through the room.

"Speaking of . . ." she whispered, "why did you wait so long to call?"

It sounded like the leather of the chair he was sitting in creaked. He didn't say anything.

Did the son of a bitch know ASL?

Before I managed to open my eye to see if he was signing, Selene spoke up again. "She's pretty, Lexi," she said in soft French.

He made a low sound in his throat. "She laid down on top of me to protect me from the people who took her."

I froze. My written and spoken French were atrocious, but I could understand a decent amount. Not that they knew that. Suckers.

"Why would she do that?" he asked, his tone tight.

"I don't know. I would've let you get beat up," she said seriously.

Alex huffed. "She's not what I was expecting." There was another pause and another clink of glass. "She didn't complain once when we were going through the forest. Her teeth were chattering, I could hear her gagging, I felt her crying from how bad she felt, and she didn't say anything."

"Is that why you're letting her stay here? We could have dropped her off at Mom's or even Alana's. You know they would keep her safe."

"When we were in the cell, I thought about it."

"Now you changed your mind?" Her tone was full of disbelief, I was pretty sure. "After everything . . . ?"

There was a huff. "I can't leave her. She's my responsibility." I heard a deep breath. "She's going to be in danger for the rest of her life because of me."

There was another heavy pause. "You think they'll figure out it was you with her?"

"I don't know, but we're never going to find out."

I must have totally passed out because I almost jumped out of my skin when I felt myself being moved.

Being . . . lifted?

Lifted?

Cracking an eye open, I startled myself even more when I took in the jawline above my head. It wasn't like I would have expected it to actually be anyone other than Alex, but it still surprised me.

"What's happening?" I asked, alarmed. "Are you taking me out back and leaving me for the pigs?"

He didn't even glance at me as he moved. My shoulder bumped his chest. The arms holding me up, shifted. For one brief moment, I worried about how heavy I was. Then I remembered who was carrying me.

That made my eyes pop open even wider.

"I don't know where you come up with this shit," he muttered, flicking a glance down at me, a hint of amusement on his sharp features. "I don't have pigs. If I was going to do anything, I'd drop you in the middle of the Pacific. I'm putting you to bed."

If he could fly. I wasn't about to bring that up though. "Where's Selene?" I managed to ask.

"In bed," he answered, sounding distracted.

It was nice being carried. Really, really nice. And I knew I should tell him I could walk, but . . . who knew when the next time this would happen would be? Much less the next time someone who looked like him would ever hold me? Never, that was when. "What time is it?" I yawned, feeling pretty shameless.

"Late," he answered. His chest was like a freaking wall against me.

"Want me to walk?" I made myself ask.

His answer was a grunt a split second before he turned into the bedroom that I recognized as the one I'd been given. Holding me up with one arm, pulling me even closer to him, Alexander tugged the comforter back before lowering me onto the mattress.

This was the first time since I'd been itty-bitty that I'd been put to bed.

And here he was.

"Hey." I grabbed his forearm.

That handsome face stared down at me. He really did look so much better now compared to how he'd been when we'd first met. His skin almost glowed, highlighting all those incredible bones and tissues that made him up. It had to be those "superior genes" he was always bragging about.

Or magic. Since he was apparently out of this world. Literally.

"Did you cut your hair?" I asked him, finally noticing that it wasn't at his chin anymore. When the hell had he cut it? How long had I been asleep?

He nodded.

It is hard to differentiate between Alexander and The Defender now, my brain thought.

I already knew there was more to him than the suit and the seemingly limitless power, but it really struck home big-time now. Here. In his house. With his mix of kindness and grumpiness. In normal clothes.

Who the hell was this person carrying me to bed, letting me hang out with him so I wouldn't be alone?

"I know this situation isn't your first choice, and you know, I wish I could say it wasn't my first choice either, but"—I blinked up at that gorgeous face—"considering how shitty my circumstances are right now, I'm grateful for it." I paused. "I hope you know how lucky you are to have people who care about you enough to go back and forth across the country to help you," I told him quietly, that lonely little ache squeezing my heart. I could only dream about having the same.

Tears popped up in my eyes, and I could tell he was narrowing his in response, but I pushed through.

"I'm not crying, okay! It's allergies," I lied.

We both knew I was full of shit.

"I just, I wanted to say thank you." I stopped talking and wiped at my eyes with the back of my hand. "I'll try not to bother you too much, but I can't promise because you're pretty much all I have left right now. But I'm going to try my best to figure out a way to get my life together so I don't have to depend on you too much, okay?" I rushed out, looking at him closely as I used my shoulder to brush my eyes too.

Those purple irises lingered on my face.

I tried to smile. "I can't carry you and run for miles at a time, but if there's ever anything I can do, anything I can help you with, you can count on me."

My loyalties were to him. He was the one I'd been through everything with. He was the one who hadn't left me when he easily could have a thousand times. The one who had split food with me and found water when I was pretty sure he didn't need it the same way I did. He'd said his kind repaid debts, and maybe I didn't feel like we were remotely the same, but my kind—me—repaid hers too.

"You? Help me?" he asked, not sarcastically or unkindly.

"Well, it's not going to be your imaginary friend doing it," I snickered. "All right?"

"If I say yes, will you quit fucking crying?"

I nodded, as he stepped back, then started to move around to the other side of the room.

What the hell was he doing?

I pulled the comforter up to my neck and watched as he pulled his sweatshirt over his head, showing me . . . showing me the most incredible body in possibly the world.

It hit me then I hadn't masturbated in forever. When he'd been staying with me, I'd managed to sneak in a rub or two in the shower while he'd slept, being as quiet as possible.

I was like a person lost in the desert, seeing water for the first time.

Supple muscles lined his chest and arms. Sleek, hard ones formed abs that would make a washboard jealous. A dark sprinkling of hair trailed from his belly button down into the formfitting sweatpants he had on.

But . . .

"What are you doing?" I croaked as he pulled the comforter back.

He slipped into the bed. "You're still sick, and I want to go to sleep."

I must have made a face of not understanding because he gave me another one of his long looks as he settled in.

He blew out one of his exasperated breaths while he was at it. "Do you remember when you were out of it and you were up against me all that time?"

He was talking about the bare-chested cuddling. I nodded. I was never going to forget that. I was going to be ninety and thinking about it.

"There's something in us that speeds up healing, like you figured out," he said. "In close proximity, it can affect others."

Ohhhhh.

Oh, oh, oh.

So it hadn't been cuddling to make me feel better. He had been trying to actually help me. Heal me.

I almost felt disappointed.

Almost.

That comforter got dragged up his chest as he kept explaining. "You're still sick; I can smell it. I know you've been trying to tough it out. You need to go to the doctor," he went on, giving me one more long look. "And you said you didn't want to be alone."

"I . . ." I mean . . . I had said that. He was right.

We were adults. I didn't need a pillow wall between us. We weren't five. I'd gladly slept on top of him while we'd been in the woods. And if I was overwhelmed at his generosity, then that was on me. He was going out of his way to be nice.

I nodded slowly, seeing him again through another lens. He really was a grumpy son of a bitch with a heart of gold. He tried to hide it, but it was clear as day.

"Okay. And you're right, I should go to a doctor. I've felt like a garbage can on fire." Setting my shoulders, I nodded at him. "Thank you for everything."

I was glad I didn't expect anything because that was exactly what I got.

Alex looked at me, and from one yawn to another, he rolled onto his side, away from me, without another word.

Not a "you're welcome," a "no problem," nothing.

I'd never admit it, but I felt pretty relieved having him here.

Old grumpy ass.

Because I could have done a lot worse.

"Gracie," he said suddenly. "Everything is going to be fine. You're safe."

I could have done a hell of a lot worse.

Chapter Twenty-One

Rolling over the next morning, I blinked blearily at the bare back inches away from my face, and then at the unfamiliar room around me.

The smooth skin . . . it was Alex. We were at his house.

Breathing out a sigh of relief, I immediately regretted when it hurt. I rolled over and rubbed at my face, taking in the light coming in around the curtains. *What time is it?* I wondered as my stomach growled, reminding me of how erratically we'd been eating for days. The one thing I didn't need a reminder for was that every single part of my body ached, inside and out.

He *was* right about me needing to go see a doctor. I'd woken up in the middle of the night, sweating, sure my fever was still lurking. I couldn't get sick anymore. I was fucking tired of it.

Rolling out of bed, I tiptoed out and shut the door as quietly as possible, even though according to what he wanted everyone to believe, he was fully aware at all times. I crept down the stairs, hearing noises coming from the kitchen. It was Selene in there, at the table, talking steadily into a cell phone, an empty plate in front of her.

Her bright blue eyes came to mine, and she smiled before pointing toward dishes piled with eggs, waffles, and breakfast sausages on the island, then at the cupboards.

It took me a long time to find the cabinet with dishes, one

with cups, and another with cutlery. All of it was nice too, heavy and not at all like the lightweight stuff that wouldn't break if it was dropped from a third story that I toted around. That I *had* toted around. In the past.

It was all gone now after all.

I filled up the glass I'd had to go to my tippy toes to reach and gulped one down before refilling it with water from a filter on the counter. After filling up my plate, I stood there and ate slowly, savoring everything. I was so hungry, and my head was starting to hurt. I'd left the painkillers upstairs.

And what time was it?

I glanced at the microwave and jerked.

"I'll talk to you later," Selene said into the phone a moment before hanging up. "Hi, Gracie," she greeted. "How'd you sleep?"

"Hi," I told her, clutching my fork. "Really well. Is it really two?"

"Yes. If it makes you feel any better, I woke up at noon, and I haven't been on the run for days," she told me easily. "You both looked like you needed the rest." Her crazy blue eyes flicked toward the ceiling. "He can go a few days without sleeping, but once it catches up to him, it hits him hard."

"And here I was worried he has a sleeping disorder," I told her, at ease but still a little uncertain about her. It was weird talking to a stranger, especially about The Defender. "He looked like hell for a while," I told her. "I don't think he's slept much in days." Possibly longer than that.

She watched me for a minute, a tiny smile playing at her mouth. "He's tough. He'll be fine."

I hoped so.

"About your things, do you want to take my car and run errands? I would take you, but I have two meetings I can't reschedule."

Oh. "Are you sure? If it's okay with you, if not, I can wait." I couldn't trust that the superbeing upstairs was ever going to have time to drive me around. That hadn't been part of our deal. "The thing is, I don't have any money." That hurt me to say. I'd come to terms with that fact at some point while I'd been clinging to his neck, except I'd thought it would be Alex I'd be hitting up for a small loan. But my gut felt good around Selene. And for whatever reason, I didn't feel so awkward asking her for it. Desperate times call for desperate measures. "Could I borrow some? Please? I can pay you back when I figure out how to get access to my bank account again."

She started nodding before I'd even finished talking. "No problem. I don't have a lot of cash on me . . ." She reached over to pick up a bright red purse, pulled out a slim, black wallet that had initials stamped all over it, and plucked out a few neatly folded bills.

Five one-hundred-dollar bills.

She didn't consider that a lot of cash?

She handed it over, along with a credit card, that I instantly tried to give back.

"This is more than enough."

Her dark blonde eyebrows rose. "Alex said you don't have anything."

I winced at the reminder of the situation I was in. "I don't, but I don't want to go too crazy. I'll just get what I need for now."

She kept the card in midair. "You sure?"

I nodded and cleared my throat, ignoring the ache. "Thanks. So much. I promise to pay you back soon."

Her expression was so friendly, it touched me just as much as her smile had. "I know," she agreed like it was perfectly normal to let a total stranger borrow her car and a few hundred bucks. I would *never*. Ever.

But fortunately for me, not everyone was as distrustful as I was.

This was going to take some getting used to.

I looked down at my clothes and lack of bra and knew exactly what I needed to go buy first. I had a long list of things to do and figure out and had to start somewhere. Sleeping Superhero Beauty upstairs wasn't going to be buying my panties.

It was close to nine o'clock when I finally drove down the driveway leading toward Alex's mansion.

I'd had to pay a lot of attention to remember how to get back and not lose track of where I was, even though her car had built-in navigation on the screen in the dashboard.

When I'd left earlier in the day, I'd only made it about twenty feet away from the house before I had to pull over to burst into tears.

I hated fucking crying, but you know what? It had been a long few weeks.

It was a good thing I'd almost made myself forget I had nothing tangible left. I'd gotten used to being independent. But now, my whole life seemed to be hinged on the generosity of others. Alex being kind to me yesterday by carrying me to bed and staying in it with me to give me his healing vibes was one thing, but the rest of it . . .

It went against every single instinct in my body.

It was basically my nightmare.

I'd been working since I was fifteen to help my grandparents. It was soon after that, that I started having to do the heavy chores around the house because my grandpa had gotten too frail. He started showing signs of dementia when I was eighteen, and that had been the beginning of me taking over just about everything. I'd worked full-time while I put myself through school. For five years, I'd been lucky to get four hours of sleep a night while I'd tried balancing everything.

I did what I had to do. I always did and always would.

And now . . .

By the time I managed to calm down, my eyes had become

sticky and puffy. But the second I found myself on my way, I'd gotten sucked into the landscape I'd missed while I'd been asleep on the way there. If his house was stunning, everything around it, just made it that much more magical. The last sign I'd seen on the way over had said WELCOME TO TENNESSEE.

It was while driving Selene's pristine white Camaro that I learned from the display we were in North Carolina. No wonder we'd been in the car for so long.

The house was situated way down a long driveway, right smack in the middle of what seemed like a forest. Huge trees flanked the paved road, and I had leaned forward, glancing every which way as I drove straight, a tall, wrought-iron automatic gate opening as I approached it. And that's where things got a little suspicious.

Instead of making it out to a busy road or a street, it was just more trees and a longer lonely road. It fanned out left and right a few times, and when I leaned forward to see where they led, there were more gates. Selene had said to keep going straight until I made it to the road—*you can't miss it*, had been her words—and eventually, after yet another even taller gate with what seemed like twenty cameras angled around it, I found the road.

How the hell I was supposed to get back in was beyond me, but I decided I'd figure it out later. Maybe there was an intercom? It shouldn't surprise me he lived in a gated community.

After following more of Selene's directions, I went straight for the first store I saw a sign for and bought a couple bras, underwear, socks, and one set of jeans so I wouldn't have to worry about my nipples and boobs bouncing around while I shopped. After that, I headed for my cell provider's store, but the phones had been so expensive, I figured I was better off reporting that mine was stolen. I had the account under the LLC I was paid with. They were a cartel; they weren't hackers, and I knew there hadn't been any information in the house about it. All those accounts were connected to a PO Box in Albuquerque with the paperwork in a safe deposit box in a bank in Arizona, so there shouldn't be a reason why anyone would find it.

After there, I'd thought about where I could get the most clothes for my buck and drove around until I found a thrift store close by. I spent half my money there before going back to Walmart and blew the rest on a couple tank tops to sleep in, some bread, sandwich meat, cheese, peanut butter, jelly, milk, and cereal. Then I got a little something else too that made me smile.

It was the least I could do after everything.

I had purposely tried not to think about my job and money while I'd been out and about, but it was hard not to once I thought about the ten dollars I had left . . . and no way to make more. I needed to get access to my account and see how much money was in there.

I was going to throw up.

No, *no*, I wasn't, everything would be fine. I would figure it all out. Maybe I could borrow more money and pay Alex back in installments?

Sniffling, I wondered what my chances were I could get another hug out of him? He'd hugged Leon and Selene. He'd been the one to initiate ours. Contrary to his crabby-ass attitude, none of the signs pointed to him being allergic to touch. He'd been the one to pull me onto his lap every time. He'd said it himself—we were *friends*.

And in the name of friendship, I'd brought him a giant cookie that said HAPPY BIRTHDAY on it in frosting as a small thank-you for everything he'd done.

Putting the car into park, I managed to slip all the bag handles onto my forearms and huffed and puffed on the way to the front door. Not sure if I should just walk in or not, I jabbed my elbow against the doorbell and waited, straining under the weight of the toiletries, clothes, and the plain tennis shoes I'd picked up to replace my wet ones.

It took way too long, but the door opened, and Selene's face was there, not looking surprised even a little bit.

I'd bet she'd seen me on the cameras. I'd only had to sit in front of the gate for about a minute, wondering how to get it open, when it had started moving. I had figured someone had buzzed me in.

She grabbed the bags hanging from my left arm. "You bought all this with that cash?" She eyeballed my other arm as I passed bags from one to the next.

"I milked every penny," I told her with a tired smile. "Sorry I was gone so long."

She turned and headed toward the main set of stairs while I toed off my shoes and left them beside her sneakers. "I didn't have anywhere to go. Agatha brought some groceries earlier. She was disappointed she missed you," she called out over her shoulder like I should know who that was. But all I knew was that she was the one Alex had told me to call.

While I was thinking about him . . . "Is he still sleeping?" I whispered.

Did her shoulders tense under the blouse she had on? "No, he got woken up a few hours ago."

Why did that sound weird? "Oh, okay," I said, following behind her. She turned into my room and set the bags on top of the bed. I set half of mine beside hers but held on to the ones with groceries in them. "I was going to put these in the fridge if that's okay."

"Sure, yeah," she said, still sounding a little off, at least compared to how she'd been talking.

"If it's not okay . . ." I trailed off, not sure what I would do. Or why that would be a problem.

Was something going on?

"No, no, sorry. I have a lot on my mind," she replied quickly. "Do whatever you need."

Something had happened. I'd bet my ass on it.

"Is everything okay?" I asked, even though I damn well knew we were strangers and she had no reason to feel obligated to tell me shit.

She nodded, but it didn't make me feel assured, at all.

"Okay . . ." I held up the bags. "I'm going to take these downstairs then."

Selene nodded again, but I definitely knew something was going on as she followed me into the kitchen. I kept an ear out for Superbutt in the house, but there wasn't a peep. I had just set the bags on the counter when her phone started ringing and she smiled at me before disappearing down the hall that led to the main part of the house with the living area.

That wasn't at all fishy. Maybe I was imagining it, but maybe I wasn't. I wasn't used to being around people. I was probably just being awkward and overthinking it.

I had just managed to put the milk in the fridge and was taking out my sandwich materials to put them wherever I could find room when I felt Alex's presence nearby. There was a signature to his energy, and we'd just spent so much time together I was sensitive to it or something. Glancing over my shoulder, I found him leaning against the doorframe into the kitchen. His arms were crossed over his chest. He had on a heather gray shirt and black jeans.

But it was that pissy-ass, crabby expression on his face that made my stomach feel weird.

This wasn't the first time I'd seen it, but it was on a whole other level compared to before.

"Hey," I greeted him, trying to sound normal while trying to think about what could have happened.

Nothing.

WHEN GRACIE MET THE GRUMP 347

I blinked, not sure why we were back to that now. "How was your day?" I asked slowly, watching his features carefully. It was the first time in months that we hadn't been stuck together.

I'd kind of missed his grumpy comments and scowls, and *that* was a strange thought.

His eyes flashed purple for a second, and he kept on staring.

"That good, huh?" I said weakly, still watching him.

Seriously, what had happened? Last night had been okay. Now there was definitely tension in the air.

"I'm sure Selene told you, but I went and bought some clothes and things," I said. "I should have asked if you needed anything, but I didn't think about it until I was out, and there wasn't really a phone I could use to call . . . and I didn't have anyone's phone number."

"I don't need you to buy anything for me," he said in a tone I hadn't heard in some time.

One of my eyes went squinty. "Good, I'm glad I didn't call then," I told him a little sarcastically.

Some way, somehow, his face went even more crabby. "You shouldn't have been gone all day."

"No, I shouldn't have, but I had a lot of things to buy. I don't have anything but the clothes I took from the first cabin and what you let me borrow, and I still wasn't able to buy a phone. I need to order a replacement through my insurance and figure out how to get another ID and access to my bank account," I told him in a rush. "Do you think I can borrow someone's credit card so I can order a phone? If I can get to a laptop, I can transfer money over."

He'd slowly started narrowing his eyes while I talked, and alarm bells went off in my head, but I ignored them.

At least I did until he opened his mouth a moment later.

"I'm not buying you a cell phone."

I blinked. "Did I ask you to?" And hadn't I literally just said

I needed to order one from my insurance? Pretty sure I'd said I would pay him back too.

"I want to make sure your expectations are in the right place."

I opened my mouth, then gritted my teeth.

"You can live here until we sort things out, and I won't let you be harmed, but I'm not here to take care of you," Alex griped, sounding like he meant every word.

Okay, I was pretty sure he had implied just that at some point, but it wasn't like I'd seriously been about to hold him to it. Give me a fucking break. It was insulting, honestly, after everything.

"Did I tell you I needed you to take care of me? I wouldn't ask you to spot me money if all my stuff wasn't gone. I'll sort out getting access to my bank, okay? I'm good for everything. I can sign an IOU if it'll make you feel better." What the hell had crawled up his ass and died? He'd been in a bad mood when he'd been at my house but not *this* bad. He'd been a little grumpy since but not anything I couldn't handle. It had even grown on me.

I'd had the nerve to kind of miss him today, and now that pissed me off.

"Good. Sort it out sooner than later," he grumbled.

I bit my bottom lip for a moment and told myself to let it go.

Just let it go. He was in a bad mood, and there was no point in making it worse. I hadn't done shit to cause it.

But . . .

I couldn't do it. I just couldn't. Just because he'd had his moments of being so nice to me didn't mean he got a free pass to being an extra jerk.

But didn't friends talk to each other when they were mad? Didn't *friends* try to understand when something was clearly wrong? I figured they did.

And just because he was being a butthole didn't mean I had to come at him like a wrecking ball right back.

Even if I really wanted to.

"I told you that, if I did something to irritate you, to tell me. I'm not a mind reader. You said I could stay here," I reminded him, since he'd obviously forgotten, trying to use a borderline polite voice. "I didn't ask."

I instantly knew that my "nice" voice hadn't done shit.

Alex's head cocked to the side at the same time his jaw went tight. "No, you didn't ask, but you took me up on it immediately."

Was this son of a bitch serious? "Is that really what you think?" I asked him, not fucking believing this shit.

He glowered as he shrugged. "You did what you had to do to help yourself."

I wanted to jab him in the throat, I really did. "Okay, sure. To an extent, yes, but I didn't ask to be put into this whole situation. I didn't shoot you down from the sky and catch you or lock you up in a cage. I could have easily gone the rest of my life never meeting you, and that would have been exactly how I liked my life." Quiet and uncomplicated.

He better not even get me started on it being his grandma's fault—or whoever the hell it was—that they wanted him to "get me" or "meet me" or whatever the hell it had been.

He straightened off the doorframe and uncrossed his arms, looking like . . . like such a good-looking shithead that needed my foot up his tight ass. Alexander watched me for such a long time that when he finally shook his head, I knew I definitely wasn't going to like the rest of this conversation even though I wasn't in the wrong. I sure as shit wasn't going to let him make me feel bad. *He* had offered. He could have left me. If he was changing his mind now . . .

Friends. We were friends. I could drudge up a little more patience. I could *understand.*

I rubbed my cheek and lowered my voice, trying to understand. "What's going on, Alex? I'm not trying to take advantage of you. I can't go back in time. I didn't mean for this to happen."

We both knew that.

Or maybe we didn't.

"You're here because I said I would keep an eye on you. You risked your life for mine. It's what I owe you."

Right . . .

"*That* was what I signed up for. Not for anything else."

My eye started to twitch.

"That's the extent of what our involvement with each other needs to be."

My eyes bugged out of my head. Hadn't he literally slept in the same bed with me the night before? Of his own choice? Hadn't he said it was okay to sleep on the couch beside him because I'd told him I didn't want to be alone? Didn't I try to let go of his hand when I'd grabbed his finger and he didn't let me?

Holding my breath, I squinted at him, embarrassment and anger and disappointment all rising inside my soul. "*You* came into my life. Do you want me to apologize for taking you in? Do you want me to say I'm sorry for getting sick? All I've tried to do is help you . . . and if I can help myself a little bit along the way, then hell yeah, I'm going to take advantage of it. I don't have anyone. I've never wanted to put anybody at risk. But you are in no position to make me feel bad. You did the same thing. I'm grateful that you offered to make the deal to give me a place to live and protection, but I didn't ask for that either. Don't turn this around. I can figure this shit out on my own if I have to."

If he didn't want me here, if he was going to make me feel bad, he could fuck right off. I would live in the woods. I wasn't going to waste a fucking day of my life feeling unwanted. He had no idea how deep my stubbornness ran.

And from the way this conversation was going and the expression on his face, I was going to have to make a decision about my future and make it fast.

His next words sealed the deal. "I want to make sure we're on the same page."

I wasn't even sure we were in the same fucking book, much less the same page.

I managed to lift my gaze and meet his dead-on. I had gotten through so much on my own. I had fed myself and supported myself. I had kept on going even on the days that I didn't want to, when I felt like I had nothing else to keep breathing for. I'd made a promise to my grandparents, and I wasn't going to back out on it, not when there was still the smallest sliver of hope that I could have a future.

I was no fucking punk.

"We're on the same page," I agreed, my mind already racing.

I stared at him, and he stared at me, this heavy silence forming between us.

His jaw moved, and I thought he was going to say something else, but Selene appeared in the doorway, her attention on the cell phone in her hands. She glanced up, saw me standing there, and smiled. "Did you find room for your things, Gracie?"

It took me a second to make sure my voice was even as I nodded at her and forced a smile onto my face. "I did."

The tension must have gotten to her because her smile fell, and her bright blue eyes flicked from me to Alexander and back.

I had to move fast. "I was wondering if I could borrow your phone, Selene? And your credit card after all? I need to get both. I can repay you what I borrowed when I'm done if I can use the browser on your phone. Could you give me an address where I can have things shipped to also? Since the community is gated."

Selene was still looking back and forth between us, her face wary, but she nodded. "Sure. Yeah," she replied even as she went back to that red purse. She barely glanced down before she handed me a black credit card.

I forced a smile and nodded again, even as my eyes started to burn. She gave me her phone, sweeping a glance toward Alex while rattling off an address that didn't make much sense, but I was too distracted to ask. I kept my gaze on her as I recited it so I wouldn't forget it.

"Thank you, I'll be quick," I promised before darting up the stairs.

I stopped right at the top, suddenly not wanting to go into the room I'd slept in.

Or the butthole's library.

Or any place else that belonged to him.

And I was way too prideful to go downstairs and walk by them to sit outside.

Fine. Sitting right at the top, I filed a claim for my "lost" phone. It wouldn't arrive tomorrow, but it would the day after.

I bit my lip, staring at the blank screen after I'd hung up.

I had no one to call. No one to worry about me. There were my students, maybe, but I couldn't begin to imagine how mad or disappointed they had to be since I'd disappeared on them, but I didn't want to worry about that right then.

Not when loneliness and a sense of bone-crushing disappointment settled on my soul. On my total existence. It was nothing new, but it hurt worse than ever.

Who would really care if something happened to me?

No one, that's who. Nobody.

Covering my mouth with my hand, I squeezed my eyes closed.

Were things ever going to change? I had no idea. I could only hope, and that was all I had left to hold on to. Tears and being upset weren't going to change shit. All I had was myself, after all.

Wiping at my face again with the sleeve of the sweater, I fanned myself and then stood up. Taking my time, I headed back downstairs. Selene and Alexander were in the exact same spot that they'd been in when I'd walked out.

I held the phone and credit card out toward her and gave her the best smile I could summon up, fucking grateful that I hadn't actually cried. "Thank you."

Her dark blonde eyebrows knitted together. "Do you need something else?"

"No, thank you," I said. "I'm actually pretty tired and not . . . not feeling so good. I'm going to go lie down."

I made sure not to look toward The Defender. No way, no how.

Selene glanced to the side, at her maybe-relative before focusing back on me, her expression troubled.

Figuring I could sneak back down for water later when the kitchen was empty, I said, "Well, thank you for everything, Selene. Good night." I thought about it and glanced in Alex's direction, focusing on his chest. My voice was flat as fuck. "I brought you one of those cookie cakes. It's on the counter. Thank you for not letting me die."

I didn't wait for a response before I was out of there.

I headed up the stairs, stopping just at the doorway to the room and wiped at my face again. It wasn't wet fortunately. He'd be able to smell if it was.

I was going to be on my own. What was new? Nothing, that's what.

I wasn't welcome? Okay. Fine. I closed the door and locked it.

I didn't need him. I could owe everyone else a favor and money, but I wouldn't add him to the list with that shitty-ass attitude. I had a lot to think about, a lot to decide on, but I was going to do it. I would rather live my life on my own terms than on someone else's.

All he wanted to do was put a roof over my head? Fine.

Pulling the cover off the bed and a pillow too, I set it on the floor so I could use it after I brushed my teeth.

I was going to figure this out.

It would be complicated and hard, but that wasn't anything new.

I could disappear again.

Chapter Twenty-Two

I could put down "sleeping on the floor" on my list of shit to regret.

It had to have been the adrenaline, fear, and desperation that had made sleeping on the floor in the cell bearable. Because this time? Things that hadn't hurt before, hurt now, and everything that had hurt before, hurt even more.

It probably didn't help that when I did wake up, all I could think about was Grumpy Ass. His words. His attitude.

How had things gone wrong so fast?

Maybe they had never been great between us, but I'd thought . . .

It didn't matter what I thought, did it?

What mattered were the facts: my existence annoyed him, and sooner or later, he was going to kick me to the curb. Maybe it would be a padded curb close by, but it was still a curb. That could be today, tomorrow, or weeks from now. Then what?

I would end up on my own one way or the other.

Promises were only worth something when there was trust between people.

Friendship didn't equal trust.

I forced myself to get up, suppressing the groans that wanted out of my mouth as my body ached. I used the bathroom, brushed my teeth with my brand-new toothbrush and toothpaste, and stared at my hair in the mirror. I brushed it out and put it up into a nubby ponytail.

Keeping my chin up, I went downstairs and found Selene in the kitchen again seated at the table with a tablet in front of her that she was staring at intently. Her gaze lifted the second I walked in, and she gave me a faint smile, like she could tell something was off. "Morning."

"Hi, Selene," I said, feeling shy all of a sudden. She'd known last night something had been going on.

"Did you sleep okay?"

I lifted a shoulder. "Did you?"

From the slight change in her narrow features, she knew I was deflecting but answered anyway. "Not long enough. I miss my bed."

"Do you live far?" I asked.

"No. We were up late, and I didn't feel like driving home," she answered, surprising me for a moment. "Alana asked me to keep an eye on him." She put her finger to her mouth before dropping her voice. "We're all worried something is still off that he's not telling us about."

Was she expecting me to rat him out? Would I? No. I wasn't a snitch. If he wanted to lie to his family, he could. Plus, I wasn't shallow with my words. I had told myself I was going to be loyal to him, and I would.

Even if I wanted to flip him off.

"He just got back a couple hours ago. He'll be asleep for a while," she kept on whispering.

"Oh." I didn't want to fish. We were back to my rule: the less I talked, the better. The less I asked, the better too. Even if I wanted to know who Alana was.

"There're leftovers from last night if you want them for breakfast. I need to head into the office today."

I wondered where she worked, what she did. How old she

was. But what was the point when I wouldn't be seeing her for much longer? She already knew more than most people I'd ever met.

Maybe in another lifetime we could have been friends.

In another lifetime a lot of things could have been different.

"Thank you, but I have cereal. You're welcome to it if you want any." See? I could be polite. I could be nice.

"I'm good, thanks," Selene answered, watching me closely.

It felt like she wanted to say something else but didn't.

Keeping my chin up, I turned to the cupboard and got my cereal and milk out. I thought about standing up to eat, but decided I was already being run out of here. I took the seat beside her at the table just as she set her tablet on the surface and leveled beautiful blue eyes on me.

I spooned the little, round, donut-shaped objects, only meeting Selene's gaze after I'd taken a few bites.

I gave her a brief smile.

"Can I help you with something?" she asked gently. "I know you've got a lot to figure out."

"No, it's okay. I think I can get everything sorted." I didn't know where to start or how I was going to pull it off, but I would, dammit.

Those eyes moved over my face like she could tell, and she probably could. I'd never been that good at hiding my feelings. I used to have to walk away so that my grandparents wouldn't notice when something was up my ass; I didn't want to hurt their feelings or get chewed out for disagreeing with something.

I fucking missed them. I missed them so much.

"It's none of my business, but I've never been good at minding my own business, you know what I mean?" the woman said. "You look sad."

I dipped my spoon into my bowl and made myself glance up.

Selene nodded.

What was I going to do? Tell her that her Alex hurt my feelings? That I didn't want to stay here anymore? No. Instead, I settled for telling her part of it. "I'm just overwhelmed with all the changes in my life. I'm sad over it." And here I'd just told her I didn't want her help. That made a lot of sense.

I was pretty sure she didn't believe me anyway. "Do you want me to show you around the property? So you can settle in? I can show you where the compost bin is," she offered. "There is a field out back with the solar panels that power the house, and he has plans for a greenhouse by the garage."

I wouldn't be here long enough for that to be necessary, so I shook my head. "That's all right. Thank you. But could I borrow a laptop? I want to send you the money you let me borrow, but I'm not sure if I can even check my account without my cell phone, and I just thought about whether I need to call the police about the incident at my house." Saying those words out loud hurt my heart.

Would I be in trouble? Would there be a warrant out for my arrest? Could my landlord sue me? Was I a missing person or did someone actually have to report you missing for that to happen?

A grunt made me tense.

Alex was there, by the door, looking sleepy in another set of fitted sweatpants and a T-shirt.

I tipped my chin up higher and decided to be the bigger person. For now. "Morning."

He grunted again.

All righty then. That's where we were. That hadn't been his usual grunt.

I faced her again and kept my expression nice and flat. "I'm going to shower. Could I borrow your phone or laptop or something later, please? I'm sorry to be so needy."

"You're not." She slid the tablet toward me. "I can use my laptop."

"Are you sure it's okay? I can wait."

The other woman nodded, her gaze going from me to The Defender and back. "Positive."

Smiling at her as gratefully as possible, I took it. I washed my bowl, eyeing Alex out of the corner of my eye as he dug through the refrigerator and pulled out what looked like leftovers. I thought Selene had said he would be asleep for a while since he'd been out doing who the hell knew what all night. Too bad for me.

I pointed upstairs. "All right, I'll be . . ."

She nodded.

I took my time walking out of there, making sure not to make eye contact with one of the biggest letdowns of my life. I had to start trying to figure things out. I didn't have another choice.

What was fucking new?

"Gracie," a deep voice called out from behind me.

I'd propped my back up against the side of the bed farthest from the door, facing the big window that showed a building behind the house that was twice as big as my trailer had been. I was fairly certain it was a garage from the size of the doors. Peeking my head up and over the mattress, I managed to keep my features straight as I found Alex there, looking just as irritated as ever.

Great.

The few hours that had passed since I'd seen him in the kitchen hadn't eased my tension or patience with him and his bullshit. We all had something going on, but that didn't mean he had a right to get such a shitty attitude and accuse me of stuff.

"Hi."

"What are you doing?" he asked, not actually sounding like he cared.

Was me sitting quietly on the floor in the room going to bother him too? I opened my mouth to ask him if he wanted me to go sleep outside, but he kept talking.

"Agatha's going to be here in a minute," he went on like I knew who Agatha was, much less why her being here had anything to do with me.

I made sure my voice was nice and even and not at all strained with a mix of frustration and hurt as I told him, "I don't know who that is."

"Robert's wife."

That still meant nothing to me.

"She's a doctor. She's going to check you out."

I learned in that moment just how petty I was. I guess I hadn't been in enough situations in life *to* be hurt or hold a grudge. I guess, just like how I'd thought the Trinity were above basic human shit like bad moods and dislike, I thought I would be the same. That I could be the better person when it always mattered.

I wasn't.

I wanted to tell him I didn't need him to do anything for me.

If I flipped him off while I did it, even better.

But I also instantly realized that as petty as I might be, I was more reasonable than that. I didn't want his help, and I didn't want to take advantage. But in my situation, it would be dumb not to do what I had to. I'd be out of his hair a lot faster than either one of us had expected. In the long run, this small thing would be no big deal since I wouldn't be bothering him anymore.

Which was what he wanted.

I could eventually pay him back for the doctor visit too.

Forcing myself to nod even though it was stiff, I took my time getting up, setting Selene's tablet on the middle of the bed. I hoped she let me borrow it again. I'd tried logging into my bank account, but without my cell phone, I couldn't verify the security steps to access it, so that was cool. Getting into my email hadn't been any easier either.

Until I got my phone, I wouldn't be able to leave.

"Thank you," I said as I made eye contact with him lingering at the door.

He said nothing.

"Do I need to go downstairs or . . . ?"

"She can come up here and give you some privacy."

Pressing my lips together, I nodded.

He watched me, the crease in his brow a stubborn line that confirmed my mood wasn't the only one that hadn't gotten better. Whatever had crawled up his ass had built a little home with a pool and wasn't planning on going anywhere anytime soon. Had I done something wrong? Had someone else done something and it just happened to trickle down to me?

Does it matter, Gracie? He'd made it perfectly clear that he thought I was a hassle he didn't want or need. To be fair, I understood. Hadn't I wished he'd landed on someone else's property? I'd taken care of two people I loved, and not once had they felt like an inconvenience, but that was because my life had revolved around theirs. I had loved them. Adored them. They had been my world.

And when you care about people, doing things for them was an honor.

The Defender didn't love me. He'd let me hold his hand out of pity. He'd originally offered to help me because he thought he owed me.

I was a responsibility, not an option. Someone had wanted him to find me because of some ancestor that gave me stomachaches. I didn't owe that person anything either.

Alex hadn't wanted to meet me in the first place.

If I'd learned anything in all the romance books I'd ever read, it was that you wanted someone to pick you.

But I could pick myself, and that's what I was going to do.

"Okay. Whatever is easier," I said to him.

Those purple eyes stayed on me.

"Thank you for calling her."

"Selene did," he claimed.

All righty then. "Then thank you for telling her. I'll pay you back for the visit, or I'll ask her if I can pay her directly in a day or two." Might as well make that clear.

He just kept on fucking looking at me.

Did that bother him too?

"Lexi?" a female voice called out.

He gave me one more look before he replied, "In here."

"I can't stay long," the unfamiliar woman kept talking from what seemed like down the hall, her voice getting progressively louder. "Asami has an appointment this afternoon, and you know how—oh. Hi."

A face appeared just behind that big shoulder. Her dark hair was tied back in a neat ponytail, her makeup clean and light. She was very, very pretty and maybe somewhere in her forties. Maybe.

The woman gave Alexander a look as she pushed around him into the room, carrying a leather backpack and a satchel in each hand. There was a little red, yellow, and green key chain hanging from one of the handles. "Hello," she greeted as she set her things down on top of the dresser.

I cleared my throat and reminded myself that she was here to help me, that I didn't have to hide, at least while I was here. "Hi," I said again, setting my hands on my lap before extending one out to her. "It's nice to finally meet you. I'm Gracie."

She took my hand instantly, her hold firm, her smile bright.

"Hi, Gracie. You can call me Agatha. We don't really use honor-
ifics in the family." Her head swiveled to the door where Alex
was still standing, arms crossed over his chest. "What are you
doing, Lexi?"

"Standing here," he said plainly.

"Do you think you're going to stand there during her checkup
is what I'm asking?" she asked him in a tone that made me
blink.

His gaze flicked to me briefly, his chin going up. "She doesn't
know you."

Agatha's eyes moved toward me too.

"I don't feel unsafe around you," I told her directly before
looking at ol' Grumpy Shit. "I'll be fine. I'm sure you have better
things to do." He had some brooding to do. Some grumpy faces
to practice in the mirror.

Those dark eyelashes fell over his eyes. "I can hear your heartbeat." He shot Agatha a look I couldn't interpret before taking a
step back. "I'll wait out here."

Fuck. "It's fine," I tried to tell him.

Without another word, he walked out and took a stand with
his back to the wall beside the doorway.

She shook her head. "Want me to close the door?"

It wasn't like he couldn't hear through them anyway, and
what did I have to hide? "That's okay."

"There's no privacy in this family, as you've already figured
out," she said, opening her backpack and starting to root around
in there. "Secrets get old. It's not so bad. You get used to it with
time."

That was a weird comment.

Either way, I wasn't going to be here much longer, so there
wasn't going to be much to get used to.

She pulled a few things out of her bag before moving toward
me. "Can you fill this out for me first? Then I'll check your vitals."

"Check her lungs," Alex suddenly spoke up. "She swallowed and inhaled a lot of water."

We both glanced toward the doorway.

"Thank you," I told her, hearing the hoarseness in my voice. I took the tablet from her and filled out the online questionnaire that covered my medical background and that of my family. At least what I knew, which wasn't really all that much. I hesitated with my last name and settled on Castro.

What all did they know about my family anyway? How had his grandmother known where to look? How the hell hadn't I wondered about that before? Was that another superpower?

Just how lazy had I gotten with staying under the radar that everyone had fucking found me?

And who the hell was the cousin who had supposedly ratted me out?

It made me upset. Made me angry too, to be honest. Because look where I was. Look at everything that had happened. Everything that I'd missed out on.

Now here I was, living on other people's charity. My life was in ruins. I had nothing. I had no one because I'd been too cautious to ever let anyone close enough to really know me. What I had was a big mouth and a chip on my shoulder, and I would have gotten drunk one night and totally told someone something I shouldn't have.

I needed to find out how Alex's grandma had found me so that I wouldn't make the same mistake again.

My hands shook, and I set them between my thighs and waited as she took my temperature, my blood pressure, checked my mouth and ears, then listened to my heart and lungs.

I could see her watching my face from time to time, but all she did was ask some general questions about my health. I stared at her hand the whole time. A big ruby ring sat on her finger, the sucker the size of an acorn.

"Robert . . ." She paused, busting me. "Gave it to me. It's a family heirloom. It gets caught on everything."

"It's amazing." Could I be less obvious? "Have you been married for a long time?" I asked her before she could turn the conversation around on me. Plus, everyone kept using his name like I should know who he was.

"Twenty-one years next month," she answered. "It feels more like forty-nine sometimes." She laughed, and it was a really nice one that made me smile.

Then I really thought about what she said and blinked. Twenty-one years? "How old are you?" Oh boy. That could have come out better. "I'm sorry."

She looked up from the tablet and flashed me a playful smirk. "I'm fifty-four."

I tried my best not to make a what-the-fuck? face but figured I'd failed when she winked before focusing back on the tablet.

"It's one of the many benefits of being married into this family and having a lot of naked time together."

Outside of the room, Alexander groaned in obvious disgust.

"Oh, be quiet," she said with a roll of her eyes. She dropped her voice. "They're so square about sex at first, and then—"

"Do you talk to all your patients like this?" he called out, his voice weird.

"Yes. You're all family, and you all hear everything, and most of you don't act like preteens about s-e-x."

"I know how to spell, Agatha," he barked out, still sounding weird.

"I'd hope so." She smiled. "Mind your own business anyway, I'm not talking to you." The doctor shook her head like she was trying to remember where she was going with her thoughts. "While we're talking about sex, I'm aware of your situation. Do you need me to fill you a new birth control prescription? You put on here you aren't on any medications."

Oh.

The last time I'd been to the gynecologist, she had written me a prescription that I hadn't filled.

Was I in a position to be that vulnerable with someone?

I thought about it.

Wasn't that the same thing I'd been telling myself for the last decade? The same lame-ass excuses? I was about to be thirty. I'd kissed less than a handful of people. I'd given a couple blowjobs when I'd been a teenager straddling the line between listening to my grandparents' orders of secrecy and being a horny little shit who wanted one more connection in life. Since then, it had been a rush of taking care of my grandparents, then just learning how to be truly alone and surviving. Making enough money with my limited circumstances to eat, pay bills, and save for an emergency.

Then all this had happened.

Of course I wanted to have sex, that was one of the things I'd been the most upset about when I'd thought everything was over. I didn't even have a vibrator anymore. What the hell did I have to lose taking a daily pill?

Maybe I could finally get over the lying and just . . . do it.

Literally.

"Yes, please," I told her before I could talk myself out of it. Maybe I could drive out of the state to fill the prescription, or have it mailed somewhere else to be safe.

There was a thump from the hallway that we both ignored.

Agatha nodded, her eyes crinkling. "Okay. What were you on before?"

I rattled off the name that my gynecologist had recommended, looking toward the door.

"I'll email it to you," she said before giving me a serious face. "Birth control is effective in this family."

What? I didn't even get a chance to be embarrassed about what she was implying because she kept going.

"Now, I heard a little something in your lungs, and your ears and vocal cords are severely irritated. Usually, I would do a chest X-ray or run some tests, but unless your condition happens to worsen, I think you're already on your way to getting better." Her eyes slid toward the doorway, and I knew she was thinking about Mr. Magical Healing Capabilities and what he'd done for me.

"If you do start to develop more symptoms, visit the office. I'd like to do some bloodwork on you anyway." She glanced toward the door. "My phone number will be in the email I send you."

"Thank you," I told her. "I still don't feel great, but I'm getting slowly better."

"I didn't hear anything alarming, but I know you've been ill. You need time and rest. I've only had to prescribe antibiotics a couple times. Your cells are pretty miraculous on their own."

How did she know?

"I just sent the email. Do you have any questions for me before I leave?"

I shook my head, wondering now if everyone knew about everything.

"If you think of anything, you have my information," she said as she packed her things up. Once she had a bag over a shoulder and the other in her hand, she gave me another one of her smiles. "It's been a while since I've been the new kid, but I know it's unreal. I didn't know my parents. I had no idea about any of this. My only gifts are that I have better-than-average hearing and I won't need glasses until I'm a very old woman; I thought I was normal until Robert came into my life and told me otherwise." Kindness radiated from her. "You're going to be fine. Let me know if I can help somehow. Robert is in India right now, but when he gets back, I'm sure he'll drop by."

I wanted to ask who Robert was, since everyone seemed to think I knew a lot more than I did, but I kept my mouth closed and pretended. I was good at pretending. I probably wouldn't be here by the time whoever Robert was got back.

"Thank you so much. I appreciate you coming to check on me," I told her.

She gave me another smile before walking out of the room, saying something I couldn't hear to Alexander, and then disappearing down the hallway toward the front staircase.

That went better than I'd expected.

I was still sitting on the end of the bed when Crabby-Ass came to the doorway, hands buried into the pockets of his pants. His face was smooth and almost impassive. What had I done now to aggravate him? Breathe wrong?

"I'll pay you back for the visit," I jumped right into telling him, trying to keep my voice and heart rate steady.

He didn't say a word; he just looked at me with that perfect face and its perfect bone structure and skin.

I hated that we were back to this bullshit.

He wasn't a total dickhead. I *could* try. I *should* try to mend what had happened, even if I'd had nothing to do with it. Not in an effort to stay but because he had gone above and beyond for me, over and over again.

It was the least I could do.

Linking my fingers together, I squeezed them between my thighs. "Did I do something? Can I help you somehow? I don't need to know what's happened, but if there's something I can do, all you have to do is tell me," I said carefully. Trying. I had to know I was trying, so did he.

But it was in vain, like just about every effort in my life turned out to be.

"No," he said, totally serious. "I've got shit to do now."

I kept my mouth shut as he turned on his heel and disappeared too, leaving me there. Alone.

It wasn't my business. I didn't totally understand everything that had happened that had led him to my house, but he seemed to. His grandmother had tried to find me, and I'd been found. Maybe once I left, I could send him a postcard to let him know I was still alive, so she would know. If I ever got my life together and managed to have a child, maybe I could let them know that too so they could keep their Atraxian family tree going.

But he or she would more than likely have too much human blood at that point, from what Alex had said.

Or I'd be smart and disappear into the wind. I could live even more under the radar. Move to the last place anyone would ever look, again. There were plenty of them.

It would probably be for the best to just hide.

Everything that made me Gracie Castro was gone now, and maybe there wasn't a point in holding on to that identity anymore. It was only in my heart after all.

The reality of it fucking depressed me though.

"What the hell are you doing?"

Fuckkk!

My eyes popped wide open. I screeched even before I noticed there was a face hovering above mine. That there were glowing eyes in the dark *staring at me*.

I didn't even realize I was swinging until fingers wrapped around my fist and pushed it back toward my chest.

It was fucking Alex. It was fucking Alex, my brain processed. I just about wheezed.

He was crouched beside me on the floor, clutching the blanket directly under my chin. I couldn't have been asleep that long because I didn't feel too groggy. My shoulder didn't feel like it was about to fall off either, not like that morning.

"What the hell?" I gasped, blinking into the darkness. "What are you doing?" My heart was about to burst out of my damn chest from him scaring the hell out of me like that cat in *Alice in Wonderland*. "Fucking fuck."

Even in the dark, I could tell he leaned to the side a moment before the lamp on the nightstand turned on, giving me a decent view of him. He was fully dressed in those deceptively normal clothes that almost made me forget what he was. Who he was.

I hadn't seen him in hours. I'd stayed upstairs practically the whole day, only sneaking down after listening long enough to make sure he wasn't in the kitchen. He hadn't been in the house, period, I'd discovered after creeping around. I'd had a feeling he was gone, and I'd been right. So was Selene.

"What are you doing on the floor?" the man known to the world as The Defender asked in a growl as he dropped into another crouch.

I licked my lips and set my palms on the floor, pushing myself up to a sitting position. "Sleeping," I told him, sounding annoyed because I was. What did it look like? I was trying my best not to bother him, so why did he have to come in here and wake me up? I'd closed the door.

"Why are you on the floor?" he asked again, like I hadn't heard him the first time.

A sudden reminder of everything that had transpired between us filled my head, and that same sadness and anger mixture made my throat tighter than it already was. "Because I'm sleeping on it. That's why my eyes were closed." *Real mature, Gracie.*

His gaze narrowed. "You want to sleep on the floor?"

I rubbed at my eyes, annoyed. So damn annoyed. "Do you need something?" He'd barely talked to me all day. I wasn't sure what he could have possibly suddenly wanted while I was dead asleep, but all right. Maybe it was something really important.

Or maybe he was telling me to get the hell out already.

"You're still sick," he said, his gaze moving from my face

down to my lap where the blanket was bunched. A little knot formed between his brows. "Why'd you want to sleep on the floor?"

I focused on a plank of the dark floor. I wondered what kind of wood it was. "I already told you," I answered, hearing the edge in my voice.

"Why?"

"Because I want to." I knew it was the wrong thing to say the second it came out of my mouth. I should have made something up. The mattress hurt my back. There were bedbugs. I didn't feel safe. Something else. Anything else.

Out of the corner of my eye, I saw his chin drop toward his throat, and those purple eyes flashed in the lamp-lit room. "You're lying."

I kept the sigh in my mouth and lifted my gaze to focus on the dresser knob in front of me. If I didn't answer him, I wouldn't be lying. There. Problem solved.

His hand moved so fast that his cool fingers were under my chin before I'd even blinked. "Tell me the truth."

I tried to look at the ceiling, but he moved his face back into my line of sight, the son of a bitch.

He was frowning. "Since when do you not look me in the eye?"

Is that what he wanted? Fine. I did it. I even made them wider than normal so he wouldn't have anything to complain about.

And those intense eyeballs did what they wanted to do. They moved over me, once, then twice, down my throat, where they lingered . . . below. I'd put on a tank top to sleep. I hadn't worn a bra; my nipples were on the bottom of my list of things to worry about. If they offended him, he could only blame his own damn self for looking at them. When I'd been younger, I'd been so self-conscious about my boobs. My grandma had made me buy shirts two sizes bigger to hide them.

They weren't hiding now.

A hell of a lot slower than I would have expected, his attention moved back toward my face. His frown was gone, a scowl in its place. Again.

Oh boy.

"I don't have the patience for your bullshit today, little monster. Tell me why you're on the floor," he grumbled, annoyed.

Oh *no*. Oh no, no, *no*.

Reaching up, I wrapped my fingers around his wrist and *pulled*.

It didn't do shit, but his eyes went hooded, and I could tell, I could *tell*, he was mad. Madder at least.

Too damn bad.

"I don't care what you do or don't have time for. Me sleeping on the floor doesn't affect you at all."

His eyelids dropped even lower over those incredible irises. "Yes, it does, because you're my responsibility, and I need to know what's going on in your head."

It took everything in me not to roll my eyes so hard they got stuck in the back of my head. "I'm not, and I don't need to be. I can take care of myself, and anyway, I'm not going to be in your life much longer, so don't waste your time. You've got better things to do, after all," I said, tugging on his wrist again.

He still didn't budge or let me get out of his hold either, but what was I supposed to do? Not try?

What he *did* do was lean forward. "What's that supposed to mean?"

This pain in the ass . . . "You've got enough going on, and I've spent my whole life hiding. I can hide for the rest of it. I know things. I know people." That part was a lie, but it didn't matter. I needed my phone. I needed to call the cops and see if I was in trouble. Find a way to get into my safe deposit box. I needed to file a claim for my insurance. I might have to go back to New Mexico to do it, even though that was dangerous.

Then there was everything else.

Alex's jaw went hard. "What people do you know?"

"People!" I hissed at him, fed up.

Oh, he didn't like that. "You're my obligation now."

I swear . . . "I don't need to be. I didn't ask for any of this."

"You think I did? But I'm trying to take responsibility—"

Was he for real? I stared at him and shook my head. "Yeah, I know, you made that clear. You knew about me years ago and didn't want to meet me, why would you want to know me now, right? It's all my fault. It's my fault for being born, and it's my fault that things happen." I made my hand into a fist, my heart hurting all of a sudden. Why did this always happen to me? Was I cursed? Was that it?

Why me?

My nose burned like Satan had lit a fire in it, but I refused to fucking cry or look away. I tipped my chin up a little higher, because fuck. This. Guy. Again. "You can do whatever you need to do without worrying about me. I don't need or want you to go through with your end of our 'bargain.' The bargain you didn't ask for or want any part of." I made quotation marks with my fingers. "Don't worry about it. It's done. We're done. I'd appreciate it if you let me stay here until I get my phone at least."

He stared at me, and his head tipped to the side, that hypnotic voice barely audible. "We're done?"

How did he have the power to hurt my feelings so much? I squeezed my hand even tighter, lowering my head to focus on my lap. He didn't want to be my friend, and he never had. This pain in my chest would pass eventually. One day, I'd come to terms with his fucking attitude and his decisions and reticence. "I'll be out of here as soon as I can get my financial situation sorted."

Why did I feel so betrayed?

Why was I so mad at him and sad?

Alex's hand cupped my jaw, and I'd swear I could feel his energy, his power, radiating through my skin. "You don't get to decide whether I live up to my promises or not," he said softly.

I gritted my teeth. "Pretty sure I do when it involves me." Now I was the crabby ass, but you know what? I didn't care. I *was* done. Regardless of what he said, what he thought, I hadn't asked for this. I hadn't wanted this ever; I never wanted to bother *anybody*.

I wanted to fucking cry. I wanted to fucking cry now, but I wouldn't.

"I gave you my word."

That got me to look up and meet him dead in the eye. "And I'm freeing you from it. You don't want to deal with me. I get it. It's fine." I'd already bothered enough people in my life.

One eyebrow went up, and then the other, his gaze bouncing around mine. I'd swear the charge his body put off seemed to ramp up like some kind of jet about to take off. An electrified vibe suddenly filled the air.

It felt so, so weird.

And I was going to ignore the fact that whatever it was made my nipples go hard.

I set my jaw. "You don't owe me anything. I chose to help you, and I'm not going to regret that I did the right thing." Even if he was a moody shithead. "You don't do nice things and expect something in return. That's not why I did it." I lifted my shoulders. "It's fine. Promise."

You could've heard a pin drop as I lowered my cheek to my shoulder and rubbed my eye against it.

His eyes were glowing so, so faintly when I lifted my gaze.

His hand moved, just an inch, his fingers sliding across the bone of my jaw, making my skin prickle. "You're planning on leaving?" he asked softly, his power making the air even thicker.

My damn nipples were the first to notice too.

I swallowed and sat up straight. "Go live your life or do whatever it is you need to do. Can I have my face back now?"

A soft puff of warm air left his nose, and he raised his other hand, cupping my throat with it.

My little heart sped up at that. What in the hell was he doing? Why was he touching me like this?

He wasn't going to kill me . . .

Or maybe he was?

"Why?"

"Why am I leaving?"

He nodded.

What did I have to lose at this point anyway? I wasn't trying to be mean, but sometimes the truth wasn't pretty. It wasn't like he held back from me either to soften my feelings. "I would rather sleep on the floor and take my chances on my own than feel like a burden," I told him slowly, softly, carefully. I didn't want to cry, and if I went too fast . . . "You have enough to worry about. The whole world needs you. You saved me from that place, you took care of me when I needed it the most. You carried me when anybody else would have left me to die." I swallowed. "Thank you. Really, thank you. I've spent the last three decades in my own little world: I can figure it out. You don't have to worry about me . . . not that you would, but you know what I mean."

That cool hand left my face, and he stood up suddenly. His chest rose and fell once before he looked down. His Adam's apple bobbed. Those perfect lips pressed together.

I stayed where I was.

"You're sleeping on the floor because of me?"

I suddenly felt tired and petty. I shouldn't have said anything. I should have kept my mouth closed. I should have pretended like everything was fine until I could sneak out of here. I was so damn dumb. Because maybe he was a grump, but he was no stranger to responsibility. Somewhere deep down in that crabby heart with teeth, he didn't let people down. He didn't go back on his word. There *was* a lot of kindness in him.

And I was guilt-tripping him.

"Gracie," he grumbled deeply.

"You don't want me here, and I'm not going to stay where I'm not wanted."

His face went cloudy. "I never said I didn't want you here."

Why did that make my chest hurt? "Yeah, you did."

"No, I didn't."

I scowled, my hand forming a fist. "I thought I was stubborn but you . . ."

A small growl formed inside that unreal chest. His hand went back to my throat. His pinkie finger grazed the soft skin between my neck and collarbone. He tilted my face at the same time he lowered his, hovering there, staring right into my eyes.

He dropped his voice, the hint of a growl there as he clenched out, "You stubborn little butthole."

I gasped. "Hey. You're the butthole." Rude.

"No, you are."

"No—" What was I *doing*? I was over this. I didn't want to talk about it anymore. I definitely didn't want to bicker with him over it.

He had his own things going on, and I understood it. If I carried the weight that he did on his back, I'd be a mush of bones and guts. I would've crumbled instantly. The last thing he needed was another human body's worth of weight to carry.

Whatever I felt now would pass.

Alexander's dark eyebrows rose though, and his face dipped even closer. So close if I would have leaned forward a couple of inches, his mouth would have brushed the tip of my nose. He was literally *right there*.

And if he had been anyone else, if we'd had a different

friendship/relationship, I would have thought something I had no business thinking of. I could have hoped that was the case. That would've been a dream straight out of one of my books. I wasn't blind. I wasn't immune to the power of his face and that incredible body. He was the most handsome, beautiful man I had ever seen and would ever see.

But this was my life, and sure we existed in a world where a person like him existed, and sure, I had some secret DNA in my body . . .

But none of that meant shit.

And I was tapped out in the miracles I was willing to believe in.

But his next words surprised me more than just about anything else would have. "You're not leaving, Gracie."

My snort hurt, but it was totally worth it to see his expression darken and his face inch a little bit closer.

He didn't let me stop him. "You said we were friends."

It was so petty. So damn petty, but I muttered it anyway. "I changed my mind. We don't need to be friends. You weren't that crazy about it in the first place."

Oh, I felt the fucking ice in his gaze. "I changed my mind."

Oh boy.

"We made an agreement," he said in that super-bossy voice, deciding to approach this in a different direction. "I said I was going to be there for you. *That's* what we agreed on."

I swear . . . I squawked right before his hand moved and his thumb settled over my lips. Was this son of a bitch for real? Was he telling me he wouldn't pay for my cell phone one day and now insisting he wanted to be there for me?

"You're not leaving." He kept going in that steady, rich voice. "We made a deal, and you don't back out on a deal, Cookie. Not with me."

He was fighting dirty calling me that, and we both knew it. But I wasn't even going to poke at it. I had to focus and not let

Dr. Jekyll and Mr. Hyde get to me. "I'm not backing out on the deal. I'm releasing you from it," I said from under his finger, feeling myself getting riled up. It was his honor making him say all this, I knew it, he knew it.

He took his sweet time shaking his head. "No. I'm not being released from anything because you forgot what I said I would do—"

"I didn't forget anything," I said, my words muffled under his finger.

"Shh."

I was going to "shh" his ass.

"Listen, Gracie."

I growled.

His nod irritated the hell out of me. Then he busted out the smoothest, most patient tone he had ever used, on me at least, as he lifted his finger from my mouth. "You're going to live here."

I didn't think I'd ever bitten anyone, but I was seriously considering it now.

"I'm going to protect you, because there might be a chance that there are people now who would want to get to me through you, and you know who those people are. You think word won't get out?" I could feel his breath, all nice and cool on my face. "I'm going to be here for you for the rest of your life. That's what I said I would do, and that's what I'm going to do."

I grabbed his wrist and tried to tug it away. He let me go but slipped his fingers through my hair right above my nape instead.

I froze, surprised. Shocked more like it. And that's probably why I could barely choke out the words, "What are you doing?" Shushing me was one thing, but this?

I was pretty sure my nipples got even harder, the traitors.

He rubbed my hair between his fingers, I could feel it. Even his breaths were soft on my cheek and nose. His fingertips suddenly grazed my scalp, and I tensed at the unexpected affection.

No. It wasn't affection. He didn't even like me.

My nipples were out of control. They needed a time-out. Maybe they needed to get grounded.

It took me two tries to clear my throat and ask weakly, "I'm not kidding. What are you doing?" Did I have to sound like a damn frog?

"Nothing," he said almost absently, still focused on my hair, back to rubbing his fingers over it.

I felt the "hmm" he let out in my chest. Those purple irises moved back toward me. "You aren't leaving."

Get it together, Gracie, I told myself and focused on his cheekbones and not the long fingers almost caressing my head. "Look, you saved my life when you took care of me and carried me away from that place. We're more than even. I don't want to take advantage of you. It'll be better this way."

"Oh, you're wrong about that," he told me, back to doing things to my hair that I was *not* going to pay attention to.

"Wrong about what?" I managed to ask.

"All of it."

I narrowed my eyes, his fingertips brushing my scalp again. Tingles trailed down the length of my spine, but I ignored them and hunched my shoulders. "Would you stop that already?"

His "No" was a straight shot as he did it again. "You aren't sleeping on the floor again."

"I'll sleep outside next time. Try me." I tried to bat his hand away, but his puff of a laugh made me stop. "What are you laughing at?"

One corner of his mouth tipped up just a little bit. "I thought I had a bad temper."

"You do. That's why I'm going to leave you alone."

That got his chuckle to dry out almost instantly.

It was unfortunate how much of a handsome bastard he was. He had the nicest skin I'd ever seen. He had the nicest everything. All healthy and virile and—

And I was a burden on him.

On everyone.

"You can't leave." His gaze bore into mine. "They'll come after you to get to me."

It wasn't like I hadn't thought about that, but I still shrugged. "That's only if they figure out how we got out, and you said you did something to their security footage. Maybe they won't know." And maybe pigs flew and I'd wake up six inches taller.

Get real. I knew how my luck ran.

"I also said that those security guards might figure out I didn't bleed when they shot me." That sneaky pinkie finger brushed the skin on my neck. "They're going to keep searching for you forever. You know that as well as I do."

He had a point, but it wasn't anything I didn't already know.

Plus, why was he being so talkative? And why was he trying to be so touchy-feely and nice? Why now? Because he felt guilty for running me out? "You just said it. They've been searching for me forever. I'm used to it. I've got this."

His nostrils flared as he tilted his head to the side. I tried to pull back again but couldn't. His pinkie rubbed my neck again, and I tried my hardest to not shiver.

"I hurt your feelings."

He'd done more than that, but I kept my mouth shut.

His sigh brushed my chin. "What happened has got nothing to do with you," he started to say before I snorted. Those fingers slipped deeper through my hair, fully cupping the back of my head. "I'm sorry, Gracie," he said.

"What?" I jerked. Did this . . . man . . . just apologize?

I stared at him. He stared at me.

"For being a butthole."

My eyes narrowed. What the hell was he up to? "What are you doing? What do you want from me?"

"What makes you think I want something?"

"Because you're saying sorry and playing with my hair. You're being way too nice."

Why the hell did he look so surprised?

"Alex, you literally implied that I planned this. That you weren't going to give me more than what you promised. That I couldn't expect more. Now you're telling me sorry and that I should rely on you after all?" I shook my head. "You've got these moments of being so ridiculously kind in your own way, and then making me feel"—I held my index finger and thumb an inch apart—"this small. I don't want to do this. I know you're a good man, but you don't need to save everyone. You don't need to save me, all right? You already did."

Those lean cheeks flexed. His eyes narrowed just a little bit. Something in his energy changed too.

And that's when I took advantage and leaned far enough away that his hand slipped out of my hair. "So, stop. Please."

That snapped him out of it. "I'm nice" was what he decided to focus on.

I wasn't even going to poke at that comment if I had a ten-foot pole. I sighed and side-eyed him, not understanding this at all. "What do you want? What are you trying to do here?" I asked him warily.

He didn't even think about it. "Apologizing."

I didn't trust this version of him.

"I regret what I said." Those eyeballs glowed faintly for a split second. "How I made you feel."

"You meant it. You don't need to feel bad."

His expression went cloudy. "I told you I've never been responsible for another person before."

Oh boy. I snorted. "You're so full of shit. You've been responsible for billions of people for years."

That got me a blink. "It's different."

"Not really," I told him. "But that doesn't change the fact that you don't want to be more involved in my life than you need to. I get it. I'm nobody. You have seven billion responsibilities, the weight of the Earth on your shoulders, and I don't have a single idea what your day-to-day life is like and what else you have to worry about. You're already bogged down. *I get it.* I couldn't handle it; 99.99 percent of people wouldn't want to either. I don't want to be an extra weight. I don't want to be a bother. Obviously, you have people that love you just the way you are. I don't know who Leon and Selene are, but they care about you enough to fly halfway across the country for you and then drive it back. I don't even . . . I don't even have an emergency medical contact anymore."

Saying that out loud broke my own heart. "You could use a little more patience, but you don't need to change who you are for anybody. Especially not me."

I watched as he listened, his aggravated expression back the moment I started speaking, but I saw it wither away with every word out of my mouth. That regal, perfect face dropped any semblance of annoyance and frustration, and . . . it didn't go soft. But it went thoughtful, I guess. He looked . . . surprised too, maybe?

For someone so self-aware of everything from how gently he had to touch things so as not to break them, to how he listened so he didn't pick up a thousand conversations, it was like this was something that went totally over his head.

Those incredible eyes flared that beautiful glowing purple

again for a long, long moment, before a crease formed between his eyebrows.

"It's okay. I promise," I whispered truthfully. "I've been taking care of people my whole life. I can take care of myself."

Alex's sigh was long. His arms crossed over his chest. "You make it really hard to not like you."

I hadn't seen that coming.

I hadn't seen that coming *at all*.

His mouth went flat. "You say whatever the hell is on your mind, and you annoy the hell out of me sometimes."

And there we go. I blinked. "Don't hold back."

Alex blinked right back. "You're stubborn as hell, Gracie, but you make it hard to not like you."

Dammit.

Dammit.

In his own fucked-up, crabby way, he was paying me a compliment.

I don't know what it said about me that I appreciated his brutal honesty, that I understood exactly what he meant.

And now it was me who had to try really hard not to like him, this pain in the fucking ass.

He was gorgeous, sure, but there was a hell of a lot more to a person than what lay on the outside. Butthole or not. And even though there were so many facets and mysteries to him that a lifetime of research and archaeology wouldn't uncover, I had meant what I said to him about not changing for someone else.

I crossed my arms over my chest, telling myself that I could replay his words on a night in the future when I was all alone again. "Thank you for the apology and that compliment, but I still don't think I should stay."

"Why?"

"Because."

"Because?"

"Because I don't want to," I told him. "Because I shouldn't. I can figure out my life on my own."

He narrowed his eyes right back at me, lingering there for a long, long moment. "I hurt your feelings that much?"

I wanted to tell him no, that he hadn't, that everything was fine. That I was used to this. That he wouldn't be the last person to ever hurt my feelings, because he wouldn't.

But I just looked at him, knowing I couldn't lie; he would be able to tell. "You don't have to feel guilty about it. This wasn't going to be long-term anyway." Which was the truth. If I'd expected anything, it was to be in hollering distance, and that distance could be a wide one with his ears. "You don't want me here. I didn't want you at my house either. I understand. You're busy, you have responsibilities. I get it."

Something moved across his face, through those incredible eyes, and I felt him exhale again right in my own chest. "If I didn't want you around, I would have left you at my grand-mother's house, Gracie. I don't give my word often, and when I do, I don't go back on it. I'm not going to start today," he said in that steadfast way that reminded me of who he was when he put that blue cape on. More than a man, an icon. A figure that brought relief and reassurance. That told countless people things would be okay.

Which was what he was trying to do for me.

The tip of his finger tapped me in the center of the sternum, bringing me back to him and that bossy face. "I'm not going to start with you."

There were some things in life that were too good to be true.

I'd already known how things were going to end up eventu-ally. With me on my own, taking care of myself. I was never going to be able to live a normal life. Unless I changed my DNA, faked my own death, totally started over with a new name and social security number, I was never going to be able to be at peace. And I accepted that that was my fate. My life. Unless a miracle occurred and a whole family and their compound got wiped out. Even that wasn't a certainty.

It fucking sucked, but it was reality.

And just as I was about to tell him that, he kept going. "I was eighteen when I agreed to help people, this planet, and over the years, I've been disappointed again and again and fucking again. I've had people throw shit at me, call me evil, tell me and my family that we're going to be the end of the world, like we don't do what we do to try and make sure that doesn't happen. I'm tired of the fucking idiots, Gracie. Most days it feels like they outnumber the smart ones. But every once in a while, I'll meet someone who reminds me of the good that people are still capable of."

I narrowed my eyes, not sure where this was going.

"You helped me when you didn't want to, when it put you at risk. I know what it's like to do shit you don't want to do, but you do it anyway because it's the right thing." The Defender tilted his head and looked at me so, so seriously. "People think doing the right thing is easy, but it's not. The right thing is hardly ever convenient." His eyelids dropped low over those eyeballs, and his Adam's apple bobbed, and I didn't think I was imagining him having to dig deep within himself to say, "Other things irritated me, and I took it out on you. I'm sorry for that."

I started to say *well, too bad* when his hand landed on my nearly bare shoulder.

"For the rest of your life, Gracie. That was my deal." He stared me right in the eye. "I'm sticking to it."

I pressed my lips together.

"You're fine." He shook his head. "You're a good person, and I didn't want to like you, but I do."

The man known as The Defender moved his thumb across my shoulder as he looked at me, that grouchy face turning open and sincere. I'd watched it too much to not notice the tiny differences in his features when his emotions changed. And I could tell that they had.

Then he reached toward the dresser and picked up a big orange bag from the top that I hadn't noticed.

Cheetos. He was holding fucking Cheetos.

I looked at him, and the son of a bitch shook the bag a little as he held it out.

Dammit, I had to be logical.

"There's another bag downstairs," he said, watching me so, so carefully.

I could be practical.

"You said you promised your grandparents that you'd live a nice, long life." He drew every word out. "Your best bet at that is sticking with me, and you know it."

Suddenly, I felt in over my head.

My stomach twisted in that funny way right before something monumental happened.

Fuck.

It twisted again, reminding me that it was always right.

Those thick, dark eyebrows rose slowly, and the son of a bitch shook the bag of Cheetos at me some more. "What's better than regular friends?" he asked. "You can be my best friend number 20. If you share the Cheetos with me, I'll think about you being number 19."

Fuck, fuck, fuck.

Was I really going to change my mind? Had he won me over with an apology, an earnest face, a bag of chips, and by reminding me of what my grandparents had wished for? By calling me his best friend number 20? *Really?*

Did he *have* to be so logical? If he'd picked any number smaller, I would have thought he was full of shit. But twenty . . . twenty was believable.

Twenty was real.

Dammit.

He shook the bag a little more. "What do you say, Cookie?"

Fuck this motherfucker.

Fuck *me*.

Oh boy.

"Fine," I snapped as a compromise, noticing that my stomach instantly went back to normal. I took the bag of chips from him.

Alex tipped his head to the side.

I pressed my lips together. "I want to tell you no. You were a real buttmunch."

His eyebrows dropped flat, but I kept going.

"I'll stay until we figure out a way that I can be okay by myself."

His gaze stayed steady.

"But if you ever make me feel that way again, I'm out. And you can live with your guilt if the cartel gets me and feeds me to their pigs."

He didn't like that, I could tell by the way his eyes suddenly glowed for a split second, but he kept his mouth closed. "No one is going to kill you except maybe me."

I didn't mean to snort, but it still surprised me when he went dark on me. "Somehow that's strangely comforting."

"I've been known to be comforting."

"Probably when you're telling someone their death will be quick and painless." I almost laughed, but I was still overwhelmed and hurt and tired and a little scared, to be honest. The future had that effect on you. At least it did on me. Regardless of what he said too, this all still felt like unsteady ground.

What if he changed his mind again? What if someone pissed him off and we had another argument?

His mouth twitched, but his eyes were serious. "Somebody made me mad, and it had nothing to do with you."

"Who made you mad?" I asked him, going for it.

His eyes flicked up toward the ceiling briefly. "My family. My elders."

I opened my mouth and then closed it.

He'd said we had ancestors. That some of the Atraxian bloodlines had died off. How long had they been here? There was so much I didn't know . . . not that it really mattered, but it would be neat to know about where some of my family had come from, since I didn't know much in the first place.

That made me sad. I opened the bag of Cheetos and held it out toward him. He took one, then I took one, and we both ate our pieces, watching each other the whole time. Each of us expecting something different, probably.

Alex held out his hand, and I tipped the bag in his direction again. He took two before asking, "We're good?"

I raised both shoulders then nodded.

"You won't sleep on the floor again?"

Why was he so hung up on that? I shook my head.

"You'll ask for what you need?"

I nodded. Practical and logical were my middle names.

"Say it."

He was *such* a pain in the ass.

But he really was an honorable one.

I rolled my eyes, leaned forward, and slipped my arms around his waist instead. Then I did the unthinkable; I hugged him close. I tucked my head and pressed my cheek against his hard chest. His arms didn't wrap around me, but at some point, something heavy palmed the back of my head.

And just like that, I rocked back and lifted my chin at him, taking in the stunned expression on his face. "Yes, best friend number 20, I'll sleep on a bed and ask you for what I need." I paused. "But I'm serious, you hurt my feelings again and I'm out of here. Then I'll just have to add you to my list of people I'm going to haunt if I die a tragic death."

Alex looked at me for a long, long moment. "It annoys me when you're fucking cute."

Was he high? I had to keep him in perspective. Keep everything he was saying and doing in perspective. We were ... whatever we were. I was here because of the things that had happened that I didn't totally understand yet and was too tired to try and process.

And maybe he was just sucking up to me because he knew I was one wrong comment away from poltergeisting his ass in the future.

The sides of his mouth curved, and he surprised me by reaching forward and tugging at a lock of hair tucked behind my ear.

I held very, very still. "What's with all the sudden touching?" I asked cautiously.

"I don't mind touching," he said, giving it another tug like he'd done it a hundred times before.

"Since when?"

"Always."

I kept watching him.

"Touch is important. I just don't welcome it from everyone."

I eyed him cautiously. "What? You're fine with it from me now?"

He didn't even think about it. "Yeah."

Did he have to look so innocent? Why did this have to be when he had the least grumpy face on? I couldn't trust this version of him.

I didn't want to.

"One more question."

He said nothing.

All righty then. "Just so that I know and don't put my foot in my mouth. You said it was your family's fault why you were grouchy. Will you tell me what happened?"

He didn't want to tell me. I could see it on his face, but he settled back onto the floor in front of me, crossing those long legs. "My uncle and grandfather came by while you were gone buying your things." Then he scowled. "I'm not going to get mad about you being nosy."

I bit the inside of my cheek. "Why? Because you are too?"

That got his mouth to twitch just a little bit. "They're on my case about making a decision I've been putting off."

Dramaaa.

I'd watched way too much reality TV to not instantly be sucked into what he was saying and what he wasn't. Plus, this was Trinity family business. *Trinity business.* I couldn't believe it was even a thing, much less that I was here because . . . well, because somewhere down the line in my family tree, someone had once been like him. It still didn't seem real, and I wasn't sure it ever would.

"What do they want you to do?" I asked. "An environmental campaign?" I eyed him. "Smile in pictures?"

The look he gave me was exactly what I expected.

"They want you to be nice, don't they?" I whispered, trying to antagonize him.

"You want to be number 21, don't you?" he deadpanned.

I smiled at him just a little bit. "I'm number 20 now, no take backsies," I told him with a straight face. "And I don't know what they want you to do, but I know if it was really important, you would. Bitching and complaining the whole time, but you would. I guess it isn't that important then, huh?"

Alex moved to lean against the dresser behind him and crossed his arms, his eyes briefly flicking lower than my face before going back up.

Did he just look at my boobs again?

"I'm considering retiring."

Say what?

"After what happened in the fire . . ." His Adam's apple

bobbed, referring to the big fire that I'd heard about a dozen times already.

It had been this apartment fire that had gotten out of hand, and he hadn't been able to save everyone unscathed. It had happened over a year ago. I had actually been in the same city that day. I had been checking my PO Box. Everyone had gotten out, but some people had gotten hurt in the process and the victims were trying to sue him, even though there wasn't anything concrete to actually sue because no one knew their names. Except a very, very select few, from what I was starting to learn.

"I didn't want to do this anymore. They made me take a break to think about it," he told me, his voice level like it was no big deal.

But that was a fucking lie because I could feel his power rising from his skin, from him.

"I was just about to go on it . . . I was on my last duty . . . when I met you. I haven't had time to think about it, and they want an answer," he explained.

Well, that was a lot more information than I'd expected.

But he wasn't done, and his power kept rising, pulsing like the Godzilla movies I'd watched, right before he laid radiation waste on another monster's ass. "I know there was nothing else I could have done." He tipped his face up toward the ceiling, and I watched him take a deep, deep breath that made his chest rise and suddenly fall. A totally unnecessary breath. "I can be replaced. I'm going to be eventually. I was never supposed to be one of the faces anyway."

Who was going to replace him? How many more Atraxians like him were there? By "one of the faces" did he mean the Trinity?

"I'm tired of helping people who don't deserve it, and I know it isn't up to me to decide who that is. One life is just as important as another. Everyone is someone's son or daughter." He shook his head. "For every thousand people we save, we're blamed for the deaths of another ten thousand." Those purple eyes flicked toward me. "Nothing I do will ever be enough, so is there a point?"

I had to try and keep my shock to a minimum and focus on what he was saying. "I don't blame you for feeling that way," I told him, thinking as fast as I could. "That's a lot to live with, and I don't think I could deal with it either. The scrutiny. The pressure. I don't even like counting change in line at the grocery store."

Did that get me part of a smile?

"But the inspectors and everyone who looked into that accident said there was nothing that could have been done. You said it. You were already saving other people. You got there as fast as you could. Those people are hurt inside and just want someone to blame, and they're stupid for putting it on you instead of the guy who is behind bars for actually starting it." I wrinkled the plastic bag in my hand. "You already know they're dumb and misguided. Anyone with any common sense does."

Alex watched me.

"But it wouldn't hurt to think about it. About your decision. I get it. It's like you said, doing the right thing isn't easy, and people who think it is haven't been in that position before. Maybe it isn't their fault either. Some people have all the luck."

It was his turn to be suspicious from the sudden face he made. "Why are you so nice to me now when you wouldn't look me in the eye a few minutes ago?"

I gave him a side-look. "You get on my nerves, don't get me wrong, but in a way . . . I don't know. I feel kind of a kinship to you. We both didn't ask for certain parts of our lives, and we're just doing our best." I shrugged. "Some battles we have to fight by ourselves, but maybe not all of them, even if it's just a little, itty-bitty thing someone can help with. Something little is still something."

I could tell he was thinking about what I'd said.

"Last question. Who is Alana?"

"My sister."

She had a name. Oh *shit*. I was going to need to give that some time to sink in.

Leaning back against the side of the bed, I ate another Cheeto and let him take one too. "Now that we've got that settled, can I go back to sleep? I slept like shit last night, and I still don't feel great. The floor sucks."

His answer was to stand and hold out the hand he hadn't eaten Cheetos with. I took it and let him pull me up. I rolled up the bag, set it on the dresser, then pulled the comforter and top sheet back and turned to him.

But he wasn't there.

He was already on the other side of the bed.

Taking off his pants.

When he caught me, he raised an eyebrow and stepped out of them. He was wearing boxer briefs; I didn't bother trying to be discreet about checking him out. He had great thighs. Great everything. I was pretty sure I'd memorized his eight-pack.

"You're still sick, and I want to make sure you actually sleep in the bed," he explained as he slid between the sheets.

It was my turn to raise my eyebrow at him.

He sighed deeply as he settled into the bed, pulling the sheets up to his chest.

Then I got in too. I reached over to turn off the lamp and sighed as I rolled onto my back. The mattress was at least a thousand times better than the floor, that was for sure.

Reaching across the bed, my fingers found his forearm and I patted it. "If you're too scared to sleep by yourself, it's okay. I'm not one to judge. I'm scared to sleep by myself too. I kept thinking I was going to get dragged under the bed by an evil spirit in the middle of the night. Just so you know though, the only thing

I'll protect you from are flying roaches. We lived in Texas for a while, and I've killed a ton of them. If the Bogeyman comes in, you're on your own."

Part of me expected him to laugh, but instead, I felt a brush at the top of my hand. It only lasted about a second, but the touch sent a shot straight up through my forearm and into my chest and . . . other places. "I bet you would," he said, his voice soft. "But I can do the protecting from now on, Cookie Monster. Bogeyman or not."

We would see about that, I thought as I drifted off to sleep.

Chapter Twenty-Three

It was over breakfast the next day, after waking up with my fingers inches from Alex's forearm and trying to sneak out of bed without waking him and failing at it, that he looked at me while holding a piece of bacon and asked, "What do you need?"

I was in the middle of eating my own slice when I started choking and had to take a second before I swallowed it down.

What do you need? What did he mean, what did I need? A lot of things. And maybe it said enough about where my mind was that I would first think about sex.

Could you imagine?

Just last night I'd wanted to punch him in the throat, but now . . . well, now I still wanted to do it. Not as hard though. It wasn't like it would actually hurt him.

A snicker from the stove where Selene was busy frying up breakfast sausages had me glancing toward her. The other woman had tongs in her hand as she stood at an angle, facing the table. She'd already been in the kitchen by the time I'd made it downstairs.

"What do you mean? With what?" I asked him as innocently as I could.

He kind of got squinty. "I meant with your life. What do you need? You said you were waiting for your cell phone."

Oh, that. I'd thought about it the day before when I'd hid in the bedroom after Agatha's visit. I had made a vague plan for the future that involved a lot of illegal things I would need to atone for in the future.

But now, I had somewhere to be. A place I hoped could buy me some much-needed time to get my life sorted. I finished eating the rest of my bacon, ignoring the too-watchful purple eyes across the table while I thought about it. Then I said, "Well, I need to figure out what to do about the 'fire' that burned the house down. I don't know if I'm going to be in trouble with the police since I kind of went missing."

"I've been thinking about that." It was Selene who spoke up.

We both looked at her.

"Get Legal in on it. They'll know what to do," she said.

Legal?

Even Alex nodded like that was a good idea.

"What does that mean?"

"The family," Selene answered, "has a legal department. There's a whole team of lawyers that sort out that kind of thing."

Their family had a legal department? How was that possible? Because of the Trinity?

"She's right. They would be the easiest way to deal with most of your issues. They have contacts in a lot of places."

I'd bet they fucking did. "Okay . . ." I told him, wondering just . . . so many things. Were they run like a corporation? Did they have presidents and prime ministers on speed dial that owed them favors?

Alex ate some eggs. "We'll go talk to them today and see what they think about your situation. What else?"

Okayyy. "I need a laptop," I told him. "I have to try to get back to work."

His features went very still. "Do you need anything else?"

"That's all I can think of for now," I told him, hopeful. I thought about my words for a moment. "I still can't get into my checking account until I get my phone, but I promise I can pay you back once I get it."

He made a dismissive sound as he finished off the rest of his breakfast like we hadn't gotten into an argument over money a few days ago. "When you're ready, we'll leave."

Here I'd thought he'd let me borrow his credit card and buy everything online, but to actually *leave* the house?

I didn't get a chance to think about it too much because Alex turned to the other woman. "Selene, I'm fine. You can go home now. Tell everybody to mind their own business. I'm set for the week; you can work from the office again."

She gave him a thumbs-up.

I blinked and finished my cooling eggs, ate my last piece of bacon, and watched Alex's face before glancing toward Selene and wondering what she did for a living.

Did he work?

I got up, rinsed my plate, and headed upstairs, taking note of their silence. I breathed heavily through a shower and got dressed in the clothes I'd bought a couple days ago. They were a lot nicer than just about everything I usually wore—just about everything was since I lived in sweats. I took a mental note to give my new clothes a wash since I wasn't leaving after all. I hoped more than I should that stayed the case.

Selene was nowhere to be found when I went back downstairs half an hour later, but Alex was there, hair damp and in jeans that hugged all the right places—which was all of them because there wasn't a spot on him that wasn't one—and a dark red, button-down shirt with a black coat.

I'd forgotten to buy a coat, dammit. The day I'd gone shopping, it had been kind of cool, and it hadn't occurred to me that winter was coming.

Literally.

But I eyed Alex real subtle. As incredible as he looked in his charcoal Defender suit, there was something about him in such normal clothes that made it harder not to stare. He might be such a pain sometimes, but he really was a gorgeous one, even fully dressed.

"Ready?" he asked, getting up from the table.

"Sure," I said, taking in the reserved expression on his face.

Alex's gaze went to my boobs, and like he'd read my mind, he asked, "Where's your jacket?"

"Waiting for me at a store?"

He blinked.

I blinked.

Then he gestured toward the door with his head. "Use one of mine. Come on."

See? Not a total heartless butthole after all. I nodded and followed after him, stopping in the foyer where he passed me a zip-up black jacket that he watched me put on. My shoes were right next to his, and we slipped them on. Then we were out the door.

But that was as far as I made it because Selene's Camaro was missing, and in its place was a black SUV parked in the front that hadn't been there before. I knew just enough about cars to recognize what the ported hood and yellow brake calipers meant. Whatever this was, it was fast.

"Is this yours?"

Those long legs were eating up the paved stones that led toward the car. "No. Come on."

I'd walked into that shit. I ran down the steps, eyeing it. "What is it?"

"A Durango."

It sure wasn't a regular Durango. He confirmed it the second he started it, the engine roaring to life, nearly blowing my eardrums out, the body of the car even shaking lightly as it grumbled. He pulled out of the driveway the second I was done buckling my seat belt.

I was focused on everything outside. I'd kept an eye on my surroundings as much as I could the day I'd gone shopping, but it was way easier to do it now that I wasn't driving. There were *so many* trees. So much green—

Someone's energy changed, and I glanced over to find him there, his jaw tense. More tense than normal at least.

Oh boy. "What's wrong?" I asked.

His attention stayed forward. "There are some people I don't want to run into where we're going."

He actually answered me. I was going to take that as a step forward. "I can talk to whoever you want me to talk to by myself," I said carefully, taking his openness to heart.

"No."

"Why?"

"I don't want them to see you either."

Shame bit at my throat, and I glared at his profile until he glanced over. I blinked. "I'm no Mistress of Mayhem, but I'm all right looking." I blinked again. "Remember? Remember you said I was 'all right looking'?"

No feature on his face moved.

Oh, right. "The actress who plays her is really pretty. She's a character on—"

"I know she's a character. I have cable."

Excuse me, motherfucker. "I'm so proud of you for knowing that," I told him sarcastically.

He scoffed. "I watch TV."

"You could have said something when you were at my house. I love her show. I could've put it on."

He huffed, facing forward again.

I pressed my lips together for a second. "What do you like to watch?" I asked him, my best friend number 20.

"Shows that teach me things," he replied.

"Nerd."

His sudden snicker made me smile as I looked out the window again. We still hadn't made it through the main gate, and I wasn't totally sure what kind of neighborhood this was, other than a very, very secluded one, but what did I expect from one of the greatest secrets of the century? A member of the Trinity to live in an apartment? Please. That wouldn't exactly work.

"It's my grandmother I don't want to see," he explained after a moment, surprising me again.

"Oh." There went that mystery grandmother again. "Is there another door we can go in that she wouldn't take?"

Those purple eyes flicked toward me. "No, but that's a good idea."

"All my ideas are good ideas." Most of them anyway. "I don't want to put you into a position you don't want to be in. I might be able to get away with not contacting the police. It isn't exactly a crime, is it? I didn't do anything, and I know the owner had homeowner's insurance. And it isn't like I'll be able to use Gracie Garcia for much longer." The only problem would be trying to file a claim with my car insurance; I really needed that money to get a new one even though it had been old and not worth a whole bunch. I had some savings but definitely not enough to buy one outright, especially with needing a new computer.

He shook his head again. "You need to deal with it. It's fine."

I eyed the grumpy side of his face. "It doesn't look like it's fine."

"It's fine."

"Your neck is turning red."

Even from the side, I could tell his eyes glowed, and I gave him my best angelic smile when he peered over, which wasn't really angelic at all.

"It is. Don't get mad. I don't want to make you do something you don't want to," I started to say before trailing off. "But okay, fine. All I'm saying is that it's okay. I can figure something else out. I just don't want to put you in a bad situation." He was trying, and I could too. I appreciated it.

He said nothing, but a muscle in his face twitched. "It's fine," he eventually muttered.

If he said so.

Half an hour later, Alex pulled his car into the parking lot of a big business building that was basically a mini skyscraper. He had been tense the whole ride, and I hadn't bothered trying to get him to talk more than necessary, not when I knew he was dreading the visit.

And not when there was so much to see while I wasn't clinging to the steering wheel of a car that didn't belong to me.

I'd never really pictured what North Carolina would look like, but even if I had, I didn't think I would have expected it to be like *this*. There were a lot more trees and steep hills than I would have ever expected. It was actually really pretty. I was going to ask him later if we were in the mountains.

I could see myself living here, even though my grandparents had always ruled out cities. It was something to definitely think about. First, I needed to start getting things sorted, and that included meeting with this "legal department" Alex and Selene had been talking about. In the meantime, I would try and make this as less of a hassle as possible for Superbutt.

I appreciated his sacrifice.

I appreciated it a lot.

So I was on my best behavior as we made our way from the parking lot, across a bridge, and into the nondescript building. We rode up the equally no-nonsense elevator to the twelfth floor, and it was when we were going down a hall with expensive-looking carpet and lots of wood paneling that he said, "Let me talk."

I couldn't help it. I snorted even though it made my nose hurt.

That got me a long look.

I gave him one right back. "You talking. We're going to get thrown out of the building now."

His grunt made me smile as we kept walking down the hall.

A thought suddenly occurred to me. "Do you own this place?"

He didn't say shit.

No. "You do, don't you?"

He made a little noise in his throat. "*I* don't own it."

"You son of a bitch. Your family does, or it's in a family trust or corporation, isn't it? Is that why your family has a legal department? Because you're all loaded?" It would explain the big house, unless he'd won the lottery.

He smiled. This big, stunning, life-changing smile that made me feel so protective of him even though he was literally the last person in the world who needed someone to keep an eye out for him. And he was still smiling, and I was still reeling from it as the hallway ended in front of a big, beautiful desk with a man behind it.

It was then I realized that we hadn't gone by any doors for different businesses.

Part of me had been joking, but now I realized I'd been right. This was a private building. Owned by someone he was related to?

Who the fuck was he related to?

The man at the desk looked up from the computer he'd been busy typing on, his face freezing for a split second before he got himself together and forced a too bright and alarmed smile on his face. "Hello, Mr. Akita."

I turned to look at Alex.

Did he just call him Mr. *Akita*?

As in the *Akita Corporation*? As in the massive electronics company? There was no way . . .

I stopped that thought right there in its tracks. Of course it was possible.

"It's nice to have you back. Is there someone I can get for you?" the man asked Alex.

He nodded his tight-ass nod. "Hep, you don't need to call me that. Who's here?"

The man cleared his throat, his gaze bobbing from him to me and back again. "At this moment, your mother is out, but Mr. Achilles, Mr. Odi, and Ms. Athena are in their offices. Would you like me to see if they're free?"

"No. I need to speak to someone in the legal department."

The man cleared his throat. "I'll see who I can get, but they might be busy—"

"Tell them to meet me in the conference room in ten minutes, or I'll make sure they aren't busy on my own."

There went bossy britches in the wild.

The man nodded. Nothing about his features registering hurt fortunately. He picked up the phone and dialed a few digits quickly. "Mr. Alexander is here . . ."

A hand grazed my elbow, and I glanced over at Alex who looked like he would rather be anywhere else than here.

I'm sorry, I mouthed, feeling bad.

He rolled his eyes just as the man behind the counter said, "If you'll follow me—"

"I know where the conference room is. Thanks."

The man sputtered like he really wanted to walk us over there, but he bent his head anyway before gesturing toward another hallway around the corner.

Alex waved for me to go first. Okay. I started down it and hadn't gone too far before he touched my back and steered me into a room with a long table, a big-screen television, and a wall of windows that opened toward the street. "Sit at the front," he said.

I took the seat he suggested. The chair was too tall, but I sat there, knit my hands together on top of the table surface, and tilted my head to get a good look at the man standing behind my chair.

His gaze was focused on something through the window.

"So I have a question," I told him.

"You always have a million questions."

"You're not lying, but really, it's been on my mind." Here went nothing. "You know who or what hurt you, don't you?"

Oh, he hadn't been expecting that from the side-look he shot me. A muscle in his face twitched before he admitted, sounding only a little annoyed, "I do."

I gulped. "Was it your brother?" I whispered.

Alex opened his mouth just as another voice, one I didn't recognize, said, "Baby brother."

My head whipped to the side just as a man came in, tugging at the sleeve of an expensive-looking suit jacket. He was tall, just as tall as Alex, with the same hair and skin color, the same features that spoke of a complex, beautiful heritage, and almost as handsome. Instead of Alex's deep brown hair, the man's hair was nearly black with lines of silver shooting through the sides.

But it was the cool expression on his face that was the most different.

Because Alex's face was an arrogant one; he looked damn near constantly crabby and irritated. His eyes though were filled with fire, with heat and life. His older brother though, instead of warmth, there was a detached cool. If Alex thought we were all dumbasses, his brother thought we were gum on the soles of his shoes.

I wasn't sure how I felt about him.

And especially not when he stopped and looked at me. The man's gaze went from me to his brother and back.

"She's the Atraxian."

He sniffed. "Barely." But that must have appeased him because he went and took a seat at the opposite end of the table and said, "I'm in the middle of something. What do you need?"

The man who had instantly moved to my side, who hadn't put on a disguise like I'd half expected him to, tensed. I could see the signs: I knew them well. To give him credit, his voice was that deceptively lazy one that wouldn't ever fool me. "I asked for someone in Legal, Achilles."

"Did you forget I'm a lawyer?"

"Just because you went to law school twenty-something years ago doesn't mean you're a lawyer," Alex grumbled in that tone I knew too well.

"Doesn't mean I can't answer whatever is on your mind."

What the hell was going on with these two? If I knew Alex's mannerisms and tone, this guy had to even better than me. Wouldn't he?

The other man's eyes strayed in my direction, lingering there for a moment before I was apparently dismissed again. He didn't have Alex's purple eyes; he had blue ones just like Selene's. "It's been a while since you've come to this floor. What do you need?"

"What's going on?" a feminine voice asked just as a tall woman came through the door holding a tablet in one hand. Dressed in a classic black suit that hugged her curvy body, she paused just inside and lifted her gaze before smiling just a little, and I mean *just a little*. "Hello, Alexander."

So people *did* call him Alexander. Who was this?

"Hi, Athena," he greeted her back with the same level of enthusiasm as she had: almost none.

This was another family member, wasn't it?

No hug? No kiss?

I hadn't imagined the big hugs he'd given Selene, Leon, and his sister, The fucking Primordial. Those had been genuine with affection. I'd been able to sense the love there. Those hugs had been so much more than I ever would have thought he was capable of. He'd said something about liking touch too . . . so this, this was surprising.

Just behind her, *another* man came hustling through the door.

And holy *shit*.

While Alex was so handsome it was hard to look away from him even when he pissed me off, this other man . . . Wow. And that was saying a lot considering Alex. This new man's features were narrower, were sharper and just . . . wow. Literally: wow. I had to press my lips together to make sure my mouth wasn't hanging open.

A fucking poke to the back of my head had me turning to glare at Alex who was frowning down at me.

I poked him back but in the rib.

"Baby brother!" the most gorgeous man in the world called out, but I was too busy giving Alex a lingering stink eye to notice him again until the moment the other guy threw his arms around him.

"Hi, Odi," Alex muttered, still high on contentment from the sound of it.

Not.

"You've been gone for weeks, can't call me, and then you show up and don't tell me you're back?" the man apparently named Odi said, rocking him from side to side in a bear hug. Odi was only an inch or two shorter than Alex, but wider at the shoulders. "You're going to hurt my feelings."

"Doubt that," Alex muttered, but I was pretty sure I saw his hand pat his brother's lower back.

Maybe they did have superior genes to have such a good-looking family. How the hell was it possible? I watched them rock a minute longer before the extra good-looking one slid his arm over his baby brother's shoulders—I was going to be giggling over that for a while, probably in his face—and pecked him on the cheek.

That was going to be burned into my brain for literally the rest of my life.

"What are you here for, Lexi?" the Odi man asked. "I heard you down the hall."

Alex's arms were still at his sides as he said, "I need to speak to someone in Legal."

It was the woman who said, one eye on her phone, "We're all lawyers here."

I tried to do the math on how much law school for three people was and almost gagged.

That had to be that Akita Corporation money there.

"I need a real one," Alex replied.

"What did you do?" the first man asked as his thumbs flew across the screen of his phone. "I knew something happened when you went off-grid without telling anyone where you were." He briefly glanced up, making a face I didn't like. "I thought you were over this irresponsible shit."

Oh boy, I didn't even need to look at Alex to know that comment didn't go down well, and one quick glance at him confirmed it. A tendon in his throat was about ready to jump out of his skin and attack the guy. "I'm not irresponsible, and I didn't do shit."

And what the hell were they getting on his case over?

The first brother, the oldest-looking one, wasn't done. He raised the single bitchiest eyebrow I'd ever seen, and I'd seen some eyebrows with attitude issues. "Disappearing for over a month isn't exactly 'responsible' though, is it?"

Ah, fuck it.

I wasn't a good girl, and I never would be. I was a decent girl, let's be real. And that was exactly what I was going to tell Alex when he pitched a fit over me butting in after he'd asked me not to. But if I couldn't stand up for him, who could I stand up for?

Last night I'd been ready to sneak Ex-Lax into his food, and now . . .

This guy didn't get to talk shit about him in my presence, even if they were family.

"He went 'missing' because he was injured," I piped up, "and we aren't here because of him. We're here because he was being responsible and helping me. So . . ." I lifted my shoulders.

Three different heads focused on me.

I gave them, or at least the snobby one, my bitchiest blink.

"Explain," he demanded suddenly.

Oh, I could feel Alex's energy radiating from him. I was picking something up from all of them, but most from him. The hair on my arms started to tingle, and if any of them noticed it, or maybe they were just used to it, no one seemed to blink twice. And I was really grateful my bra was padded because my nipples were the first thing to react when he got like this.

"I don't need to discuss this with you," Alex replied in the bossy Super voice I'd heard so early on in our acquaintance. "What I need is to talk to someone in the legal department."

The woman screwed up her face. "Your business is our business. It's family business, Alex." She shot me a side-look like she wasn't sure how much to say, but too late now, motherfucker.

"If it affects you to the point where you were injured, then it affects us," the woman said. "What does that even mean? What happened?"

"None of your business," Alex answered as he set a hand on the chair I was sitting in.

It was nice to see there were some people he didn't hold back with either.

"Everything about you is our business," Athena said, totally serious.

"Wrong."

I peeked over at the extra handsome one and found him staring at me.

My face went hot.

All three faces focused in my direction again for a second, but Alex didn't give them shit. From his expression, he wasn't going to either. I knew that level of stubborn, and I knew it well. I'd been dealing with it for the last however many weeks.

"We're going to hear what you talk to Legal about anyway," the woman said after a long beat of silence, her attention still on me. "If you need help, we can help you. You don't need to be difficult. Tell us what happened."

He looked at me for a moment before lifting his gaze to his siblings. "My back was broken. My power drained," he told them, getting straight to the point. There was definitely more to that sentence that he was trying to express, and I knew they instantly understood what he meant because three sets of nostrils flared. "Gracie took care of me. While I was recuperating, a group of people who have been looking for her, found us. They burned down her house and took us; we left once I was well enough. Leon and Selene picked us up from my cabin in Colorado, and we got back a few days ago. Alana is already aware of the situation," Alex said matter-of-factly. "Gracie can't go back to her life because they'll be looking for her. I need to speak to Legal to see what we can do about her situation."

Three sets of heads turned to me again, but I was too busy focusing on what he'd just said.

His cabin? He'd lied! All right, maybe he hadn't lied, but the sneaky son of a bitch hadn't said a word about it being his place. I knew he'd been acting weird while I'd been snooping.

"Your power was gone? Are you sure?" Athena asked cautiously.

Someone suddenly sounded really concerned.

But really, *his cabin?*

There was some kind of big fucking secret here that no one wanted to talk about out loud. What in the hell could be bigger than the Trinity? Because whatever it was, they were guarding the shit out of it.

"I'm positive. Are you going to help me help her now?" he demanded.

His sister's eyes widened more and more by the second. "You've recovered?" Her question was soft.

Alex grunted. "Not fully." A muscle in his face twitched. "It was the worst pain I've ever felt in my fucking life."

The oldest brother grunted, something flashing across his face like he agreed with him.

Yeah, this was some Area 51 level confidential shit right here.

"Why is someone looking for her?" he asked.

"She was in witness protection."

I was going to start calling him The Defender of Deceit at this point.

"How long were you out?" The handsome one, Odi, threw the question out.

"Five weeks."

All three faces went stunned and pale.

It was so, so suspicious.

"Can I get someone in Legal now?" Alex asked.

His sister glanced at me, but the jerk and the one who at least seemed to like his younger brother were focused on him.

"I'm going to talk to Alana and Robert about it soon. Selene is going to see what she can do. They might have footage of us, and it needs to be taken care of."

"It does," Achilles answered seriously, his face stormy. "Have you spoken to . . . ?"

Ooh, I felt Alex's aggravation instantly rise. "Also none of your fucking business."

"Do you really need to be that low class?" Achilles snapped.

"Fuck no," Alex said without missing a beat. I didn't think I'd ever been so attracted to him before. I kind of wished I had some popcorn. "Are you done asking questions?" he barreled through.

"Fine, get it sorted," the older brother said in exasperation.

"Keep me posted," Athena said before the two of them walked out. They seemed wound up about something.

At the door, they glanced at me, and she whispered something I couldn't hear.

"Damn, Alex," Odi said with a sigh the second they were gone. "Let me get someone, because I have no idea what to do." His eyes drifted in my direction.

For one brief moment, I was pretty sure I saw his eyes glow, but it disappeared so quickly I might have imagined it. Then he walked out too, slapping his little brother's shoulder on the way.

I waited patiently.

Mostly patiently.

Insulted. Confused. A little annoyed.

Alex was silent.

After a moment, those purple eyes flicked toward me.

I put my chin on my hand and made my mouth go flat. "So, they're rude," I whispered. "No offense."

Both corners of his mouth went up into the slightest smile. "Ruder than I am?"

I snorted and winced. "I don't know about all that. You usually grunted at me and acknowledged my presence every once in a while. And you figured out my name eventually."

"I always knew your name. I just didn't want to use it."

I shouldn't laugh, but I did. He was *such* a fucking shit.

The side of his mouth curled up a little. "Achilles and Athena are the worst about it. The rest of them aren't so bad," he explained, sounding almost apologetic.

From the door, I heard the Odi man's voice say, "I've got someone coming in here in a minute, but I have a call in five. See you tomorrow?"

Alex's curse was swift.

"Yup, see you, baby bro," the other man replied, already sounding like he was down the hall.

Baby bro, huh? I couldn't picture him being someone's little brother, much less baby brother. Or even letting someone call him that in the first place. I was going to have to think about that later on.

I waited all of two seconds before asking, "What's happening tomorrow?"

That familiar crabby face was back, except this time I was pretty sure I wasn't imagining the dread mixed in with it. His body stiffened, and his tone was off. "We're going to my mother's."

We?

Chapter Twenty-Four

We were going to his mom's.

Alex had a *mother*. Why that blew my mind made no sense. He had brothers and sisters. It wasn't like they'd hatched from eggs.

The Defender, The Centurion, and The Primordial had a *mom*.

I couldn't stop thinking about it as we headed to the nearest store that carried the laptop I wanted. I thought about ordering one online, but I didn't want to wait any longer if I didn't have to. I'd spent some of the ride to the mall on his phone, distractedly trying to find who carried one. I hadn't even been able to muster up shock that he *owned* a cell phone. It looked brand new. His background image was the default one. Who called him? Just his family?

When I wasn't processing the "mom" situation or staring at the small screen, I wondered what in the *hell* he meant by "we."

Did he really expect me to go with him?

The thought alone had me sweating.

Leaning back against the headrest, we drove by a giant parking lot with a carnival set up on it. It had a Ferris wheel, rides, booths . . . My breathing made a big circle on the window that I wiped with the sleeve of Alex's jacket. I'd always wanted to go to a carnival or a fair, but my grandma hadn't liked crowds.

After a while, I peeked at Alex again as I forced my thoughts

WHEN GRACIE MET THE GRUMP 413

away from shit in life I'd missed out on. Something was up his butt.

The problem was, I wasn't sure I wanted to know what.

"Why are you being weird?" he asked suddenly as he turned into a mall.

I straightened in the seat. "I'm not being weird. I was just wondering if you're done being grumpy."

"I'm not grumpy. You're the one staring, trying to be discreet but sucking at it," Alex said. "Why? You worried about meeting my mother?"

How could someone be this perceptive? There was no point in me lying. "Yes."

"Then stop. I don't like the way it smells when you worry."

I lifted my arm and took a quick sniff. All I caught was a trace of my deodorant. Seemed fine to me.

"It's different than your normal smell. It doesn't stink."

Hm. "Is it a curse? Having such a good nose?"

He turned the car into just about the farthest spot you could get in the lot, a quarter of a mile away from the actual mall building. "It can be," he answered. "But I've been training my nose to ignore most scents my entire life, so it isn't overwhelming."

I turned to him. Maybe a normal person would have asked what kind of training he'd endured, but that wasn't what pressed down on my nosy soul. "Who has the worst farts you've ever smelled?"

He blinked before sliding me a look. "You're really asking about farts?"

I shrugged. "I'm sure you've smelled some terrible stuff. I didn't really want to go dark that fast." I also didn't want him to confirm he could smell when someone was turned on. That was definitely something to keep in mind.

He tilted his head to the side. "Alana's make me gag," he answered unexpectedly.

I laughed. "I wondered if you pooped in the first place."

He made a noise in his throat. Was he smirking? "We do, not as often as you do. We burn through most of our calories and use it as energy."

That explained so much. "That's almost as amazing as being super strong."

Alex snickered. "Let's get this over with."

I got out right after he did, tugging his jacket closer around my body as I waited for him to come around the side. I shivered as a strong breeze blew by, and I took a half step closer to Alex, using his body to block it. He glanced over but didn't say a word about me being so close as we hustled toward the store.

Wait a minute.

I stopped and grabbed his arm, peering up at his face. "You've got contacts in?"

"I put them in when you used the bathroom."

I grabbed the collar of his jacket and tried to tug him down.

He went, lowering his head willingly, his eyelids widening over *dark blue* eyes.

With my other hand, I touched the tip of his eyebrow and took in the color some more . . . and the smooth skin beneath them.

Those cheekbones.

That jaw.

"Are you still looking at my eyes or the rest of me?"

I let go. "The rest of you. The color looks real."

"They only last a few hours. We've got to leave before they dissolve."

"They *dissolve*?"

He stood up straight. "Yeah, come on."

"Why don't you wear a wig?" I asked. "You don't need to?" I'd always wondered how they got around, how they survived among people. I'd thought for sure they wore wigs or simply just . . . hid from the world in general.

But Alex just looked like himself minus that charcoal suit and blue cape. Was that why he didn't let his face get photographed or recorded? In the movies, Electro-Man wore a wig when he was in "normal" clothes to protect his identity. Even the Mistress of Mayhem had a little strip of cloth over her eyes.

"Alana goes all out with a disguise, but that's because she's tall so she draws more attention. Robert wears glasses and combs his hair different. They were both homeschooled. They rarely go out to be cautious." He held up his wrist, showing me a plain rubber band. "When it gets long, I tie my hair back. Nobody notices."

I gave him an incredulous look before taking my own hair tie off my wrist. I held it out toward him. "I'm sure your hair is super strong, and it's too wonderful to even think about breaking but come on. Use a real hair tie."

Those temporary dark blue eyes flicked toward me, and he took the elastic. He kept his eyes on me as he pulled his hair back and tied it into a short half-ponytail that was basically a nub.

Not many men could pull off a tiny ponytail, but Alex, he could pull off anything.

I smiled. "Now you'll catch 99 people's attention instead of 100. Good job." Were people really that oblivious? How the fuck had no one ever figured it out?

Alex huffed as we walked through the automatic doors of the electronics store. I peered up at him, liking the security of him being right there, as we headed toward the computer department.

"What exactly are we looking for?" he asked when we got there.

I told him the name of the model, looking around to try and find an employee. There was one talking to a customer close by, but she was busy.

"I'll start over there," he said. "You look here."

We split up. The section wasn't large at all. I guess most people bought their stuff online now, but Alex headed toward the row farthest away, and I started on the opposite end. It said they had one in stock; they couldn't have sold it already. But this was my luck, so they might have.

"Can I help you find something?"

I jumped.

"Is there something specific you're looking for?" the employee asked from where she stood at the end of the aisle.

"Yes. Please." I rattled off the name of the laptop I was looking for.

"You're close, next row over. I'll show you," she said. "It's on sale right now—*oh my God*."

A big hand landed on my shoulder a split second before I heard, "Did you find what you were looking for?"

The girl made a noise that I totally understood.

I would have "oh my God" too.

"Yeah," I confirmed.

Alex pulled out his wallet, handing me a card. "Buy what you need. I need to get something. Meet me in the food court." Then he leaned forward, whispered a four-digit number into my ear, squeezed my shoulder quickly, and took off, heading straight to the exit that led into the mall.

I stared after him.

After that tight butt mostly.

"Wow," the employee whispered so quietly I wasn't even sure she knew what she'd said out loud.

I didn't even have to glance over to know what she was talking about. "I know," I agreed. Oh, I knew.

Twenty minutes later, with my computer in tow, I headed through the mall and followed the signs to the food court. There were so many *stores*. So many people. I'd been to malls a couple times before—behind my grandparents' back because there were too many people—but I'd never seen so many people at one.

Plus, I had a card in my hand from a bank I'd never heard of. What was up with this family and their special credit cards and foreign debit cards? How much money did you have to have to qualify for one? Would Alex tell me?

Part of me had expected the cashier to ask for my ID or call the cops, but he hadn't even made eye contact when I'd paid.

Clutching my heavy bag tight, I moved through the mall slowly, taking in everything. I was already worn out. At the food court, I used the last of the ten dollars that Selene had loaned me on a cinnamon coffee drink with drizzled chocolate over a mountain of whipped cream. Taking a seat at a table, I sipped on my drink and kept an eye out.

I didn't have to wait long.

I'd only been sitting there a minute when I spotted the tall body striding through the crowd.

I bit my lip and kept watching that long frame move. I also got to witness how the women he passed reacted. Some of them totally stopped to check him out, and some of them tried to be discreet but checked him out anyway. I couldn't blame them. I couldn't blame them at all.

I smiled as we made eye contact. There was a big department store bag over his forearm and another smaller bag that looked like it may or may not have a shoebox in it. I didn't take him to be a shopper, but he was still one of the great mysteries of the world, apparently. I held the drink out and he took it, instantly putting the straw between his lips and taking a big sip.

"Did you get what you needed?" I asked, not even trying to be sneaky about staring at his bags.

He narrowed those blue eyes, and I was pretty sure he held the bags closer as he nodded. "You?"

Of course that was all he was giving me. "Yes," I told him, disappointed.

He smirked.

I didn't trust it.

"Ready to go?" he asked, holding the coffee out.

I nodded and took it as I got up, picking up my own bag from where I'd stashed it between my legs because I didn't trust someone to not run up and steal my things. Stopping beside him, I peeked at his bag, and he definitely pulled it even closer to his side.

"Nosy," he said, his fingers brushing mine as he plucked the strap out of my hand.

I tried to take it back. "I can carry it."

"You need to work out those puny arms," he said, tugging it out of my hand again. "But you still smell sick. Let me carry it."

He was right on that part. Walking through the mall had worn me out. "Okay," I said, letting go. "But question."

I was pretty sure his mouth twitched.

That was my cue to keep going. I dropped my voice. "Does that even feel like anything to you? You know, because you're so strong?"

Those eyes that weren't as dark blue as they'd been half an hour ago flicked toward me as we walked back the same way I'd come. He made a thoughtful sound. "It's more work for me to carry this because I have to think about not overdoing it, than it is for me to . . ."

"Pick up an eighteen-wheeler?" I asked, referring to a video of him carrying a semi that had driven off a bridge a few years ago. He'd just happened to be at the right place and time, on the way back from an incident off the coast of California that I couldn't remember.

Alex nodded. "Yeah. That's nothing too."

I whistled. "And I think I'm a bad shit when I finally open a jar that's a pain in the ass." I raised my arm and flexed, even though he couldn't see anything under the big jacket.

He flicked that strange but beautiful gaze over to me. "I break jars as much as I open them," he admitted quietly.

I bet. "What's the heaviest thing you've ever lifted?"

That smooth forehead furrowed, and out of the corner of my eye, I saw a couple of girls coming toward us, tilting their heads in our direction, their eyes glued to Alex.

He didn't notice, or if he did, he ignored it.

"A fully loaded cargo ship."

"Was it hard?"

He looked at me and raised an eyebrow.

So it was like that? I reached over and squeezed his forearm.

The muscles beneath my fingers flexed, and I whistled again, pleased with him for playing along, before I let go.

I guess now that I wasn't on his shit list, and maybe since he understood I wasn't trying to kidnap or take advantage of him, he'd decided he could be friendlier. I'd take it. Gladly.

We caught up to a family walking in front of us, four people across. A teenage boy wearing a shirt with the symbol of the Trinity on it was holding his arm out, letting his grandma use him as a cane. It was so sweet.

"How do you stay in shape? It's not like you can go to the gym," I asked as soon as we passed them. I took the final sip of our drink and threw the plastic into the nearest recycling bin.

"It's natural."

I groaned. Superior genes, my fucking ass. "Incredible, beautiful, rich, and naturally fit. The world is so unfair."

Out of the corner of my eye, I saw him glance at me, and his voice was a little funny as he asked, "You think that about me?"

"I was talking about your sister."

I was pretty sure he wasn't even expecting the chuckle that snuck out of him.

I tipped my head and grinned at him.

The slight smile he'd made while he laughed slowly fell off, and I looked away.

We finished going through the mall and out the electronics store, heading to the parking lot where he put our things in the back seat. We got inside, and I purposely kept my mouth closed as he pulled out of the lot and drove in the same direction we'd come from. He drove and he drove. My mind must have been too busy originally to notice just how far away we'd been from his house.

But all of a sudden, the Ferris wheel I'd been eyeballing on the way to the mall got bigger and bigger. The next thing I knew, he was pulling into the dirt lot for the fair.

We were at the carnival.

I slowly swiveled in the seat to look at him. "Really?"

He put the car into park and turned it off before turning toward me too. "Yes, really."

I shouldn't have been so excited. I knew it. It was just a carnival, like all the others I'd driven by countless times. There were plenty of things I was used to doing alone. The movies? No problem. Out to eat? Every once in a while, but only because I was cheap and ate at home. Since my grandma had passed, I'd gone to two concerts, even though I'd been paranoid the whole time for no good reason.

But that was it.

It was stupid how excited I was, I thought, as I took in the Ferris wheel some more, and the rides that looked kind of sketchy but fun with all their multicolored lights on. There were booths with games and a couple cart-looking things with signs that claimed they had funnel cakes, corn dogs, and popcorn.

"You ever been to one of these before?" I asked, lifting my hands toward my mouth and blowing into them. The temperature was getting a little cooler. How fucking lucky had we been that it hadn't been this cold while we'd been trying to get away?

"Nope." He put his hands into the pockets of his jacket but not because he was cold.

He didn't ask if I had, and I had a feeling he knew the answer. "We don't have to stay for long. I'd be happy just getting a funnel cake, if you'll let me borrow money. I only have four dollars left."

He nodded.

Putting my own hands into the pockets of the jacket I had on, I hustled faster to catch up with his long stride. It was just barely starting to get dark, and there weren't a ton of people around, but there were some. Little kids clinging to their parents. Couples holding hands. Groups of teenagers clustered together, sharing cotton candy and pointing at different attractions, like they were trying to decide what to do. I watched Alex keeping an eye on an older man pushing a wheelchair with a woman about the same age in it.

"Let's get tickets first," Alex said suddenly, putting his hand on the back of my neck and steering me toward a cart with a short line in front of it.

I guess he'd been serious about being okay with the touching thing. It wasn't like I minded it. I liked the way he made my skin kind of tingle.

"Really?" I asked him, peering up at his profile. Part of me still couldn't believe it.

His hand tightened a little as his gaze dropped to mine briefly before he looked around. "Yes, really."

"We can leave whenever you want. I'm just happy to be here." I thought about it. "But could we get a funnel cake for sure? Please?"

He snickered, but the corner of his mouth hitched up a little as he gave my neck another little squeeze. "You got it, Cookie."

"It's rigged," I whispered right before shoving a handful of cotton candy into my mouth as we stood in front of a booth with figures lined up in rows that you were supposed to knock down with softballs.

"No, you just suck at throwing things," Alex said, holding the cotton candy in one hand and pulling pieces off it with the other.

I must have been hanging out with him too much because I grunted. "Some people didn't get to play softball," I muttered.

"I can tell."

I shot him a dirty look, but part of his mouth was flat in that amused expression of his.

"Money was tight?" he actually asked though.

Oh, he was curious about me. "Yes, but that wasn't why. It took me six months to petition my grandparents into letting me wear pants. I can only imagine how me asking to play a sport would have gone," I told him. "If I could've played something, it would've been volleyball." I snuck my hand over to pluck some more cotton candy before I asked, "Did you play sports ever?"

"Soccer in high school," he answered. "It helped me learn more control."

"Were you any good?"

Oh, those eyes were crinkling. "I couldn't be too good, that was the whole point."

I groaned even as I smiled at the employee that I'd given a handful of tickets to—for the balls I'd gotten—and turned to the shit-talker who'd sat on the Ferris wheel with me a few minutes ago, looking super interested in his surroundings, like he had never been so high in the sky before. He was a good actor. But more than anything, I appreciated how much of a good sport he was being letting me do this. I'd half expected him to wait around while I got on.

He'd bought so many tickets, I'd almost asked if he wanted to get a refund on some of them.

He had no idea that it meant the world to me actually, and when I'd tried to tell him that, he'd shoved the cotton candy in my face and told me to help him eat it.

So I'd dropped it.

"Let's see you do better then, hotshot," I said.

He held the spun sugar out, and I took it. I couldn't see his eyeballs, but I knew we didn't have too much time left even though it was quickly getting dark. I figured we could get away with no one seeing the real color once it happened, at least as long as they didn't do their glow thing. Alex handed the guy a few more tickets and took the balls from him.

"I have to knock them all down to win the big one?" Alex asked him.

The young man scratched at his neck, clearly bored. That's when I noticed there was a tattoo on the back of his hand: three black triangles. The "sign" of the Trinity.

I didn't miss the way Alex's cheek kind of twitched, and I definitely didn't miss the determined glint in his eyes as he casually lifted his arm and threw the first ball, apparently not caring he had a fan right here.

He knocked down a clown.

He threw the next and the one after that and knocked them all down too.

And when he did the other two too, I whistled, pinching off another piece of cotton candy and eating it.

The employee gave an even more bored face. "Which one do you want?" he asked with zero enthusiasm.

Alex pointed at a big Hello Kitty mounted in the corner. The guy pulled it down and handed it over, and Alex tucked it under his arm.

"Why did you pick that one?" I asked him, my mouth trembling at the memory of him in my T-shirt.

He smirked. "Why do you think?"

"It was the biggest shirt I had," I explained, trying not to smile.

"Sure it was." He lifted his chin toward the booth next to the one we were at. It had cups filled with water on a table. "Maybe you won't suck at that one."

Maybe I wasn't the only one in a good mood, and that was fine by me. "I miss the days you didn't talk to me," I joked.

Alex huffed, and we walked over to it. Apparently, you were supposed to toss little balls into multicolored cups. If you got enough balls in, you won a prize. If you landed a ball in one of the red cups, you won something better. I took the ping-pong-like balls, and Alex took another bucket with them too, balancing it on the edge of the panel separating the players from the cups.

He still had his huge cat under one arm and had put the handle of the cotton candy in his free hand.

I pressed my lips together before whispering, "Where's that big, bad telekinesis at now, huh?"

His eyebrows slowly rose. "You really think you've got a chance at beating me?"

No. "Absolutely."

He scoffed and tossed his first ball, not even looking in the direction. The cup clinked. *Really?*

I lightly threw one and made it in. "You can let me win if you want, but if you don't, I'll beat you fair and square."

Another ball went flying and plopped perfectly in a cup right in the middle of the group. "I'll close my eyes, will that make you happy?"

"Don't you have a photographic memory?" I laughed. Who the hell was this person playing around with me? Joking? He'd been in such a mood earlier while we'd been at that building, that I hadn't been sure how fast he was going to shake it off.

"Don't worry about it. Toss the balls," he said in a tone that made me smile wide.

We tossed our balls, and he won. He tucked the small stuffed animal into his front pocket, looking way too proud of himself.

But it was pretty cute.

"What do you want to do now?" he asked.

"Nothing that takes any skill." I gestured at the booth next to us, a game where you took a seat and had a water gun that you pointed at a target. "That one."

The expression on his face said *really?*

"Well, we aren't playing that strength game with the hammer, Hercules."

His snicker made me smile again, but he handed over tickets, and we took a seat beside each other. His legs were so long, his knee and most of his thigh brushed mine.

"Whenever you're ready," the worker said, looking slightly less bored than the last one had.

I turned to Alex. "On the count of three, okay?"

He nodded. "One—"

I started shooting.

"You fucking cheater," he hissed under his breath. But was that a laugh I heard?

"You snooze you lose, motherfucker." I laughed, keeping my attention on the measuring stick above the targets.

"I can't believe you."

"See it and believe it." I kept on cracking up, so close to winning, so close . . . "Yes!"

I turned my chair at the same time he turned his. "Again," Alex demanded.

I leaned toward him, grinning so wide my fucking cheeks hurt. Why did this feel like I'd won a gold medal? "Are you being a sore loser right now? Because it's okay if you are."

His mouth was slightly open, and he was shaking his head, those bluish-purple eyes glittering as the bright, colored lights hit his irises.

I leaned just a little closer. "Do you want me to let you win the next one?"

His snort was soft, his gaze following my face. For one millisecond, his eyes glowed before the color snuffed out. "You better not."

I held up the plate of fried dough and powdered sugar and tried not to smile.

Then I failed three seconds later when an annoyed set of eyes landed on me, the eyebrows above them flat in jealous sauce.

"Oh, don't be a sore loser," I said. My cheeks were still tingling from smiling so much. "You're good at everything. Just not at being a better cheater than me." Sucker.

Alex gave me the dirtiest look in the whole world, and it just made me smile harder. "None of your wins count because you cheated."

I shrugged and held the plate a little closer to him. "But you fell for it *three times*. It's not my fault you did."

He shook his head slowly, but I caught the quick flick of his gaze toward the plate I was still holding out as a peace offering. "You said you were done cheating each time, you liar."

Okay, I had done that, but part of me had expected him to know I was full of shit.

It was his fault for believing I was that good of a person.

Alex snickered, then reached for the funnel cake, tearing off a piece of the dough and plopping it into his mouth.

I smiled and ripped a piece too, eating it slowly as I watched the sore loser. We were standing a little away from the cart we'd bought the funnel cake and bottle of water at, right beside a fun house. Now that it had gotten darker, more people had arrived at the roadside carnival. Alex's contacts had officially bitten the dust, and I'd purposely made to stand in a dark spot without a lot of lights. I figured we were going to be done soon; we'd blown through the tickets playing the water game over and over again.

"Thank you for doing this with me," I told him seriously, taking a sidestep closer so he could have better access to the plate.

His eyes flicked to me as he slipped his hand under mine and took the plate. His voice was gruff. "You're welcome."

"I really appreciate it."

That got me a long look as he chewed a huge piece.

I opened the bottle of water and took a swig before holding it out to him too. He took it, watching me the whole time. That pissy little face still present.

"You still lost," I reminded him under my breath, not able to help myself.

His eyebrows went up, and just as he opened his mouth to talk shit, we both turned toward the attraction behind us.

"Mommy, *please*." The little girl standing beside her mom pleaded as they stood beside a game that said TEST YOUR STRENGTH! The woman lowered the oversized fake sledge-hammer down and shook her head, saying who knows what to the little girl.

The goal of the attraction was to hit the hammer against this scale thing on the ground and get the giant light-up thermometer-looking sign above it to go all the way to the top in order to win the whopping prize of a giant unicorn.

"One more time! Please! I know you can do it!" the little girl said, squeezing her palms together under her chin. "Please, please, please, Mommy."

The mom shook her head, saying something else that even without super hearing, I could tell was going to be a definite "no." I couldn't blame her. I figured those games were rigged so that you couldn't easily win them.

Unless . . .

Unless you were Alex.

I tipped my head up to look at him.

He tipped his chin down to look at me.

"Should you?" I whispered.

"I should," he agreed with a serious nod. "Don't tell anybody though."

"Best friends number 15 don't rat each other out." I pressed my lips together. "I moved you up on my list after today. Don't get too excited, but you might just make it to the number 14 if you get that unicorn for her."

His face . . .

With his giant Hello Kitty under one arm, another stuffed animal halfway hanging out of his pocket, a fourth of a funnel cake on the plate in his hand, and a bottle of water under his other arm, we moved. The little girl was still there begging her mom the three seconds it took us to make it over. Alex stopped, bit off half of what remained of the funnel cake, then held up the rest in front of my mouth.

Oh, okay.

We had taken care of each other. We'd slept in the same bed; we'd snuggle-healed. We were friends. Or at least . . .

At least he was my friend.

And he was trying to let me be his.

He didn't have to do any of this with me, and it meant a fuck of a lot that he did. How was it possible someone could have so much goodness inside a grouchy little heart? I didn't know and wasn't sure I ever would.

I opened wide and took the rest as he threw the plate away, dusted his hands on his jeans, then held the white cat toward me. I took it. "I'll protect her with my life," I promised.

He put the bottle of water into his jacket pocket as he said, "It's for you anyway."

It—

I didn't even get a chance to make a comment because he

handed over his tickets to the worker. The man took them and gestured to the hammer by Alex's feet, the guy's face totally fucking skeptical, probably thinking Alex was a dumb chump. He was fit, but he wasn't built like a powerlifter after all. It was really deceiving.

Out of the corner of my eye, I saw the little girl standing a few feet away, her eyes following Alex, who was listening to whatever the employee was telling him. Were there rules to the game? The mom made eye contact with me, and I smiled at her. She returned it just as her little girl tugged at her hand and pointed toward the game as Alex hefted the hammer over his shoulder.

Muscles under his shoulders bunched, and my nose tickled. What an *actor*.

We all watched as he raised it overhead and brought it down on the scale. The colored icons on the thermometer lit up like fireworks on the Fourth of July, going allllll the way to the top. Even a little bell went off. On the first try.

The little girl started jumping up and down, and I smiled.

"Mom! Did you see that? See! He can do it!" she squealed.

I squeezed the cat—my Hello Kitty?—tighter to my side before whistling.

Alex turned as he dropped the sledgehammer, and I know I wasn't imagining the smirk on his face before he took the giant stuffed unicorn the employee handed him. He turned and came over to me, making eye contact with the mom when he stood at my side. It took a moment before she nodded in understanding.

He held the stuffed animal out to the little girl.

She gasped.

"My girlfriend already has a Hello Kitty. Do you want this one?" he asked, the edges of a smile turning his mouth up into the biggest one I'd seen him make yet.

Who the hell was this playful, kind smart-ass?

She nodded enthusiastically, her arms reaching out, snatching it up before he could change his mind. She hugged it tight to her face. I was pretty sure she might have licked the cheek like she was marking her territory.

"What do you say?" her mom asked, her smile wide.

"Thank you!" the little girl shrieked.

"You're welcome."

"Thank you, thank you, thank you!" she repeated, clutching that unicorn like it was going to run away from her if she relaxed even a little bit.

Thank you, the mom mouthed.

Alex nodded, giving the girl another smile that was small but blinding.

Did he have to be so beautiful and nice when he was in the mood?

I couldn't help myself. I wrapped an arm around his waist and gave him a side hug, pressing tight against that solid frame.

He really was a good man. A total fucking sucker too, but a good man. And I hoped he could see that on my face as he dipped his head while I hugged him.

"You're a real hero when you use your powers for good," I told him before dropping my arm just as quickly as I'd gone for him.

He blinked. "I always use them for good, even when I don't want to."

"I know." Because I did.

Alex made a hoarse sound, but I hoped he understood what I meant.

Doing the right thing was never easy, but doing the right thing when you didn't have to was even harder. Most people would never be able to set aside their pride, to do what should be done. And I think that said everything about his personality.

About him.

It gave me a lot to think about.

His eyes scanned the crowd, and in my gut, I knew it wasn't just to be cautious. He'd said it himself, there was nothing in this world he had to worry about . . . other than others like him. But I understood how he'd become so disillusioned. One of these people might need him someday. Would they badmouth him too? Try to sue him?

"Alexander?" a foreign voice spoke up.

Alex's arm came over my shoulders, pulling me into his side so fast I stumbled into him. Into that rock-hard side that felt like a damn brick wall.

"Hey," the voice said a moment before a man took a step forward, a toddler-sized boy in his arms, a woman at his side.

The arm on my shoulders stayed right where it was.

"Hey, I guess you don't remember me. It's Phillip. We went to Andover Prep together," the man said.

The fingers dangling by my collarbone twitched, and for a second I thought he was going to deny knowing the guy, but the hand not around me gradually extended toward him. "Yeah . . . I do."

He sounded the opposite of excited.

The man named Phillip took Alex's hand and gave it an aggressive-looking shake. "I almost didn't recognize you. How's it going? I haven't seen you since graduation."

Yeah, Alex went all tense again, and his voice sounded off, sounded different as he answered, "Well, you?"

This was reminding me of the first few weeks we knew each other.

The man laughed like what he'd said was funny. "I'm great. This is my son, Pip, and my wife, Ashley."

Alex simply nodded at the two. "This is my . . . Gracie."

The guy looked at me, and his gaze flicked in the direction of my boobs. In front of his wife.

The hand on my shoulder tensed.

"I'm a cardiologist," the man said like someone had asked. "What are you doing now?"

"I work," the son of a bitch with his arm over my shoulders answered.

I almost choked.

But this man who used to know Alex in school wasn't deterred. "Did you just get here? I'd love to catch up. I haven't seen hardly anyone since graduation. We just moved back from San Francisco. Where did you go—"

The more people you knew, the more you had to lie. And Alex's contacts weren't in anymore. How many did he used to have to go through when he'd gone to school? Hundreds?

"We need to get going, actually," Alex cut in smoothly. "Take care, Greg."

Greg?

"Nice meeting you," I helped him as we turned. Alex instantly ignored the small family as we speed-walked away, me clutching my cat as tight as I could.

We pretty much ran to the car, and it wasn't until we got inside that I said, "You know damn well his name wasn't Greg."

"No, it's Phillip Kennedy the Third. I couldn't stand him in high school. I could tell from his cologne I still wouldn't like him. He had so much of it on. I didn't recognize him until the last second," Alex muttered, turning the car on.

I hugged the stuffed animal on my lap and pressed my cheek against it. "I could tell." I thought about it. "You went to a fancy private school? You don't act or talk like a spoiled rich kid."

"We weren't spoiled. We had chores. My parents had no problem telling us 'no.' We ate dinner together as a family almost every night. They made us do community service every other weekend. We watched TV. Only Achilles and Athena act like they're better than everyone."

"I can't picture you scrubbing a toilet for allowance money or putting up with people at Andover Prep." I put way too much enthusiasm into the name of his school. It sounded made up.

He looked at me, and I could tell his shoulders relaxed. "It wasn't easy. Phillip tried to get these guys to beat me up our freshman year."

"No," I gasped.

He nodded.

"What happened?"

"Odi pulled the fire alarm to stop it."

"But you could have beat the shit out of him." He could have done way more than that. What an idiot!

His laugh was so genuine it felt the same way in my chest as an ice cream cone did on a hot day. "Yeah, then I would've gotten the shit beat out of me."

"By your brothers?"

Alex huffed. "I wish. Alana. But it'd be easier than picking on a baby. It's the first thing we're taught: the strong don't pick on the weak. Even if we want to and they deserve it."

That was something else to think about. I side-eyed him. "I can take his wife and kid if you want me to."

Alex leaned against the back of the seat, his eyes glowing briefly in the dark cabin of the car. "You would fight the kid too?"

I hugged the Hello Kitty a little bit tighter. "You don't take care of the kid, he'll grow up and come after you in the future. Come on, Alex, you're better than this. You probably don't read comics, but everyone knows this. The Electro-Man movies are really good; you might enjoy them if you gave them a chance."

His eyes briefly glowed bright again, and I was pretty sure I saw a smirk on that perfect face. "Yeah, I might." His smirk got even bigger. "I just might."

Chapter Twenty-Five

It was settled. I was going to see how long Alex could hold his breath when I held a pillow over his face later.

When he wasn't expecting it.

It was either going to be that, or I was going to choke him out.

Had his sister, The Primordial survived in space? Yes. Were chances in his favor that he could do the same? Yes.

And could he realistically overpower me with his smallest toe? Most definitely. But I was going to give it my all anyway.

He was going to learn a lesson some way, somehow. He couldn't just do whatever he wanted.

"Why do I have to go with you?" I asked for about the twentieth time.

The son of a bitch, who I was purposely not looking at for longer than a second or two, repeated the same thing he'd said half the other times I'd thrown the same question at him. "Because."

That was his answer: *because.*

Real helpful.

I wasn't sure how I felt about meeting his mom, and that's probably more than half the reason why I kept asking. I'd thought about pretending to have a migraine so I could stay, but that was cowardly. I was running at 50 percent capacity now, and maybe I should have insisted, but . . .

I owed him.

"Hear me out," I started to say before he groaned.

"We're five minutes away. You're dressed. I'm dressed. We don't have to stay long. I know you aren't feeling great. It'll be an excuse to leave," he told me, sounding ultra-crabby.

I wanted to bang my head, but that would mess up the makeup that I'd had to watch an hour-long tutorial to learn how to put on.

Makeup that he'd left on my bed.

Along with a beautiful dress.

And shoes.

All of which were perfect for me, even the foundation that matched my skin tone perfectly.

I'd been so surprised the night before when I'd come out of the shower and found the bags from the mall sitting on my bed. I wasn't sure what members of a bomb squad felt like, but it had to have been close to how my heart had pounded as I opened every bag and box. It kept pounding slowly while I'd looked for him and found him in his library.

I was holding everything in my arms when I stopped in the doorway. "What's this?"

His attention had been focused on the computer on his lap. "Clothes."

This mother . . . "For me?"

"They're not for me, Cookie Monster."

That didn't help any. "For funsies or a reason?" I asked, my voice going just a little high.

His fingers flew across the keyboard as his lips moved along with it before he replied, "For tomorrow."

What was . . . ? His *mom's*. I'd purposely made myself stop thinking about it. The idea of meeting The Primordial's mom . . . Alex's mom . . . was intimidating as hell. I gulped. "I thought we were going to your mom's."

"We are." He still hadn't looked up. "You don't go to her birthday celebration in jeans and a T-shirt," he said, sounding irritated about it, but that did nothing for me.

I hadn't been to a birthday party in years. Much less a *birthday celebration*. Was that a grown-up version of a birthday party? I was pretty sure the last time had been for this nice girl in high school. My grandparents had needed to go to their bank, which had been two towns over, and I'd snuck over there in the meantime. Her dad had made barbeque, and we'd drank root beer out of bottles and played pool. We had been living outside of Phoenix then.

I'd thought about looking her up once or twice, but I hadn't seen the point.

Only then had Alex's eyes strayed to me. "I don't get to wear jeans either," he'd said like that explained everything.

I had been *speechless*.

My mouth had moved, but nothing had come out, and then his phone rang, and I'd slowly backed out after he'd said Alana's name.

I'd spent the rest of the night being stunned.

I'd pretended to be asleep when he'd come into the room hours later.

And now we were here.

I pulled at the silky black material of the dress that fit me surprisingly well and sighed.

For so long I'd dreamed about what I would do once I didn't have to hide. How I'd go out and *do* things. But now I wanted to go back to my temporary home base and put on the jeans and the shirt that I'd been wearing earlier while I'd been in denial over this happening.

"Are you sure this is a good idea?" I asked him. "Shouldn't I be hiding at your place?"

He glanced at me. "You don't need to do that here. Not

anymore. No one here knows or would think about betraying you. You're safe."

I hoped he was right. I really did. But somehow I knew he wouldn't put me at unnecessary risk, not after everything.

"We don't have to stay for long," Alex reminded me, sounding so, so irritated it only slightly made me feel better.

I pulled at the material of the dress again and looked out the window. I didn't want to get riled up. The last thing I wanted was to start sweating or smell scared. "Is there anything I need to know? You haven't said a lot about your family, so I don't want to screw up in case I have to talk to someone without you." I thought about that. "Please don't make me talk to people. My social skills are rusty. I would rather deal with you than have to stand there awkwardly all night or get nervous and tell someone about how I almost used poison ivy to wipe my butt when we were on the run and you barely stopped me in time."

His fucking laugh startled the hell out of me.

I hadn't even thought about the incident on purpose out of shame. At least the tiny amount of it I had left.

And he was still laughing as he said, "I won't leave you alone."

I almost asked him if he promised but kept the words in my mouth.

He made a noise in his throat as his laugh wound down while he approached what seemed like a gated community. We weren't far from his house at all, but we had left the "neighborhood." I hadn't figured out this whole living situation and hadn't found the right moment to ask either, but I would. Sometime soon.

He punched in a code at a gate, then went forward, and a few minutes later, nodded at a man working behind yet another booth. Only then did he start talking again. "Achilles, Kilis, was at the office. He's my oldest brother. He has good intentions, but he's bossy and a stuffy shit."

A stuffy shit.

Here we were, driving to his mom's "birthday celebration" dressed like something out of a spy movie, and he was . . . the way he was.

He really was something. "Is he special like you?" I asked him. "Or do the 'superior genes' skip around?"

"They do in some ways and don't in others. We're all like this, but he wasn't chosen after all."

"Because he's a stuffy shit?"

The side of his mouth closest to me curved up. "Basically."

I had so many questions about that.

"He was supposed to be one of the faces, but . . ." Alex shook his head. "When he was in high school, he lost control and hurt a classmate. Our grandmother had to get involved, and that's why she chose me."

The questions. The fucking questions I had. I almost choked on them.

He kept going. "Athena, Thena, my sister, is the second oldest. She's also a stuffy shit. She only likes Achilles and Alana. The rest of us annoy the hell out of her. She's mad she wasn't chosen either, but she isn't as strong for some reason. She's the smartest though."

He had to be kidding me.

"Then there's Alana—"

"The Primordial?" I asked in a squeaky voice that got me another side-look.

"Yes. She's everything she seems to be but better."

Wow, those were big words from someone I didn't think handed compliments out easily.

"Odysseus, Odi, is the fourth one of us. He's a stuffy shit sometimes, but he's a good guy." He made a thoughtful sound in his throat. "After that is Robert, or who you all call The Centurion. He's a kiss-ass, but he's everything he seems to be. Then there's Leon. He owns a farm an hour away. He's good. He doesn't like people much though."

Said Old Grumpy Pants. I almost snorted.

"He might be here if our mom pressured him into it," Alex kept going.

"Then you, since you're the baby," I told him with a little cackle. "It explains so much."

"I was until Selene. She was the surprise no one saw coming."

"She's your *sister*?" I squawked.

He gave me a crazy look. "What did you think she was?"

"I don't know. A cousin or something."

"No, she's my baby sister."

I hadn't seen that coming either, but now that I thought about it, I guess she did look like The Centurion. I was going to have to ponder that one. "At first, I thought you and Leon were twins. You look a lot alike."

"He's a year older than me."

"Are you the closest to him?"

He thought about it for a second and tipped his head.

"So Achilles, Athena, and Odysseus all work for the same business?"

"Yeah. Everyone that works on that floor is family."

What was the family business? Was it the Akita Corporation? I wanted to ask and hoped he would say, but he didn't. Fine. Maybe I'd overhear something tonight. "Is there anything to worry about with them?" I patted the little knife I'd snuck into my underwear. I hoped it didn't stab me in the thigh.

"No." Alex trailed off, obviously noticing what I thought I was hiding from the way he sighed. "Still?" he muttered, almost sounding disappointed.

"I'm not going to stab you with it," I told him. "It makes me feel better, all right?"

He grumbled. Then he sighed, and a moment later he said, "There's something for you in the glove compartment."

I looked at him before remembering why I wasn't supposed to focus on him for too long and focused back out the windshield. "What?"

"Do I have to repeat the entire thing or . . . ?"

I rolled my eyes before stopping and wondering if that might mess up the eyeshadow that it had taken me three tries to get decent. "Sometimes I think I do miss you being pissed off and just grunting," I muttered. "But please, repeat the whole thing. I don't think I heard you correctly. There's something in the glove compartment?"

The man I wasn't supposed to be looking at, who was dressed in a suit that looked like it had been made specifically for him, sighed. "Something for you."

For me? "Really?"

"That's what I said. You bought me that cookie; we're even now."

"Just so we're on the same page, a gift isn't a gift if you expect something in return."

Alex didn't say a word.

"And again, just to be on the same page, I wasn't expecting anything. I got you the cookie because you'd said that one night that you wanted a cookie when I said I wanted Cheetos. You got me the Cheetos already."

"Did you argue with your grandparents as much as you argue with me?"

"Hell no. I'd go into my room and talk into my pillow so they couldn't hear me. My grandma was old, but her stink eye was just as good as yours, and she was scarier than you." I peeked at him again for a split second. "And you're the one who likes bickering. I just like giving you a hard time because I think you enjoy it."

Got him.

"Open the damn glove compartment, Gracie."

Leaning forward, I opened it almost timidly. Inside, there was a slip of paper that was his insurance card—the name on it said ALEXANDER SHŌTA AKITA—and a small, brown, rectangular box.

Why I wanted to ask if that was his real name explained everything that was wrong with my life.

I mouthed it out and shot another quick look at his profile.

I could see it. It was classy, just like him. Most of the time.

Putting the card back, I took the box out, slid another glance toward Alex who was still focused on driving down the longest brick driveway in the world, and I took the top off.

There was a multi-tool inside. A Swiss Army knife on steroids.

"For me?"

He slid me a quick glance. "No, it's for the other demon that insists on sleeping in my bed."

Now he was calling me a demon, and I was about it. "That was you who went into the room when I was asleep and got into *my* bed."

"You're still sick, aren't you?" he asked.

I swear . . . "How long can you hold your breath for?"

His eyes flicked toward me. He'd put his blue contacts in again. Was that a tiny, itty-bitty smile on his mouth? "A long time."

Oh boy. I plucked the tool out of the box, noticing how light it was. What the hell was it made out of?

"It's safer than you carrying around that knife in your underwear. Take it out before you stab yourself. I don't want to hear you crying again."

I snorted as I tossed it up and down, wrapping my fingers around it, squeezing it tight. A little beam of light shot out from the tip. It even had a flashlight!

I swallowed, tossing it up one more time.

I was not going to cry.

I was not going to cry.

I was not—

"Don't even think about it."

I pressed my lips together, and it took me two tries to finally say, "That's what I'm trying to do, and you're not helping." I clutched the multi-tool tighter and tried again, ignoring the fact that my voice still sounded all breathy and weird. "Thank you, Alex. This is wonderful. I love it."

"I know it is."

I was starting to think if he stopped being a smart-ass, I might miss it a little. "I've been worried about the knife in my underwear since I sat down," I admitted. "Thank you."

His entire upper body turned toward me. "I was joking. You really put it in your underwear?"

"I'm not Lara Croft. I don't have a thigh holster for it."

Out of the corner of my eye, I saw he faced forward again, and I let myself glance over at him for longer than a second. I had a perfect view of the smooth edge of his jaw. His hair was styled nicely to the side with some hair products. He'd put some effort into tonight, that was for sure.

Keeping my shit together and ignoring the *GQ* model beside me, I started shimmying the dress up my hips and unbuckled my seat belt. His dark eyes flicked over, but I ignored him until the skirt was high enough, then I snuck my hand up the outside of my thigh and carefully pulled the knife out from the band holding it down. Then my hand went back in and I slipped the multi-tool in the same spot. It wasn't exactly an easy reach, but that was all right. It was lighter than the knife, but I'd keep checking it to make sure it didn't fall out.

"You might be the most distrustful person I've ever met."

"I don't have a purse, otherwise I would have put it in there." And I wasn't really relying on the knife to save me but more as a backup plan if we got into a pickle. I was never going to leave myself unprepared again. I'd even taken a knife from his kitchen and stuck it between the mattress and base of the bed. I would put it back if he noticed. "Thank you. I love it."

"I heard you the first time."

I groaned, but it was his light huff that instantly reminded me he was just being a pain in the ass.

That he was joking.

This man who bought me a multi-tool to make me feel safer.

Oh boy.

"No crying," Alex muttered in his Superbutt voice.

Time to change the subject then. "Is your mom going to hate me?" I managed to ask. "I don't think your siblings liked me very much yesterday."

He didn't even think about it. "Yeah."

My shoulders dropped.

"You don't need to worry about it. I told you, I don't think they like half our family either."

Great.

There was a pause. "She only likes about five people, and I don't even think I'm one of them."

The snort came out of me before I could stop it. "Is that where you learned it from? Not liking people?"

He huffed, but I saw the corner of his mouth curve up. "I like more than five people."

Excuse me. "Six?"

"I just expect the worst in people."

Oh. I could see that. I squeezed my knees and eyed him quickly. "So why did you want me to come with you? So no one kidnaps me while you're gone?" I joked.

"Nobody is kidnapping you."

"I was kidding. What I was trying to say is that I thought you'd be close enough to your family to not feel that way. You said you liked Alana and The Centu—Robert. Selene and Leon too, I thought."

It took him a long second to answer. "I do. I am close to them, but . . . it's different."

How?

"You're still sick too. Being close by will help you heal faster." He thought about it for a second. "You're not bad company either. I like talking shit with you."

I jerked in my seat. "I'm growing on you, huh?"

"Like an ingrown hair." His gaze slid over to me. "Not that I've ever had one."

I reached over numbly and grabbed his forearm, my eyes tingly, my whole heart starting to feel a little funny too. "I thought the multi-tool was my favorite thing I've been given, but I think . . . I think you saying you can talk shit with me just beat it. Not that long ago, you didn't even want to make eye contact with me."

Eyes with blue contacts slid to me. "A lot changed since then."

I squeezed his arm.

Then I was sure.

A world-class half smile drew up the corner of his mouth.

Then he took it to the next level when he said, "I could have done a lot worse than ending up in your yard."

I laughed. "Thank you?"

"You're welcome. We're here," he claimed as he turned down another long driveway.

Where were we? We drove by a tall fence, and I felt my heart kind of start to gallop a little, especially when I spotted the massive house up ahead. Well, more like the light coming from it.

Alex's house was big. This one was . . .

It was one like they showed on historical drama shows where dukes and duchesses lived in the summer with a thousand employees. Where rich people ate Grey Poupon. This was that.

It was *huge*. There were a few cars in front of us with people exiting them and slowly making their way inside.

"I thought this was a birthday dinner for your mom," I muttered.

"Celebration."

Okay, that was exactly what he'd said. "How many people are here?" I croaked, suddenly nervous.

Didn't they live reclusive lives to not bring attention to themselves? They carried the biggest secret in the world in them. Shouldn't they be secretive?

"I don't know."

I was going to throw up.

"What's wrong with you?" he asked suddenly, as if he could smell my nerves flaring to life.

I didn't even bother trying to hide it, my voice shook a little. "Alex . . . I thought . . . I don't know. Maybe this was a formal family dinner. That we'd sit at a long table like in *Beauty and the Beast* and there would be a very nice maid who might serve us food, and there'd be some silver candlesticks.

"I must have been in denial. I . . . I . . . I haven't been around more than a few people in a long time, other than going to the store. You know that. I've had one pair of heels in my life. Fancy for me is eating Olive Garden. I haven't lived in a house bigger than 1,200 square feet until coming to stay at your house." My voice had gotten quieter and quieter with every word.

Up ahead were two people in tuxedos, either valets or security of some sort, which would have been ironic considering who he was. Who *they* were.

Alex pulled the car over to the side, threw it into park, and turned his whole body after unbuckling his belt to face me. There was a strange expression that wasn't a frown or a scowl but somehow both and neither at the same time.

I swallowed and tried to give him a brave smile, but my heart was beating too fast for that, and I suddenly didn't want to get out of the car. "You know I'm not . . . socialized." I swallowed hard. "I've barely talked to people since high school. Since my grandparents passed away. I'm quiet so that I don't say things I shouldn't. You're the first person I've ever been able to run my mouth around. That I've been able to have a real conversation with . . . joked with. The first person in forever I've been able to be mostly myself around. I'll probably tell a stranger a fart joke if I'm given the chance."

I could wait here.

No, *no, I couldn't.*

After everything he had done for me, I could handle this. It was just a gathering with a lot of people, not climbing Mount Everest. What was the worst that would happen? I'd embarrass myself? Embarrass him?

These people didn't know me. They didn't know my circumstances.

I sucked in a weak breath through my nose and let it back out again, ignoring the shakiness in that too. "I'm sorry I'm over-reacting. It's fine. I'm just . . . I suddenly had a bad memory of being young and having other kids calling me ugly names because I was the new kid, or because we didn't have a lot of money. You're you. I've never even been out of the United States. I'm proud of it, but I have a college degree from the cheapest online university I could find." Wow, I had thought for the longest time that I'd toughened up a lot over the years, but maybe that wasn't totally true. "Anyway, I didn't know there were going to be so many people here, and that's a Rolls-Royce in front of us. It's okay. I'm okay."

I took a breath through my nose and tried to shake it off right at the same time he said my name.

I met his gaze, sucking in another breath and letting it rattle out through my mouth. Oh boy, I wasn't feeling so great.

"You are no less than any person in that house," he told me.

I knew that.

And oh fucking boy, *that was his mom's house?*

He turned even more toward me. "All the money in the world doesn't make someone a better person, so knock it off with that bullshit." He paused, and his eyes glowed bright for a moment. "You're loyal, and even when you're scared, you're brave. I'm not joking, don't make that face. You think I use those words lightly? You're brave when it counts. That's what matters. Nobody's going to have a problem with you anyway. Don't worry about that." Alex nudged me. "You can be more than just 'mostly' yourself around me too, I guess."

He was joking.

My eyes started tingling, and I could feel my nostrils start to flare as a sound built up in my chest.

"Don't even think about it," he growled.

I pressed my lips together and nodded slowly. "I won't even think about it. Promise." That was a lie; I was totally going to think about it. I was going to think about it for the rest of my life.

And at this point, he knew I was full of shit, but he still said, "Good."

I eyed him.

"I'm not going to let anything happen to you," he reminded me softly.

It was exactly what I needed though.

I held my breath, took a second, and then asked, "Is Selene coming? I liked her. I got a good vibe from her."

"No, she's in New York right now, and she got a good vibe from you too."

"Is she like you? Or like Athena?"

He shook his head. "She's stronger than Athena but not like Alana."

What the hell? "Not everyone in the family ends up being so special then?"

Something awful funny came over his face. "Not anymore. From what I understand, our bodies, our genetic makeup, have been adapting over time." The way he cleared his throat was a lot more aggressively than I thought he needed to, and I was pretty sure his funny face got even funnier. "It's part of the reason why my grandmother is trying to find the rest of the Atraxian lines. To make sure some of us continue on; to give the kids the best shot at continuing the genes as long as possible." I was pretty sure he glanced at me so fast he didn't mean for me to notice, but I had.

Why did that sound loaded?

Before I could ask, he kept talking. "Let's get the hell out of here so we can leave faster," he said before turning forward again, putting the car back into drive.

A great, big question pecked at my brain: why he would admit all of this to me and at what cost? None of this information was out in the open. I understood his grandmother wanting to keep track of the bloodlines, but there were still some holes in his story that didn't add up to me. I could worry about my chances of getting murdered for knowing too much later on.

And a part of me didn't doubt for a second that if I breathed a word of this to someone, Alex wouldn't be the only person to end up with a broken back.

And I knew I wouldn't be able to heal from it the same way he did.

The passenger door opened, and a valet held out a hand to help me out of the car.

I took it and got out, wobbling on my heels after I thanked her and moved forward on the path to wait for the man-being making his way around his car.

I gave him a smile that was a lot less nervous than it would have been five minutes ago as I undid the buttons of the wool coat that Alex had left on the bed for me. It was heavy and so fine that I was scared of getting it dirty. Which was why I was taking it off ASAP.

And that's when Alex stopped walking. Right there, in the middle of the pathway. He just stood there.

Staring at me.

More like in the direction of my chest.

And his voice was deeper than usual as he asked, "What are you wearing?"

Slipping my hands into the pockets of the coat, I spread the sides wide and looked down at myself. "The dress you got me?"

Oh, he was definitely looking at my boobs.

I had done the same thing after I'd put it on and realized that even though it had looked modest on the hanger, my boobs decided they wanted to be the center of attention. And they were. The sweetheart neckline dipped in there, not actually showing a ton of skin but hugging the shit out of them. But he'd seen me in tank tops. He'd seen me in my bra of all things. And he'd definitely seen me without a bra on. He'd seen all kinds of parts of me.

But none of that seemed to make a difference because he wasn't looking away. Why the hell was he frowning?

"That's not what it looked like on the mannequin."

I shimmied my shoulders just a little. They were already C-cups when I was in middle school. He could stare at them all he wanted, and they weren't going to get any smaller.

His gaze flicked up toward mine. He scowled. "Keep the jacket on."

It was my turn to frown. "Get real. I'm not risking getting this coat dirty; I read the label. And maybe there's a sugar daddy or two that might be interested in an all-right-looking, almost thirty-year-old virgin. Do you have a lonely, rich cousin?"

His scowl went nowhere, and it might have even got meaner. "No, and don't do that shoulder shake again."

I blinked, and his scowl hit yet another level. He eyed my boobs one last time and finished coming over, walking beside me toward the double doors, where a man in a dark suit stood. He must have recognized him because he stood up straighter, cleared his throat, and said, "Welcome, Mr. Akita."

A woman came over and helped me take the coat off, handing over a small slip of paper to Alex who pocketed it. That was when I got my first look at the inside of the house.

Mansion.

Estate.

I had never used the word "opulent" before, but that was the best adjective I could think of to describe the house. Everything was massive and expensive. The hallways wider than normal, and even the artwork on the walls seemed like something I should have recognized in a museum.

I pressed my lips together to make sure I wasn't walking down the hall with my mouth open.

"How rich is your family?" I whispered.

His elbow bumped mine, and I glanced over at him to see him raising his eyebrows.

Oh.

I slipped my hand into the crook of it.

That was nice. Some of the tension left my shoulders as I squeezed the hard muscle beneath his clothes. It felt like a rock under there.

"Rich," he answered simply.

I snorted. "The fact you didn't even try to play it off says everything, huh?"

He grunted, but I knew it was an amused one.

"I meant to ask when we went to that building . . . are they, your family, the same Akita family that—"

To give him credit, he didn't try to play that off either. "Yes."

"You didn't let me finish. The electronics, the cars—"

"Yes. Both sides of the family have successful businesses and investments."

"No shit," I breathed. That was going to take me another second to process. "And the rest of the families? The other Atraxian people?"

"The head of the house in Eastern Europe is a steel magnate."

I blinked.

"The family living in India is in biotech."

"Huh," I muttered. "Wait. Did everyone that came from Atraxia look different, and did that determine where they settled? So they could fit in better?"

He nodded just as we made it to another set of double doors where yet another man in a tuxedo stood.

I needed to start a list of all the things I was curious over so I could ask him in a better situation. Not when we were surrounded by other people who might have his incredible hearing.

"Are those security guards?" I asked him instead.

"Yes. We don't need it, but it's more the impression."

I'd fucking bet. "I was thinking, if you want to get out of here sooner, I can pretend to faint so we can leave faster. Wink at me or something. That can be our sign. But you have to promise to catch me."

"I'll think about it."

"What? Catching me or me fainting?"

"Catching you."

I tightened my hand over his inner elbow and groaned. "Never mind. At least point your mom out to me so I can pretend to use the bathroom when she starts to make her way over."

"Too late," he said just as I spotted a tall woman making her way over with Achilles and Alex's almost twin, Leon.

Shit. "I can't make a run for it then?"

"Sorry."

He wasn't sorry.

Fuck.

First of all, if this was her, she didn't look old enough to be his mom. The woman seemed to be in her fifties, her hair a shade of blonde that no bottle in the world could recreate. It was styled in an elegant up-do, her makeup not exactly light but done really well. I felt like an expert now that I'd spent so much time looking at makeup tutorials on my new computer. A couple inches shy of the sons at her sides, she was formidable-looking. Her skin tone was a deep tan like The Primordial's, and I totally understood how her DNA wasn't 100 percent human. Even from a distance, she had *presence*. Her features made her heritage indescribable. I was fairly certain she had contacts in, but whether they were naturally purple or bright blue, I had no idea.

Her children were beautiful just like she was.

What the hell did their dad look like?

"No," I said, pretty sure she could hear us, and I wasn't above sucking up. "That's not your mom."

"Yes, it is," he replied.

"Are all your brothers and sisters from the same mom and dad?" I asked.

That got me a glance out of the corner of his eye. "Yes, we only marry once. We can't exactly get divorced."

That led to me having more questions, but I managed to keep them in my mouth just as the woman and her two sons stopped right in front of us.

Oh man, someone was not a fan of me, and I hadn't even opened my mouth yet.

Then again, now that I had a better look, her expression was Alex's default one, so maybe not.

His arm flexed under my hand.

"Happy birthday, Mother," he greeted her.

The woman turned her cheek to the side, and Alex leaned

forward just enough to brush his mouth across it, my hand slid-ing down until I touched his wrist.

Her smile reminded me of a shark.

No, not a shark.

That wasn't aggressive enough. Something older, bigger. She was whatever it was the T. rex had fought in one of the *Jurassic Park* movies.

If they weren't all capable of smelling my pee, I would have probably gone on myself a little bit.

"I'm pleased that you finally decided to come see your con-cerned mother, Alexander," the woman said in a voice with just a hint of an accent I couldn't pinpoint. "You should have called me. I had to hear from Selene instead."

"I know that you've been busy," he replied stonily before his gaze flicked to the two men on either side of him. "Achilles," he said flatly.

"Alexander," the uptight butthole greeted him back, all dull.

Leon tipped his chin up, the most mischievous smirk on his good-looking mouth.

Their mom tsked.

"Mother, this is Gracie," Alex said.

Her head swiveled toward me like she had all damn day.

"Happy birthday, ma'am," I said.

Long, dark blonde eyelashes fell over dark blue eyes that def-initely had to have contacts in them.

"You are really beautiful and terrifying, and it's nice to meet you. You have beautiful children, and I see now where they get it from," I rambled in one breath.

Her gaze moved toward Alex. "This is who you were with?"

"Yes," he answered.

Her sleek eyebrows flicked up just a little bit as she glanced back in my direction.

Slowly, oh so slowly, a long, thin hand extended toward me.

Was I supposed to kiss it?

"Just shake it," Alex muttered under his breath.

Oh, I did just that, a low, cool power zinging straight up my arm like I'd just touched a glacier. I gulped as I pulled my hand back and instantly snuck it back into the crook of Alex's elbow. Then I smiled weakly at his almost-doppelgänger, and said, "Hi, Leon."

"Hi, Gracie," he said with an amused smile on his stunning face. "Did you meet Lexi's first wife yet?"

The arm I was holding on to tensed as I grinned right back at him. "Not yet, she hasn't escaped the attic yet."

"Lock your door before she gets jealous," he joked in return.

Alex growled. "Are you two done?" he snapped. "Why are you flirting with each other?"

We were flirting?

Out of the corner of my eye, I could see Alex's mom's face change, and I thought that maybe, just maybe, his older brother might have stood up straighter.

A big, solid hand landed on top of the one I had on his arm. "If that's all, Gracie needs to use the facilities," Alex kept going, his gaze settling on Leon, who had a super-smug expression that I didn't know what to do with.

We took a step back just as Achilles said, "I need to speak to you."

Shit. "I'm bad with directions and get lost really easily . . ."

"It's right out the doors, second door on the left," the snobby butthole explained.

The award-winning actor nodded, but I could tell he was resigned. "I'll meet you there."

"Okay," I said, taking a step back. I'd tried to save him. If I hurried, maybe I could pretend to roll my ankle or something, so he would have to help me. "Nice to meet you, ma'am."

"See you, Gracie," Leon called out, that ornery look still on his face.

Oh, he was a pest too.

But it made me smile when I spotted Alex's scowl as I got away. I took my time walking through the doors, meeting some people's eyes. Everyone was dressed in clothes like people in *The Great Gatsby*. Long dresses with heavy beading and expensive materials. Jewelry with gems the size of my pinkie nail. Tuxedos that were just as nice as the one Alex had on.

When I'd first seen him standing in the foyer, my knee had almost given out. Sure I'd said his other brother Odi had taken over the top spot of being the most attractive man I'd ever seen, but Alex in that suit? It was why I'd forced myself not to look at him more than I had to. It was too much.

I didn't want my body to do something embarrassing either, which meant, I needed to focus on something else.

A woman beside me let out a fake, high laugh.

I felt so out of place.

And I was hungry.

I turned right out of the doors and took in the empty hallway, counting the doorways until I found the one with literally a bathroom sign for women on it.

I pushed open the door, half expecting a half-bath, but it was a full-on bathroom with stalls. Was that marble on the floor and the sinks? Ducking into one of the stalls, I did what I needed to with my clothes; I clutched my brand-new multi-tool so it wouldn't fall into the toilet and squatted. I'd just started peeing when I suddenly stopped.

Because peeking at me from the gaps in the slats that made up the door was a little face.

I covered my midsection with my hands.

"Hi," the little girl said.

Watching me pee.

I kept holding it and said, "Hi."

"Whatcha doing?" the little blonde girl asked.

I kept holding it, not sure whether to pull my dress back down or not . . . but I wasn't done. "Peeing." I paused. "What are you doing?"

"Nothing. Looking for my grandma."

Grandma? She had to be . . . little? I hadn't been around all that many kids, but she looked like she might be freaking cute.

"Do you . . . need help finding her?" I hadn't seen any other kids in the ballroom now that I thought about it.

"Uh-huh."

"If you let me finish peeing, I'll help you look for her after."

I saw her bob her head through the slats. "Okay," she answered in a sweet, squeaky voice.

But she didn't move.

Was she . . . ?

"You don't have to keep watching me if you don't want to . . ." I trailed off. I didn't want to hurt her feelings. Maybe watching people while they peed was no big deal. I wasn't going to be the one to shame her. Her parents could have this conversation with her.

"I want to," she said, totally seriously.

I tugged the front of my dress down, knowing all she could see were thighs anyway, and kept going. As much as I could at least, because apparently, I could go in front of Alex but not in front of a Peeping Tom of a little girl. I finished and wiped carefully before flushing and opening the door just as she backed up.

She *was* adorable.

Her hair was down, straight to her shoulders, bangs were cut straight across her forehead, and in a mint green dress that looked like it had been made by some fashion designer, she blinked bright blue eyes at me.

Selene and Achilles's eyes. How was she related to Alex? Was her grandma his mom?

"Hi."

"Hi," I told her, going straight for the sink to wash my hands. "I'm Gracie. What's your name?"

"Asami," she answered. "I like your boobies."

I was in the middle of rubbing soap between my fingers when I snorted so hard my head hurt. "Thank you. Me too."

"My mommy doesn't really have boobies. I hope I do," she let me know.

Thrusting my hands under the water, I couldn't help but grin as I said, "Well, I hope you do because you want them, but if you don't, they are still boobies, just smaller ones."

"Uncle Leon calls them jubblies."

Did she just say *jubblies*?

I started cracking up again and could barely say, "I like the word boobies more." And if Leon was her uncle, Alex had to be too.

"Me too," the little girl agreed. "Can we go find my grandma now?"

I reached for a towel and stalled just as I saw there weren't *paper* towels but cloth ones. That was the epitome of rich. I dried off, taking in the soft texture as I said, "Sure. My friend might come with us though."

"Okay," she agreed, reaching for my hand, threading her tiny fingers through mine.

It made me smile.

We marched forward, and I felt something in my chest at her easy friendship and soft little hand in mine. Like she knew I was thinking about her, she beamed up at me.

Oh, I knew that smile.

It was a no-good one.

And it looked awful, awful familiar.

There was a tiny zip of energy coming through her palm too, I noticed.

Oh boy.

I opened the door for her and let her go out first. Part of me expected to find Alex right outside, but he wasn't there, and the little girl started tugging on my hand, heading in the opposite direction of the ballroom. "She's over here," she said. "Come on."

So she knew where her grandma was?

Well, Alex could sniff around to find me, I figured.

"You wanna play Trouble with us?" she asked, leading me in the direction of a big, ornate door on the left.

"I need to find my friend first," I told her, pleased by her invitation and that deceivingly sweet smile she kept shooting at me.

"Uncle Lexi?" she asked, confirming exactly what I'd already put together, before pulling me straight for the cracked door she pushed open. "Grandma?" Asami called out. "Grandmaaaaa?"

"You were gone too long," a dry, almost raspy feminine voice said.

"I found my friend," the little girl replied, pulling me into a space that resembled a really grand living room. There were two couches, a rug that might have been Persian, and two walls of bookshelves. A big TV was mounted front and center. There was even a fireplace with two spacious chairs in front of it.

But it was at a table with four seats around it that I found a woman sitting. Her hair was pure silver-white, her skin the same deep gold as The Primordial's. She had to be in her . . . I had no idea. Seventies? Eighties? Nineties maybe?

"Hello," the woman said, the slightest accent to her words.

The hairs on the back of my neck and on my forearms rose.

And it wasn't fear exactly that peppered through my spine, but . . .

I'd gotten used to the energy that Alex put off. It was almost second nature now. Even Asami's slight buzz had been a pleasant tickle. I wasn't sure I could get used to the vibes that Alex's mother radiated, but chances were, I'd be able to. But the power, the intensity coming off this woman . . .

Part of me expected to grow a third eye, or at least some hair on my chin.

"It's okay," the little girl assured me as we made it to the table, like she knew why I'd hesitated.

I gulped and tried to focus on something else to calm down.

That was a sturdy-looking table. Was that redwood it was made of?

"Grandma, she's nice, and I like her boobies," Asami said suddenly as we stood on the opposite side of the table from where her grandmother was.

I let myself try again and slid my gaze back to her.

The woman looked at us with eyes that were way too percep-tive, too clear and bright, and honestly frightening when they lingered on me. A bright purple glow flared from them before she focused, then smiled, revealing a mouth full of white teeth I had a feeling weren't dentures.

"She needs to find Uncle Lexi, but maybe she'll play Trouble with us," the little girl went on as she climbed onto a chair beside her.

The grandmother kept looking at me, still smiling her creepy, too strong smile.

I wanted to back out of the room slowly without giving her my back.

"Hello," I croaked out.

"Hello," she greeted me again.

Oh boy. "It's nice to meet you, ma'am." Was *this* Alex's grandma?

"He can wait. Sit down," the woman said as the chair beside her was pushed back.

He? Could she smell him on me? I really hoped that had been her foot that had moved the chair.

"Yes, ma'am," I replied in a hurry, not wanting to irritate her.

Her eyes ran over my face, and I watched as she smiled even wider after a moment, like there was some joke she'd thought of.

I wanted to hide under the table. Use Asami as a shield, and *that* was embarrassing. It took everything in me to smile and even then, it was weak as fuck.

"She's pretty, huh?" The little girl took a long inhale like there were croissants in the room and let out a dreamy sigh. "I like the way she smells."

"Because she smells like intelligence and cunning. Well done, Asami," the older woman praised her, her focus entirely on me.

I was still considering hiding under the table, but . . . intelligence and cunning? If she was going to break my neck, at least she thought I was smart and crafty? Did Asami have the same abilities?

"I'm Gracie, ma'am," I forced myself to say, ignoring the fact it came out kind of hoarse and that my heart was starting to beat fast enough that she'd be able to sense it.

"Gracie," she repeated slowly as if savoring the word. "You children with your English names."

I wanted to apologize. "It's Altagracia on my birth certificate."

Her eyes glowed faintly purple.

"Ximena is my middle name."

A little smile played at the corners of her mouth, but it didn't feel that friendly even though it looked like it wanted to. "Altagracia Ximena Castro. You may call me Grandmother."

I had full-on goose bumps.

This was his grandma. How the hell else would she know my last name?

"I met your grandfather once."

The fear suddenly left me, and I sat up straight. "You did?"

"Oh, yes. When he was young." She smiled big, and I had to tell myself not to pee. "I lived in Limón for a time. You smell just like him, and he smelled just like his mother and grandmother."

He had always smelled great, like almonds or something

sweet. "He passed away a few years ago," I said, even though I had a feeling . . .

She didn't look surprised. "He had a long life. It's the best end any of us could ask for." Her gaze moved over mine again before her eyes flicked creepy quick toward the door, a moment before I heard a knock, then Alex's careful voice as he called out, "Gracie?" There was a loud clearing of his throat before he spoke again, his voice stiff. "Greetings, Grandmother."

"It's about time you came to see me, Alexander," the older woman said. "I had to get Asami to borrow your Gracie to get you to come."

His Gracie?

"Don't be angry with me," she continued on, not asking, but telling him. "I assisted you as much as I could."

Absolutely nothing registered on his stoic features. "I'm not. I understand."

Understand what? And what did he have to be angry over?

"Hi, Uncle Lexi. I picked up Uncle Leon's tractor yesterday. Can we play Trouble now?" Asami's sweet, little voice asked. "Please?"

She'd picked up a fucking tractor?

I heard Alex's steps, but my mind had already stuck on to what she had said.

Luck was one thing.

And this . . . this definitely didn't feel like that at all.

Chapter Twenty-Six

"Bye, Gracie!"

"Bye, Asami!" I called out over my shoulder as I followed Alex out of the game room an hour and a long—and eerie—game of Trouble later.

Seeing Alex sitting beside me at the table in a beautiful tux, pressing the little bubble in the middle and moving his pieces around the board, smiling occasionally at the ruthless girl sitting between me and who I was sure was her great-grandmother had been something else.

He called her "stinky," and she'd hooted, and I'd almost fainted. But that was beside the point.

On the other hand, watching said grandmother sitting at the table, her back totally straight, her long fingers plucking at pieces as well, while the most primal, raw power radiated from her in invisible waves was probably also going to be stuck in my head and body for a long time.

In my nightmares more like it.

I felt nauseous.

I was pretty sure I'd seen her mouth the number that appeared every time the dice was rolled a second before it settled.

She had nodded often, and her expressions were pleasant, but when her gaze landed on you . . . it was like being spotted by a shark in the middle of the ocean with no way of escaping. Like being in the middle of a field during a lightning storm. Honestly, she scared the *shit* out of me, and I had no real reason why she had that effect on me, but she did.

And that's exactly what I told Alex when we were reentering the ballroom.

"So, your grandma is terrifying," I whispered. "I thought your mom was intimidating, but she took it to a whole new level."

His attention was up and forward, but I watched him huff. He'd seemed distracted throughout the game, and I had a feeling it had to do with the tension none of us had been able to ignore between him and his grandmother. I'd noticed Asami, the tractor-carrying child, peeking back and forth between them. There had also been that weird comment about him being mad at her. It hadn't been an angry type of tension, but I had seen a smug smile cross her features when they'd made eye contact once or twice.

It had been like seeing a car about to hit an ice patch, knowing it was about to spin out of control and hit a road barrier, and not be able to look away.

Alex's grunt was off, rougher than usual. "She likes it that way. I'm surprised you lasted as long as you did in her presence. Most people can't."

Maybe that explained why I felt so weird. "Really?"

Alex glanced down. "Selene says she's like looking at the sun. Agatha met her once and hasn't seen her since. She says she saw her life flash before her eyes and claims she knows the day she's going to die."

My eyes went wide. "That's amazing and scary as hell at the same time."

He raised his eyebrows in a mix of pride and wariness and maybe something else.

"What is she?" I asked.

"She says she's the last full-blooded one of our kind. She's the strongest . . . the most powerful of all of us."

My mouth dropped open. "Oh shit."

Then I processed what he'd said. He *was* part human.

Those bluish-purple eyes flicked toward me, and he nodded. "She can't be around most people because they sense what she is. Or at least, they know she isn't like everyone else unless she wants to hide it, and she rarely bothers. Her abilities go . . . further than the rest of ours."

I didn't want to ask, but chances were a drop of sweat was about to roll down my spine.

"She's the one who wanted you to find me, right?"

Somehow his grunt sounded suspicious, but I wasn't about to poke at it too much. I already had too much to think about. Turning my attention toward the ballroom, I spotted a waiter making his way over, holding a tray of something. "Say, Alex, she knew my grandpa."

I peeked at him. He raised an eyebrow, not looking surprised even a tiny bit.

"She said she met him in Costa Rica."

"She lived in a lot of places before coming here seventy years ago."

"I wanted to talk to her more about it, but you know, she's kind of scary. I wonder if she was friends with my great-grandmother."

He turned to me slowly, measuring his words, thinking a thousand words a minute from the look in his eye.

I got this feeling again, just a tickle in my stomach. "Just out of curiosity, how powerful is she? Like really?" I asked.

"She's the reason why the Trinity was formed, Gracie," he answered. "We think she might have had a vision of what would happen if some of us didn't come out in the open, and that's why she pushed it."

Oh boy.

"I only know a fraction of what she's capable of. My mother

told us to never ask for more information unless she offered it first. There's a reason she picks and chooses who she meets."

I squinted at him. "You're scaring me."

He tilted his head to the side, something about him suddenly feeling heavy and extra thoughtful. "I won't let anyone hurt you."

Yeah, that drop of sweat went straight down my spine. "I haven't done anything to anyone. I don't want to die," I whispered.

That got me an instant eye roll. "Why would my grandmother want to kill you? She's why we met. I told you that."

"You literally just said you'd protect me . . ."

"I was trying to make you feel better," he said in exasperation. "Anyway, I don't think the three of us could stop her if we tried, but I still wouldn't let anyone hurt you." He picked up my hand and put it back on the crease of his elbow. "I promised."

I was going to shit myself.

The *Trinity* wouldn't be enough to stop her?

At the same time, I thought that was nearly the neatest, most amazing thing I'd ever heard. What was she capable of? How refined was her gift of knowing the future? Why didn't Alex have it? Hadn't my own supposed great-grandmother been able to do the same?

"She's interested in you but not in a way you need to worry."

Yeah, that wasn't helping. I squeezed his inner arm. "I kind of want to ask her what else she knows about my family."

"You want to talk to her more?"

"Yeah, unless you think she might be able to suck my soul out."

His tiny smile got under my skin, especially when he was in that freaking tuxedo. It was too much, like looking at an eclipse. My retinas might burn off if I focused too long.

Fortunately, the waiter I'd been eyeing earlier happened to walk by right then, and I got his attention, snagging what looked like two crackers with stuff on them off the serving tray in his hand. "Thank you," I told him before turning toward Alex. "What is this?"

He took one. "Caviar."

I made a face and handed the other to him.

He took it and ate that one too. "I doubt anyone is passing around Cheetos tonight," he said once he'd swallowed.

"You say that like you wouldn't eat them if they had them," I muttered. "I saw you had that microwave macaroni and cheese in your pantry, Chef Boyardee."

That top lip disappeared into his mouth, but I saw the corners move.

"I'm still not sure I can trust your smiles, but I like your smirks," I told him honestly.

His speed at scowling had to break some kind of record.

I laughed. "So who is Asami's dad?"

"Achilles."

I screwed up my face. She was so . . . sweet and cute, and he reminded me of sourdough bread.

The way he snickered told me he wasn't surprised I couldn't see it. Maybe she took after her mom.

"Did your parents like Greek legends?" I asked him.

He huffed. "I'm surprised it took you so long to figure it out. They named us all after legends and people they admired."

"Are you Greek on your dad's side, by any chance?" I dropped my voice. "Is he normal? I mean human."

"No, he's Japanese; his line is one of the stronger ones, so he's more Atraxian than human." He rolled his eyes. "They met in Greece. That was where our line settled when they arrived here." Those medium-blue eyes moved toward me. "You'll meet my dad soon. His sister had a stroke a few days ago, otherwise he would be here."

I nodded, trying to picture how attractive he had to be.

"Twenty minutes and then we can leave."

"Wink at me when you want me to faint," I whispered, following after him as we moved through the loose crowd of people. There was no way all of them knew what they were. His mom had been wearing contacts. Were they just hiding in plain sight? I wondered.

There was a quartet playing in a corner, but no one was dancing. They were all just standing around, talking. I met a few people's gazes, but mostly everyone stared at Alex from a distance.

"Why doesn't anyone come say hi to you?" I asked.

"Because they know I don't want to deal with their bullshit."

I snorted, earning me a side-glance.

"Most of my brothers and sisters are good at dealing with these people, but I don't have any patience for it. For them. They don't ask questions because they care, they ask things for information. They're bored and have nothing better to do."

The nausea got a little worse, and I'd swear another drop of sweat rolled down my spine. "Are they family or family friends?" I made myself ask so that I wouldn't focus on it.

"Both. Some business associates that my mom has known for a long time." He glanced at me. "What's wrong?"

"Nothing."

He gave me a fucking look.

I don't even know why I bothered. "My head hurts a little, and I think I might need to find a seat sooner than later, but I'm okay."

He didn't need to say he thought I was full of shit because his face said it all.

"Being here just feels like a bit . . . much. I'm not used to being around people. Much less, rich people. It's just like the historical dramas I like to watch, except there aren't wallflowers and people aren't waltzing. There's *caviar*. I think I'm fancy when I put my Pizza Bites into the oven instead of the microwave. I saw the price tag on the dress and the shoes, by the way. This whole thing feels like a dream, but that might be me feeling off because of your grandma. She made my heart start beating really fast. But I'm fine. No one here knows me or cares to, other than your grandma and Asami." I pressed my lips together. "And your brother Leon."

Someone didn't like that joke.

All right, maybe I shouldn't mess with him. "So, I keep trying to figure it out . . . how does no one know who you all are? It's a well-kept secret, but it isn't like any of you are hiding. At least you aren't since you're here, and neither are your siblings or your mom. How the hell is that possible?"

"We take an oath to never spread the secret. We all understand the responsibility of our heritage. We know why others can't know—it would destroy all of our lives. It's one of the first things we're taught growing up, that you can never tell anyone.

"Our families are small, but second and third cousins would be kidnapped and experimented on. They'd be tortured. Their very normal kids would be hunted down. Extended family members don't tell their spouses or their kids. The secret dies with them. It's what happened with your family too, I'm guessing." Those impressive shoulders rose beneath his beautiful jacket.

"I get that it's dangerous, but I don't know how that's managed to be enough to keep people from talking. Not for so long. I mean, you said that old great-great-great-grammy was one of the first to get here. That's a long time."

"It was easier to keep things a secret before technology, but it is an oath." He was watching me closely. "In each generation, there are family members who take the responsibility of making sure the secret is kept. In ours, it helps that they all get quarterly payments from the family's businesses."

A total dummy I was not.

I got what he was implying. I got it well. So I mouthed, *Are you the hitman in the family?*

Alex smiled and slowly shook his head.

Who was then? Maybe asking that in a room full of people with his same level of exceptional hearing was a bad idea. I'd ask him later. I'd bet it was Athena, or maybe Odysseus. He'd fool people with his looks and then bam! I could totally see that.

I'd worry about it later though.

A quick peek around the room confirmed that yeah, I should leave that for when we were back home. I swallowed hard. "Does the government know?" I whispered.

"The important people do."

Hmm. My brain went back to what the hell he'd just said. "You're sure you're not going to kill me for knowing all these secrets?" I pressed my hand against the multi-tool by my hip. "I haven't taken an oath."

Cool fingers pulled my hand off. "Nobody's going to do anything to you."

Oh, I felt light-headed now. My knee started shaking too. Glancing toward the side, I spotted the table with a bartender with a lot of delicate glasses sitting on it, thirst punching me straight in the throat.

"I think I need a drink." I'd never said that before, but the moment felt right. "I've never had champagne. Do you want some?"

Alex shook his head, and I gave him a weak smile at the knowledge bomb he'd just dropped on my ass. Oh boy, oh boy, oh boy. I rubbed my hands together and made my way toward the table with the white tablecloth, my head spinning with thoughts and questions.

I was sweating. Great. I was really starting to feel funny too.

I smiled at the bartender as he handed me a glass, or was it a flute? "Thank you."

Not exactly sure what I was expecting, I took a sip. I didn't drink much other than an occasional beer, but . . . not bad.

It wasn't a Dr Pepper, that was for sure.

I took another sip and figured I had to finish this shit to not be rude. The last thing I wanted was for Alex's mom to see me making faces or handing back expensive champagne. Then I'd really get my throat slit.

This was a family of gods and demigods. I could barely wrap my head around it. It was pretty much insane really.

Alex was *The Defender.*

His grandmother would have been some evil villain deity that it took heroes twenty-five comics to try and vanquish, and then, they would have only found a way to contain her for 100 years or something like that.

And here I was. The country bumpkin with a stomachache that made me slightly interesting to them.

That was bullshit. Maybe I was a country bumpkin, but so what? I wasn't going to feel bad about it.

Fuck these snobby fuckers if they thought otherwise. That made me feel better. I smiled at the bartender, and he gave me one right back.

I took my time making my way to Alex, who was in the same spot I'd left him, but wasn't alone anymore. Beside him was the Odi brother.

I walked even slower, slowly sipping and looking around as I skirted the room the long route back. I took another sip, making eye contact with Achilles as I went by him as he talked to a petite older woman in . . .

He was speaking Japanese, and the woman was replying to him in it. Her gaze met mine, and I nodded just a little at her, earning myself a nod in return. I happened to make eye contact with Achilles again and did the same, but just barely bending my head at him, and got one right back too.

I didn't think I liked him much yet, but I could appreciate him being what he seemed like.

I kept walking, going by another waiter, and took three of what I confirmed were beef kebabs, ate two, and saved the third for Alex. He was still talking to his brother, and I was running out of reasons to avoid getting over there. If his grandma hadn't made me feel so funky, I would have gone back over there and talked to her for longer.

He had no idea how lucky he was to have so much family. Maybe they weren't all best friends, but they were still there for one another. They still worried about each other in their own ways, and the good relationships he had seemed to actually be special.

I took another tiny sip and wondered why the hell the room felt extra hot suddenly.

Was I running a fever again? I'd been doing better. Agatha had said she thought I was on the right path for recuperating. It had seemed that way to me too, except for being exhausted over the smallest things.

A different kind of shiver than the one that Alex's grandma had caused ran down my spine, and I cleared my throat, taking another drink of the champagne before looking at it. I held it up to my nose and took a sniff. It didn't smell weird, but it wasn't like my olfactory senses were all that great. Not like theirs. But someone here would have noticed if there was something off with the champagne. There was no way they wouldn't have.

I walked a little faster, licking my lips and not exactly liking the taste.

Why was it *so* hot?

My head was really starting to feel weird. Was I dizzy? I reached down and pulled the dress away from my chest a little, blowing down into my boobs as I approached Alex and his brother.

He had no idea how good he had it having people in his life, I thought, as a sense of longing filled my chest.

The lucky son of a bitch was already looking at me and frowning. I wrinkled my nose as I stopped right next to him. I held out the boujee version of beef-on-a-stick and gave him a weak smile, my tongue a little numb.

He took it from me and held it there, in the air. Alex leaned forward and sniffed.

"I have deodorant." I licked my lips again and blinked slowly. "Is it really hot in here or is it just me?"

He sniffed again. Those strange blue eyes were aimed at my face when he suddenly plucked the champagne from my hand and, with the kebab, shoved both at the frowning brother beside him.

I angled my face down to blow into my boobs again before saying, "Alex, I don't feel so good."

My knees went soft.

I full-on grabbed his forearm and flicked my gaze up to him. I opened my mouth . . .

And that was the last thing I remembered.

Not again.

Peering up at a ceiling that I didn't recognize, I groaned.

What had happened? Had I fucking *fainted*? Again?

I opened my eyes even wider and started patting around the area beside me, feeling . . . a bed? Sheets?

WHERE THE HELL WAS I?

"About time," a crabby voice muttered.

Oh. Angling my head, I found Alex right there, sprawled out on the bed next to me, on his side with his head propped up by a hand on his cheek. His face was smooth and relaxed, but his eyes . . .

"What are you pissed off about?" I asked, hearing the roughness in my voice and swallowing hard.

Moving my gaze around, I realized I was on a bed in a room I didn't recognize, but it wasn't *just* a room. There was crown molding. The wallpaper looked like it was made of silk. Even the furniture seemed like it was made of some ancient wood.

Flicking my eyes back to Alex, I barely heard myself ask, "Am I dead?"

If I thought he'd looked crabby before, he definitely did then.

Dragging my hand across the surface of what felt like an embroidered comforter, I rolled onto my side and pressed my fingers against a spot on his chest between his pectorals. His jacket was off, and that white, button-down shirt that was more formal than a normal one was stretched across his chest. It had to have been tailor-made for him because not a single button was on the verge of popping off over all those spectacular muscles.

I blinked slowly. "Is this hell? Are we stuck together forever?" I whispered.

His scowl was monumental. "You'd be lucky to be stuck with me for eternity."

I blinked again.

"You're not dead. Would you stop with that shit already?" he grumbled.

"I'm not?" I asked, moving my fingers to the side a little and finding . . . oh yeah. It was there, that ultra-slow thump pumping beneath the shell of his bones. "Oh."

"Yeah. You see," he confirmed, raising an eyebrow before flicking his eyes to the hand I still had pressed against his fancy shirt.

"What happened? Where are we?" I folded my arm beneath my head. "Did someone poison me?"

"What happened is that you came up to me, said you weren't feeling good, and passed out. We're still here. Agatha checked you out, your blood pressure was low. Maybe being around my grandmother had something to do with it." His nose scrunched up. "No one tried to poison you."

Oh boy. "I passed out?" That was fucking embarrassing.

He nodded. "How do you feel?"

"My head is funny, and I might die of shame, but my vision isn't blurry anymore."

He didn't like that shit. His eyes narrowed. "I should have known. I didn't think it was that bad."

I hadn't thought I was that bad either. I'd been through worse with him, way worse.

His voice was gruff. "You'll tell me if you start to feel bad again?"

"Yes." Was he worried? Or was he embarrassed that I'd done that in front of his family?

"Promise," he grumbled.

"I promise."

His eyelids dropped over his eyes, and I knew he didn't totally believe me.

"Promise," I insisted, earning me another long look from a face that made the guy who played Electro-Man in the movies look like a knockoff superhero. "What?"

His lips pressed together. "I thought you were dying."

I knew it!

"You went limp, and you smelled wrong. I don't like the way that made me feel." His gaze moved to meet mine, and he pointed his index finger at my nose. "I mean it. No more fainting."

It was so hard not to laugh. He genuinely sounded so put-out.

He'd been worried about me.

Friends worried about each other. Friends cared. They wanted the best for you.

And here we were.

"Control my bodily functions after spending time with your

grandma and learning a bunch of crazy top-secret knowledge, got it," I whispered sarcastically, watching his face, trying not to take it too much to heart.

But failing.

Because . . . I was sure he cared. About *me*. Alex cared, and I couldn't show it on my face or I'd ruin it.

But it was like learning the earth really was flat.

"Exactly," he agreed in that low, grumbly voice.

I had to keep my face straight. I couldn't let my heartbeat get all funny or let my eyes water as I looked at the flawless features right in front of me, all concerned and irritated at the same time. I couldn't react to the tip of the finger that was now barely brushing the tip of my nose. Definitely couldn't do that.

His expression was sober. "No more fainting."

I pressed my lips together. "No more fainting . . . if I can help it."

"Promise me."

I had to cling to my sarcasm so that my body wouldn't betray me. I couldn't fucking smile. "You're really annoying when you're bossy, but yes, I promise." Okay, I smiled just a little, but just a little.

He narrowed his eyes, fully aware of my bullshit.

I guess we both knew each other too well at this point.

The door creaked open.

I held my breath as I took in the figure there.

"Grandmother," Alex greeted the woman standing at the doorframe, her fingers wrapped around a cane that looked . . .

Was that a huge emerald on the top of it?

The amount of power she managed to pack in her body, it electrified my cells. It was a rough buzz beneath my skin. For some reason though, this time it made me a little less nauseous and more . . . awake?

"Is there something we can do for you, Grandmother?" Alex asked, still not moving from where he was.

She raised her chin. "You can leave the room. I want to speak with your Gracie."

I had a feeling about that "your Gracie" thing.

"Alone, Alexander. You can wait outside," the older woman said. She obviously knew a door and some drywall wasn't going to block out our voices, but all right.

I felt his gaze shift back toward me, and I met it, giving him a nod that was 98 percent reluctant.

Did I want to be alone with her? Hell no. But I wasn't going to be the one to tell her no either.

Plus, maybe she wanted to tell me about my grandpa, not that she really knew him, but it seemed like she might have known his parents. Who were also family. I knew his mom had passed away right after I'd been born.

"I don't think that's a good idea. You made her faint earlier," he said in that same funny voice he'd pulled out of nowhere before.

Was he telling her *no*?

The woman tipped her chin up even higher. "There's hope for you yet, child. Fine, yes. She'll be safe in my presence," she almost seemed to concede.

But I was still too stuck on what the hell else had happened.

He was trying to care for me.

My heart . . . my little fucking heart gave a thump that both of them had to hear.

Alex set his hand on mine. I nodded before he rolled off the bed, giving me a long, long look as he walked out and closed the door behind him.

She held the cane with the maybe apple-sized emerald loosely and landed her bright purple gaze on me before saying abruptly, "This family grew too large in the last generation."

"Ma'am?"

She set her free hand on top of the other holding the cane.

"I had one brother, and he lacked any motivation to marry. We kept our families small to protect our identities. It might be my fault for allowing my daughter to have so many children, but I don't appreciate the concept of blaming myself."

I barely held in the cough that rose in my throat. Whatever she was, she was a predator. You didn't tell a predator you were injured or sick, especially when I had no idea where the hell she was going with this.

"These children rarely trust, and I blame technology and the times that we live in." She aimed that intense gaze at me that made it seem like stars had been born in her pupils in the span of a second.

My mouth went dry.

She was ancient and eternal. At least some part of her was. Maybe every part of her.

I could totally see why Agatha would have said she saw her life and death in the woman's eyes.

My hands were starting to sweat.

"Humans are more complicated than they look. People aren't just good or just bad. Nothing is as black and white as it seems. The boy, Alexander, is a perfect example. His heart isn't as pure as his sister's or his brother's, but it's a strong, ferocious heart that wants to protect those it sees as weaker. He reminds me of my father in that way."

I still had no clue where she was going with this, and I didn't have the balls to ask. She could rant all night about mathematical theories, and I would force myself to listen and pretend like I knew exactly what she was talking about.

"Your brain isn't weak, but your body is compared to ours." Those eyes that suddenly seemed even more clear than Alex's zeroed in on me. "I've seen what you are, and I've seen who you will become. You wondered if it was fate that your life has brought you into ours, and it isn't. I had a dream of you the night you were born, and I've followed you loosely over the years, child."

My leg started shaking.

"I've had visions of my children and their children's mates."

Did she say the word "mates"?

I had thought she'd wanted to meet me because of my great-grandmother.

Her fingers curled over the giant rock on her cane, and I'd swear her eyes glowed pure fucking white for a moment. "This is my one offer," she went on. "You are under my protection, blood of Ximena and granddaughter of Felipe. My mother once owed your great-grandmother a debt, and it's my responsibility to repay it. If you need me, say my name and I will be there," she finished, like I knew what in the hell was happening.

I could feel my eyes getting bigger by the second. By the syllable. I was pretty sure I couldn't breathe.

Because the old woman had started to stare me right in the eye, and I saw . . .

I saw . . .

I saw something in those glowing white-purple eyes that was timeless. Power like I'd never experienced before and would never experience again, that had nothing to do with super-human strength or speed or telekinesis covered my soul. For one brief moment, my body felt like it was floating in space.

And I saw it.

I saw it in her eyes.

The future.

A brief glimpse of it.

There and gone in the longest second of my life.

Taking my breath away and then sucker punching me back within its span.

And in the greatest feat of strength I was capable of, I didn't allow myself to look away. If this was anyone else, I would ask if she was sure, but I knew this wasn't the moment or much less the person. My nose started watering. I wouldn't have been surprised if it'd started bleeding.

"Do not forget my offer," she said, the glow dwindling. "You are important to our future, and an Atraxian always repays a debt." She stared, hard. "As you already know."

My voice shook as my brain managed to think just enough ahead. My voice wobbled and cracked. "What's your name?"

Her smile was glorious and disturbing at the same time, and I understood what Alex had mentioned and what she had implied.

She was unstoppable if she chose to be. The façade she seemed to show to the world was a fucking ruse to make her slightly less intimidating. Her skin might not be butter smooth anymore, but this woman could destroy the planet if she chose to.

Where The Primordial was good and radiant, this woman was life and death equally. The sun and the moon. The beginning and the end.

Whatever The Trinity were, she was so much more.

There was a reason this woman was the last full-blooded Atraxian, and I couldn't begin to fathom . . . to picture there being more people like her. More *beings* like her. Where she came from, what she was . . . good god.

I didn't want to think maybe it was a good thing she was the only one left, but . . .

The name she told me was lyrical and beautiful, and I knew I could never say it out loud unless it was an absolute emergency. The end of the fucking world. Or at least the end of my world.

Maybe it was fear that made me delusional or some kind of high from the power she'd just imbued me with that was completely different than what I'd picked up on earlier. Or maybe I was just dumb as hell. But I asked the last thing I had any business asking.

The absolute last.

"May I ask why you hurt Alex?" Even I could barely hear my voice. "Why did you take his power away?" I wasn't positive how she'd done it, but I knew, I knew in my bones that she was capable of it. "Why did you do it then?"

It was like she was expecting the question because it didn't faze her even a little bit. If anything, she looked nearly pleased. "It had to be done."

I was smart enough not to make a crazy fucking face, because why the hell had it *needed* to be done? How was hurting her grandson necessary? *How the hell had she done it?*

"He should have met you the day of the incident with the fire. I'd had a vision of you meeting at a post office in Albuquerque, and I had finally convinced him to look for you. That was why he was in the area in the first place. I didn't anticipate how hard he would take the situation, the blame. I had to get his life back on track since he wouldn't do it himself after that. If I had waited any longer, there was a chance he was going to make a decision he would regret. Alexander wouldn't have been the same person afterward. He needed to be reminded about why we do what we do. It took me much longer to find you than I had expected. I knew you were somewhere in New Mexico, but I only had a vague idea of the area. You were very smart to live so secluded," she explained in a tone that didn't leave room for questions or arguing. "I left him in good hands."

And with that, her fingers closed around the cane she was clearly using as a prop, and she headed to the door, opening it, then continuing to move on out.

And then Alex was there. A hand on each side of the doorframe. His expression wild.

And I ignored the four faces that lingered behind him. Odi, Athena, Agatha, and their scary mom.

I lifted my exhausted fingers at him. "So that was intense."

Alex looked pale.

Me too, buddy. "I think my brain just exploded," I told him weakly. "Can you tell if it's hemorrhaging?"

The faces behind him went straight stricken, and for some reason, that made me feel better.

There was a reason for me to feel the way I did. I hadn't imagined it.

"Are you okay?" he asked in a raw, raw voice.

I nodded.

My friend licked his bottom lip and took a step forward. "It felt like a nuclear bomb in here."

I nodded, my heart pumping just a little harder than normal it felt like. I clenched my hands into fists. "Alex . . . when did you figure out it was your grandma who hurt your back? How did her breaking it take away your powers?"

He didn't seem even a little surprised. "A few days after I got there. When I was able to think about how Alana and Robert couldn't have done it . . . wouldn't have done it. When I realized most of my abilities were drained. Only one person is strong enough to do that kind of damage quickly. I was in too much pain when I got there. Then I saw your eyes, that cat clock on the wall, and I knew it had been my grandmother. I hadn't sensed her following me, and all I saw was a bright light before I think she punched me in the back. She had to have carried me all the way to your house, and banged me up along the way so you would feel sorry for me. She's smart like that." His chest rose and fell. "We don't understand how it works completely, but Agatha thinks that an injury to our spinal cord of that magnitude, doesn't allow our brains to send those important signals to the rest of our body until we're healed. It's the same idea as vertebrae damage in a human body. It takes time to heal from that kind of thing, even for us. When did you figure it out?"

That's what I'd thought. "She told you not to be mad at her.

Then you said all those things about her being the most power-ful of all of you . . ." I gulped, my skin still tingling like crazy, my heart still running a marathon.

He took another step forward, and I ignored the faces behind him. "Are you sure you're okay?"

I only had to think about it for a second. "I'll be better with a hug. With one of your hugs. They always make me feel better. Probably because of your healing mumbo jumbo." I shrugged, knowing it wasn't the healing stuff at all, but I was going to run with it anyway. "Please? I feel like I just got into a car accident and barely survived."

To give him credit, he didn't hesitate. Alex came to the side of the bed and held out his arms. And then I didn't hesitate either. The moment I got up to my knees, he wrapped his arms around me like it was second nature. Tight, tight, tight.

"You're sure you're all right?" he asked, hugging the hell out of me.

I nodded, pressing my forehead to that perfect nook between his shoulder and neck.

A big palm spanned the middle of my back, and I barely heard him say sometime later, "Gracie?"

"Hmm?"

"You were supposed to wait for me to wink."

Chapter Twenty-Seven

I was just close enough to the window for my breathing to fog up a small circle on it when Alex's familiar voice scared the crap out of me. "What are you doing?"

I'd been so jumpy since meeting his grandma, dammit. I'd been distracted and skittish and just off. And I had been trying my best to hide it from him. Which was how I managed to keep my eyes on the vision of white on the other side of the glass. "Looking at the snow," I told him, still riveted by the sight.

He'd warned me there was a big snowstorm coming, but I hadn't taken him that seriously.

I was still all off. I was better but not great. My body now felt like it had been run over by a small sedan instead of a tank, so I was taking that as a win.

I'd woken up not too long ago by myself, even though that wasn't how the night had started. It wasn't how any night the last week had started: with Alex in bed beside me. Sleeping shirtless, sometimes in sleep pants or, every once in a while, in those tight boxer briefs that left absolutely nothing to the imagination.

It was an image that haunted me a lot. A fucking ton. But I didn't beat myself up for it too much. I didn't think there was a single person who could have gone to bed with a man like him beside them and not been affected by it.

If he wanted to sleep in his underwear, who was I to complain when I kept to my tank tops most nights too?

That specific morning, I had laid in bed for half an hour trying to hype myself up into this next stage of my life, telling myself everything would work out. That everything would be fine. I listened to my grandparents' voice mails like I had every morning since I'd gotten my replacement cell phone and thanked God I still had them. Only then did I trudge downstairs for a bowl of cereal. I'd noticed that the house felt colder and that the floors too were cooler, but it hadn't been until I'd pulled out a bowl and fished my box of cereal out from a cabinet that I had finally peeked outside and seen it.

What had to be a few inches of snow had fallen overnight. Literally just a couple, but it was something. It was everything I'd ever imagined and hoped for when I finally got the chance to see snow. I couldn't believe something could be so beautiful sprinkled over tree branches and the ground.

It wasn't until he stood nearly directly behind me that I realized he had moved.

He wanted to look out the window too, I guess.

A few flurries were still coming down, and we both stood there, sucked into the sight of snow covering the plants and trees that made up his incredible forest-like backyard. He had taken me out yesterday and shown me where he wanted to build a greenhouse in the spring. He had also given me a tour of the solar panels that powered the property, and even shown me his composting situation and water recycling system.

A slight puff of warmth hit that spot between my shoulder and neck, and I clung to my composure.

For about the hundredth time, I fought not to think about what Alex's grandmother had shown me at the party. Of all the things I'd learned, that had been what hit me the hardest. Even in my dreams, I hadn't been able to ignore it.

The problem was keeping it so that he couldn't tell something was on my mind.

Despite everything that had happened between us, the level of comfort we both felt around each other now, I wasn't positive I wanted to have that conversation with him. I didn't know if I wanted him to know.

Correction: I was *sure* I didn't want to tell him. My pride might not survive it. Then I'd have to try and suffocate him to preserve what I had left, and nothing was in my favor for that going well so . . .

I either needed to ask someone else about it, or I needed to move on and pretend it hadn't happened.

Right. Super easy.

"I'm sure you've seen more than this, but I've only seen a sprinkle before," I told him quietly, like if I spoke too loud I'd break the effect it had. "I want to go out there."

I could feel his breath on my neck, all soft and slow. "Go out there then," Alex said, for some reason reminding me of how I'd fallen asleep on the couch the night before and how he'd woken me up by crouching beside me, just starting to slip his arm under my back like he'd been about to pick me up.

I'd walked up the stairs myself, but it would have been an experience.

A real nice experience.

Dammit, I needed to stop or find some other way to get past this weird shit going on in my chest now every time I thought about him. He'd been in and out of the house a lot; when he was around, he'd be in the room he'd called his office with the door closed for long periods of time. When the door was open, he was on his big, two-screen computer with a pen in his mouth, jotting down notes in a notebook. He'd come out in the evenings and make something for dinner. So far he'd made burgers and spaghetti, and one night he'd made the best carbonara I'd ever had in my life, even though I'd only eaten my own. I had only teased him a little about how he knew how to cook and had kept it a secret. And every night, we'd sat there and watched a movie together while we ate. Not awkwardly, just quietly. Then sometimes, afterward, we talked about it.

We'd watched one of the Electro-Man movies, and he hadn't had much to say about that one, but the rest we discussed, mostly talking about all the shit we didn't like about it.

I was pretty sure we both had a hell of a lot on our minds that neither one of us wanted to talk about.

Fine by me.

With so much time to kill, I had started rebuilding my website under another business name from the very comfortable location of the living room downstairs. Even though I was fairly confident the cartel hadn't found out anything about my banking information thanks to my paranoia which led me to use the browser window that didn't save any of my history, and never staying logged into anything, I had decided to play it on the safe side and buy a new URL for my business. The one and only breadcrumb I would have left them were the workbooks and notebooks I used with my students. Would they be able to figure out what I did? Where I got students from? I hadn't thought about that issue until recently. Would they eventually be able to figure me out? IP addresses could be tracked down, and I just wasn't sure if it was worth launching the site, so even though I was working on it, I was going to sit on it until I thought it through.

Having to think about the long-term effect of things seemed to be the story of my life now.

"I don't have a waterproof jacket or boots," I told him. I'd already been trying to figure out how to make it work since I'd been standing there. I'd tossed my old pair of shoes when they'd fallen apart after I had washed them, and I wasn't going to go out there with the nice heels he'd gotten me.

Alex huffed, and I glanced over my shoulder to find him leaving the kitchen, sleep pants low on his hips . . .

The son of a bitch didn't have a shirt on.

His waist was trim, shoulders broad. His rib cage tapered perfectly as a segue from one part of his body to another. His skin looked deceptively soft.

I needed to calm down and quit checking him out before he noticed and got suspicious. We both knew I found him attractive—who the hell didn't? It wasn't some shameful secret. That didn't mean I had to be so obvious about it.

Subtle could be my middle name. I had this.

I was in the middle of washing my bowl when he came back into the kitchen, a T-shirt straining across his shoulders and chest, holding . . .

"The boots are too big, but I brought you three pairs of thick socks; if you tie them tight enough, you'll manage. This jacket is more waterproof than the one you've been using; zip it up and you'll be fine," he said as he lowered a pair of brown leather boots with fleece lining on the floor beside one of the chairs of the breakfast table. Then he draped a big jacket over the back of the same chair before lifting his face and giving me a wary expression. "What?"

"Nothing," I told him defensively, trying to hide the way my little heart swelled at his kind gesture. "Thanks, Alex." I was pretty sure my voice came out normal.

Maybe not.

He frowned. "You need some boots your own size."

"I know, getting my credit card sent was a pain in the ass, but it's on its way," I confirmed. It had taken a while, but getting my banking sorted was a huge weight off my back. I'd run out of groceries already, but one morning, I'd found the refrigerator and pantry restocked. The cereal I usually ate sitting there, looking at me. I'd tried to ask him how much I owed him, but he'd changed the subject by asking me if I'd heard from the legal department yet.

I hadn't.

"I'll survive until then as long as you keep letting me borrow your things," I told him.

Alex grunted, and I finally noticed just how tired he seemed. There weren't dark circles or bags under his eyes, but it was something about his energy that was just off.

"Are you good?" I asked. "You look a little ragged. Did you wake up at the crack of dawn?"

That funny expression came over his face again. "I woke up in the middle of the night. I had someone I needed to talk to," he said, voice tight.

In the middle of the night? I didn't ask, but I nodded. "Well, thanks for letting me borrow everything. I'm gonna go out there for a little while. Maybe make some snow angels," I told him, watching his face closely.

Did he have to be so damn handsome all the damn time?

I need to stop. I was pretty sure we were friends at this point, but that was all there was between us. A give and take. Two people bound together by obligation and . . .

Maybe other things I didn't want to poke at too closely.

He was a good best friend number 15 or wherever we were at. Whatever he wanted us to be. I'd take anything.

That realization had me thinking about his grandmother's vision again.

Fuckkkk.

"I promise I'll start trying to figure out a way to be able to move on soon." I still hadn't come up with anything, and that day in Legal hadn't done much to give me any ideas better than what I'd already come up with. They were setting up another identity—whether it was legal or not, I had no idea, and I was in no position to be picky—but they'd warned me it would take some time. Then we'd gotten caught up with his mom's birthday, and I'd almost forgotten about it since I had other things to focus on.

Alex nodded at my plan, still seeming just . . . off.

Maybe I could make him some cookies and cheer him up later.

Shoving the pairs of socks he was letting me use into the boots, then picking them up along with the jacket, I made my way toward the front door and started layering up. First the three pairs of socks went on. Then I crammed my feet into boots that were still too big, so I tightened the hell out of the laces until I was sure they wouldn't come loose after the first step out there. The jacket was heavy and hit my knees, but it was warm, and there was a big pair of black gloves in the pockets that I put on too. Then I was out of there, closing one of the two doors behind me and carefully making my way down the steps until I stood at the bottom. My pants were going to be soaked.

I tipped my head back, closed my eyes so a flurry wouldn't blind me, and stuck out my tongue. It took a minute but eventually a couple flakes landed in my mouth. I smiled. It didn't taste like anything.

A few more flakes hit my cheeks and landed on my eyelashes, and I smiled even wider. I took a deep, deep breath full of cold, clean air and held it in my lungs, relieved I was finally feeling so much better. Then I did it again a few more times. I scooped some snow into my hand and pressed it to my cheek.

And just like I'd imagined myself doing my entire childhood, I waddled a little farther away from the door, and I started making snowballs.

Well, tried to. There really wasn't more than a few inches, and the snow was too fluffy, and I hadn't realized there was a right and wrong kind of snow, but I tried my best, making a few tiny ones that fell apart, and then figuring out how to make them slightly better. I managed to make two bigger balls and stacked them on top of each other, cackling to myself over how small and cute they were.

I was in the middle of attempting to make another tiny snowman when one of the front doors opened and Alex stepped out, wearing a brown jacket that didn't look thick enough, a light pair of jeans, and dark winter boots.

"What are you doing?" he called out, closing the door behind him.

"Fulfilling my childhood dreams of making a snowman."

His gaze swept toward my two figures. "You call that a snowman?"

"They're mini on purpose, okay," I muttered. "And I'd like to see you try to do better."

Was that a kind-of grin? "I can't. It's something with my skin. They melt almost instantly."

I blinked. "No shit."

He nodded.

An evil little thought climbed into my head. Another thing on my list of things I'd always wanted to do. But he was literally one of the last people in the world I could do it with.

"I don't like that look on your face," he said warily, stopping just to the side.

I shrugged. "I had an idea, but it's a stupid one."

He tipped his head to the side, interested.

I went back to trying to form another small snowball. "It's pointless."

"Tell me anyway."

"Well, I thought about throwing a few snowballs at you, but I forgot that you're super fast so none of them would actually land," I explained. "See? Dumb? And you'd probably fracture my skull if you threw one back at me."

He didn't say anything for so long that I glanced over to see why.

Were his shoulders hunched up? It seemed like they were. He had a thoughtful expression on his face as he met my eyes.

"What?" I asked him.

"I've spent my whole life moving like a human."

What was that supposed to mean?

And did he suddenly look kind of excited?

Was he . . . interested? Really?

"Did you want to . . . ?" I gestured toward the small collection of snowballs beside me, trying not to look like I was on the verge of being over the moon. I was probably failing big-time though.

That incredible gaze lingered on mine, and his hands slipped into his pockets. "I'll count to ten before I come after you."

Would it be worth it? Eating some snow if I could peg him a couple of times?

Yes, yes it fucking would. When the hell would be the next time I'd get a chance like this? I had no idea where I would be a month from now. Fuck it.

I yelled before jumping up to my too-big feet and crouching in front of my small mound of snowballs. Then I attacked. The first one I threw far to the right, the second and third landed closer.

He barely moved to the side to avoid the fourth, letting his guard down with a smirk aimed at me like he'd thought he'd gotten away with it, when I threw two back-to-back, fast as I could.

He batted the first away, and bless his soul, he purposely let the next one hit him in the forehead when I knew in my heart he could have dodged that too.

What I did know for sure was that I was way too excited and threw two more at him before he said slowly and breathily, "Time."

Yeah, I knew I was in for it.

I tried to run, I really did, but my main problem was the

shoes. My foot slipped out of one of the boots on the second step I took trying to get away, and it was over pretty much instantly. His hand caught me by the back of my pants, and he was suddenly holding me up by them, by my pants, leaving my body parallel with the snow and the ground.

Alex lowered me back down, and I was on my hands and knees, about to try and crawl away, the cold sneaking in through the thin material of my pants, when I felt the waistband get tugged again. My ass went *freezing*.

"Alex!" I screeched, shoving my hand inside them to dig out the snow he'd shoved into my underwear.

The son of a bitch was laughing. Laughing his *ass off.* There was a sock covering his hand! When the hell had he managed to put that on? Where had it even come from?

I pulled his leg out from under him and pushed his stomach as hard as I could so he landed on his ass. It wouldn't hit me until later, way, way later, that he'd *let* me do it.

He stopped laughing, but then I started cracking up, tossing a little bit of loose snow at him even as I shivered. I grinned. Alex took the sock off and shoved it in his pocket.

"Why are you smiling?" he asked, wiping the melted snowflakes off his face and hair with his bare hands.

"Because my ass might be suffering from hypothermia soon but that was fun." I blinked. "You didn't have fun? You were laughing."

I'd swear there was a twinkle in his eye as he admitted in that gruff voice, "I had fun."

See? I tossed a little more snow in his direction. "Picking me up like I'm a little kid or shoving snow between my butt cheeks?"

"Both."

Figures.

He leaned back, planting both hands behind him, propping himself up. "What else have you wanted to do in the snow?"

"I'd like to try skiing one day. I've always wanted to go sledding," I told him. "Did you grow up here?" It was hard to picture him small in the first place, but when I did, I imagined him as an emo kid in all black. Maybe one day I could get away with asking him.

He tipped that handsome head back toward the sky, and I watched as a few snowflakes landed on his cheeks. "We moved here when I was four. We lived in California until Kilis broke that kid's arm; then our parents moved us out here. I've never tried sledding. What do you need?"

He'd never . . .

I kept my lips pressed together to not make a face of disbelief that he'd never gone sledding before, or that he'd given me another sliver of knowledge about himself. "I don't know," I told him. "A trash can lid maybe? Cardboard?"

He thought about it. "I've got cardboard boxes in the garage."

I brightened as he got up, dusted off his pants, and reached for the boot that had fallen off my foot. Without missing a beat, he bent over, lifted my leg up by the heel, tugged it on, tied the shoelace, and held his hand out to me, pulling me straight up to standing.

It took everything in me to just smile at him a little—almost shyly—and he gave me a weird look before turning. I followed him around the house toward the massive garage I'd only walked by, set off to the side of the house. It took me longer to follow because it was hard to walk in his boots without them getting stuck and falling off.

"Are you all right?" he asked as he opened the side door to the building and waited.

"Yeah, I'm tired and a little icky, but so much better thanks to you and your healing vibes," I confirmed, going through the doorway, trying not to huff and puff so much. "I'm not exhausted enough to skip out on having fun."

Inside, he stopped by the right wall where there were indeed a few flattened boxes leaning against it. There were two cars covered in tan canvas material, and enough room for at least another car or two. He always left his out.

He picked a box up, set it aside, and grabbed a bigger one behind it. Alex held it, then looked at it in a different angle, then held it by me before leaning it against his hip. Then he started picking through the rest of them. He was quiet for a while, so I wasn't expecting him to casually ask, his attention still on the cardboard, "Why haven't you told me what my grandmother showed you?"

I reached over to take the box he'd set aside and held it up, fake inspecting it. It was stiff and sturdy. *Keep it cool. Keep it cool, Gracie.*

Could I get away with ignoring him? Feign being hard of hearing? Maybe I could . . .

I started wandering off to the side, pretending to see something in the corner of the garage.

"Gracie," he called out in his too-calm voice. "What did she show you?"

Shit.

I didn't want to tell him, that was a fact. Part of me wanted to talk to Agatha about it first, even though we'd only met once. I wanted . . . I wanted to make sure I hadn't imagined what I'd seen.

Even though I was certain I hadn't. It had been too vivid. Too real.

It was fucking troubling.

And it explained way too much.

"She's shown me two things," Alex added almost softly, at least for him.

"What?" I broke my silence to ask, even though I knew damn well his comment was bait.

He didn't hesitate. "Your house," he actually replied.

I moved to the side and looked at him. "Really?"

He was still facing away, picking up another box and inspecting it. "The cat clock on your wall. The print of your couch. I told you about the cat."

He had? When? My throat went dry. The skin on the back of my neck prickled. It took me two tries to talk again. "You were so mad . . ."

"I told you I was in a lot of pain, but some part of me must have remembered." He didn't look at me as he picked up another big piece of cardboard. "It's why I didn't ask you to contact anyone for me. I knew I was supposed to be there."

The hair on the back of my neck rose. "When? Did she show you that, I mean?"

"A few years ago. That's when I learned about you," he answered easily.

Goose bumps rose on my arms too, but I wanted to tell myself it was because my pants were soaked through and I was cold. But that wasn't the case. I swallowed hard. "If your grandma is so powerful, why didn't you call for her?" I asked him. "When we were in the cell?"

It took him a second to answer. "I almost did. Your heart rate got real slow there, and I thought about it once or twice, but the situation never got bad enough. You don't mow down a whole field when you can pluck a single weed. And I'm positive she's the reason there was an incident with the cartel that made them stay away."

I thought about that, coming up with a dozen more questions while I did. I settled for the most annoying one. "Why, Alex? Why did your grandma want you to find me so bad that she would have hurt you like that? You said that stuff about being Atraxian too, but some of you have made these comments . . . and I feel like there's more you aren't telling me."

All he said was "Yeah."

"Yeah what?"

"There's more."

This motherfucker. "Are you going to tell me what that other stuff is, or are you just going to tease me with it?" He was just going to tease me with it; I didn't know why I was asking.

His answering huff said it all. I had a feeling . . .

"What else did she show you?" I croaked. Did I have to sound like I was dreading his answer?

He smirked.

Son of a bitch.

I didn't want to tell him.

I really didn't want to tell him.

He would laugh. Or roll his eyes. Or shut down again. Maybe worse.

I wasn't even sure how *I* felt about it.

My neck started to itch.

"You're going to tell me eventually," he egged me on with that smart-ass expression, dragging me away from the knowledge he'd just dropped on me.

"Why would I do that?"

"Because we don't have secrets."

"Since when? I'm pretty sure we've got like twenty between us, and nineteen of those are yours."

Those big shoulders rose and fell in a too casual shrug. "It's only about sixteen now."

I raised my eyebrows.

"Best friends number 10 don't lie to each other."

Why had he moved me up on the list?

"What did she show you?" he asked again, all calm and cool. Daring me. He was fucking daring me.

My heart started to beat faster, and I wasn't sure whether this was a fun game or torture.

"What did she show you?"

Someone was fucking relentless.

And I didn't like him pushing me like this.

Did he think I wouldn't tell him? Or was it reverse psychology? I wouldn't hold it against him.

I mean, he'd seen my house. His grandmother had dropped him with me on purpose. And if he really was going to get bent out of shape, it was going to happen now or six months from now. Six years from now. I had my phone, and all I needed was my new credit card. As far as bad positions went, this wasn't the worst one to be in. I'd already been through that.

And I was still here.

I'd lived just about my whole life pretending to be meek and keeping to myself and always tiptoeing, and where the hell had that landed me?

"You," I made myself admit in a rush before I could talk myself out of it.

He slowly turned to look at me over his broad shoulder. His face was even, smooth. His body way too relaxed.

I lifted my chin. "You were holding a baby." I shrugged a shoulder. "You asked. What else did you see?"

"You," he answered.

Alex stared at me, and I stared right back.

My heart started beating even faster, and I knew he could hear it. There was no hiding it. My face went warm. "Me how?" I asked as loudly as I could. "You said no secrets," I reminded him.

His eyebrows went a little up, pink suddenly tinting his ears.

For a moment, I thought he wasn't going to say shit.

But this was a man who went into burning buildings without blinking an eye, and now I knew he would have done it even if he wasn't invincible.

"You were on your hands and knees," he said.

What the hell did that mean? *What was I doing on my hands and knees?*

My face went even warmer. Hotter. So hot.

"Come on," he said suddenly, holding up an even bigger cardboard box.

What the hell had I been doing in his vision?

I couldn't ask. I couldn't fucking ask. And why wasn't he questioning the baby in my vision?

I kept my eyes down, ignoring the beating pattern my heart had decided to skip along to with this between us, and followed him out of the garage and down the driveway we'd waddled through, heading toward the downward slope part of it on the other side of the house. I kept my eyes on his wide frame. I thought about the vision I'd seen.

Him holding a dark-haired baby with my eyes, smiling. Alex's hair was longer than it was now. There had been something different about his face though. He'd looked a little older? Or maybe just . . . less grumpy? More . . . happy?

We made it to the top of the gentle hill, and I stood beside him.

"You go first," I said, trying to act cool when I felt everything but.

Those purple eyes flicked toward me. "Me?"

"Or we can go together?" I suggested. "You can be my Atraxian shield. Make sure I don't break an arm."

He bumped his arm against mine. "Let's go down together. No arm breaking."

I smirked and laid down the cardboard I'd been carrying, pushing it into the snow. I took a seat as forward as I could get without falling off, legs straight out in front of me.

To my surprise, he climbed on behind me, his long legs bracketing mine between his. I had expected him to make me be the big spoon. He pressed his chest to my back, settling his chin over the top of my head. "Ready?" he asked, his voice soft and almost mellow. Different.

I nodded tightly, and he slipped his arm around my waist. I grabbed the sides of the cardboard, feeling his free hand grab on to one of the sides too. And with our feet dangling over the front, we pushed ourselves forward and took off.

I laughed. He chuckled. Wind whipped us in the face. And when our makeshift sled stopped halfway down the bumpy hill that didn't have enough snow, Alex held out his hand and picked up the broken-down cardboard box with the other. We climbed back up the hill and went down again, me between his legs, his arm around my waist, and we got even farther.

We did it again and again, and I laughed and heard his laugh low beside my ear. We molded the snow with our forearms and made a longer racetrack, then gave each other a push for momentum, trading back and forth going down before going down it together again. We got soaked, and I got light-headed from hiking back up the hill so many times.

I grabbed Alex's forearm as we hiked up, and when my hand slid down it, I clung to his wrist, and he didn't shake me off. Then we did it again and again.

And I thought about that baby with my eyes.

I thought about what that meant a lot.

Chapter Twenty-Eight

I came out of the shower and strained, thinking I was imagining hearing voices.

Just a little while ago, Alex and I had been downstairs eating chicken tacos in front of the television with the second Electro-Man movie, called *Electro-Man United*, playing on the TV. It was the movie where they'd introduced his secret brother, a smart-ass that simply called himself Steelflyer. It was my favorite movie. The two actors had such incredible chemistry. I'd tried my best to watch it at least. I'd been lost in my thoughts for half of it, and I was pretty sure he had too from the faces he'd made when I'd peeked and caught his attention already on me.

Mine happened to revolve around him.

I knew it was a waste of time to like him. My heart was being dumb by speeding up every time we were together. My brain had better things to do than try and put this puzzle that was our pasts and why we'd met together.

But it happened anyway.

The second the credits started rolling, I'd trudged upstairs to shower, hearing the quiet rumble of Alex's voice as he spoke to someone on the phone. Who he was talking to or what he was talking about was beyond me. He'd been awfully quiet since our snow day, and it hadn't escaped me that he still hadn't gone back to "work." I guessed he was still trying to make a decision about his future, but I had a feeling it had to do more with him not being totally healed yet than him not wanting to continue being a member of the Trinity.

So I was surprised to come out and hear voices other than just his.

I yawned and peeked at the alarm clock on the nightstand. 9:28. I was still taking my time showering, making sure not to get water on my face unless I splashed it myself. I had been spoiling myself by taking a bath every other day, alternating it with a shower. Getting my face wet had gotten slightly easier, but I meant *slightly*. I still breathed heavily the whole time, and my heart beat crazy enough that Alex had come and knocked on the bathroom door a few times to ask a random question while I was in there. I knew what he was doing though. He was checking up on me. Distracting me.

Tugging my sleep pants up a little higher on my hips, I snagged the oversized sweatshirt I'd taken out of Alex's library that he'd left hung over a chair. I slipped it on, grabbed my multi-tool from the top of the dresser, and moved toward the doorway in my socks, still hearing the slight murmur of talking coming from down the hall.

I hesitated. Should I stay in my room? It sounded like they were in the library.

"Gracie," Alex's voice called out.

Busted. Always busted. I forgot I couldn't get away with anything here. I'd started muffling my farts and turning on the exhaust fan so that he wouldn't hear me being human so easily.

I made my way toward the library and stopped before I went in. Alex was there, but so were two other heads. Both of them stood and turned toward me.

One of them was long and lean, his blond hair cut short. He was handsome, but it was his bright blue eyes that were the most amazing. They were just like Selene's. And the other person . . .

502   Mariana Zapata

The other . . .

The woman was sitting in the spot perpendicular to the chair Alex was on. Her hand was on the armrest, her body angled toward him. I felt like the biggest country bumpkin in the land, standing there in his sweatshirt, oversized flannel pajama pants, and socks, my damp hair probably making me look like a drowned rat.

And she was there, in a turtleneck, her hair pulled back into a bun, being just as ethereal as Alex.

"Hi," I said, suddenly more awake than I'd ever been. "I'm Gracie." My voice broke, and I tried to glue it back instantly. They already knew that. Idiot. I cleared my throat and focused on the man first. "Hi, Robert." That's what everyone called him after all.

The blond man smiled so bright and sweet, it instantly made me happy. "Nice to finally meet you, Gracie."

The being known as The Centurion, with his gold and red suit, held his hand out, and I took it. I shook it. Low, cool power flowed from his pores as he smiled a little more before letting go.

Then I turned.

The woman held out her hand just as I pulled away from her brother. Another bright, shining smile came over her mouth, and I almost fainted from intense fangirling. "I've heard so much about you. I'm Alana."

She knew my name.

The words got stuck in my fucking throat. It took me two tries to say, "Hello, madam . . . Miss Primordial . . . Alana."

What was wrong with me?

She took my hand, her already big smile getting even bigger, and I'd swear a breeze swept into the room because it sure seemed like her hair flowed backward for a second.

But it was the big head that popped around the side of her body, giving me the flattest, most incredulous look he'd ever given me, and that was saying something because he'd given me some crazy looks in the time we'd known each other, that snapped me out of it. Alex's mouth was cracked, but somehow the corners were tilted just a little. "What did you call her?"

The motherfucker was wheezing.

I could hear the laughter in his tone. In his fucking eyes.

I met his gaze and lifted my shoulders. "I don't know, I just . . . panicked," I told him.

His palm covered his mouth, and I couldn't hear it, but I knew he was laughing.

Somehow, I forced myself to look at The Primordial, at *Alana*, while ignoring the idiot cracking up more by the second, and said, "I'm so sorry, ma'am."

Oh boy.

Alex's fucking body was shaking.

I hated him sometimes. I swear.

But the powerful, beautiful woman shook her head, her expression still so friendly and kind. "It's all right, but you can call me Alana."

Shit. "I'll try," I whispered. She'd given me permission to call her by her *first name*. That made me scream inside a little.

Her smile was angelic, I swear.

I gulped again and focused on the man still laughing. Son of a bitch. "I heard voices, and I just wanted to make sure everything was okay."

Alex's head rose. He was grinning. "Everything is fine." His eyes were twinkling.

I was glad someone could enjoy my humiliation. Was he drunk? Was that something he was capable of?

Alex leaned back, away from his sister, and spread his legs wider. "They came by to talk to me about the cartel," he said.

I smiled mildly like I wasn't in shock and started to take a step back before he held his hand out.

I guess it was second nature that I took it and took a step closer to him.

His face . . . his face went from mocking to just . . . soft. Open. Different from just about every other look he'd ever given me.

And I knew I'd screwed up. "You wanted the multi-tool, didn't you?"

He lied to me. He flat-out fucking lied to me, and I knew when he said, just so, so seriously, "No."

I tried to take a step back, but he didn't let me.

Instead, Alex pulled me toward him, just fast enough that I couldn't stop myself, turning me at the same rate until he tugged me down onto his lap. Sitting me up high on one of his thighs like I belonged there or something. One of those muscular arms wrapped around my lower back, and I knew I wasn't imagining that he was holding me down on him, like he knew I was going to try and get away from sheer humiliation.

My spine went straighter than it had ever gone before.

We sat right next to each other all the time. Laid beside each other so many times by that point it meant nothing. We'd slept in the same bed a lot.

What was sitting on a lap? He'd said touch was important. I'd seen him be physical with others. With me too, I could admit.

Even though I'd been wrong about what he'd wanted.

But I still whispered, "Are you drunk?"

What had to be his palm settled low on my back near my hip. His free hand he set on his other leg. "Alcohol doesn't do anything to me."

"Then why . . . ?"

"We can argue about it later."

"We can argue about it now."

The son of a bitch grinned.

I swallowed hard as I caught the faint smiles of the two members of the Trinity looking at me sitting there. On his thigh. In their street clothes. *Robert* had a T-shirt that said WELCOME TO MOAB on it. *Alana* had *bobby pins* in her hair.

And I was on Alex's fucking lap.

All righty then. I could focus. If he didn't think this was a big deal, why should I? If he got a boner, that would be another thing. I almost wanted to check. "Thank you . . . for helping," I told them, not sure what to say since I could barely think with a granite-like thigh under me.

"You saved our little brother," Robert replied. "You put your life at risk for him. We're all in your debt."

Oh.

"You can trust us. Your secret is safe," Alana said in her warm, ethereal voice that reminded me of an angel . . . that could demolish your ass. "It's family business now. We'll help any way we can. Selene is already doing what she can."

Family business.

I couldn't help but nod.

I had been on my own for so long now that it was almost overwhelming to have someone else willing to help me. Especially when that "someone" was him. *Them.*

And if the ball was rolling now on getting something else done to make my life a little safer, that was a good thing. I was supposed to move on eventually. Why not sooner than later?

And if that made me sad, it was okay too. I'd been spoiled already being here. I was grateful for it.

A big hand settled on my hip, giving it a gentle squeeze and pulling me back to the present. Peeking over my shoulder, I found those purple eyes. I could tell what he was trying to say: that it was okay. That I could trust them.

Why did that feel so monumental?

I was kind of in a daze as I kept sitting there as Alex spoke about the cartel and then repeated what the family's legal department had planned for me, which was basically sorting out whatever issues had risen from the loss of the house, my car insurance, and setting up a new identity. I was going to close my business account as soon as I got it, I decided, regardless of what happened with my translating work.

That was what I had too much hope riding on. If I could change my name, that might be enough to get under the radar for the rest of my life. It would be as good as it could be.

Then I could move on, like I'd promised him.

I was so hung up on thinking over the details of what they had planned that I was caught off guard when Alana eventually asked, "Gracie, have you considered reaching out to law enforcement?"

My whole body stiffened.

The hand on my hip moved to my back, and Alex gave it a long stroke upward, right along my spine.

"Umm," I stuttered, already feeling like a chicken.

"With the right people, they might be able to help put cartel members away," she said gently.

Oh, I knew that.

"She'd be putting her life at risk, hoping someone won't sell her out," Alex said, stiffly. "She'd have to have someone she can trust involved to make sure something wouldn't happen to her."

I reached down blindly and found his hand. I covered it with mine. "I . . . I've always thought hiding was the best option I had. My grandpa used to say that they would never quit looking for us even if they got their money back. When we were in the cell, they told me that my cousin had given them the information they needed to find me. I don't know if that's true or not, but if it is . . . if I can't trust a family member I've never met, it's hard for me to believe that there's someone who's never met me before, who doesn't have any loyalty toward me, that wouldn't sell me out for money. That was what that woman told me.

"I know I have to sound like a coward for not being willing to put myself at risk like that but . . ." I opened my mouth and closed it. "I can think about it. I don't want what's happened to me to happen to anyone else. But I'm scared to be a martyr." My voice got shaky, and I swallowed hard. "I'll think about it."

Of course she would think about others. She would never hide. She'd never run.

Me, on the other hand . . .

The hand on my back went up, all the way up between my shoulder blades, before sliding back down.

"Gracie will do it when she's ready," Alex said.

I couldn't help but peek at him over my shoulder, earning myself a serious nod from him like he really believed that one day I'd get there.

But his words must have been enough, because out of the corner of my eye, I saw both The Primordial—*Alana*—and Robert nod, something funny on their faces.

She changed the subject immediately. "Lexi, are you back to normal now?"

The leg under me tensed harder than fucking ever, and it was only because I was looking at Robert that I saw the confusion come over his features.

I guess the lack of reply was enough to make her features melt into a concerned expression. Even her voice changed. "You still can't?" she asked.

She'd asked.

She'd just asked about his flying.

"Oh, Lexi," she told him gently. "Did you ask Grandmother about it?"

The thigh under me tensed even more, but he didn't beat around the bush as he said, "I haven't tried, and I didn't ask her. I did speak to Grandfather about it the other night. Everything else is almost back to normal."

Everything else? I knew there had still been something off about him!

You could have cut through the silence with a butter knife. I hadn't even realized I still had my hand on top of his, and I gave it a pat.

"Let's try," she suggested in a voice that reminded me of my grandma from how no-nonsense it was.

I moved my hand and set it on top of Alex's knee, partially expecting him to whack it off. He didn't though. He didn't do or say anything. His leg stayed stiff.

"Might as well get it over with," she said encouragingly, like she genuinely believed anything was possible. I totally understood how she was his favorite. She really did seem like an angel.

But if she was an angel, it was because her inner brightness had to block out old Grumpy Goose over here.

I squeezed his knee as his leg got even harder, feeling like concrete under my butt.

At my side, his chest expanded in a breath he didn't need to take; then it deflated in what I knew was resignation.

And to my surprise, when he started to rise, he picked me up and slowly lowered me to my feet. A few fingers brushed against my palm in a gesture that took me about half a second to recognize.

It was my turn to be there for him, like I'd promised when we'd been on the run.

I wrapped my fingers around the three digits closest to me: his pinkie, ring, and middle fingers. I squeezed them tight too.

Was he that worried?

Alana and Robert moved toward the balcony doors, and Alex followed. When I tried to let go, he turned his palm and caught all of mine in his. My hand was a ball inside his as he tugged me along.

I kept my fucking mouth shut as we went through the doors.

I stopped so suddenly, he did too.

Alex glanced at me.

"You've said that I saved your life, but you saved mine. You did it without being able to fly. Okay?" I told him, knowing it wasn't much, but it was something. It was everything to me. "You can be my number 9 best friend regardless of what happens, all right?"

His lips pressed tight.

I smiled, or at least I tried to. Then I took a step forward, wrapped my arms around his ribs, and gave them a quick squeeze before stepping away just as quickly.

His Adam's apple bobbed as his gaze moved over my face. A muscle in his cheek might have even moved too. Then he said it, sounding almost disappointed, "You make it really, really hard to not like you."

Oh boy.

I smiled and thought about that vision his grandmother had shown me. "I know exactly what you mean," I replied, hearing just how high and squeaky I'd sounded but not able to control it.

Because I mean . . .

What life was this? How was this moment even possible in the first place? It broke my heart and mended it together at the same time.

There wasn't one thing in any life that defined a single person. We were all a mixture of a lot of different things. Alex wasn't just The Defender. He was a brother, he was a friend, and he was sweet when he wanted to be, just like he could be such a fucking turd when he did too.

And maybe he would rarely ever need me for anything, but I could be there for him regardless. I'd be on call for him. I promised myself that right then one more time. To always be there for him if he needed me.

The sound of his sister or brother clearing their throats reminded us both what was happening. They were on the balcony, both of them looking up toward the moon. With the beam of white hitting their features perfectly, they really did look like gods.

"Why didn't we go downstairs to do this?" Robert asked.

"We're already here," Alana explained. "Whenever you're ready, Lex."

"When was the last time you tried?" Robert asked.

"Couple nights ago."

He had?

The blond man frowned. "Everything else is almost back to normal?"

Alex nodded again, this time tipping his own head back to the moon. His chest rose and fell, and his jaw went tight. I wanted to give him another hug.

"When she did it to Achilles, it took him six months to recuperate. Dad told everyone that he'd been in a car accident," she said in a way that sounded like she was telling me about it.

That's what had happened to Achilles when he'd hurt his classmate? When their grandmother had to "get involved"? She'd done to her teenage grandson what she did to full-grown Alex? *What? She'd broken his back?*

Alana wasn't done. "Do you remember how long it took Leon to figure out how to do it? It was all in his head. He fell out of a tree when he'd been little, and he hadn't been able to get out of that fear, even though nothing happened to him. He wasn't able to do it until he was seven. You were three the first time. You were adorable, Lexi," Alana said carefully, a concerned expression on her perfect face.

Could it all be in his head?

I looked at Alex who stood there, still soaking in the moon as he closed his eyes.

I took in the solid frame of his body. The strength that radiated so deeply from within him. The pure energy of his soul.

He was incredible.

Dammit.

And he *was* concerned.

Did he really think he couldn't fly anymore period?

Moving toward the edge of the balcony, I peeked down. The snow had melted so fast, you couldn't even tell it had ever been there. My heart started beating a little faster as I measured the distance to the ground and made a plan in my head.

There were two super-fast superbeings here who weren't injured.

This wasn't my place by any means, but . . .

I'd lived so safely for most of my life that I had never actually done a lot of dumb shit before. The dumbest thing I'd ever done was lie to my grandparents about who I was with and what I was doing a few times. I'd avoided putting myself into situations that would end up with me going to the hospital or possibly getting into trouble. That had never been me.

Yet this was a man who liked to protect. It was what he'd been born to do. Maybe he'd been second-guessing continuing to do this, but some part of me understood now that it was more out of a concern of failure than anything else.

I knew what I had to do.

I did the sign of the cross before I glanced back to see that the three of them hadn't moved, but I wasn't a fool enough to believe they didn't know exactly where I was. They wouldn't be expecting it though, not unless their ESP was a lot better than mine. I tested the guardrail around the balcony to make sure it was sturdy as inconspicuously as possible.

"You know what to do," Robert started talking.

I peeked over to see that Alex still had his eyes closed, and the other two weren't physically paying me any attention. Perfect.

I pushed up onto my arms, using my foot on part of the railing to get up onto the top of it, channeling my inner cat. I had to be fast and hoped they didn't stop me too soon.

I crouched on the guardrail and didn't let myself peek down. What I did do was glance back again and instantly meet Alana's gaze, and I smiled at her. Then I stood up, balancing as best as I could, and said, "Hey, Hercules?"

Alex grunted, and when I didn't say anything again, he opened his eyes.

Time to shine. Holding my breath, I said in a rush, "Bye!"

And I jumped off the edge.

I was pretty sure I heard him curse. I think he might have even spiced it up by saying, "Dammit, Gracie," just as I started to fall.

And in the split millisecond that my body fell—and I prayed that he either caught me or one of his siblings did, and I tried to reassure myself that I wouldn't die if they didn't, I might just break an arm or leg, maybe both, maybe all of them—I knew that regardless of what happened, it would be worth it.

I hoped.

He was going to be so mad if he tried to fly and couldn't, but it was my choice.

I still wasn't 100 percent anyway.

Somehow those thoughts managed to enter my head and leave again before I stopped falling.

I stopped falling?

Sure enough, I was about two feet off the ground. If I stretched my arm out, I could touch the mud.

I looked up and realized that I'd been grabbed by the back of my pants again.

And it wasn't Alana or Robert holding on to me. It wasn't The Primordial or The Centurion who had saved me.

It wasn't The Defender either.

It was crabby-ass Alex there. Grumpy Goose Alex who muttered in midair, "I'm going to go get some pigs now just so I can feed you to them."

I laughed, and then I lifted my arm and gave him a thumbs-up.

I looked behind the nightstand for maybe the fifth time and frowned.

Where the hell was my charger?

It had been here in the morning because I'd charged my phone overnight, and I knew for a fact I hadn't taken it out of the room. I didn't want to leave my stuff everywhere. It wasn't like it could have grown legs and walked away.

Which meant . . .

Alex had the same brand of phone I did. He hadn't asked for my number, and I hadn't asked him for his either. Not that I was upset over it.

Creeping over to the doorway, I stopped and listened. There were noises coming from the direction of his study or maybe his room. I headed over, crossing my arms over my chest to hide my boobs as much as possible. The library was empty, his office door closed, but the light in his room was on. I went to the doorway, and my whole body suddenly jerked.

Alex was changing. He was in the middle of pulling his shirt over his head. Golden skin rippled. Muscles I didn't know existed twisted and contracted as he tugged a plain gray T-shirt down that incredible body.

And he knew I was there.

Keep it together. Keep it together. Oh boy, keep it together.

I cleared my throat super dramatically and knocked on the doorframe. "Hey, did you see my charger?" I asked, knowing he could hear how rough that came out but trying to play it off. So I'd seen him shirtless. That was nothing between us at this point. It wasn't even the first time.

Alex turned, giving me a quick view of his oblique muscles as he finished pulling his shirt down. "On my nightstand," he answered, those big hands already back to moving as he started to take his watch off.

I glanced toward his bed and stopped again.

I hadn't done more than peek into his room that first day we'd arrived. His door was usually always closed, and I hadn't had the balls to go in there without permission. I wasn't about to go and violate his trust like that.

So I wasn't expecting to see the stacks of what looked like magazines on his nightstand.

And along the floor.

There was even a small bookshelf crammed to the max with hardcovers and paperbacks.

And most surprising was the framed poster on the wall with a trophy sitting in front of it.

I glanced at him. He was watching me as he set his watch into a box on top of his dresser. His face was relaxed, but something about his features told me that wasn't totally the case with the rest of him.

Making my way toward the furniture, I spotted my charging cable sitting on top of the tallest of the stacks there. I unplugged it and then stopped again, looking at the opened notebook sitting on top of the stack of books. It was that same notebook he was always scribbling in when he was working in his office.

I shouldn't have. I know I shouldn't read what he wrote in it. But I did.

I read it twice.

No.

I flicked my gaze to the poster and squinted at it. Then I looked down to read the title for the magazine below it. Only it wasn't a magazine. It was a comic book. I froze before taking in the one below it, then the one below that.

Out of the corner of my eye, I saw Alex cross his arms like he was waiting.

I crouched and slowly picked through the stack, finding another notebook wedged between some of them, shaking my head the whole time.

And that was when I got a good look at it.

The trophy in the shape of a star. I didn't need to get closer to read the plaque below it either.

PLEITSKY AWARD
BEST WRITER
ALEX AKITA

I'd heard about the Pleitsky Award because one of my students had taken lessons from me in preparation to start to work with a recipient. They were comic book awards. They were the Oscars of comic books.

I couldn't believe it.

This sneaky—

His chuckle caught me almost as off guard as what the hell I'd just read.

"What are you laughing at?" I barked.

He laughed even harder. "The expression on your face right now."

This sneaky *motherfucker*. I pointed at the trophy, then held up the book closest to me. "I don't even know who you are anymore."

Alex laughed even harder. It was brilliant and beautiful and everything I could have ever imagined a genuine laugh from him sounding like. "You never asked what I did for a living."

I blinked. "Our whole friendship seems like a fraud now."

Alexander Shōta Akita started cracking the fuck up.

"You have at least twenty Electro-Man comics right here!" I held up the one in my hand even higher. "You have a first edition of *Steelflyer* sitting around like it isn't worth a fortune."

The smile Alex gave me right then, midlaugh was something I was never going to be able to forget. Not ever. But I was too busy being fucking *flabbergasted* to really process it. Not surprised. Not astounded. Flabbergasted.

Who the hell was this man?

"I told you I understood your Mistress of Mayhem comment."

"You said you had a TV," I muttered, not believing this shit at all.

"I do. You've watched movies on it."

I set the book down and shook my head. "How could you deceive me like this?"

Oh, his smile. "I thought you would've noticed them when you snooped through the rest of the house."

"The rest of the house but not your room or office," I explained again quietly.

It was like he plugged himself into an outlet, he glowed so brightly right then as his smile widened. "It's more fun when you figure things out on your own."

"We watched the fucking movies because I thought you hadn't!"

"I haven't," he said, smiling. "I just read through the script to make sure they stayed true to the storylines."

I put my hand over my heart as I stared at him.

And he . . . he fucking smiled even more. "My grandfather will love knowing you liked them too. He's the creator of Electro-Man."

It took me a moment to put that family tree together. "On your mom's side? Your world-killer grandma's husband? She's *married*?" I squawked.

Curly eyelashes fell over incredible purple eyes. "Gracie . . ."

What?

His face was . . .

Oh boy, I wasn't going to like whatever he was about to say.

"My grandmother has unimaginable power, but she didn't . . . reproduce . . . asexually," he deadpanned, eyes wide, that fucking smirk on his mouth. "Do I need to explain the birds and the bees?"

"You know what, Alex?" I asked him sarcastically before shaking my head. "How can someone handle who she is? What she is? I feel like I've walked through Chernobyl when I'm with her, even when she says she won't make me feel sick. I swear I had this scar on my hand and it wasn't there the next day."

He didn't look surprised. "They've been together seventy-eight years."

How? And how old *was* she? I couldn't wrap my head around it. I was going to process that later. It was going to take some time.

He switched back to the other bomb he'd dropped on me. "It was my grandmother's idea, but he was the artist. It's a family secret. He was glad when I told him I wanted to do that instead of going to law school."

"That's what you're always working on in that notebook? What you're always mouthing to yourself?" I croaked.

"Yeah."

"It's so obvious though! How do you not get caught? I know you aren't directing the movies and walking the red carpet, but you won a Pleitsky!"

"They mailed it to me. Plenty of manga artists keep their identities a secret. It helps that family runs the business so no one can force me to do something I don't want to do, or be somewhere I don't want to be."

I hated when he made sense. I patted my heart twice as I shook my head. "I can't believe you."

"Yeah, you can."

This mother . . . I couldn't help but snort. "You're right, I can." I laughed. "You sneaky shit. All you told me was that both sides of your family had successful businesses and investments . . . That's incredible, Alex. Do you work on the Steelflyer comics too?"

"They do. Before Shinto Comics, my grandmother bought a lot of real estate then developed it. The family trust owns shares in a few companies too, most of them involved with renewable energy. But no, I only work on Electro-Man, but I read the scripts before they go into production."

I squeaked. I didn't give a shit about how much money or land or whatever his family had, but it was neat to know. "I always wanted to be a superhero, you know, but I think that's just about everyone. But the only thing I'm really good at is lying to people even though I hate it."

His head tipped to the side. "The Damsel of Deception?"

I blinked. "I prefer Sorceress of Secrets, thanks."

"I like Lady of Lies."

I thought about it. "Yeah, that's pretty good."

Alex grinned that fucking grin that had the power of a nuclear bomb.

"You're the Defender of Deceit after you lied to your siblings that day, telling them I was in witness protection. Now this."

He shrugged, still wielding that grin. "They don't need to know everything."

"You never told me that was your cabin we stayed at, by the way."

"You know now."

I sighed as I shook my head, taking a couple wobbly steps toward his bed. I laid down. "I don't even know what to say to you anymore. I don't know if I can forgive you for not actually telling me you're the Electro-Man writer."

"You can. You will."

I couldn't believe him. I really couldn't. I knit my fingers together and set them on top of my stomach.

A brief thought entered my head, making me feel like a hypocrite for a second, but . . .

No, no, I didn't want to tell him. Not yet. But maybe someday. Maybe someday soon.

"After that stunt earlier, you can't give me any shit about anything," he said, as I watched him out of the corner of my eye. "We're even."

Oh, now he wanted to talk about it. "I knew you wouldn't let me hurt myself," I told him, still hung up on him not telling me what his job was.

The mattress dipped, and I looked over to see that he was sitting on the edge. "You did?"

I nodded, inspecting his traitorous, deceiving face.

His eyes glowed for a split second.

"But if you couldn't, it would have been worth it," I told him. "I really can't believe you."

Alex's laugh was a puff. "It's not my fault you ask the wrong questions."

I hated it when he had a point.

The mattress dipped again as he stretched out beside me on top of the covers, on top of his bed, and before I could talk myself out of it, I scooted over until I was right next to him, literally lined up against him. I pressed my cheek against his shoulder. He'd tell me to beat it if I got annoying.

"You're still not feeling good?" he asked quietly, the back of his hand wedged between my thigh and the mattress.

He thought I just wanted him to make me feel better. I did, but not . . . like that. Not like that at all. I didn't want him to know that though, did I? "Yeah," I lied, knowing he could more than likely tell. "I'm feeling a little off. But hey, I'm really glad you were able to fly again."

His silence had me finding his grouchy face.

"It worked. You don't need to be mad," I told him.

"You could have broken your neck."

"Maybe." I pressed my cheek a little tighter to his shoulder, focusing up on the beams of his ceiling. "I had faith. You told me you wouldn't let anything happen to me, remember?"

He tensed for a split second. "I remember." I felt his exhale. "I'm never going to let anything happen to you."

Oh boy. I swallowed that statement for safekeeping. "For the record, that was the most exciting thing to ever happen to me."

"You all right with that?"

I snorted and closed my eyes, taking in the sweet scent of him. "Are you kidding me? I dreamed of that my whole life. Thank you for not letting me down. It was my choice, and that's all I've ever wanted." I paused. "It was totally worth it."

His "hmm" puffed against my hair.

And I hoped he believed me when I reached over and wrapped my fingers around his index and middle finger.

I held on real fucking tight.

Chapter Twenty-Nine

He was gone.

Tapping the pad of my finger against the note on the kitchen counter, I blinked. Then I read the note again like there could possibly be some kind of secret message hidden on the back of the grocery store receipt.

Call Selene if you need something

Other than a cell phone number and a four-digit code below it, that was all that was written on it. Right beside the paper, he'd left what I was pretty sure was a house key, what definitely was his car key, and the same card he'd let me use to buy my laptop.

Had he made his decision about continuing to be The Defender? Was he back on duty? How long would he be gone? Where was he going? Last night, we hadn't talked about what it meant that he was able to fly again, and we'd laid on his bed and talked for a while, mostly about his secret comic book career.

That sneaky son of a bitch. Of course he'd told me the truth in the most disbelieving way.

I really admired him.

Too much, and that made me mad.

We were both skirting around the vision thing again, and I damn well knew it. I was going to keep doing it too. So was he, from the feel of it.

He liked me as a friend. He liked my boobs, but so did random strangers. Him staying in my life in a positive way was the most important thing, and I wouldn't let myself forget it.

Because in what universe would a man like him end up with someone like me?

I folded the note and slipped it into my pocket. His handwriting was scribbly, and it made me smile that there was one thing he wasn't good at. I could make fun of him later and remind him about that time he'd lost at the carnival over and over again.

It was while I was thinking about that, that a knock came from the front door.

My first thought was that I shouldn't answer, but then I remembered where I was. In the safest place I could be. But just in case, I grabbed my phone and pulled my new multi-tool out of the back pocket of my jeans as I crept toward the front door just as another knock rattled it. I flipped the sharp blade out.

My skin prickled suddenly. A strong buzz shot through my spine. And I felt it.

Oh boy. I didn't need to use the peephole to know who it was. I flipped the blade back into place and put my multi-tool in my pocket. I opened the door, already mentally bracing myself for the force of nature on the other side.

I wasn't disappointed.

Standing there, holding a cane with a big red rock that might or might not be a ruby, dressed in a simple cream button-up shirt and navy slacks, was Alex's grandma.

At her side, in overalls, was a little blonde girl with her hair tied up in buns on each side of her head. She was beaming, holding a board game in her hands. "Hi!" she greeted me.

I hadn't seen this coming. I smiled at her. "Hi, Asami." Then I held my breath and gave the other woman the same kind of smile. "Good morning."

"Hug?" the little girl asked, setting her game on the floor.

Oh. I dropped into a crouch and wrapped my arms around her, feeling hers go around me and—

"Oh *shit*." A grunt slipped through my lips as she hugged me back. Tight. Really fucking tight.

Too fucking tight.

"Careful," the scary one said at the same time Asami's hold loosened.

"Sorry!" she apologized, dropping her arms instantly.

"We're still learning our strength, aren't we, Asami?" the grandmother asked, sounding stern.

"Sorry, Gracie." Her face screwed up into the purest form of apology.

If the comment about carrying a tractor hadn't been proof enough, here it was. Wow. This tiny thing was amazing.

I held my arms out again. "It's okay," I assured her, a sucker for that bright face. "Want to try one more time?"

Oh, she looked happy, and so, so gently, those little arms went around me, hugging me back just perfectly. We smiled at each other when I pulled back and slowly stood to face Alex's grandmother. She tipped her head to the side, and I recognized that expression. Up on my tiptoes, I leaned forward and kissed her cheek.

My lips stung afterward, and it took just about everything in me to keep my expression even.

"Come in," I said, like the house was mine.

The older woman went in first, then Asami, and when I started to push the heavy door closed, she helped me . . . and I knew I didn't imagine how much easier it had been.

By the time we faced forward, Grandmother was halfway to the kitchen.

The little girl slipped her hand through mine and tugged me to follow.

In the kitchen, I gave Asami a glass of apple juice, made

Grandmother a cup of tea—she told me where to find it before I even had a chance to wonder—and refilled my own glass with water. While I did that, she set up Candy Land on the table. I had to breathe in through my nose and out through my mouth, trying to get used to the way the woman made me feel as I took a seat too.

Scooting my chair closer to the table, I cleared my throat and met Alex's grandma's eyes for a split second before refocusing on Asami. I wasn't ready for that shit—for her. If I could make it through sitting here with her during a game of Candy Land, I would be proud of myself. Most of my instincts told me to run. My body probably remembered how she'd made me feel after that game of Trouble.

"You're doing much better than you were the last time we met," Grandmother said the second after I'd looked away.

Asami gave me a little smile from across the table that I couldn't help but return.

"Yes, ma'am, I am," I answered, quickly peeking at her again.

She was watching me closely, her back ramrod straight, the cane leaning against the wall behind her. "I'm pleased to see that Alexander has been helping you. Soon enough, you'll be healthier than ever."

It was the subtle amusement in her voice that put me on edge. Was she smirking?

And why was she implying I'd be healthy? Because he'd been giving me his healing vibes every night sleeping so close? Not that she knew that. Or did she?

"If he would have met you when I told him to seek you out, all of this could have been avoided." Her gaze went glassy and flat for a second before a single blink brought her back. "It will all work out now."

Why did that feel so premonition-like?

I focused on the elegant stud in her ear, curiosity running

right through me at her words, at her tone, at everything. "My grandpa used to tell me that everything eventually works out the way it's supposed to." I wasn't sure I believed it but he had.

"Eventually, yes, but there are easier ways for things to come to pass."

If that wasn't cryptic as shit, I didn't know what was.

"Though knowing the future doesn't make decisions easier, does it?" she asked.

In front of me, Asami's eyes bounced back and forth between us, and I knew that despite being so young, she was eating up every word of this conversation. I was relatively certain Alex didn't have any kind of premonition, but why? And did anyone else in his family have it?

I cleared my throat. "I don't have that ability like I think you do."

"It only runs in two lines of our people, and it's the strongest in your family. Some abilities work that way. I inherited it through my great-grandmother on my father's side, but my daughter took after her father," she clarified. "With the right mix, I think it would continue. I would like to see that happen." There went another sneaky little, loaded word.

I eyed the board hard though I wanted to focus on her instead. "Mine is mostly just a stomachache when something bad is going to happen, or when something monumental is, but usually only right before it does. Maybe a few hours depending." It felt unreal to be having this conversation with her. To actually admit that maybe there was something in me that might actually be Atraxian.

Asami's bright blue eyes glowed suddenly for a moment, like she didn't control it, reminding me of just what was possible and what wasn't.

"That talent is too diluted in you. It's a testament to the strength of your line that you still retain some of it," Grandmother said.

That had me meeting her incredible purple gaze. "Really?"

A small smile tweaked her mouth. "Oh, yes. My mother admired your family greatly. She wanted her brother to marry your great-grandmother, but she wouldn't have him."

My great-grandmother had to be the baddest bitch there was, because I had a really hard time picturing anyone telling this woman or anyone like her no.

"She knew our lines weren't meant to cross then. It wasn't until decades later that I understood why it wasn't supposed to happen with them." Grandmother's attention moved to her great-granddaughter and lingered there, contemplative. "Your ancestors were the ones who led us here, who promised us that this was where we were meant to go when they left Atraxia. It may have cost them in the end, but I don't think they regretted their choices. Not many can say that about their decisions."

"What decisions? Letting their . . . strengths die off? By marrying humans? Having children with them?"

"Yes. They were the first to distance themselves when we arrived here. They insisted on integrating. So the story goes," she said.

"Grandma said you and Uncle Lexi are gonna get married," Asami whispered with a gleeful look in her eye. "Can I be the flower girl?"

I almost fainted, and I know I wasn't imagining the dry chuckle that rose from Grandmother's throat.

"I *think* you're going to have"—she held up two tiny fingers—"two boys."

I swear I swooned, and I might have fallen out of the chair if her hand hadn't shot out and grabbed me by the side of the shirt to keep me in place.

"I don't . . . I don't know about all that, Asami," I tried to say and heard it come out high and wheezy as I gripped the table to keep from falling over. "We're friends, and I like him, but I don't think . . ."

The little girl's eyes flicked toward her grandmother, and I saw the smug, smug smile form on her face. I didn't need to look over to know the older woman was probably smiling at her too, mixed up in their own little secrets. Secrets I was pretty sure I partially understood.

"Remember what I told you about choices," Grandmother said. "Life is full of them, but there are some that matter more than others."

Chapter Thirty

A few days passed, and I still hadn't heard a word from Alex. Not a call or text. Not even a smoke signal.

It was fine. It was cool. It wasn't like he knew my number anyway.

Knowing his sneaky ass, he might have gotten it somehow behind my back though.

In the meantime, I took my time putting the finishing touches on my new work site. The same one that I really wasn't sure I would be able to use. I planned on talking to Alex to see what he thought.

I'd also wandered around the property. I had annihilated a lot of his food supply too, not wanting to leave the house and drive his fast car. I'd swear I went through a pack of cookies faster than I thought I would and that there had been more sodas in the fridge, but I figured I just had my mind on more important stuff and wasn't keeping track.

I slept a lot too. I *was* feeling better, but my body was still so tired. My soul was as well if I was going to be honest. That conversation with Alex's grandma had really gotten under my skin and into the cavities of my heart.

I was just as confused as I was lonely, and it was weird to be both when I thought my past would have prepared me for all the time being spent in a quiet house.

And that was the excuse I used when I finally broke down and dialed the number that Alex had left me. It only rang twice before a familiar-ish voice answered, "Hello . . . ?"

"Hi, Selene. It's Gracie."

"Hey, Gracie." She sounded so cheerful. "What's going on? Do you need something? I know he's in London right now. I just got back yesterday from Vegas, otherwise I would have come by to check on you. I heard Grandmother dropped by to surprise you."

How had she heard?

Asami. I'd bet my life it was her who spilled the beans.

The memory of her holding up two fingers haunted me suddenly.

Did she say he was in London? Huh. "Yeah, she did a few days ago. She said she would see me again soon." I swallowed. "I was actually calling because I need groceries, and I was wondering . . . ?"

"I need to go grocery shopping too. We can go together," she suggested.

Go together? "I don't want to be an inconvenience. I'm just not sure how to get in and out of the neighborhood—"

Selene cut me off. "You're not. I want to. I hate going grocery shopping by myself. I make bad choices," she said. "I'll be over to pick you up around six."

"Okay . . . are you sure?" I didn't like asking for favors, but I didn't hate the idea of spending time with her. I'd gotten a good feeling about Selene.

"Positive."

I scratched my nose and reminded myself that things were different now. That no one had any idea where I was. That here I could be someone else. Branch out a little more.

Maybe I could make another friend here.

I nodded to myself and said it. "Thanks, Selene. I'll see you then."

"Hey, don't thank me. That's what family is for."

The next few hours dragged by, mostly because I was unusually restless. I had some money saved, but not enough for long-term. Plus, I wanted to give Alex money for utilities and have enough to start over. I had already wired Selene what I owed her, and my new favorite superbeing brushed me off every time I brought up what he'd let me use.

Money, money, money, fucking money.

And all this uncertainty was driving me fucking nuts.

I'd spent my whole life with a singular goal in mind: staying inside my bubble as happy as anyone could. Now I was just antsy. Something felt off, and I had no idea what it could be.

That was a lie. The truth was, I had an idea, but I didn't want to focus on it too much.

So when I heard the doorbell ring and a minute later heard Selene call out, "Gracie?" I was already ready.

I ran down the front staircase with my purse and *Alex's* card and stopped when I found Selene in the foyer. My plan was to pull out cash from an ATM and pay him back. It would be safer than using my card in actual places.

She was wearing dark gray sweatpants and an oversized sweatshirt, her hair in a bun.

The cute blonde smiled just as another voice called out, "I don't know how the hell I can hold so much pee in my body. I could have put out a fire with it."

Just like that, Selene rolled her eyes the same exact way Alex did. "I didn't mean to bring her, but she was waiting for me at my car, and I couldn't convince her that she doesn't buy groceries." Those bright blue eyes slid slightly behind me, and I was pretty sure I saw her mouth a prayer under her breath.

"*Bonjour*, Gracie!" the same voice bellowed out as a woman, a young woman, even younger-looking than Selene, strolled up beside me and instantly threw her arms around me.

I only froze for a second before I hugged her back.

Who the hell was I to say no to a hug from a friendly stranger?

They were a touchy-feely bunch, I was starting to learn, which surprised the shit out of me. Even their grandmother had wanted another peck on her cheek when she'd left. Asami had planted one on mine along with the most gentle, big hug in the world after we'd played two tense games of Candy Land.

"Gracie, this is my niece, Hiromi," Selene said.

Oh. "Oh, hi," I told the curly-haired, dark blonde.

She pulled back and then gave me another tight, unexpected hug. She was shorter than Selene and had more of The Primordial's frame than Selene's long, lean one. Her skin was a shade close to mine, but where mine was more bronze, hers was a unique golden. She was beautiful. This whole family was. Their genetics were miraculous.

"It's nice to meet you. I wanted to come by before, but Mom wanted to give you and Lexi some time to settle in. Sorry I had to use your bathroom. I drank a venti on my way to wait for Selene, and it makes me have to go pee like a busted fire hydrant." Hiromi pulled back and dropped her arms, wiggling her eyebrows at Selene. "Wow, you weren't joking. Uncle Lexi got really lucky."

This family and their fucking secrets.

"It's not my bathroom," I told her, feeling shy all of a sudden. "Coffee makes me have to go pee like crazy too."

A big, beautiful smile took over her equally beautiful face. "You live here. It is your bathroom."

"Just for now," I tried to clarify.

They looked at each other. Selene smiled *almost* innocently, but Hiromi just smirked.

I could smell bullshit a mile away, and I'd been dealing with Alex long enough to know when someone was being sneaky.

And this was his family. Sneakiness must run in it.

I didn't know what was going on with these little looks, but . . .

Most of these people, they all gave me a good feeling.

Some more than others.

"Does it have to be so loud in here?" I yelled across the table.

"People don't like to talk to each other anymore!" Selene yelled back at my question, nursing her bottle of beer beside me.

The niece and aunt, who really acted more like sisters, were sandwiching me between them at the bar we were at. I might have been the oldest, but they treated me like I was The Precious that had to be protected. I liked it more than I should have.

I'd told them a few days ago that I had never been to a bar with friends that were girls, and they'd taken it upon themselves to give me another experience. It was funny though because Selene couldn't get drunk—just like Alex had said—and Hiromi had just turned twenty-one a few weeks ago. Selene only drank fruity beer—just like me—but not really anything else, and Hiromi mostly just guzzled Sprite with a lemon wedge. It was what she ordered the couple of times we'd gone out to eat dinner.

Because they were two of my newest friends.

"Speaking of not talking to each other," Hiromi started, those bright eyes flicking toward me. "You still haven't heard from Uncle Lexi?"

I shook my head, trying to be as casual as possible. Accepting reality wasn't that difficult. I got where his priorities had to lie and why.

It had been a month since I'd last seen or heard from him.

At least in person.

I had laid eyes on him via television. Twice. The first had been when he'd helped with a collapsed building in Wales, and the second time had been during footage of a train accident in France.

It wasn't like he was exactly crazy busy.

Which only meant one thing: he was avoiding me. I'd realized it and accepted that about two weeks ago when Selene and I had gone to lunch and she'd mentioned talking to Alex and how he had asked how I was doing. He didn't call *me* to check in; he'd called his sister.

Yeah. Cool, cool. I wasn't bitter about it or anything.

Maybe I'd weirded him out telling him about his grandmother's vision. Or holding his fingers the night before he'd left. Maybe I was cramping his space.

He'd already warned me that he wasn't used to taking care of people. That he didn't want to like me. If it had taken his family weeks to start worrying about him and his disappearance, it was for a reason. Why worry about people who were 99.9999999 percent invincible?

So why would Alex even think about calling someone to check in with them? Why would he think about calling *me* to let me know he was fine? We were friends, yeah, but we were top 10 best friends.

At least he was my top 10 best friend.

A little higher than that if I wanted to think about it.

I tried not to get too hung up on it.

Fortunately, I'd been busy while he'd been away. I still hadn't decided how to proceed with my career as a teacher, which bummed me the hell out. If I launched a new site with conveniently all the same languages the cartel had found books for at my house, they would find me. Probably pretty easily unfortunately. I had changed focus to starting to learn the basics for Japanese. I'd known it was going to be hard, but I hadn't anticipated just how difficult. I had taken for granted how easily I had picked up every other one I'd learned. One night, Hiromi had confirmed that my "talent" for languages was part of my Atraxian gift.

On that same night, Selene had taken my hand and told me about a cousin of mine that she'd found in Costa Rica named Valentina. One year ago, this Valentina deposited ten thousand dollars into her bank account in cash. Almost immediately, she used every penny to pay a hospital bill.

I couldn't even muster up that much anger over it. If she had given away my name to pay off her debt, I understood. I was no one to her but a name.

She was a traitor, but I didn't blame her.

I didn't have a whole lot going for me being in this weird limbo situation, but I did have one thing that lifted my spirits.

I finally had people in my life. People I liked a lot. I had friendships with a twenty-five-year-old, a twenty-one-year-old, a three-year-old who was stronger than me, and a terrifying woman I had a feeling was a hell of a lot older than she looked.

It made me wonder how old Alex would eventually be. How old my grandfather had actually been. I knew now that he hadn't been lying when he'd whispered to me that he was turning one hundred so many years ago.

He'd told me the truth.

The knowledge made my heart so full.

Over the last month, I usually spent time with at least one of Alex's family members every day. On that first evening with Selene and Hiromi, we'd gone to buy groceries . . . and gone back to his house with a couple frozen pizzas and a pack of raspberry beer that we'd destroyed in record time while we watched a reality show about an attractive man on the hunt for the love of his life.

The day after that, Hiromi had shown up and taken me with her to get my hair cut and colored. I think they'd called it a "balayage job" or something like that. I didn't remember, but apparently I'd told her all about wearing a wig the day before. She hadn't let me pay for it either, saying it was an early birthday present. In hindsight, I couldn't believe I'd drank enough to do that, but it made me glad I hadn't trusted my big mouth around people, otherwise who the hell knows what I might have told a total stranger.

After that, Selene showed up with a USB-looking stick, and we'd watched a not-yet-released Shinto Comics movie about Justine Justice. That was the night I learned that she handled "privacy matters," or as Hiromi had explained immediately after, she was a "fucking hacker." Apparently, she had set up some kind of program or algorithm that alerted whatever member of the Trinity was closest to natural disasters and specific kinds of emergencies. And here I'd thought they had some kind of team with a hotline that people called into.

I'd also figured out the night before that Hiromi bounced around jobs because she couldn't get to work on time, and the family wouldn't hire her. The Akita side or the Shinto comics side, which was also known as the Drakos part of the family.

Another day, Grandmother and Asami had paid me a second visit with a different board game. Then she had asked me to drive her to her daughter's house. I'd wanted to say no, but my balls had picked up and walked away, so I did. That's where I got to meet Alex's dad, a tall, lean man with dark, serious eyes but a warm smile that told me exactly where The Primordial got it from. The energy coming off him had been a warm, steady one that was the complete opposite of his wife's. I had wondered just what gifts he had.

One evening, Hiromi brought Asami over, and the little girl found an Xbox in the TV stand that I swore hadn't been there the last time I'd gone through the cabinets. On top of it had been a brand-new copy of a racing game and one with a blue hedgehog. We played that night, and when they left, I played by myself afterward too. It had made me smile. Another afternoon, I met up with Selene for lunch and had been surprised when that "snobby shit" Achilles showed up with Asami, and he'd been surprisingly loving toward his daughter and little sister.

To my continued fucking surprise, he'd called me three days later and asked if I would be interested in tutoring Asami in Spanish. I hadn't even thought about it, I agreed instantly. He brought her over the very next day, and from the way it sounded, he and his wife were interested in having me teach her more languages in the future. I had warned him I wasn't sure how much longer I would be close by—and he'd frowned before his phone rang and distracted him—but it still gave me hope. The truth was, it made me feel even more included. More a part of them. It was the nicest feeling but at the same time, it made my heart yearn for all kinds of things.

And that was how the last month had gone. I'd gone to another mall and my first outlet mall, even though I hardly bought anything because I couldn't spend extra money with the future up in the air. I'd gone to the movies with company twice and had even gone with Asami and Hiromi sledding after another snowy day. That was when I'd learned that they were sisters, which blew my mind.

And now, today, we were at a bar that felt way too packed.

So it was because everything was going so damn well that I was trying not to take it personally that Alex hadn't reached out once. Why should he? There was no need to think about my whereabouts when I was living so incognito, and he knew first-hand I was on my way to being back to normal health-wise. I'd even stopped leaving notes at the house in case he got there and wondered where I was. I hadn't wanted him to worry.

"Really? He just sent me a text like fifteen minutes ago," Selene said.

I rubbed my lips together.

We'd had some nice moments together. We were friends. And if I liked him? Who wouldn't? Especially once you got below that prickly-ass exterior.

As grumpy as he was, the man had a heart of gold and the face of an angel.

And the body of a superhero.

He'd been the first person in a long time to show me care and kindness, and my poor, deprived heart had only reached toward him with open arms once I'd started to feel safe around him. I could dream a little dream. Rebuild my life step by step.

That's what I was focusing on.

The attorney who had helped us the day we'd gone to Alex's family's office had called and told me where they were at with my situation. They had sorted out whatever it was that needed to be done with the local police. They had dealt with my car insurance, and I'd have a check coming in hopefully sooner than later. She had also brought up that they were still working on changing my name.

It wasn't the first time it had happened, but some part of me hoped that it would be the last.

Which was the reason why I had decided that the second I had my new license, passport, or whatever identification they gave me, I would leave. I'd decided that I liked North Carolina. Unlike what my grandparents had always tried to stress, I figured I would be just as safe in a city as I had been in a tiny town in the middle of nowhere. There were enough people where I could hide. There were also plenty of smaller towns where I could hopefully find a reasonably priced place to live.

Plus, I'd be close enough to still see my new friends, Selene and Hiromi, when they were free. Asami had been making it real clear that we were going to be friends too, so it sounded to me like that was in the books. I would also be close to Alex's grandmother. Not that I thought calling on her was something

I would ever use lightly. You didn't have the nuke codes and throw a hissy fit.

And Alex would be within hollering distance if I needed him.

I was trying my best to build a life, and here was just as good a place as any.

Better really.

If I was a little . . . lonely over his absence, it was my fault for getting attached. I knew better. I definitely knew better, and if I saw him again—if he came back before everything was settled— I could go back into our friendship with my expectations in place. The world was a big place, and I'd finally sort of been able to take my blinders off and experience it.

And it was pretty wonderful.

I took another sip of my beer, feeling just a little bit more relaxed. There was no reason to be sad. I was here, out, trying new things, and that was exactly what I wanted. What I had always dreamed of.

". . . he want?"

"He wanted to know where we were," Selene answered.

I kept my attention on the crowd of people around us. This wasn't my scene at all, I'd decided right after we'd gotten here. But I had to get a little more used to being in crowds. I still couldn't put my face under the shower spray, but that was different.

For once, things were looking up instead of forward.

And that's what I was thinking about when I squinted.

Because by the door to the bar, shouldering his way through the crowd, was a face I recognized.

Alex?

"Look who showed up," Hiromi said, either seeing him or sensing him close by.

"Aww, you're in trouble," Selene whistled. "What'd you do, Gracie?"

I jerked. Was he scowling or was it my imagination? "I didn't do anything."

What was he doing here, giving us that face like he had something to be annoyed with? I wasn't doing anything wrong. Hadn't done anything wrong. He'd been the one to tell me to contact Selene if I needed something. If my friendship with her was a problem, then too damn bad. I wasn't giving it up.

That didn't seem right either though, and my brain moved along to the next mystery.

"He goes out in public?" I asked them, knowing he could hear me despite all the sounds in the bar. The mall was one thing. This was another.

"Once a blue moon," Selene answered, lifting her arm and waving it wildly like he hadn't seen us the moment he'd come through the door or before. "He doesn't like being around big groups of people usually. Too much noise."

I blinked just as the tall, dark-haired man came to a stop at our table. In a light button-down shirt under the familiar black jacket he usually wore and jeans, he could have been a gorgeous anyone. A perfect anyone.

But he was so much more than that, and it was weird to think, as I looked around the room, that no one knew the truth about what else resided within those muscles and tissues and bones. He didn't even have a beanie on. Could people really be that oblivious?

It wasn't so hard to give him a friendly smile and say as casually as I could, "Hi, stranger."

He looked from me to his sister and niece and gave them both his tiny, warm smile.

Selene, who was the closest to him, gave him a side hug.

"You didn't say you were coming!" she told him with a bright grin as he moved to pat Hiromi's back. "It's not even my birthday!"

His gaze flicked back toward me. His smile wavered. "Gracie."

A gruff "Gracie" was all I got? I'd had my head on his shoulder a month ago. I'd held his hand back then too.

"Come with me to get a drink," Hiromi said suddenly, poking her aunt before pushing her chair back.

It wasn't the fact Selene got up immediately that prickled my senses, but the fact that she did it with a smile on her face I'd only seen her use when she was being sneaky.

"Want something?" Selene asked Alex.

"Any beer is good," he answered in a rough voice.

The aunt and niece looked at each other before disappearing into the crowd.

Alex slid into the seat that Selene left beside me. Lights flickered around, striking his face in different angles. Everything about him seemed normal. The same. I saw just enough to notice he had his contacts in.

He angled his body in the chair, giving me a good view of his thighs in those dark jeans. The nice black boots he had on. As handsome as he'd been in his tuxedo, and as perfect as he filled in his Defender suit, him in everyday clothes put everything else to shame.

I pressed my lips together before asking, "What are you grouchy over?"

"I'm never grouchy," he said, dead serious.

I burst out fucking laughing, and it took me a minute to calm down. When I did, I said, "All right then. You look nice, by the way."

He stared. His throat bobbed, and the second shit he said to me was, "I didn't know where you were."

I'd missed the sound of his voice, I thought as I shrugged, not trusting my own.

"You didn't leave a note," he kept going, his voice still that low, crabby one.

"I did at first, but I stopped leaving them . . ." That was a weird statement. How did he know about my notes?

"Why?"

All righty then, we were going straight into this. He wasn't going to ask how I'd been doing, what I'd been up to. Okay. So I told him, "You were gone. I didn't think you'd care if I left the house for a little while."

For one millisecond, his irises did that unreal glow before just as quickly going back to normal behind his contact lenses. The urge to look around to make sure no one had seen it rode my chest, but no, he knew what he was doing. "Why would you think that?" he asked.

It wasn't that much of a mystery. "Because you were gone," I repeated slowly.

"I could've gotten home any time."

Like I didn't know that. I set my elbow on the tabletop and cupped my chin with my palm, deciding to be the reasonable one. He could be annoyed with whatever he wanted to be annoyed with, but I wasn't going to let him drag me down into Crabby Town. "But you didn't."

His eyes moved around my face, over my throat, across my chest by my breasts. I'd bought a cute top at the outlet mall, and I'd decided to wear it tonight. It dipped low enough that my grandmother would've been scandalized, but then again, she thought T-shirts showed off too much arm.

"How are you?" I asked him, trying to be calm and cool like he hadn't dropped me cold turkey without even saying goodbye.

"Fine." I was pretty sure a muscle in his cheek might have tensed. "Did you have a good time while I was gone?" Alex asked slowly, so strangely, it felt like a test or something.

I nodded.

"Hiromi and Selene were good company?"

"The best company."

Oh, that got me a raise of an eyebrow. "The best?"

"Yep." I smiled.

"Nobody else is better?"

Was he . . . ? "No, they've been the best."

His cheek did that thing again. He knew I was fucking with him. Keeping my chin up, I looked him right in the eye and told him the truth. "I didn't think I could really feel that alone anymore, but they made it go away. I like them a lot. They're nice."

Something about my words must have not been what he'd expected to hear because those elegant features suddenly went stricken. "You were lonely?"

He made it sound like I'd broken a hip. "Little bit." I tapped my fingers against the beer bottle. "We were together for so long, I guess I got used to knowing you were usually close, even if you were in your office for hours."

"You mad?" he asked after a moment.

I was going to play it innocent. There really wasn't a point in making him feel bad. For what? Working? Staying away? I couldn't do it. I wouldn't. "About what?"

But his shrug got on my nerves even though we both damn well knew what he was talking about.

So I pretended not to know either and took a sip of my beer while his gaze followed me, and then I held it out toward him.

He took it. Bringing the glass to his lips and taking a slow drink, still watching me the whole time like it was me who was about to do the disappearing act. He made no sense.

But now that we were here and talking, and he wasn't running off, I might as well take advantage of it. He might leave in a minute and be gone for another month. And then what? Would I see him again?

The possibility of that happening made my nose tingle. But I'd known this wasn't permanent from the beginning. And this had to be done. "Umm, just so you know, in case you have to leave again soon, your legal department called while you were gone—"

"I know. I talked to them."

So he'd communicated with them but not me. "Okay then. They said they were going to get my things transferred from my safe deposit box in Arizona to a bank branch that your family does business with. Also, I think I'm going to stay in this part of the state. Housing isn't too bad, and *maybe*, if you could rent me a place out under your name, or if you know someone who owes you a big favor and can do it, I should be fine. I can pay for it, but I just don't want it even under my business, or an alias if I can help it. The fewer breadcrumbs I leave, the better," I told him. "We don't need to talk about it right now, and if you don't want to do that, it's all right too. I just wanted you to know before I forgot to mention it and you need to go."

I didn't miss the way his eyes briefly glowed again.

Was that it? Was he fine with it? Why wouldn't he be after all? I was just a friend living in his house, using his utilities. With his permission, but it still was what it was.

I would treasure the time and the experiences we'd had together. The laughs we'd shared when it felt like the world was on the verge of collapsing. He said he would be my ally for the rest of my life. He'd promised, and I knew he would keep his word. That was what kind of man he was.

A very, very special one.

And one that hadn't wanted me and still didn't. He'd made that real clear being gone for so long. I understood.

Alex reached forward and grazed the ends of my hair with his fingertips. "Your hair looks nice like this. Pretty."

The noise that came out of my throat was unholy.

He pinched some of the strands and spread his legs a little wider as he settled that heavy gaze on me, snapping his hips and the stool forward, trapping my knees between his. "But I liked your hair the way it was before too." He rubbed those strands between his fingers a little more as he watched me so, so closely.

My skin buzzed with his energy.

Alex's head tilted to the side as he gave my ends a tiny tug, and I didn't think I imagined the way one corner of his mouth went up.

It took me two damn tries, but I finally got it out. "What are you doing?"

"Nothing," he replied just as Selene and Hiromi parted through the crowd, on their way back.

But my stomach . . . my stomach disagreed. It didn't feel like nothing.

"Thanks for driving me home—I mean back to your home," I told Alex later on, my throat a little raw from basically yelling, but I was in a good mood. We'd hung out for another hour, with Selene and Hiromi telling me funny stories about the family that had me wiping at my eyes. It was usually what we did every time we went out; they told me stories and gossip.

I loved learning everybody's business, and they had no filters.

All the while, Alex sat there, listening and occasionally smirking his way through Selene and Hiromi's versions of their family's shenanigans. My head hurt a little, and part of it was from laughing so hard. The other part was because I'd drank more than I should have. More than I would have if he hadn't shown up. Eventually, once the bar got even more crowded, Selene and Hiromi suggested we go to another one, a quieter one, but I hadn't wanted to go, and when Alex said he didn't either, it only made sense to catch a ride with him since I hadn't driven. I'd tried my best not to drive Alex's car unless I absolutely had to, and that'd only been a handful of times. I'd driven around his grandmother's Mercedes and clutched the shit out of the wheel each time she asked me to chauffeur her around. The rest of the time, Selene or Hiromi always picked me up.

I caught his glance as we walked from the car to the big, dark house. The ride back had been quiet. I knew what I was thinking about but had no idea what was on his mind. Melting ice caps. The islands of trash in the ocean. Who knew?

Out of the corner of my eye, I saw him glance over. "It is home," he said, sounding so solemn.

I pinched my lips and kept my face even. I had to keep everything in perspective. Keep my cool. *Give him his space. Don't ask anything. Don't expect anything.* Those were some of my new rules. *Try not to be scared* was my favorite one.

He unlocked the door and pushed it open, turning that body just enough for me to squeeze through first. I kept my gaze forward as I stopped to pull off my newish boots as he locked the door. I snatched them up and met his gaze, giving him a little smile. "I'm going to go shower off the beer Selene spilled on me."

"Yeah, you stink like it."

There he was.

I smiled just a little, more than a bit relieved he was back, at least for a while. I really had missed him. Even though I had made myself at home while he'd been gone, having him around just felt . . . right.

And that's why I needed to give him his space and keep everything in check.

Alex tipped his chin up. "Go shower, Cookie," he told me as he set his keys and wallet on the console table by the front door, giving me his muscular back.

I turned and ran up the steps as fast as I could. I wasn't going to be sad. We were together because of some fluke of fate. Because I had an ancestor who had had an ancestor that had been special.

His grandma had dropped him into my life—literally—but life did have choices. And you couldn't control them all; I refused to believe that.

We wanted different things. He hadn't wanted to meet me; he hadn't wanted someone to tell him what to do. I knew him well enough at this point to understand how much he would like someone telling him what to do. Which was not at all. And I wanted . . . I wanted fucking everything. I wanted to live my life, I wanted sex, but I wanted love more. It was why I'd waited. Why I hadn't settled for just anyone.

I had a future, and soon, I'd be given more freedom than I ever could have expected before.

I wasn't going to be sad. Disappointed, okay, for a little while. But not unhappy. You didn't tell someone they had bought a winning lottery ticket and then remind them they'd thrown away the ticket and expect them to be ecstatic about it.

And that's what I kept telling myself as I showered and slipped on the loose, flannel pajama pants I'd stolen and a tank top. Getting into bed, I started to reach for one of the paperbacks that Hiromi had brought me the other day, after I had learned she enjoyed reading too, when I felt that tingle that warned me Alex was close.

Because he was.

Right at the doorway. I didn't mean for my smile to be weak as I set my book down, but I guess I couldn't help it. "Hey."

"Were you sleeping in the library? It smelled a lot like you in there," he asked, crossing his arms over that impeccable chest, there in a tight T-shirt and sleeping pants he'd changed into that were probably the same size as the ones I was wearing, just longer.

"I've been taking naps on the couch." Busted. "I've been sleeping in the living room downstairs with the TV on sometimes too," I told him. "I figured if you came in through the front door, I'd be able to hear you better."

I didn't want to admit it, but he'd be able to smell me in there too. I might as well be upfront about it.

"You can sleep wherever you want." The muscles in his arms flexed. "When I'm gone. When I'm not gone."

This man and his wording.

"You good?" Someone was feeling chatty. Or bored.

"Yeah, I'm almost back to normal now. I've started running again a little." I could do this. I could draw this line and make sure to stay on the other side. "Are you okay?" I asked, hoping to sound about as normal as usual.

"Glad to be home. You showering okay? No panic attacks?" he asked.

Oh. I tipped my head to the side a little. "It hasn't gotten worse."

Alex nodded like he wasn't surprised. "Nothing is ever going to happen to you again, but if you want to talk to someone about it, Asami's aunt is a therapist. She's just a call away."

Despite everything, I couldn't help but smile at him a little. "Thanks. I'll think about it and let you know."

He pushed off the doorframe with his shoulder and came to stand beside the bed, with an expression on his face that I hadn't seen before. Ultra-serious. The most serious of serious. "Alana said I owe you," he said.

"For what?"

"For that night out on the balcony."

"Didn't we already talk about it?"

He shook his head.

I was pretty positive we had made a joke about it, but fine. "I'm living in your house, using your water and electricity, and hoping you'll protect me if anyone ever comes for me. Your family is going to help me figure out a fresh start to my life. Your brother wants me to teach Asami Spanish. You don't owe me anything."

He exhaled, not seeming even a little surprised about my mention of Achilles. He was probably aware of that too since he seemed to be able to get in contact with everyone else but me. "I do."

"No. I'm good. If anything, I owe you rent."

"No."

"Pretty sure I do."

Alex shook his head. "I like to repay my debts."

That I knew.

Wait. "Are you leaving again already?" I asked him, trying to keep my tone even. "For a long time?"

His eyebrows curved as he frowned. "No, not again, Gracie. I won't leave you for that long again."

"I was just wondering," I told him, knowing this whole conversation just felt off and weird and strained.

I missed my Crabby Pants, I thought just as my heart freaking pulsed.

Oh no. Oh, no, no, no.

I couldn't think about it. I wouldn't. "I know you have things to do. I just . . . don't know how much longer it'll be until my ID stuff gets sorted, and I wanted to tell you bye just in case. You know, if you're gone doing Defender stuff, and I'm moving out . . ."

Alex's face tightened. "I'm not going anywhere."

I gave him a weak smile that I was sure he could tell I wasn't holding my breath on that actually being the case.

"I'm not going anywhere," he insisted. "I was only gone that long because there were things I needed to think about."

That didn't sound ominous as fuck.

"I had to think about the future," he said, like he could read my damn mind. "I had to come to terms with some things."

The future, huh? And what things? I hummed and dropped my attention to my hands, reminding myself of what was and what wasn't. "I'm really glad you decided to keep being a member of the Trinity, by the way."

The way he grunted was so suspicious, I flicked my gaze up. His eyes moved over my face so slowly . . .

My stomach churned.

"What do you want?" Alex asked suddenly.

"For what?"

"To repay you," Alex answered seriously.

Oh boy. He wasn't going to let it go, was he? Clenching my hands into tight fists, I shrugged at him. "Just make sure nothing happens to me. If you're around."

He'd started shaking his head before I finished talking. "I'm already going to do that. Tell me what else you want."

Time. To be a different person. Love.

But I patted the spot on the bed next to me instead, going with the next best thing.

Those dark eyebrows rose straight up his forehead.

"What the hell are you thinking about?" I snorted. "Talk to me."

I couldn't tell if he was smirking or smiling.

"What? I missed arguing with you. I missed your grouchy little face too. And I have so many questions I couldn't ask Hiromi or Selene, even though I like them a lot." I smiled. "They aren't you."

Part of me expected him to grunt, but he gave me a long look instead and made his way around to the other side of the bed. From one blink to another, he was lying next to me, his long legs stretched out in front of him. He'd even pulled the pillow up to pad his back from the headboard before crossing his arms over his chest.

There went my Grumpy Goose.

Honestly, he was my favorite. This version of him. All bark and no bite.

He slid those purple eyes toward me, and even though his mouth was flat, I didn't think he was really all that crabby about having to talk to me. Or maybe it was just wishful thinking. "What do you want to talk about?"

I rolled onto my hip and twined my fingers together. "Things I had too much time to think about since you snuck out of here a month ago."

"I didn't sneak out."

I snorted. "You were gone by the time I woke up the next day, after you slept in the same bed as me. If that's not sneaking out, I don't know what is."

"Not sneaking out."

My mouth went flat, but *fine*. It didn't matter. I knew what had happened, and so did he. We didn't need to talk about it. "Were you really three when you learned how to fly?" I asked, bringing up that conversation from a month ago.

"That's what you want to talk about?" He sounded so surprised, like he didn't understand how or why I remembered that tiny fact.

But he wasn't the only one who paid attention. "I'm just getting you warmed up. Don't get excited. I've been thinking about it for a month, and you said I could choose so . . ."

His biceps bunched under his T-shirt. "Yes."

"Flying-flying? At three?" I hadn't believed it then, and I didn't believe it now.

"With my mom. When I was six, they let me go with Alana."

I'd bet it was the cutest thing in the whole world. So cute it was hard to picture. "How amazing is it? To be able to do that?"

"It's the same as walking. Until I couldn't, it wasn't something I really even thought of. You just . . . do it."

You just do it. Like breathing. Oh, how I fucking wished.

"What?" he asked.

"Nothing, I'm just a little"—I lifted my hand and held my

index finger and thumb about an inch apart—"jealous. I would trade ten years off my life to be able to fly." I side-eyed him. "Do you ever offer rides?"

"Rides where?" he asked like he didn't know exactly what I was talking about.

I pointed upward, mostly joking.

Mostly.

That got me a subtle snort. "Hell no."

"Never?"

He shook his head, and I completely believed him.

At least I'd asked. It wasn't like I'd genuinely believed he would take someone on a joy ride up there. "I'm sure you already know by now, but I spent some time with your grandma and Asami. She told me that you promised to go up with her soon."

Go up, like it was an elevator. Oh boy.

Those purple eyes lit up a little. "I did tell her that." His eyes crinkled. "She's going to be something. She's already strong."

"I know. She gave me a hug and my ribs were sore for a few days."

He frowned.

"It was an accident. She said she was sorry, and we tried again," I explained. "Your grandma seems to really love her."

"They spend a lot of time together. We all did when we were small. She's the best teacher we could have."

I'd bet she was.

"What else do you got?" he asked.

"I'm thinking about it." I smiled a little, letting the easiness between us guide me through this conversation that left a funny little flurry of a feeling in my stomach. "All right, I've got one. If you could have another power, what would it be?"

"Nothing. I'm already perfect," he said, with a straight face too.

There was no hesitation. I reached under my head, pulled the pillow out, and whacked him in the face with it.

Well, I tried to. He grabbed it right before it touched him.

"You're such a shit, Alex." I laughed. "Your brother and your sister are so nice and humble, and you are just . . ."

He tugged the pillow out of my hand, smirking.

I had to fight the urge to squeeze my eyes closed so that I wouldn't have to see it.

"It's not useful, but I like the guy in the Shinto comics who could put magic into objects and throw them," he told me.

I took the pillow back and stuffed it under my head again. "That's what you would want?"

"It looks fun."

Fun. I couldn't help the smile that stretched across my mouth. "You are the most complicated person I've ever met in my life. When we first met, I thought you were so damn grumpy all the time, but you're not. You've got a little bit of everything in you, huh? Being a superhero is just a tiny part of who you are." My heart gave a single, hard beat. "Anyway, did you choose your costume? Is your cape just for decorative purposes?"

"It's not a costume," he answered. "And no, I didn't. My grandfather did. He insisted on a cape to follow along with the Electro-Man image, it doesn't help us fly any better."

"Did you burn your suit with your secret laser eyes at my house by the way?"

His smile confirmed it.

"Why didn't you want me to call you Alex at first?"

"I had wanted to keep some distance between us. The only people who don't call me Alexander are my family." He didn't lose his smile. "You get it."

I did. He hadn't wanted us to become friends. I hadn't either. Not at the beginning. I tugged the covers up higher over my shoulder. "Why were you in a bad mood when you showed up at the bar?" I asked.

There was no hesitation. "I got home, and I didn't know where you were."

That was . . . not what I expected him to say. "You make no sense, you know that?"

"That's why I was gone for a month."

I didn't understand him. I didn't understand him at all. I had to clear my throat and pick my fights: this wasn't one of them. "If you say so. All right. How many people have you dated?"

"Next."

"No, this is my time. You told me you owed me. Tell me. I'm not going to judge you." I would, but he'd figure that out later, if he didn't already realize I was full of shit.

He grunted.

I was pretty sure he knew damn well how full of shit I was.

Unfortunately for him, I wasn't about to give up. Maybe he *would* leave tomorrow regardless of what he'd promised. Maybe we wouldn't get a chance to talk like this again if he was in and out of the house, even though that wasn't how the Trinity worked.

But if there was one thing I'd learned in my life, *you never fucking knew shit.*

And this was my shot. "Alex, in this moment, you're in my circle of trust. I'm not going to make fun of you or call you anything. You're a gorgeous, pretty much perfect man. *Physically,* calm down, cowboy, your attitude could still use an adjustment. But all jokes aside, how many women have you been with?"

He'd lifted his gaze to the ceiling when I started talking, and it was still there when I was done.

Fine. "Okay, okay, you don't have to tell me."

He made a growling noise in his throat before saying, pretty much spitting both syllables out like they tasted bad in his mouth, "Zero."

"Zero?"

He side-eyed me. "I told you we only marry once."

No.

No.

Was that possible?

"You"—I pointed at him, scrunching my face up—"haven't been with anybody ever or anybody recently?" I asked slowly, not sure I was going to believe either.

He turned to look at me, not fucking amused at all. I'd swear he might have even been glaring at me too. "Never."

I swept my gaze from his face down to the girth of his strong neck, to the shoulders stretching his T-shirt, across his pectorals and flat stomach, to those long legs and the black socks covering his feet.

This *GQ* motherfucker was trying to tell me he'd never been with *anyone*?

"Why are you looking at me like that?"

I focused on the muscles in his arms, in the general direction of a midsection that I knew was a masterpiece of an abdomen, and said in the dumbest, most distracted voice of all time, "I'm just . . ." I was fucking *speechless.* He'd said zero. "For a second, I was wondering how someone that looks the way you look could never have . . ." I waved my hand at him, still not comprehending how the hell that number was possible.

"Are you complimenting me again already?"

I scoffed. "Don't let it go to your head."

"Why is that hard for you to believe? Why haven't you been with anyone?"

Of course he'd ask. "Why do you think?"

"Because your grandma probably told you that you needed to wait until you were married, and because you didn't want to disappoint her, you decided to wait. Then once she was gone, you felt like a fraud lying to people and—"

"Whoa, whoa, whoa," I cut him off. He'd come at me like a

fucking hurricane with that. Was it all true? Yes. Did I want to hear him figuring me out like that? No.

"Tell me I'm wrong."

"You're annoying is what you are," I muttered.

His smirk was just as nice as a smile. Maybe better.

His expression eased into another solemn one. "You're not the only one who's had to hide their entire life, Gracie."

Oh, shit. He totally had a point.

"I wasn't homeschooled, but I went to a private school. I've had to lie to every person I've ever met that I'm not related to. I couldn't let myself get too close to anyone, because the more I interacted with them, the more possibilities I had of fucking up and doing something that would give me away."

This sounded strangely familiar.

"I'm lucky I have a big family; otherwise, I wouldn't have any friends." He didn't look troubled at all, just more matter of fact. "I've had to stay under the radar my whole life. I couldn't get too good of grades; I couldn't do anything out of the ordinary. We've all waited until we have found our partners to be with someone, because we can't risk screwing up. We can't put our families or our identities at risk if we hope to have any semblance of a normal life."

This intense sensation of kinship rose up between us, strong and powerful. I felt my eyes widening at everything he was telling me because it was hitting way too close to home.

"I had no idea."

Apparently, he had because he gave me this face that said he thought I was dumb for not coming up with it before.

Maybe I was.

How the hell had I not realized just how similar our lives had been? The only difference was that he'd had more people in his and more duties. My only responsibility had basically been to keep going. To be quiet.

The weight of a family, of a whole life, rested on those shoulders, and he was a hell of a lot stronger than I was, that was for sure.

"Why the hell are you tearing up?"

I didn't bother wiping at my eyes. I just shrugged. "Because we're so different, but at the same time, we're almost the same person."

Alex blinked. "Are we?"

"Yeah."

"How?"

I shrugged. "We're both a little mean."

That got a corner of his mouth to lift. "You're mean. I'm blunt," Alex corrected.

"Honesty can be mean sometimes. That's what white lies are for."

"White lies are bullshit."

I groaned. "Two. We both like to bicker."

"Picking on each other isn't bickering. We're having fun."

Picking on each other, was it? I had to keep from smiling. "We've both had to live with a thousand lies on our souls."

He didn't say anything then.

"And we're both members of the V-club."

Oooooh, that got me a side glare.

"I'm not making fun of you. I'd be making fun of myself. But it's the truth." I thought of something. "How many women have you kissed?"

If I could measure the length of the look he gave me, it would have been at least a mile long.

I knew what that expression meant.

I had to try hard not to gasp. "No one?"

"Why do you sound excited?"

My eyes went straight to his mouth. "Do you watch porn?"

It was the noise he made in his throat that made me glance up at his face. His red face. The tips of his ears were that color too. "What kind of a question is that?"

Oh b-o-y. "I'll tell you what kind I like. It isn't that big of a deal."

The color in his cheeks, the tip of his nose, and ears went nowhere.

I smiled at him. Then I leaned forward, so, so close his earlobe was an inch away from my mouth, and I whispered right into his ear.

I could see the muscles in his neck and his biceps tighten as I moved back onto the pillow.

I smiled at him again.

He glared.

"See? It's no big deal. Everyone does it."

He went Glare 2.0 on me.

"I've done more than pee in front of you, Alex. It really isn't weird."

Nothing.

I squinted at him. "You're into butt stuff, aren't you?"

The hair on my arms started to rise as he stared at me, and I laughed. "Stoppppp."

He stared at me for a minute longer. "That's really what you're into?" he asked then, going back to what I'd whispered.

I nodded, not feeling even a little bit embarrassed about it.

That purple gaze stayed on my face, and his voice was just slightly lower as he said, "I'm surprised you're not into pegging."

OH BOY.

I howled. "I knew it! The fact you even know what pegging is says everything! In books, it's always the big, buff, controlling guys who are the kinkiest."

My hands were covering my eyes from how hard I was laughing, but I know I heard him snicker. "I knew you were full of shit when you said it was no big deal. You're crying. You're fucking crying right now, you little liar."

"I wasn't expecting you to say pegging!"

"That's not what I'm into," he spat back dryly.

"It's okay if it is. I just . . ." Oh shit, I couldn't even finish that sentence; I started laughing even harder. So hard I rolled onto my stomach and buried my face into the pillow.

There were fucking tears coming out of my eyes.

He sighed clear as day. "I'm not even going to bother insisting that's not what I'm into. It's not. You're just being a little shit."

With my mouth pressed against the material of the pillowcase, I mumbled, "I thought you telling me you liked my hair was the best part of my night, but now—now it's this." I turned my head to look at him and found him shaking his head, staring straight forward. Reaching over, I tickled his lower rib.

Well, I tried to.

He snatched my finger in his hand.

My face ached from smiling so hard, and it was one of the best feelings ever. "It's okay if you don't want to tell me. I guess it is a little personal." Then I couldn't fucking help it, I snorted again.

The word "pegging" had come out of Alex's mouth. I was never going to be the same again.

He gave my finger a tug, still not looking at me. "How many people have you kissed?" he asked, sounding annoyed.

I rolled onto my back, still smiling. "Three."

His hold tightened just a tiny little bit. "You haven't had a boyfriend or long-lasting friends, but you've managed to kiss three people before?"

I moved back onto my side to face him. "One was this boy who lived next door when I was in the fifth grade. I used to go outside and play with him and his sister when my grandparents weren't home. When I was seventeen, I met up with a gaming friend I'd had for a long time. His family happened to be visiting where we lived. It was a nice, first real kiss. I met up with him a few times." I thought about how else we'd messed around and felt my face go warm.

Alex's grunt made me wonder if he knew what the hell I was picturing.

So I kept going. "I liked that guy, but my grandparents found out and they grounded me for a year. I'm not exaggerating either; it was a whole year. They made me cancel that account and never get on it again. That's when I stopped playing *Call of Duty*. And the third was a delivery driver when I was twenty-one. I knew I shouldn't talk to him, and I didn't really, but he was cute, and I was lonely and horny and wanted a boyfriend so bad, you have no idea. It was okay, neither one of us knew what we were doing, and I moved away right after that. He thought my name was Esther."

A frown formed over his mouth and stayed there as he rolled onto his side to face me too. Those purple eyes bounced over my face. A muscle in his cheek moved. He wasn't glaring, but he wasn't not glaring either.

"So that's my tale," I told him. "A whole three, and one of them probably doesn't even count because it was a peck."

There was a pause and a glow of those eyes before he grunted.

What the hell was he thinking?

One of the tendons at his neck popped right before he said, "Sure."

I blinked. "Sure what?"

"You can kiss me."

It took my brain at least a good five seconds to catch up. To *realize* what in the fuck he'd just said. And maybe if I had been more meek or shy, I would have acted all coy.

But I wasn't.

Not with him. Not anymore.

"You're giving *me* permission to kiss your precious lips?" I asked him in disbelief.

He dipped his head.

Was he being serious?

He was, wasn't he?

"Huh," I muttered.

He blinked.

I blinked.

And my fucking heart just . . . it didn't soar; it freaking bunny-hopped its way across state lines.

I lifted my head and propped it up on my palm. "Alex?"

"What?"

"Why?"

"Now is as good of a time as any."

I rolled my eyes. "No, why me?"

Those curly lashes fell over his eyes again. "Why not you?"

"There are about a million different reasons," I answered seriously.

"You're really asking?"

"Just did, didn't I?"

Part of me expected him to make some sarcastic comment. Maybe to glare. I even kind of thought he would say "never mind."

What I didn't expect *at all* was for him to say, "Maybe there are two million reasons why it should be you."

He couldn't have stunned me more if he'd pressed a taser to my neck.

And he took advantage of it. Those purple eyes glowed, and his voice was dead serious as he said, "Your lips look soft."

The bunny in my chest turned into an Olympic champion, long-distance jumper.

And it was me who sat there without a single comeback.

I knew he'd been looking at my mouth . . . but like that?

I could make a joke. I could be the one to brush it off. I could even be the one to say that this was too much pressure—kissing The fucking *Defender* for the first time?

But he was so much more than that, and I knew it.

He was Alex. He was my hero. My friend. My protector. At least a handful of other things first before he was The Defender to me.

I'd been forced to be closed in my whole life, and so had he.

And the fucking monumental weight of being his first kiss . . . well, I'd shouldered heavy shit my whole life too. Maybe it didn't physically weigh as much as the things he'd been burdened with, but they could have been crippling for me.

This . . . it'd be an honor and a privilege. And if it was all I'd ever get, then it was all I'd ever get. A kiss from Alex. Who knew what life would throw at you?

My voice was wary as hell as I said, "Only 1,999,999 other reasons to go."

His nostrils flared. "Your mouth is pretty too."

Of all the things he could have said . . .

"You know you're more than all right looking, don't you?" he asked in a low voice. "Everyone says you're pretty, but they don't know you look that way even when your face is covered with mud and you feel like shit."

The breath I let out shuddered, and I gulped, making a split-second decision. And before I could convince myself of the million reasons why this was a shitty idea, I scooted across the mattress, crossing the distance between our pillows.

That power that radiated from him brushed my skin gently. It wasn't hair-raising anymore, maybe because I was getting used to people like him, but more of a tickle. A nice, pleasant tickle.

His eyes followed my every movement as I got closer and closer, my heart doing fucking laps around a football field at superhuman speed. But he didn't make fun of me for being nervous. He just . . . stayed there, with his head on a pillow, watching and watching and watching.

I was pretty sure he was holding his breath.

"Are you positive?" I asked.

Alex just nodded. That gaze settled right on my mouth.

"Promise you won't regret this or disappear on me if you feel uncomfortable afterward?"

His features went rigid, but he dipped his chin in agreement.

I wouldn't regret it. I hoped he wouldn't either.

I scooted a little closer, then a little closer. When he was a couple inches away, then just an inch, and finally, right there, right there, right there, I pressed my lips against his. Soft and gentle, like he wasn't made of the strongest cells in all the galaxies, I kissed Alex. A peck.

I heard him inhale.

I drew back a little, then moved my head and pressed my lips to the corner of his.

He didn't move as I angled my head to kiss the opposite side of his mouth, still as can be.

I drew back, uncertain, just a couple inches.

He moved so fast toward me that I didn't realize what was happening until he was right there, brushing his mouth over mine.

His lips were soft.

A big, cool hand curved around my jaw, and he guided me closer. But it was me that licked his bottom lip. It was him that licked my top one. And it might have been both of us that met in the middle afterward.

His tongue touched mine, and mine decided to touch his right back.

Those firm but soft lips . . .

And his tongue . . .

I pulled back as much as I could with his hand on my face and asked in a fucking deranged whisper, "I thought you said you'd never kissed anyone before?"

"I haven't," he said . . . laser focused on my mouth.

He was awfully fucking good at it.

I wanted to kiss him again.

And he was focusing on my mouth like . . .

"Again?" he asked.

I didn't answer. I leaned forward, and there was no brushing then, no casual peck. My tongue went into his mouth, and his palm was there, holding me in place, and Alex kissed me like the world was fucking ending and this was it. The last moment of our lives.

He ate at my mouth, enthusiastic, his tongue brushing mine, kissing me like he had kissed a million women before, all for this fucking moment with me. His hand held me there, gentle but firm, not letting me retreat. Not that there was anywhere else I would rather be.

Because there wasn't. There absolutely wasn't.

This was stupid, this was dumb, but too fucking bad.

I snuck my hand between us, palming a spot on his rib, curling into his T-shirt like he might try and back away.

He didn't.

We kissed and we kissed, and my breathing through my nose was rough, but I wasn't about to pull away until I absolutely had to.

And when I did, I was panting, and Alex's face was pink, and his eyes were heavy-lidded.

His throat bobbed hard.

"Okay," I croaked.

He was still looking at my mouth.

"Okay?" I asked like an idiot.

That got him to lift his gaze, nostrils flaring.

Okay, okay. I'd been the chosen one. My job was done.

If he wanted to do it again . . . for practice, he would say something, wouldn't he?

Wouldn't he?

Since he didn't tell me to come back, and he hadn't found something else to focus on . . .

I had to get it together. Change the subject so I could think about something other than the way his tongue felt in my mouth, like he hadn't minded at all. Like he'd actually enjoyed it. Like I hadn't heard his faint groan.

But I couldn't think about that anymore.

Not able to handle being the center of his focus, I zeroed in on that big hand, on the nice fingers stretched wide. I started poking at the sides of his palm. They felt normal. There was nothing about them that seemed all that different. When he didn't move away, I started squeezing the sides of each finger.

He let me.

"So." I tapped at the fingernail of his index finger before moving on to the middle one, pretending like my voice wasn't all high and breathy and we hadn't just been making out and my nipples weren't hard. I knew he had to be aware I was turned on, but what was I going to do about it? I cleared my throat. I focused. "Do you wear your not-a-costume around the house, or do you change into it every time you need to bounce?"

His dry laugh made me glance up. He was smiling that faint little smile.

I smiled back weakly, still thinking about his tongue.

"I change into it. It only takes a second."

I went back to messing with his fingers. He had just a little patch of hair by the first knuckle of each one. I grazed the pad of my finger over it. "I never did understand how you squeeze in and out of that thing. It was falling off you when we met. Is there a zipper hidden somewhere?"

Alex snickered. "No zipper." He paused. "I'll show you one day."

I snapped my head up. "Really?"

"The things you get excited over . . ." The corner of his mouth curled. "Yeah, I'll show you."

I just wanted to mess with him. "Can I try it on?"

That got the reaction I wanted. He laughed. He straight fucking laughed.

"Yeah, it'd probably be too big for me," I joked.

"You're annoying."

I focused back on his knuckles and started trailing my finger over each ridge. One little mountain after the other. "Spoiler alert: I don't think you think I'm really that annoying."

He didn't say anything.

I peeked up self-consciously.

And that's when he curled the hand I'd been messing with under my chin, drew my face up, and brushed that mouth over mine.

Alex kissed me some more.

And my heart, it took off long jumping that time.

Maybe it meant nothing. Maybe this was just two people who both liked affection. Two people who hadn't allowed ourselves to grow attached to others. Two horny virgins.

Or maybe it was something else.

I didn't know, but I would take what I could get.

I'd enjoy it for as long as I could.

Chapter Thirty-One

I was watching him.

Well, more like I was watching that tight ass move around the kitchen.

It was an obsession really. I tried to look away, I really did, but I couldn't stop. I was weak.

My inner horny stalker had been unlocked.

Did his sweatpants have to be that tight?

Alex glanced over his shoulder as he brought a blue mug up to his mouth. He took a long, long sip of the coffee I'd watched him make with fascination—it was basically creamer with a splash of coffee. I'd never asked, but I bet if he could manage to only sleep a little bit and be fine, he didn't need caffeine to stay awake. Must be nice.

"What are you staring at?" he had the nerve to ask.

Was there a point in lying? "Your butt. Where'd you get those pants anyway? GapKids?"

Alex bent his head, and the only reason I knew he was laughing was because he held the cup farther away from him.

He was still laughing as he glanced up at me, those bright eyes glassy. "I dried them on high heat too many times."

I put my chin on my palm, feeling pretty much shameless around him. "I'm more impressed you do your own laundry than the size of your butt."

"You realize that you used to barely talk to me. That you went out of your way to not tell me your name, and now you're talking about my ass," he noted with a snicker.

"I thought I told you, but once I get going, I don't stop, and after everything we've been through together . . ." I shrugged and told him the truth. "I don't think I've ever felt more comfortable around anyone than I do you, Alex. Even my grandparents. Even though you disappeared on me, to me, you're still my number 7 best friend. All I wanted for years was that. For someone like you. For you. You Alex, not you The Defender."

Alex's eyebrows went up slowly. That couldn't be surprising to him. Could it?

"You changed my life. Regardless of what happens, I hope you know that." I smiled again, realizing I'd been smiling a lot more in the last two months than I had in a really, really, really long time. "And it's a nice bonus that your butt is hypnotizing and you're a good kisser."

My chest instantly went a little funny at the fresh memory of the night before. Of how we'd laid in my bed, facing each other, kissing and kissing and kissing a little more. Softly but not that gently. It had built up and up, until I'd clutched the bottom of his T-shirt in my hands like he was going to fall off a cliff if I didn't.

I hadn't wanted to stop. I hadn't wanted the best kiss of my life to end. Sure, there were only a few to compare, but even if there had been a thousand, it would have still been at the top of the list without a doubt. Best of the best. I was a fast learner, and so was he.

Shit, it was the first thing I'd thought of when my eyes had opened that morning. I wanted to do it again. And *that* was a dangerous thought, but only if I let it. If I took it too seriously.

Last night, when we'd finally broken apart, we'd laid there quietly before I'd made myself ask him a few more random questions.

Alex narrowed his eyes right then though and took another long sip, settling that gaze on me as he leaned against the cabinets and crossed one ankle over the other. I picked up my own cup and took a big drink of it.

"What made you decide to keep being The Defender after all?" I went ahead and asked.

The moment he pulled the cup away from his mouth, he said, "I remembered why we do what we do. Why it's so important. For the future." He licked his lip. "I'm going to be on call from here on out."

"Okay?"

"I'll have to run out from time to time," he warned me.

I nodded, not sure where he was going with this.

His gaze moved around my face. "I don't know how long I'll be gone but it won't be a month."

"Okay." Why was he watching me so carefully? Did he think I was going to tell him it wasn't okay?

He took another long sip of his sugar coffee before saying, "I'm not used to telling anyone when I'm leaving."

I took another sip too. "I figured. I mean, if I don't see you, I know what you're doing. I didn't expect you to sit around all day, writing Electro-Man storylines." I bit my lip, pushing aside the fact that I still couldn't comprehend he was a writer for a living. "I wasn't trying to make you feel bad yesterday, Alex. I was mostly joking. But it did hurt my feelings you were gone for a whole month and you couldn't send me a text." I paused. "Even though you don't need to tell me where you are. It was just because it was a long time that you were gone, and I thought we'd been getting closer. And I'm being fucking awkward now. The point is, I wasn't trying to make you feel bad. You don't owe me anything. You can be gone as long as you want. I already told you what I wanted to tell you. Thank you, I mean."

He nodded slowly, and I could tell by his face he was thinking.

About me sticking my foot in my mouth? Maybe. But I hoped I made a little bit of sense at least. "All I'm trying to say now is good luck with all your Defender stuff. You don't need to warn me when you have to leave."

He was back to thinking, I could tell, as he took yet another drink from his mug. "I'll make sure to leave the car keys by the front door."

"Honestly, I was surprised you left them for me last time."

"I don't expect you to get around in your invisible car."

I snorted, which reminded me. "I should be getting my check soon, from my insurance." It wasn't enough to pay for a new car, but I didn't want to share that concern with him. "Hopefully I'll be getting my life back on track so I can get out of your hair."

His eyebrows knit together. "About that. You can have the car in the garage. The silver one. Or we can share the Durango. I don't drive much—" His cell started ringing. Alex cursed as he pulled it out and peered at the screen for a second before answering it, his gaze dead on mine. But all he said was one word, "Yes," before he hung up.

I smiled at him, and in the time it took me to blink, he was out of there, and a heartbeat later, the front door slammed shut.

I ran to the big window in the kitchen, but there wasn't even a dot in the sky.

He was gone.

Wow.

Wow, wow, wow.

Smiling, and purposely ignoring what in the world he might have wanted to talk about, I finished my breakfast and showered. Once I was done, I grabbed my laptop and headed downstairs to the living room, where I turned on the television.

My hand froze in midair holding the remote.

I'd forgotten that I had turned on the news to see if I could find anything about Alex.

"... *sentenced to five back-to-back life sentences without the possibility of parole*," the television anchor said as an image of Camilo Beltran filled the screen.

Five life sentences.

I felt my breath go out in literally a whoosh.

Then I changed the damn channel as fast as I could as my stomach churned.

It didn't mean anything. He could escape. He had before.

But what if he didn't? What if he was one less person to worry about now?

I couldn't stop thinking about what I'd learned the day before.

Alex hadn't come back, and I'd turned on the news to see that he'd been helping deal with a nuclear reactor. It wasn't the first time, or even the tenth time, one of the Trinity had dealt with nuclear issues, so I knew the radioactive gases and radiation didn't harm them, fortunately. Or at least not in the same manner or level it did humans. I was planning on asking him one day how that worked exactly. Did it affect him a little and just make him weak instead of blatantly killing him? Or were their bodies just that amazing that they repelled all that toxic stuff outright? My money was on that.

On the bright side, Selene had shown up and taken me to Robert and Agatha's house for dinner, and I'd been reassured that the man known as The Centurion really was terrific and sweet. He had a polo shirt and khakis on, and just looked like . . . a hot uncle.

I knew all about hot uncles now.

For one moment, I'd thought about asking Agatha about that vision, but I'd kept my mouth shut. The more I'd worried over it, the more I'd realized and then come to accept the fact that it didn't matter. It didn't change anything. Having these feelings for Alex was the equivalent of having a crush on a celebrity.

That you knew and lived with.

And kissed.

Or maybe a boss at work.

What his grandmother wanted didn't change his heart or his desires, even if we'd made out. Attraction wasn't love, and I couldn't go too crazy with my thoughts or feelings, that was a damn fact. Alex Akita was a pro football player in the National Football Organization, and I was the best player on the pee-wee team.

But the problem was that no matter how much I tried to convince myself that was the case, no matter how much my brain recognized the truth, the rest of me was hung up on the things I couldn't have.

Including the little bit of relief that I wanted to experience at the possibility that scumbag might be behind bars for the rest of my life.

And *that* was what upset me the whole day.

All those fucking things I couldn't have . . .

So that morning, I'd woken up to a quiet house and, after breakfast, focused on the one thing that was so difficult it wouldn't let my mind stray: I worked on my Japanese.

It wasn't until early in the evening when I heard the door open and shut, then felt the faint hum of Alex's power coming from the doorway a heartbeat later.

"Hi, Lexi," I greeted him as I popped another Cheeto into my mouth and chewed slowly.

"What's wrong?" was the first thing he asked.

I paused as I took another one out and eyed the puffy orange snack. "Why do you think there's something wrong?" I asked, even though I knew the damn answer.

"Because I can smell it."

Exactly what I'd thought. I put the snack into my mouth and took my time eating it.

As much as I'd tried not to think about it, that was literally all I'd been able to focus on every time my mind strayed: how unfair shit could be. I couldn't remember a single thing I'd tried to learn. "Nothing bad. I shouldn't have watched the news. It's no big deal. I'll be fine. How are you? Are you okay? How did it go saving humanity from being poisoned with radiation?"

That buzz of power heightened in the room, and I turned to see where the hell he was. Alex was halfway in the kitchen, still in that incredible charcoal suit and cape, looking like some mythological god from another planet. A savior of civilizations.

He was incredible. His skin seemed to glow even brighter than usual, every bone and angle in his face was more pronounced than before. No part of him seemed like it could be real.

If I'd tried to look away, I wouldn't have been able to. No way.

And I couldn't help but peek at his mouth for a split second. Remembering I'd kissed him. Those lips. That face.

Alex crossed his arms over his chest, his expression a sober one.

I gave him the best smile I could dig up, which didn't say much.

Then he huffed as he headed toward the pantry. He tucked something under his arm, opened the fridge, and pulled a Dr Pepper out. And in the next blink of an eye, he had pulled out the chair beside me, plopped his cookies with chocolate candies in them beside the bag of chips, and sat in it at the same time he opened the tab on the drink and took a big sip.

Those incredible eyes met mine, and he held the drink out.

I watched him right back as I took it and swigged it too,

setting the can between us. Then I turned the bag toward him, watching as he reached inside and grabbed a handful. I ate more, and we swapped the drink before he pulled out a handful of cookies, handing me two.

Was this how he wound down after Trinity business, I wondered?

I'd barely finished my cookies when he crossed his arms over his chest and flattened me with a few sentences. "You don't have to worry about me. I'm fine. The only thing that can injure me is my grandmother, I told you that. I burned my suit and changed so I wouldn't risk bringing anything home with me that can hurt you, otherwise I would've gotten back sooner."

I blinked.

He kept going. "But so we're clear, you being upset about something is important to me," he told me. "Just as important as saving people from a nuclear meltdown."

I hadn't seen that shit coming.

Not by a mile. "Just as?" I echoed.

He tipped his chin down, those eyebrows flat on his smooth forehead. "More. What's wrong?"

More?

Some small part of my brain wanted to deflect. To change the subject because I didn't want to talk about it, not with him, not over something so petty that I thought I had already moved on from. Something that shouldn't have upset me. I should have been throwing a fucking party or something.

But last night, while I'd laid in bed, I had wanted to talk to him. I'd wanted him to grunt at me and tell me not to cry.

Hot, sticky tears filled my eyes. I wanted to ask him to repeat himself.

But he didn't need to.

I'd heard what I heard.

"Well, that means a lot to me." My damn voice was wobbly.

I eyed him sitting there, The Defender and Superbutt and Alex all in one. "It means everything to me. I just . . . you have enough going on. I don't want to drop shit on you. You don't need to hear me being upset over things I should let go."

He opened his mouth to argue, but I managed to lift my finger and point at him.

"No, I'm not done. I don't want to, but you know what? I'm going to."

Both of those dark eyebrows rose in what wasn't exactly surprise, but maybe . . . relief?

"I don't think I can teach online anymore," I told him first.

He dipped his head knowingly.

"You already knew that?"

"I couldn't think of a way for you to do it without them eventually finding you. You had notes and books in your office, it's too much of a trail," he replied, watching me closely. "I didn't want to make you sad and crush your dreams."

My shoulders slumped even though it wasn't like I hadn't come to the same conclusion on my own.

"If you still want to translate, we'll figure it out. My brother is going to pay you for teaching Asami. That's nothing for you to worry about, we can work that out, find something that makes you happy," he tried to assure me. "What else is wrong? What's really bothering you?"

How did he know me so well? I wondered even as his words eased a tiny bit of my concern. He was right though, as worried as I was about money and how I needed a job to make some, it was nothing compared to the bigger picture. The hole in my heart that had only gotten bigger and more brittle.

"That drug lord, the head of the cartel, was sentenced to a few life terms in prison," I told him. "That son of a bitch ruined so many people's lives . . . *my life*, my grandparents' lives . . . and he just gets to live some cushy life in a cell where he'll probably bribe prison guards and still be able to live a pretty decent . . . what? Another twenty years? And the rest of us just get to live with the shit he left us with." I made my hand into a fist. "I have nothing because of him, and he won't even know a quarter of the way I've had to feel my whole life. He'll never know how scared I always was, how lonely I was—"

My voice broke. I stopped talking as I clenched both my fists and tried to reel in the anger flaring within my veins.

"It's not fair, Alex. It's not fucking fair that I have *nothing*, and it's his damn fault and my parents' damn fault," I spat out, angrily, cutting myself off as Alex's energy suddenly flared, forcing me to focus on him as even my scalp started to tingle.

Out of the corner of my eye, I'd swear I saw the can of Dr Pepper levitate.

"You don't have *nothing*," he said slowly, carefully in that rich, demanding voice of his.

Fingers wrapped around my fist, and those long fingers pried mine open.

Then he slipped his through mine.

I pressed my lips together, trying to take a breath through my nose so that I wouldn't tear up even more.

"You don't have nothing," he repeated, staring me right in the eye as he held my hand.

Oh, fuck. I reached up and wiped under my eyes. My nose stinging. My eyes stinging. My heart just . . . just fucking hurting in anger and grief.

And I shouldn't have asked, I shouldn't have been so pathetic, and my self-esteem shouldn't have been so low, but I couldn't stop the question. "What do I have?" I croaked, because it didn't feel like a whole lot.

His expression went dark, and he scooted closer, his cape lapping at his calves on either side of the seat. Alex leaned forward, dropping his head so low, the tip of his nose brushed mine. Those eyes of his glowed. "You've got me."

Oh hell.

Oh fucking hell.

My eyes went full-on traitor. All Benedict Arnold. Then my head did the same when it fell forward and hit his chest so hard it actually hurt a little. It was like hitting a brick wall.

I didn't even think about it. I slid my arms around the lower part of his ribs, and I hugged him as close as I could without crawling into his lap. I took the deepest breath I'd ever been able to take in my life, I was sure.

And I just soaked him up. That body, his scent, his energy. Mostly the safety that he convinced the rest of me was possible.

It wasn't my imagination either when he lowered his face and pressed his cheek to the top of my head. I didn't make up the feel of his breath on my temple or what I'm sure was the brush of his mouth as he pressed it to my forehead. I definitely didn't hallucinate him putting his arms around me, both of them around the middle of my back, as he held me tight.

And I barely heard him murmur, "You get on my nerves so damn much."

I huffed into his chest and hugged him a little tighter, this fucking knot in my soul.

His breathing fanned my temple. And I didn't imagine how his arms squeezed me just a little bit closer. "Let's go outside," he told me.

"Why? You want another snowball fight?" I asked, staying exactly where I was. "It'd be more of a mud fight."

"No. We're going somewhere."

That perked me up a little. "We are?"

"We are."

"Okay," I agreed, but I thought twice. "But it's not your mom's house, right? I liked your dad, but she still scares me."

His huff was a light one. "No, not my mom's. I heard he liked you though."

He had? "Okay," I whispered, leaving that for another time.

Pulling away, he grabbed my hand and led the way, and I followed him outside, grabbing a jacket on the way and putting it on with his help. We headed toward the clearing by the garage where I'd learned he had a silver electric SUV and a plain older sedan that Selene had explained had been his first car. I wrapped my arms around me just as he stopped a few feet away.

Had he really said I could have one of his cars?

Alex stared for a minute before gesturing me forward. I took a few steps closer until I had to tip my head back even though it was so dark out I could barely see his features. The moon was tucked away and hidden tonight. Maybe she was sad too.

"Get on," he said.

Huh? "What?"

Alex waved me closer again. "I can catch you if you fell off me going piggyback, but I'd feel better doing this if I can see since I've never taken anybody up before."

My heart started beating fast first, but my brain slowly caught up. "Are you serious right now?"

"Dead."

"But you said you don't do this," I gasped.

He held his arms out. "I changed my mind. Come on, Cookie."

He meant it.

He fucking meant it.

I leaped at him like a flying squirrel, forgetting all about my heartache and the future and the other ache that I wanted to pretend didn't exist.

And if I screamed at the top of my lungs as I did it, well, he was the only person around to hear it or laugh.

Because that was what happened.

Alex laughed, that slow, deep chuckle of his as he grabbed me right before I landed on him, my arms around his neck, legs around his waist. He didn't rock, he didn't move, grunt, nothing. I would've worried if he had.

"I meant in my arms, but this works too. Reminds me of old times," he huffed into my ear as I squeezed the crap out of his neck, burying my face into the curve of his shoulder. He smelled so good. Was that an Atraxian thing too? "Ready?"

"I've never been readier for anything in my life," I told him, joy boiling in my fucking veins, incinerating everything bad that had been in them before.

He was going to take me up!

I squeezed him that much harder, tipped my head back, and pressed my lips to his cheek before putting my face back where it was, chin on his shoulder. Breathing him in all over again because why the hell not?

The hands that were on my thighs moved up even more, settling low on my butt, and he pulled me up even higher on him, the cradle of my hips pressed to his lower stomach.

I felt it, I felt the energy in his cells right before his knees bent just a tiny bit and we went *up.*

Slowly, not at all like when he took off to go somewhere, our ascent took its time, and three feet off the ground turned into ten, then twenty, and pretty soon, his big house looked like it was a foot wide, we were so high.

I couldn't even fucking talk as I peeked over his shoulder, taking in the world, the land, the trees; the lights getting smaller and smaller.

Oh my God. *Oh my God.*

My ears *popped.*

I should have been scared. I knew I should've. The only thing keeping me from falling to my death was Alex. We weren't harnessed together. I didn't have a line connecting me to something stationary. A parachute? Fuck a parachute.

I was just there, in the air, with The Defender.

And I thought, *My heart is going to burst.*

I was in awe.

I couldn't fucking believe it.

His huff was soft in my hair. "I know you're having fun when you aren't running your mouth."

My great comeback was a simple "uh-huh" that made him huff some more.

"I don't want to go too much higher. Want to stay here or go around?" he asked.

"Around, please," I told him all meekly, still just . . . shocked.

I wanted to stick my hand out and see if I could actually touch a cloud. Could you imagine?

"I don't know if I like you quiet, but I know you're having fun, I can feel it."

All I could do was nod, and I felt his breath again before we started moving. This wasn't the position he normally flew in. Usually he was belly down, going as fast as possible—for aerodynamics, I'd seen some people guess—but I knew why he was doing it this way. So I could see without him having to take his arms away from around me. It felt like we were free floating.

I ate it up.

Every single second as he flew slowly, still in an upright position, I clung to him, and I looked down at the twinkling lights of homes from over his shoulder.

I was fucking *flying.*

"I like it up here. It's quiet," Alex said out of nowhere. "There are some places where the clouds hang low, and I used to go out there when I was tired. It reminded me of why we do this. It's to protect humanity, but it's mostly for this planet. We're here to take care of her too. Some day we won't exist, and we won't be able to help, but we have to try while we can."

I pressed my mouth to the spot on his neck closest to me, and

I felt the arm around the middle of my back give me a gentle squeeze.

"For someone who said he's never taken care of anything before, it sure does sound like you've had a whole lot to take care of," I told him.

His breath was slow, slow, slow. "Nothing that was ever just mine though. Nothing that ever really mattered to me."

I pulled back just enough to peer into those eyes. Mine had adjusted slightly enough to catch the faint outline of them, of his features, despite how dark it was so high up.

Alex gave me a long, long look but didn't say a word, weighing down the moment that much more. Forcing it to be heavier and heavier by the second. I had to swallow hard.

"Did I ever tell you I've always wanted to go skydiving?" I whispered.

That instantly changed the moment, bringing back the shit-talker I knew and loved. His tone almost sounded innocent. "Yeah?"

I knew exactly what kind of fire I was starting, I really did, but I still didn't expect it.

I nodded.

And in the next heartbeat, it was like someone cut the invisible cables holding us up in the atmosphere, and we were plummeting. Like all those rides at theme parks. Like we really were skydiving from the way he managed to fall with his back to the ground with me still clinging to him like crazy.

I screamed as we fell.

I screamed and I screamed and . . .

The fucking butthole holding me, with his cape whipping up around us, started laughing. What was more than likely two seconds later, but felt like ten minutes, we suddenly stopped halfway to the ground.

Alex kept cracking up as his arms tightened some more and we changed to vertical again.

Maybe I was going to kill him, but it wasn't going to be today, I thought as I swallowed up the glee in his rich laugh.

It wasn't going to be today, I confirmed to myself as he moved me around in those arms so he was carrying me, and then he tossed me into the air and caught me again, and I laughed too with pure fucking delight. The truth was, it was absolute joy. So much of it I thought I was going to burst.

Alex did it one more time before we went straight up into the sky and plummeted all over again, screaming and laughing.

It was a thousand times better than skydiving could ever be.

Not for a single second did I feel a pinch of fear.

I trusted him.

I trusted him completely, I realized.

And it was then that I knew without a single fucking doubt, as I screamed my lungs out, that I was in love.

Not just a little bit either.

My-life-will-never-be-the-same love.

And it had nothing to do with the vision or being Atraxian or the Trinity or my safety.

It just had to do with Alex.

Chapter Thirty-Two

I had my arms looped around Alex's neck when he dropped to a stop in front of his house.

My throat ached from screaming, and I was cold even though he'd pulled his cape over his shoulder and let me use it as the most ridiculous, incredible blanket of all time. I decided one day I was going to ask him what it was made of because the material was so strange. My jaw was sore from clenching it too, and my arms were exhausted from clutching him for dear life, even though I trusted him not to drop me.

But I'd never felt more alive. More energetic. I couldn't remember ever being happier.

And that was the thing that snuck under my skin the most.

How happy I felt. I was almost delirious. I'd never done drugs, but I figured this was what being high had to be like. Like you were in a cloud made of cotton candy riding on a sugar high.

But there was that other feeling too. The one that felt too big for my body. For him. For this man who huffed and puffed and had more than likely blown some houses down at some point in his life—for a good reason. A man who was a total pain in the ass.

And I was thinking about that as he lowered us back to Earth, and I wished I could have recorded it. I wished I could have seen if it looked like how it did in the movies when Electro-Man descended.

But I doubted it. I was sure I looked like a fucking wreck.

I reached up the second my feet touched the ground, and I palmed his smooth cheek as I wobbled. My cheeks were achy from how hard I'd smiled for so long. "You made my dream come true." I smiled even wider. "I'll never be able to thank you, but I'll buy you some cookies, deal?"

That perfect face was tipped down, and I didn't think I was imagining the fact he turned his cheek deeper into my palm. "You're welcome," he grumbled softly.

"Are your ears okay? I think I might have torn something in my throat from screaming."

"They're fine." Alex's gaze moved over my face. "You're going to sound like the Cookie Monster again."

I snorted, sucking in every inch of those features right then. His cheekbones. His brow bone. The shape of his unreal eyes.

His mouth.

Something bright glittered in his irises, and if I hadn't heard him laugh, I would have still known he'd had a good time too. "I had a lot of fun," he said gruffly.

"Me too, but you're lucky I didn't faint."

His nostrils flared just a little. "You're lucky I didn't faint."

I smiled.

"Are you feeling better now?" he asked after a moment.

"Yeah. I was sad and mad, and the reminder of how hopeless I've felt for so long because of him and his family really hit me hard. I had my grandma and grandpa, but it's never been easy. I wouldn't wish it on anyone." I shrugged. "Spending all this time with you and your family, just reminded me of how tired I am of being alone. Everyone's spoiled me. They've been so nice."

Alex frowned. "You aren't alone anymore."

My heart yearned, and I had to give it a gentle prod to keep it in place. To remind it not to fly too high. "I know. I know you said that, but what about . . . five years from now? What if he escapes?" I had to be realistic about this.

Our living arrangements wouldn't stay the same for much longer. We could be friends forever, but he had massive responsibilities. Sure, his siblings managed relationships, but Alex could have anyone.

Plus, he knew the same thing I did about what his grandmother had wanted for him. What she'd shown him. I'd had my choices taken away from me, and I would never participate in doing that to someone else.

He was the last person I would ever do that to.

"You're not alone anymore, Gracie," he said, still frowning.

I just lifted one shoulder that time. "What about ten years from now?"

That got those eyes narrowing.

"Twenty, Alex?" I smiled at him, not wanting to ruin the night with this crap. I'd just had the time of my life. "I get it. People leave people all the time. One day you'll find someone you care about, someone you love"—and oh that didn't feel right to say it, it pissed me off the second it came out of my mouth—"and maybe she'll understand what you promised me, but maybe she won't. We already screwed up kissing. We could have played the friends card if we hadn't, but we did. You're not going to lie to her either.

"You wouldn't be able to blame her for being unhappy about it. I wouldn't. I'll just be some person hanging on to you for something that happened in the past. Nobody likes a third wheel who knows how their husband's"—oh boy, my voice broke saying that word—"tongue feels in their mouth."

Why the idea of someone else putting their tongue in Alex's mouth made me irrationally fucking angry was something I wasn't going to poke at too much.

Trying my best to settle for giving him a tired smile instead of a frown that reflected how upset this shit was making me, I shook my head. "I'm rambling. I had the most fun ever, and now I'm going on about shit that we don't have to worry about right this second. Yes, I'm better now. Thank you for that gift. It's the best gift I've ever been given. You just made my whole life."

I squeezed his forearm, trying my hardest to keep my voice even. "You're kind of the best, Hercules." Then I let go of him. "When you're not aggravating."

And I would try my best not to hate his future partner's guts, but let's be real, I would probably have to move across the country when the time came.

My hand formed into a fist on its own just thinking about it.

Alex's eyebrows rose and stayed up, and I knew I didn't imagine the growl that came from deep within his chest. "You can't be that dense," he sighed suddenly.

Uh, rude. "Excuse me?"

"You can't be that blind," he repeated with a scowl that might have made me want to hide if he hadn't just played with me for half an hour.

"Hey, fuck you, I'm not dense," I spat.

"Yeah, you are," he argued, gently but somehow looking genuinely insulted.

What did he have to be upset over?

Those purple irises blazed, telling me just how aggravated or annoyed he was, and then confirming it with the way his voice went so deep it sounded like it came from the base of his throat. "Gracie, do you think there's a future for you without me in it?"

Why would that get his panties in a twist?

"Do you really think there's a future for *me* without you in it?" he asked that time, enunciating every word, his gaze blazing into mine.

I'd thought for sure it would have been my heart that reacted to that comment, but it was my gut. "I don't understand why you're mad."

His jaw ticced to the side, and I could see the battle on his face. In those eyes. Alex's chest rose and fell before he said, very, very calmly, more controlled and gentle than I'd ever heard from him before, "It hurts my feelings that I'm right here, that you're right there, and you still think that you're ever going to be alone again."

I blinked.

He did too.

I blinked again, and his head tipped to the side, those perfect cheekbones tight.

Had he just admitted that I'd hurt his feelings? Me? He might as well have . . . he might as well have told me his deepest, darkest secret.

I was stunned.

"Do I need to explain this in a different way?" Alex asked so carefully.

I nodded.

His gaze flicked upward, and he set his hands on those charcoal-colored hips, looking like The Defender and sounding like I'd thought The Defender would sound, but acting like . . . like fucking *Alex* as he muttered to himself, "Okay."

What the hell was happening?

He pinched the bridge of his nose, dragging his fingers down the tip. Then he dropped his hand and looked at me. "Gracie?" he asked slowly.

"Yes?"

He was straddling that line between sounding grouchy and cool. "Guess what?"

I hesitated just a little, not sure where this was going but too curious to not wonder. "What?"

"Listen to me clearly."

"I'm listening clearly."

His mouth twitched first. Both his hands formed fists, but his voice was absolutely steady and so rich. He leaned in so his face was the only thing I could see as he said, "I always like you the most."

OH BOY.

My whole soul went weak.

"What?" How was it possible that my eyes could start watering so fast?

He took a step closer and wrapped an arm around my lower back like it was the most natural thing in the world—it felt like it was—and he said evenly, in his Super voice, "I *always* like you the most."

I tried to form a word, any fucking word, and nothing happened. I tried in English. In Spanish. In Portuguese.

All I came up with was *mapsosa*. It was Korean. It meant *oh my God*.

Alex's breath was soft against the top of my head. "Not just sometimes. Not just when I tell you that you annoy me or when you make me laugh or when you're talking back to me. Always. More then," Alex told me quietly. "Do you understand that?"

Of all the ways I could've responded, I made a fucking squeaking, choking sound in my throat.

But he spoke Gracie apparently because he said, "You understand."

I licked my lips, my heart already beating so damn fast. "I mean, I'm pretty cool, and I think you care about me, but . . ." I swallowed hard, this whole thing feeling like a damn dream or something.

He always liked me?

I was never going to be alone again?

Those were big fucking words. The biggest fucking words.

Alex shook his head against my hair. "I thought for sure you'd figured it out by now since you usually get everything else by yourself."

"Figured what out?" I asked, too focused on the feel of him right there, of the weight of his hand on my back.

"I gave you every clue I could think of."

Turning my head just a little, I let my cheek press to the strange texture of his suit. "What clues?"

The hand on my back moved up and down. "I told you I didn't end up at your house by accident. Told you my grandmother made it happen. I heard her tell you that we were supposed to meet before then."

"Uh-huh." Why did I ever think he wasn't that warm? He was.

"I told you about Agatha and Robert. Alana has a husband."

I put my palm on the solid wall of his ribs.

His whisper sent goose bumps up my back as he breathed the words directly into my ear. "We both know what my grandmother showed you."

Every single part of my body stiffened, and it took me a second to say, "Right, and we both know you didn't want to meet me."

Alex's huff of a laugh went right to my ear, just as nice as his whisper. "I know I didn't word it like that."

"No, that's word for word what you said."

The palm on my back moved until his fingers curled around my hip, and I felt his laugh.

"Fucker," I said, muffled against his chest.

That just made him laugh more, made him streak his hand up and down my spine, with what felt like his fingernails gently following along too. His breath brushed my ear again. "We both know that you like being told what to do as much as I do. We're almost the same person, remember? You wouldn't have believed me if I'd told you we were supposed to be together, and you know it."

He'd gone there. He'd really gone there. He was acknowledging it.

Another set of goose bumps rose along my back, on my arms, even my scalp felt funny. But I pressed my cheek a little tighter to the material of his suit as I thought about it for maybe three seconds. Should I pretend like he was wrong?

Or should I just fucking own it?

I knew the answer like I knew that I would do just about anything for this son of a bitch. "Probably not, but I might have come around." I spent another three seconds thinking about it. "All right, you're right. I would've thought you were on mushrooms, but I would have come around if I thought I had a chance in hell of maybe making it work. If I thought that maybe you would have been open to liking me a little, maybe more in the future. Do you know how many marriage of convenience books I've read, Alex? They're my favorite. It's not that crazy of an idea to me."

It was the fucking truth too. I wasn't about to deny it. Him liking me didn't seem possible, but plenty of cultures had adopted that plan and made it work for them. It worked for some people.

And the fact that Alex looked the way he looked . . . and his heart was the way it was . . . really, nobody would have said no.

He was no ray of fucking sunshine. He was the moon. A full fucking moon so bright no amount of clouds could fully block him out.

I pulled back just enough to tip my head at the same time he did too.

"You're my first real friend," I told him, wanting him to understand.

"And that's never going to change."

I dropped my voice and gulped. "Meeting you has been the best thing that's ever happened to me—"

He had the nerve to smirk. "I think that was the whole point of having my back broken."

"Alex. Listen to me. You should be with someone you *want* to be with, not—"

"You think that I would do something, feel something, if I didn't want to?"

I pressed my lips together, knowing that answer immediately. "You don't do anything you don't want to."

He didn't even have to say "duh" to get his point across.

But right at that instant, his cell phone started ringing from somewhere on his body and had me wondering where the hell it was hidden. His hand dipped under his cape before he pulled it out like magic, giving me a long look as he did, and tapped at the screen before putting it up to his ear.

I pressed my lips together, trying to calm my thoughts and brain.

His cobalt blue boots were molded to his feet and shins. The dark gray material hugged absolutely everything. He was tall, ripped, incredible, and beautiful. One of the most well-known figures in the world.

And he had said he liked me. *Always* liked me.

This gorgeous, amazing, complicated man was supposed to be mine, according to his grandmother.

He lifted that heartbreaking face toward the sky, listening to whatever he was being told. Suddenly, he hung up before leveling a look at me. "I need to go. I'll be back as soon as I can."

"Okay."

His eyes glowed. "We'll talk when I get back?"

"Sure." I smiled at him, and I tried my best to put all the affection in my body out for him. Just in case.

Because he might have said what he said, but . . .

Alex took a step forward, his eyes blazing so bright I had to blink for a second. And then he dipped his face, putting his forehead against mine, and said, "I didn't leave you alone for a month, Gracie. I came to check on you every other night while you were sleeping. You think those Dr Peppers showed up magically? I thought you'd like the Xbox."

I felt my eyes just about bug out of my head.

"I want you in my life, this mate shit aside. Don't come up with a million different bullshit excuses why I don't. I care about you. I worry about you. And I'm going to come back as soon as I can so we can finish this conversation, you got it? We've put it off long enough," he whispered fiercely.

I nodded, fucking stupefied, and then he was out of there. He took a step back and shot straight up faster than I could comprehend.

A human-shaped comet.

One that apparently was supposed to be mine.

Chapter Thirty-Three

We'll talk about this when I get home, he'd said.

Squeezing my hands together, the sound of a door opening had me sitting up straight on the bed. I'd been on the edge, trying to talk myself into reading my book after jumping into the shower, but I'd been too busy thinking about our conversation. And staring at my giant Hello Kitty in the corner.

I hadn't expected him to get home so soon.

But I didn't think it was such a bad thing either.

I listened, not totally surprised when a big shadow appeared at my door. I only had one of the bedside lamps on.

"What are you doing?" Alex asked, stepping into the room.

Oh.

His suit was pulled down to his waist, leaving most of that incredible upper body bare to my poor unprepared eyes.

I blinked and made myself focus on his face. "Oh, you know, I've just been sitting here for the last thirty minutes, wondering what in the hell all that stuff we talked about really meant."

He raised one arm to palm the back of his neck, giving me an even better view of those hard pecs. "You know exactly what I meant. You always do."

"Do I?" I asked him slowly.

He nodded back at the same pace. "Do you need me to tell you again?"

This motherfucker was serious. But so was I. I nodded.

That's when I finally noticed that Alex's beautiful cape was on the floor behind him. The sight of it almost felt sacrilegious. He should at least carry it and not drag it around.

Alex took another step into the room, then another and another until his shins bumped into my knees, and a half naked Alex in a skintight suit loomed over me, and he was nudging my jaw with his index finger. "Why's your heart beating so fast?"

I lifted a shoulder and met his eyes. "Because I'm scared."

His head jerked back a little, and the smile that came over his face . . . it tipped the edges of his mouth into the sweetest expression I had ever seen. He even let out a little huff, and in a move I wouldn't have expected, he leaned forward, slipped his arms under me, and scooped me up. In the next second, I was on his thighs, on his lap, and he had a forearm bracing the middle of my back, and Alex was looking down at me with the most unbelievably affectionate look on his face. "We talked about this already. You've got nothing to be scared of when you're with me," he said, sounding absolutely serious.

It was too natural by then to lean against his side and let my head fall with a clunk against that spot between his neck and shoulder. "You say it like it's supposed to be easy," I told him. "You were gone for a long time. What did you have to think about for a month? Whether you liked me or not?" Did I have to sound so irritated?

"I thought we already covered that I like you."

I frowned. "You sure haven't acted like it sometimes."

"I didn't know what I expected you to be like, but it wasn't like this. Alana's husband doesn't curse, Agatha is great, but she's serious, and I'm pretty sure Achilles's wife shits rainbows. Could you imagine me being happy with someone like that? You were ready to stab people to defend me. You like talking shit to me." The son of a bitch smiled. "I thought you were okay when you didn't run and leave me behind when they took us. Then you kind of won me over when you tried to protect me in that cell. And you've kept on winning me over since," he said quietly. "I needed some time to think about what was best for both of us. That's why I was gone."

I frowned even more.

"I did," he insisted. "I've been told my whole life what to do, how much I could say, how I should behave. Who I should be and so have you. Neither one of us always did what we were supposed to do, but for the most part, we did, didn't we?"

Where the hell was he going with this?

"My brothers and sister both went looking for their mates the second my grandmother told them to. My mother and father barely knew each other when they got married. None of them asked questions, they didn't argue; they went and found their partners, and have been happy since. You mumbled something before about wanting to have a choice, and I get it, Gracie. Better than you'll ever understand. But unlike you, I was never lonely," he explained calmly.

I closed my eyes.

"Until I was. Until I was on another continent and wondering what you were up to. Until I was in bed, by myself, and I didn't like it," he told me.

The urge to faint was right there in my heart but I held on to listen to him.

"I missed your three thousand questions and the way you hold my hand. I missed my little monster. Missed her a lot," Alex admitted with a huff, like he couldn't believe it but it didn't bother him after all. "I was never going to leave you, but I needed to be sure, Gracie, of what we were going to be to each other. And once I was, I made myself think about you. How fair would it be for me, for my family, to take that kind of decision away from you?" he asked.

I pressed my head closer to him, not sure how to answer that.

"It isn't, but *I know you*. And you're not supposed to be anyone else's Gracie, you're my friend. My Gracie. I'm too heavy to be a good swimmer, but I'll never let you drown. I'll never leave you. I'll never keep secrets from you again."

"Alex . . ." I started.

"Hold on, let me finish. Then my grandmother called me, right when I picked up the phone to call you, and told me to give you a little more time. That I had to let you see that you could be happy here by yourself. That you could have friends and build a life," he told me seriously. "If I've learned anything these last few months, it's that I should listen to her if I don't want her to break my back again. So I left you alone. I made it two weeks before I started craving Cheetos, and I only wanted to eat them with you around. You've ruined tuna and pears. Snow and laughing. Being by myself. Nothing is the same without you now." He dropped his voice. "You little butthole."

My world rocked. For a moment, I thought I couldn't breathe. I thought that maybe I was never going to be able to breathe again.

But I did. "You mean it?" I whispered.

He squeezed me tight, giving me his answer that way.

I didn't mean to say it but I did, and I know I sounded like I'd lost my mind. "You're fucking scary, Lexi. You know that?"

The smooth skin of his chin brushed my temple. "You're one of the only people on this world, in this entire fucking universe, who never has to be scared of me."

I reached for the part of his cape I could touch and grabbed a handful of it. "But I am because nobody else has to trust you with other stuff. With the stuff you could hurt without even using your strength, you know?"

His fingers curled over my hip. "If I wouldn't hurt a stranger that could use a foot up their ass, why would I hurt the only person I'm not related to that I've ever been able to be myself around?"

Oh boy. *Oh boy.* I pressed my face even closer to his chest, to that smooth fucking skin right there. I opened my eyes. "I don't know where this marshmallow filling inside you is coming from, but I'm all about it," I mumbled, hearing how shaky that came out.

Even my bones felt his laugh. "You know you have nothing to be scared of. I'm your sneaky shit."

I grunted, and he laughed again.

"Come here. I'm going to tell you a little secret," he whispered, and I sat up straight. His face was intense. He wasn't smiling. He wasn't mad. He was just focused. On me. "What my grandmother showed me was you crawling on the floor with a baby on your back. My baby. Our baby. It was so real, he smelled just like you."

I leaned back. Way back.

Then I blinked up at him.

"There is no place I wouldn't look for you. Seven miles deep in the ocean. On a planet in a distant galaxy. I would go anywhere for you if someone took you, Gracie," Alex said, his voice intense. Then he leaned toward my ear again and said in the barest whisper, "I know your parents let you down, but I would never. All those things I promised I'd never do, wouldn't mean shit to me if it came down to you or anyone we made together in the future. All those things we worry about Grandmother doing wouldn't be anything compared to what I would be capable of. Nothing and no one is ever going to hurt you again. I won't let it happen."

The center of my fucking existence rocked.

If there was such a thing as a good kind of heart attack, that's exactly what I would have been having.

So I wasn't surprised that my voice came out high as a

fucking kite as I said, "You're talking about mass destruction, and I don't think I've ever been so attracted to you."

His laugh was another puff against my skin.

My throat swelled up, but I found the strength to say, "But I don't want you to think you want to be with me because someone told you that you should."

Alex's head jerked backward, and oh, those eyes were glowing. "Didn't I just finish explaining that's why I stayed away?"

"Yes, but I had to say it again."

He scowled. "What I feel for you, it's got nothing to do with what anybody else wants or needs. I don't give a fuck about any of that. That's what I give a shit about. Being with you makes me happy. I know you know what that has to mean to me."

I squeezed his cape tighter.

"I didn't want to like you. I didn't plan on feeling this protective of you and your smile and your heart. Definitely didn't want to fall in love with you and your secrets. But then you had to go off and say, '*You snooze you lose, motherfucker,*' and I knew my life was never going to be the same after that." He dipped his head again and snuggled me even closer as he said, "And I don't want it to be."

Of all the things he could have said . . .

Of all the things he could have done . . .

I pulled back to take in his face, that perfect fucking face, and I made my own choice.

I didn't want life to be the same ever again either.

And if I couldn't trust this son of a bitch, there was no one in the world I would ever be able to.

But that was the fucking thing—he hadn't wanted to like me, and I hadn't wanted to trust him.

Yet I was still here.

I reached up and cupped his face. "I swear to God, Alex, if

you break my heart, I'll find a way to break your back worse than your grandma did."

His laugh healed something in me that I didn't know I was missing, I guess, and he was still laughing as he said, "Best friends don't break their best friend's hearts."

Oh, this son of a bitch and his fucking words.

His *words* . . .

Then he smiled at me, and I knew exactly what it was like to finally look forward to the future.

I turned on him, not waiting for an invitation, and swung around on his lap. Alex's hands went to my thighs, and he pulled me straight into his body as my legs wrapped around him. With a hand on each side of his head, I leaned forward and brushed my mouth against his.

And oh, he didn't let me down. Not at all. His tongue didn't wait for an invitation as he moved his head to the side and brushed his against mine. Alex kissed the fucking hell out of me, kissing me and kissing me, sucking my bottom lip with a wild groan that had me returning it.

I pulled back just a little, clutching those smooth cheeks for dear life. "Are you sure about this?"

That gorgeous smile curved his mouth before kissing me again. "Are *you* sure about this?"

"I don't want to go too fast for you," I told him quietly. "I've waited this long; I can wait longer if you're not sure."

His eyes glowed, and he brushed his mouth over mine. "I might not be sure about a lot of things in my life, but I'm positive about you. About this." He shook his head. "You think I'd let anybody hit me in the face with a snowball? You think there's anybody else special enough to put up with me? That'll tell me when I'm being a butthole?"

If I wasn't so damn horny, I might have cried. Instead, I told him barely loud enough for him to hear, "You need to know then, if we don't break the bed, I'm going to be disappointed."

His smile and laughter changed my life. "I think I'm going to be focusing on other things tonight, but if not this time, next time."

Next time.

There was going to be a next time with him.

Oh fucking *boy*.

Then I kissed him. His hands curved around my thighs greedily, and his tongue went straight into my mouth. His tongue stroked mine and mine stroked his, his chest pressing and rubbing against mine while we made out. There was no way my nipples had ever been harder. His hand slid up and down my back while the other molded itself around my hip, holding me against him. *Him*.

I could hug him all fucking day. Kiss him for the rest of my life, and it would be a fulfilling life.

And that's what I thought of as I kissed him and he kissed me back, filling my spirit with everything I had ever wanted and dreamed of.

I started grinding on him.

I didn't waste any time going for the material of his suit clinging to his ribs and tried to tug it down. He stood with me wrapped around him, and with a forearm under my butt, he leaned over and somehow took off his suit so fast, I didn't even get a chance to watch him.

But I didn't need to use my eyes after that.

Reaching under my thigh, I found his leg and then the rest of him.

Oh, the fucking rest of him.

I skimmed my hand over the silky-smooth skin, feeling just how long and thick he really was, then closed my fingers around him. I stroked his hard dick as Alex dipped his face to my neck, giving it an open-mouth kiss.

I stroked him a little faster, surprised to feel him lengthen even more, get even harder somehow as he moaned with each stroke up and down of my palm. "You're so big. How are you so hard?" I whispered before moving my mouth toward his, slanting it over his soft lips.

I wasn't the only impatient one. I pulled back as he tugged the front of my shirt down and went straight into sucking my nipple into his mouth.

Oh shit.

His buzzing skin had started to be second nature for the most part by that point, but when his lips went there . . . when they pulled at me with that wet electrified mouth and tongue . . .

I almost came.

My breasts were never going to be the same.

I thought *I might pass out if he ever goes down on me.*

"I know what you were doing while you showered when I stayed with you," he whispered, curling his tongue under my other nipple, pulling it into his mouth too.

If it was possible, my nipples went even harder.

"I saw what you had in your nightstand," Alex said, going back to my other breast and sucking that nipple again.

"*Oh shit*," I wheezed, arching my back to get him closer. He did.

I was going to die from being so turned on.

"I've been dreaming about how good it's going to feel pushing inside you," he whispered, his wet mouth going back and forth, sucking harder than before.

Oh shit, shit, *shit*. He'd remembered. Of course he'd remembered.

I shuddered, arching my back closer to his mouth as I slipped my hand into his hair and curled my fingers over the back of his head. If I'd thought my heart was beating fast before, it was nothing compared to now. "Deep inside me, right?" I asked him, my voice husky and low. If he was doing this for me, talking dirty to me, I could participate. I could do it right back. "You're going to give me every inch, Alex?" I squeezed that unreal dick, shivering at how it throbbed in my hand. My fingers were tingling with the energy coming off him. "You've got a lot of them, huh?" I sucked his earlobe.

His groan was hoarse and wild, and his hands got tight on my hips, bringing me even tighter against his low abs. That whole big body shuddered before he lifted his head and nailed me with a look so hot, I shook too. "Every inch, Gracie," he rumbled before taking my mouth again in a kiss so fucking consuming I was panting when we pulled away from each other.

I nipped his lip. "You're going to have to work the tip in first, real slow."

He leaned over and licked my neck.

"None of my vibrators were as big as you, you know."

Alex growled, his tongue sweeping over my throat one more time.

"I can't wait for this big, hard thing to go in. To stretch me out for the first time. I bet it's going to feel incredible inside of me. My skin can't make yours tingle, but I bet it'll still be nice."

He started panting.

I wasn't the only one who liked dirty talk. And I could do this. Oh, could I fucking do this. "I'm sure it'll be real tight, but you can do it."

He took my mouth, sucking my tongue as he pulled my hips in more against his so I could rock into him.

"After you pull out, we'll have to work the tip in again."

His groan was fucking savage. "You're going to be the death of me, Gracie. Swear. Fucking swear."

"Hope so," I whispered before nipping his ear.

I wasn't the only one who had been waiting for this for a really long time. Alex's hands tugged my shirt up over my breasts, and he took my nipples into his mouth, one after the other, sucking on them harder than before, over and over again.

Oh *shit*. Oh shit, oh shit, oh shit.

I reached back and gripped the hard width of him one more time. His groan was music to my ears as he dropped onto the bed. Yeah, I'd waited long enough. Tugging my pants off, I threw them across the room and sat back on his thighs and finally got my first real look at him.

Oh, even his penis was beautiful. As golden tan as the rest of him, his head was a rosy-pink, big and plum shaped, fine veins lacing the sides of it. If this was going to be mine for the rest of my life, maybe my luck wasn't as bad as I'd always thought.

No, maybe not. Things were finally turning around.

I gripped his hard shaft, stroking up and down, watching a glistening drop rise to the tip. I ducked my face and gave him a single hard suck before lifting him straight up and stroking that soft skin up and down. I pressed him against my stomach, seeing how far he reached.

I smiled at him. My body clenched with the feel of all that tingling energy so close to my bundle of nerves.

His eyes were low and hooded, and his neck was pink.

I had to close my eyes when a buzzy finger slid between my lower lips, over my clit and deep, deep in me. It moved in and out, in and out. *Holy shit.*

"Want me on top?" I panted, nearly fainting when he pulled his finger out and gave it a lick. "Maybe that's what you like? Want me to ride every one of those inches?"

The groan he let out . . . "Please." He tugged me toward him, whispering into my ear just what exactly he was into.

Oh, this naughty motherfucker.

I should have known.

"On top. Fucking please," he exhaled. Those big palms reached up, cupping my breasts, the size of them spilling perfectly into his hands. Filling them up. And I didn't know who moaned louder, him or me.

How lucky was I that he was a boob man?

I laughed and gave that hard dick one more suck before lifting him straight up once more, going up to my knees and slipping the head right where I wanted him. Where I was wet and so ready, he had no idea. I moved down just enough for the tip to lodge itself right at my opening, just the head disappearing inside me.

The way that alone felt . . .

His grunt was going to be burned into my head until my last breath. Alex's hips curled a little, slipping another inch in before he wrapped those arms around me. I arched my back and slipped a little lower on him, a shiver racing up my spine because this was everything I'd ever wanted. Everything I'd ever dreamed of. Just this big, incredible body sprawled out below me. All smooth, golden skin, lean muscle, and everything I loved.

All that time I'd spent with my vibrators had been for this. To warm me up, prepare me for him.

The inches in me were throbbing.

That incredible skin too was even better than every vibrator I'd ever owned. It was the sweetest tickle. Perfect, just fucking perfect.

Shifting my knees, I leaned forward as another couple more slid deeper, and I hissed right before I kissed his chest and whispered, "Does that feel good for you? Because I'm already wishing we'd been doing this since we'd met."

Alex huffed, those hands lifting me up a little and lowering me back down more so that half of him was stuffed inside of me. "You feel so damn good. So fucking good, Gracie," he said, his voice ragged. "Unreal. Nothing's ever felt better. Nothing is ever gonna feel better."

I squeezed those lower muscles and got myself a fucking choke that made me smile and kiss his chest again.

He curled his hips, slipping even deeper, those incredible eyes moving from my face to my chest and back again. The pink on his neck became richer in color as his Adam's apple bobbed, and he said in that sandpaper-rough voice, "Tell me what you need. How to feel good. Do you need me to rub your little clit?"

I shuddered on top of him, taking a little more of him. *Oh my God, oh my God, oh my God.* "Oh, oh—"

I dropped even more until he was in to the hilt. To the balls. All those fucking inches.

The grunt that left his mouth was going to be in my fantasies for the rest of my life.

I shifted again. With my hands on either side of his head, I rode him slowly, figuring it out, watching his face, meeting his stare, his hands lingering on my waist. Legs moving until his feet were flat on the bed. He lifted his hips and dropped them, just a little, and I ground against him, letting his base rub me just where I needed. He was thick and perfect and incredible.

He was fucking everything.

And that's when he raised his head and started sucking on my nipples again, going from one to the other and back, like he was trying to pick a favorite. Desperate, his hips pumped into me from below. "Can you feel how hard you make me?" he asked hoarsely.

I moaned, nodding wildly, working my lower body desperately against his. I was shivering. Sweating. Feeling so damn good. "I bet you can't wait to feel me coming on you, squeezing you when I do."

He rode me from beneath, snapping his hips up, sliding in and out, the base of him glistening with me and how wet he made me. And I rode him right back, watching him disappear in and out, a creamy ring at the root of his shaft. Going all the way up until it was just the head of him in me before going back to take him all. Up and down. I moaned when he was totally in me, the bubbling sensation of an orgasm lighting up the middle of my body like the Fourth of July. I'd had hundreds of great orgasms. Probably thousands, but this one . . .

And from the way he was gritting his teeth, I wasn't the only one.

Alex leaned up and took my mouth then, kissing me.

I came, my muscles pulsed around him, and I felt him groan loud and felt him pulsing, throbbing, coming inside of me.

Wet, we were so wet, and I squeezed him and squeezed him as he kept pumping into me.

Alex came and came, pressing his forehead between my breasts as he moaned and panted.

It was incredible and amazing, and then he started chuckling.

The biggest fucking smile took over my whole face as his hands snuck under my armpits and he pulled me up on him until I was sprawled totally over him and that incredible body. My cheek was half on his pectoral and half on his shoulder, and I could feel his cum and mine slip out of me and onto him.

"That was so fucking hot."

"So. Fucking. Hot," he agreed, almost sounding dreamy.

I pressed my mouth to his skin and shivered.

He wrapped an arm around my lower back, his chin dropping just into my line of view. "I think I tweaked something in my back, I came so hard."

I snorted. "You're going to be okay doing that with me from now on? For a long time?"

Lips touched my forehead, and Alex hugged me even closer. "A long, long time, Cookie." He nuzzled me. "A very long time."

"Speaking of a long time. Are you going to live fifty years longer than me and get together with someone half my age after I'm gone?"

His laugh was the loudest one yet. "Are you going to haunt me if I do?"

I scowled, thinking about how I would do more than that if he did.

Alex pressed his mouth to my forehead one more time. "I don't think my grandmother would be cruel enough to find us a partner and have us lose them so soon. My healing will help us age together. You'll live as long as I do. We can haunt whoever you want after that."

I didn't think anything had ever sounded better. Not even close.

Chapter Thirty-Four

I tapped my fingers against Alex's skin, soaking up just how amazing he smelled.

How was it possible to feel this good? This hopeful? Which reminded me . . .

There was something I had to do. Some *things* I had to do. It wasn't like I hadn't planned on it. I'd thought about it, but there hadn't been the right moment, and I'd chickened out. I had to tell him though. I couldn't put it off any longer.

"Alex?" I asked, sounding almost meek.

That big palm went from my back down to my butt, where he cupped it. "Hmm?" he asked, sounding . . . sounding so happy.

I didn't want to ruin it. I didn't want to tell him. But I had to. He wouldn't get mad. He probably wouldn't even be surprised. But I didn't want to carry this shit on my chest or my heart any longer. "I need to tell you something. Two things."

No part of his body tensed; he was languid, and I could feel his joy coming from his skin. "Okay," he said like it was nothing.

"I've been thinking about it, and . . . you promise you'll never let anyone hurt me no matter what I do?"

He patted my butt, and I swore I felt him laugh. "I promise, but what the hell are you planning on doing?"

I think it said everything that I wasn't scared. "I think . . . I think I want to reach out to someone in the FBI or something. Someone who can put at least a few people in the cartel behind bars. I don't know how we should do it, if I should use myself as bait and have them kidnap me, and then you come in and save me, but we can prosecute them because kidnapping is a felony . . . but I've been thinking about it. Even if only a few people get arrested, it's still something. I don't want them to do to someone else what they did to us. It doesn't have to be kidnapping, but it was just an idea."

I bit my lip. "I know it's not very brave of me to only want to do it if you're there, but I don't want to risk this. I don't want to risk what I have now. At the same time, I swore to myself I was going to make them pay for what they did. Since we can't blow up their buildings or give them all hemorrhoids, I figured this might be the next best thing." I paused. "What do you think?"

His chest rose and fell, and the hand on my butt moved down for him to cup my hamstring. His rich voice though was still lazy and almost sweet as he said, "If you want to do that, I'll be there, but only do it if you want to."

"I do."

"Then you tell me when you're ready, and we'll find the right person."

I nodded, feeling pretty at peace with that plan for now. I knew we'd have to talk about it, think about it a lot more, but whatever had to be done, I would do it. But there was still something else. I poked his arm. "Alex?"

His grunt was low, and it made me smile.

"You remember that time you said you loved me but snuck it in real quick like I wasn't going to notice?"

Oh, that chest puffed in another silent laugh. "What I remember is that time I said it and you pretended like you didn't hear it because you didn't tell me you were in love with me back, even though I know you are."

I lifted my head to look at him for a second, finding those eyes sparkling, his mouth forming into that smirk that was as familiar to me as my own hand was. "I do. I didn't want to either, but I do."

His smirk disappeared for a second, melting into a tender, tender expression before it was back. "I knew you would. It was only a matter of time before you realized it."

"How'd you know?"

"When you told me you trusted me," he said. "When you said that if you could trust anybody, it would be me, I knew we were getting there." His fingers brushed my jaw. "You jumped off that goddamn balcony and let me drop you in air."

He was fucking right. I pressed my lips together before I stroked that nearly unbreakable cheek.

That jaw straight from another galaxy.

Skin that made my own tingle.

Alex wasn't just anybody. He wasn't just The Defender.

He was mine.

And I had to tell him this last part.

I gave him a smile that probably looked like a grimace. "So, I need to tell you something else."

His eyes went wide but not in fear or wariness. "You can tell me anything."

He had no idea how much that touched me, and that was exactly why I had to tell him. Because I trusted him. I trusted him so much. "It's the last secret I have to tell you before I can retire Sorceress of Secrets."

Alex's mouth curved. "You don't need to retire her with everyone else. Just me. We're forming an alliance," he told me, making my fucking heart swell and swell.

"For the record, if I could lie to you, I probably would."

That made him fucking laugh.

"I'm kidding."

That big hand stroked from my hip and up my rib cage as he smirked. "I'm ready when you are, Cookie. What's on your mind?"

I hoped he was. I whispered, feeling the weight lift off my chest with every syllable that came out of my mouth next. I said it in Korean too because I might trust him, but I didn't trust anyone else. "I think I know where the money is," I told him. "I have this letter my mom sent in my safe deposit box and . . ."

He laughed. Oh, he laughed. He laughed even as he hugged me. Naked on naked.

I didn't know then that was going to be the story of our lives . . . but it was.

That's what happens when you find your best friend.

Epilogue

Shinto Studios Presents *Electro-Man and the Lady of Lies*.

The world needs them again.

It's been twelve years since Electro-Man and Lady of Lies hung up their capes to take on their greatest challenge: raising the next generation of superbeings. All two of them. But when a surprising old friend reaches out to Eric and Esther with news that an ancient power might have awoken, the supercharged parents know there are only two people who can handle this type of rival . . . them. Their family and mankind depend on it.

Coming This Fall.

Acknowledgments

Thank you so much to my incredible readers for your love and continued support.

An enormous thank you to the greatest designer in the world, Letitia at RBA Designs; my wonderful agents Jane Dystel and Lauren Abramo, and everyone at Dystel, Goderich and Bourret.

Judy, I can't thank you enough for always answering all of my audio questions and for just being wonderful. Thank you to Virginia and Keeley at Hot Tree Editing and Ellie with My Brother's Editor for your editing skills. Sita, I can't thank you enough for swooping in to save the day. Kilian, thank you for all your help.

Eva, I sound like a broken record, but I don't know what I'd do without you and your memory. Thank you for talking to me about nipple colors.

To my friends who have helped me in some way (who I know I'm forgetting): thank you for everything.

To my Zapata, Navarro, and Letchford family, you're the greatest families a girl could ever ask for. I couldn't do this without you. Isaac, thank you for always being so quick to give me an opinion. Eddie, thank you for everything. Mom and Dad, I owe you a million dollars. Thank you for letting me take over your dining room.

To Chris, Kai, and my forever editor and angel in the sky, Dorian: I love you guys so much.

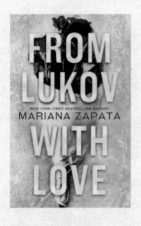